Poison Promise

by

Paul Evancoe

Based on the screenplay, "Shiprock,"
by Paul Evancoe and Paul Schneeburger

Mon Reve Media

Proudly printed in the United States of America

Published by Mon Reve Media, Gaithersburg, MD.

ISBN: 978-1-59594-458-0 (pbk.)
ISBN: 978-1-59594-675-1 (hardcover)
ISBN: 978-1-59594-779-6 (ebk.)

First Edition 2012

Library of Congress Control Number: 2011943833

For more information about the author, questions and answers, previous and future books, scheduled book signings, etc., please visit the author's web site at: www.paulevancoe.com

Also by Paul Evancoe
Own the Night
Violent Peace

Cover art and design: J. Keohane (imtstudio.com)

In memory of Stanley J. Holloway
August 17, 1945 – May 18, 2009
My SEAL teammate, my best friend and the brother I never had.

Acknowledgments

This story, in part, is based on the screenplay, "Shiprock," that I co-authored with Paul Schneeburger just prior to the 9/11 attack. Thank you, Schnee - I hope this book makes you proud. To my family contributors and critics, Ann Evancoe, Sean Matthews and Jon Roark, who read my draft manuscript and provided brutally honest review, chop and feedback to make this a better story - I am most grateful. To my friends COl Jim Caldwell, USAF (ret) and LCOL Jay Cook, USAF (ret), thanks for all the flyboy help. To my friend and former colleague, Elaine Bullington, your enduring insight is remarkable, thanks. To my OCS classmate, fellow officer, and longtime friend, CDR Connie Killion, USN (Ret.), your recommendations were invaluable – thank you. To Geri McCarthy, a fellow author, great editor and friend – Thanks. To Beth Terrell, Olympic-class story editor and fellow author. Thanks for focusing me on the character's point of view. To Sean McCarthy, former USMC Force Recon who served two tours in Vietnam as well as taking part in other covert operations that followed – you da man! Thanks for the superb editorial feedback. To Mike Laroi, my cigar smoken' buddy, thanks for your excellent recommendations. To Jennifer Keohane, thanks for your insightful recommendations and great book cover (I'm still working on the moon projection idea). To my author friends and mentors, Gary Brosch, Vince Flynn, Steven Pressfield, and Ben Small, I humbly thank you for the coaching and for always being there for me.

Most of all, thank you to those who serve. You know who you are.

How to read this book — a note from the author.

In recognition of the fact that not all my readers have a military special operations, counterterrorism, or technical background, I have provided a glossary of terms in the back of this book. I have otherwise attempted to be as descriptive as possible throughout the dialogue.

It is my hope that this story challenges your thinking and increases your awareness and understanding of historical, current and likely future world events. The events suggested in this story, though frighteningly possible, are nonetheless fictional. I hope they do not come to pass, but realize they could.

Enjoy the read.

Prologue

Leaving the CIA's Langley headquarters behind, the president's motorcade sped along the George Washington Parkway back to the Whitehouse. Retired Army General, Gregory Cline, the president's National Security Advisor, sat directly across from President Banner, who stared mindlessly through the heavily armored limo's blackened windows. Through the tint, the Potomac River and Georgetown University, which sat on the other side, looked like they'd been draped in shadows. The president's chief of staff, Robert Holiday, sat on the president's right side facing Cline. Holiday, a forty-something career politician, wore his bleached blond hair styled and long. His features were soft and effeminate, and Cline thought he probably sucked wind just running to catch the White House elevator. Sixty-five and bald as an eight ball, Cline was sure he could take down the little prick with one hand tied behind his back.

He turned his attention back to the President, trying to keep the tension from his voice. These boys in men's clothing lacked the experience to fully appreciate the situation, but it was Cline's duty to explain the facts as he knew them.

"They're still at it, Mr. President. We continue to get reports about pirate attacks against American flagged merchant vessels on a near daily basis. I'm sure you were briefed on the Russian freighter that was believed to have been hijacked last Tuesday in the Atlantic somewhere off the coast of France."

"Remind me again, General, won't you please?"

"The on-line maritime bulletin, Sovfracht, reported a Russian merchant freighter, by the name of the Arctic Mist, disappeared mysteriously and all communication with the ship was lost. It was reportedly bound for Syria with a planned replenishment stop in Algeria. It was supposedly carrying a load of lumber it had picked up in Finland."

From his blank stare it was obvious that the president had no recollection of his briefing on the incident.

Cline slowed his explanation. "Well, the ship never made it to Algeria as scheduled. Sovfracht claims to have reports that masked men boarded the ship off the coast of France and took the crew hostage. Russian naval vessels spent the better part of last week searching the Atlantic with no luck. The intelligence community speculates the masked men may have been Israeli commandoes."

"Israelis? Why Israelis?"

"Because the ship was allegedly carrying nuclear weapon precursor materials along with some very sophisticated rocket engines and guidance systems intended for Iran."

"Have they found the ship yet?" Holiday asked.

"Yes. The Russians found it off West Africa this morning and they took control of the ship. Russian commandoes reportedly killed six hijackers and repatriated all fifteen members of the Russian crew uninjured. The hijackers were all Sierra Leone nationals."

"So what happened to the Israelis and the contraband cargo?" Banner asked stroking his chin.

"We don't know, but we think the Israelis either removed the cargo or dropped it over the side and may have abandoned the ship close enough to shore so some unwitting pirates would board it and cover their tracks. The ship is now headed toward the Russian port of Kaliningrad in the Baltic Sea and the Russians are keeping close wraps on the crew."

"I want it stopped."

"You want the Arctic Mist stopped?" Cline asked in stunned surprise.

"No, General, I want to send a loud and clear message to those who are contemplating piracy that we will not tolerate any attacks on our ships."

"Yes, Sir," Cline said carefully. "We all would like to see that, but our hands are tied by Admiralty Law. Our Navy has very limited options on what it can and can't do to preempt piracy against merchant vessels, especially if the ship is within the territorial waters or jurisdictional authority of African and Middle Eastern littoral nations."

The president again gazed out through the limo's window at the passing treetops as if he was searching for divine inspiration.

"Boucher," Holiday suggested softly with a nod.

A few silent moments passed before Banner slowly nodded to himself, affirming his own thoughts.

"Tell Secretary of State Cummings to get Boucher and his men to do it."

"Boucher?" Cline asked. "The rogue who stopped the nuke attack in the Canary Islands last year?"

"Yeah, that's the guy," Banner acknowledged returning the nod to Holiday. "She'll know what I'm talking about. And, gentlemen, this conversation stays between us."

Holiday nodded approvingly back at the president. Cline gave them a disbelieving glance realizing they were both clueless egocentric children - very dangerous children.

Chapter 1

The Pearl Lady, one hundred miles off the coast of Somalia

Boucher had taken this MSC ship security contract at the express request of Secretary of State Cummings. Secretly, he realized that last year's operation in the Canary Islands had profoundly affected him. It ended with the death of Sandra, for whom he had great affection, and his best friend, Leon "Pat" Patterson, in a coma. He blamed himself for his failure to protect them and as a result, he had become reclusive and withdrawn - a loner. His longtime trusted men, whom he had commanded as a SEAL officer, urged him to take on a challenge again lest he, himself, atrophy from self-guilt and boredom. He hadn't lost his nerve, but he was now risk-adverse. He had become overly protective, insisting that only he take risks. He secretly swore he would never lose another under his charge. His men knew he was suffering and tried to help him get back into the game. For them, this job was necessary therapy for Boucher and a welcome adventure for them.

Standing on the ship's portside bridge wing, Boucher lowered his binoculars. The three fishing boats he was observing had been shadowing the Pearl Lady for the past two hours. They had remained just close enough to observe but far enough not to threaten. Boucher estimated that each boat was about forty feet long and manned by a crew of four or five. Although he was suspicious of their intent, they hadn't demonstrated any aggressive behavior – at least not yet. Maybe they were indeed just fishing. Nonetheless, retired Navy SEAL Commander Jake Boucher was both concerned and prepared for anything they might attempt. He and some of his men had been riding the Pearl Lady since she left Port Said, Egypt, and transited through the Suez Canal and Red Sea the previous day. They were onboard to ensure that the Pearl Lady, an American-flagged ship owned by the Lykes Lines, would carry its cargo of Rapid Deployment Force bombs and fuses to Saipan in the Marianas Islands unscathed. There, the Pearl Lady would wait three months in a stand-by status for further orders. Little did they know those orders would soon take them to Diego Garcia.

Boucher raised his binoculars and carefully studied the three boats bobbing along on the eastern horizon. A much larger fishing vessel – a mother ship – had now appeared. Boucher knew piracy had been running virtually unchecked in an area between the Gulf of Aden and the Arabian Sea. He reckoned, from his previous map studies, the area to be approximately the size of Texas.

"No damn wonder it's so hard to keep piracy in check," he mumbled to himself. He subconsciously considered the background briefing folder provided to him by the State Department. He knew a number of Lykes Lines freighters like the Pearl Lady were contracted by the U.S. Military Sealift Command (MSC) as floating warehouses for the Rapid Deployment Force. As such, ships like the Pearl Lady were moved constantly around the globe to secure strategic ports where they could be called quickly forward when their war fighting cargoes were required. Their cargoes consisted of tanks, fighting vehicles, maintenance logistic support equipment, and of course, ordnance items like bombs, rockets and ammunition. They were floating mega bombs and slow moving low hanging fruit for pirates.

For the purpose of explosive safety, these MSC ships were loaded according to cargo compatibility and Captain Palmer, the ship's captain, had provided Boucher and his men a tour to show them. The ship had her below deck holds crammed full of bombs, fore and aft. Since fuses are never stored with their bombs for obvious safety reasons, the captain had explained, the bomb fuses were stored on deck inside locked, environmentally-controlled, forty foot cargo containers.

Boucher smiled to himself at the thought of explosive compatibility. One rocket propelled grenade put in exactly the right hold and the entire ship would be blown into low orbit somewhere around the International Space Station.

"Commander," a familiar voice boomed from behind, "sure don't look like them boats are fish'n. What do you suppose they're up to?"

Boucher lowered his binoculars and turned to see Mojo Lavender's five foot eleven inch frame. His flowing white beard buffeted in the wind.

"I'm not sure, Mojo, but I'll bet you they're going to make a run at us before dark."

"Ya know," Lavender said, adjusting his prescription bifocal sunglasses, "I just don't get it why these dickheads think they're going to intimidate an American-flagged ship. They gotta be smart enough to realize ships like these here ain't gonna just stop and drop their trousers so they can get bent over and corn-holed."

"Nah," Boucher smiled, "they're not smart enough to know better. They apparently don't even know ships are built to float. The stupid bastards think they can sink a ship with anti-tank rockets and small arms fire."

"Yeah, I hear ya boss, but these guys want to board and then hold the ship and crew for ransom. Maybe cut everybody's heads off or somethin'."

"Let'm try. We'll hand'm their asses if they do."

"For sure. Maybe you could get the captain to slow us down a bit to make it more enticing. I'm kind'a look'n forward to meet'n those boys face to face."

"No, Mojo, no can do. You know if we keep our speed above fourteen knots it's almost impossible to board a ship with a high freeboard like this one from a small boat. We're not here to murder these camel jockey part-time pirates. We're here to ensure this ship makes it safely to Saipan."

"Yeah, I know but I was just hoping to cap a few of them along the way. Hell, Jake, I ain't shot nobody in almost two years. I'm think'n I might be lose'n my touch," he light heartedly commented.

Boucher didn't laugh as he stared into Lavender's steel gray eyes. Lavender had served with Boucher as a SEAL in Vietnam, and he knew he would never lose his touch no matter how old he got.

He took a deep breath of moist salt-air and raised his binoculars. Memories of the previous year's nuclear counterterrorism operation invaded his thoughts. The Caspian Sea, Jordan, La Palma and Dakar - Boucher had killed a bunch of people and for the first time in his forty-four year career as a gun slinger, he took revengeful pleasure in it. But he also saw some of his own people fall in the process.

He remembered vividly the sticky wet blood that coated his hand as he pressed his palm against Sandra's sucking chest wound. He closed his eyes and saw it again. Her body, limp against his. The smear of blood across her cheek and forehead. A familiar ache spread through his chest. Then he pushed it down and opened his eyes, again scanning the horizon.

"Enough," he said aloud.

The Pentagon, Office of the Secretary of Defense, the same time

A flat screen television mumbled on the wall in front of Secretary Hammond's desk when a BREAKING NEWS banner flashed brightly on the screen. From the desk, Hammond, the Administration's newly appointed Secretary of Defense, pointed a remote at the TV, increasing the volume just as the anchor began his report.

"In a moment, we'll be going to our correspondent, Christian Sparrow at a border outpost in an undisclosed location close to the Turkmenistan - Afghanistan border for a breaking story."

Sparrow's grainy picture appeared flickering on and off a few times before the blur transitioned to clarity. He was standing in front of some military trucks and a heavily sandbagged fortification. Men dressed in hooded, white anti-contaminate outer garments; wearing air filtration masks that completely covered nose and mouth, scurried about. Sparrow dramatically pressed his earpiece deeper into his ear.

"Do we have audio yet?" he asked as though the audience could impose some sort of control over the circumstances at his location. "Are you there?" he asked quizzically. "Yes, I can hear you now." He nodded in affirmation. Hammond had been a political hack his entire thirty year career and knew that act was the network's way of building drama into an otherwise meaningless report. He paid little attention as Sparrow squared himself to the camera and began his report.

"Tension has escalated here in this remote border village located between Turkmenistan and Afghanistan following yesterday's seizure by local Afghani agents of weapon-grade special nuclear material." Hammond sat up straight and alert and quickly increased the TV's volume. "The nuclear material is believed to have been smuggled from Russia via the Caspian Sea through Turkmenistan. According to highly placed officials who spoke with us on condition of anonymity, the special nuclear material was bound for Keleft, Afghanistan where several al Qaeda terrorist training camps are reportedly trying to develop an 'Islamic nuclear bomb.' U.S. military officials report they confiscated twelve lead-lined, barrel-sized containers. The U.S. Nuclear Emergency Support Team, known as NEST, arrived here last night to investigate, identify and safely package the material contained in the confiscated barrels." Various picture file clips of military helicopters and troops appeared on screen. Sparrow continued, "A high ranking official within the Department of Energy's National Nuclear Security Administration, revealed that the containers were filled with enough weapon-grade, special nuclear material to make at least a half dozen crude nuclear weapons." Hammond cussed beneath his breath as his desk phone rang. The CNN report continued. "The President's National Security Advisor intends to hold a news conference after meeting with the…"

Hammond again pointed the TV remote at the flat screen and muted the audio, then answered the ringing phone.

"Hammond," he answered, pressing the phone against his ear. "Yes? Okay," he stoically replied and replaced the phone. As he stood from his desk chair, his office door swung open. An Army colonel took one step inside and braced to attention, saluting.

"Secretary Hammond, Brave Night is underway."

The two men quickly walked down several adjoining hallways to the National Military Command Center, or NMCC. A plain clothes security officer followed close behind. Several four-star generals joined the ad hoc procession from other hallways as they entered the ultra-secure area. They each showed their special, red-striped, ID badges to the armed guards at the door, signed in the logbook, swiped a card reader with their badges and entered the NMCC.

Hammond always marveled at the NMCC's theater-like interior. The long VIP-executive table where he always sat was predominantly located in front of everything else. Secure telephones, microphones and work stations ran along the side of the table facing the front wall. A dozen high-back, overstuffed leather executive chairs were evenly spaced along the table behind each work station. The front wall consisted of a series of large, composite, flat screens all tied to an operating system that could display multiple different pictures of any size, or could be integrated as a single wall-size display - like a movie theater. Behind the executive table, desks filled the room in a panorama that radiated from side wall to side wall. A glass-enclosed gallery filled with staff, desks and computers was located above the back of the room.

All personnel in the NMCC stood at attention until all VIPs were seated at the executive table in the front row. General Cage, the Chairman of the Joint Chiefs, was seated on Hammond's right side. A two-star Air Force general from the National Security Agency stood before them in front of the composite flat screens with his eyes on Hammond and General Cage. Hammond nodded to the general.

Laser pointer in hand, he began.

"Mr. Secretary, Chairman, gentleman, this overhead imagery of the target locations was taken from a Global Hawk several hours ago."

The composite flat screens flashed to life with incredibly detailed color imagery of specific target locations along the Afghan-Pakistani border between Khowst in Afghanistan and Wana in Pakistan.

"Note the activity at targets two, five, and seven," he said running his laser pointer across the three highlighted locations. "Our intercepts confirm that Saif Al-Adel, al Qaeda's man-in-charge of Pakistan and Yemen operations, will move from target five to target seven, the training camp, tonight." He followed a path with his laser pointer from target five to target seven. "Mr. Secretary, as you know, he's again been linked to the most recent U.S. embassy bombings in Kenya and the Hilton bombing in Islamabad."

"In Afghanistan, he claims he shot down our troop helicopter and that he personally executed six of our Rangers who were taken prisoner after surviving the crash," an Army general sitting on Hammond's left, authoritatively added.

Hammond always remained silent when he wanted to hear more opinions. In fact, he found silence a very useful tactic.

A four-star Air Force general sitting on General Cage's right leaned toward him holding his note pad in front of his mouth so only Cage and Hammond would hear him.

"Mr. Chairman, what are we waiting for? We know he travels at night between his three camps. I say we strike tonight. Hell, we might get lucky and kill his whole senior staff as well."

Cage glanced over at Hammond and leaned back into his chair considering the Air Force general's recommendation. "Al-Adel and his deputy never travel together," he said aloud. "If I knew with any certainty where his headquarters is I'd order an immediate strike and throw everything we have at him. But we don't know and we need Al-Adel alive. And we must also ensure there is no civilian collateral damage," he cautioned. "We're trying to win the hearts and minds of the Afghan tribal population and killing them won't help that effort. Besides, we don't need this escalated into a holy war by the news media."

"So we use precision-guided munitions and surgically strike only his bomb-making and training facilities," the Air Force general added.

Hammond was amused as the generals at the table began to argue, but Cage stopped them.

"Gentlemen," he said loudly, hushing all other conversation instantly, "finalize strike plan Brave Night. This is a unique opportunity to take out al Qaeda's nuclear development capabilities, their training camps and capture Al-Adel alive in one fell swoop. I don't want this rich kid to become a martyr. I want him alive, broke, and in our custody if that's at all possible." He turned to, Eric Osborn, the Navy SEAL four-star admiral who commanded the U.S. Special Operations Command. "Eric, are your forces in position to strike?"

"Yes, Sir. They're at our forward operating base on a two-hour short leash. I spoke with Central Command thirty minutes ago. General Wayne is standing by for your order."

"Mr. Chairman, we can expect losses if we put men on the ground," the Army Chief of Staff solemnly reminded.

"General, that possibility always exists," Cage responded. He paused momentarily before turning back to Admiral Osborn. "See to it that there are none."

Osborn adjusted his wire-rimmed glasses and silently acknowledged with a confirming nod.

Hammond, interrupted, "Are we prepared for retaliation? I have heard no discussion of that aspect."

"We have taken all necessary precautions for an operation of this magnitude, Mr. Secretary," Cage replied confidently. "We'll watch this closely and go to readiness level four immediately following the strike if warranted. Gentlemen, I want it airtight."

Hammond nodded in agreement. "I'll approve the order and brief the President immediately," he said loud enough for all to hear. He leaned back and took a deep breath, "Pray that we are successful. Godspeed everyone."

The Pearl Lady, one hundred miles off the coast of Somalia

The three fishing boats had slowly approached the Pearl Lady and were now matching their course and speed at a range of about two hundred yards off her port side. Boucher had divided his nine men into three, three-man fire teams. With the exception of Boucher who was in the ship's pilothouse, they were all observing from covered positions along the ship's stern quarter – the preferred area where a boarding attempt could be made while the ship remained underway. Boucher had radio communications with his fire teams and they would not take action, even if fired upon, without his express direction. Until the boats attacked or attempted a boarding, they would patiently wait and observe.

Boucher smiled confidently at Captain Palmer, the Pearl Lady's captain, who was standing nearby a pilothouse porthole also observing the small boats.

"Let's kick our speed up a few knots," Boucher suggested.

Captain Palmer obliged, ordering the mate on the helm to advance the ship's throttle to AHEAD FULL. Its powerful diesel engine growled up to twenty three hundred RPMs with tattletale blue-black colored puffs of exhaust that occasionally billowed from the ship's funnel high above the superstructure. As the ship slowly picked up speed the small boats closed to one hundred yards and formed a line parallel to the ship, one directly behind the other.

Boucher saw a man in the middle boat raise an RPG rocket launcher to his shoulder, aim and fire. The rocket-propelled grenade hit the Pearl Lady's hull low amidships and harmlessly exploded a few feet above the waterline. Then a man in the lead boat stood and did the same. His rocket was aimed at the pilothouse. Boucher instinctively ducked as the rocket detonated with an ear shattering blast against the outside bridge wing, spewing burning hot fragments against the outside bulkhead. The familiar smell of high explosives wafted over Boucher sending a jolt of adrenaline through his entire body.

The boats sped closer; now to within fifty yards of the ship's port side. Boucher's heart pounded. He watched a man in the first boat stand and begin raking the ship's deck area with full automatic fire from an AK-47. The guy shooting looked like he was little more than a teenager – if that. For Boucher, a kid with an automatic weapon was deadliest of all because kids generally don't process fear the same way an adult does.

Boucher clicked his radio mic open, "Okay gentlemen, here they come. On my command."

The last boat in the line peeled off and made an approach toward the ship's port stern quarter. The pirates had learned that boarding from the port stern quarter was the "sweet spot" as far as ship boarding was concerned. That location put the boarder's boat behind the ship's amidships pressure wave and enjoyed the relative calm water it provided. The clockwise turn of the ship's propeller also created a hydrodynamic effect that tended to suck the small boat in against the ship's hull at that particular location, making it easier to hold the boat's position against the ship.

Two heavily armed men with scarf-covered faces, dressed in dirty white muslin pants and shirts, were standing in the bow area of the approaching boat. They were holding a long bamboo pole with a homemade grapple tied to its tip. A crude rope ladder with bamboo rungs stretched down to the boat beneath the grapple. Fortunately, the ship's speed made it almost impossible for the small boat's helmsman to hold his boat against the ship's side. After four unsuccessful approaches, they finally grappled the deck safety rail some twenty feet above. The two men clung to the ladder and began the treacherous climb up the ship's side.

As the first boat peeled off a second boat approached the ship and pulled in alongside the dangling ladder. Boucher watched three more men toting AK-47s and RPGs mount the ladder and begin the climb. They were young men too and very dangerous.

Boucher shifted his attention to the third boat which was maintaining its position and was apparently acting as a spotter and security force should anyone on the ship's open deck attempt to repel the boarders.

Boucher patiently watched and waited. Throughout his twenty-five-year SEAL Team career he had conducted numerous underway ship boardings. He understood the limitations and the vulnerabilities far better than the pirates now scaling the side of the Pearl Lady. In fact, it was almost comical watching their novice tactics. He clicked open his radio mic.

"Standby boys, they're almost on the spot."

As the last pirate pulled himself over the rail joining his henchmen on deck, Boucher gave the order.

"Execute, Execute, I say again, Execute, Execute."

All at once, six soda can-size grenade-like canisters of OC pepper spray exploded on the deck forward of the pirates with their choking contents clouding aft, completely engulfing the boarders.

Boucher specifically chose OC, short for Oleoresin Capsicum, because it is a natural chemical found in hot peppers and it's the stuff OC pepper spray is made from. It's used like tear gas and is a strong and persistent irritant to the eyes and mucus tissue of the nose, throat and lungs. Plus, it was effective and could be removed from the ship's weather decks with a simple wash down.

The five pirates immediately began coughing and running toward the stern to get away from the choking cloud. Their eyes were stinging and they couldn't breathe. One of the men turned and blindly fired a full thirty round magazine from his AK-47 up the deck towards the source of the cloud. As the men ran around the stern to the opposite side of the ship, they were met with another overwhelming cloud of OC pepper spray.

One of the men tried to open a watertight door leading into the ship from the deck, but it was bolted and locked from the inside. The ladders leading up from the main deck to the deck above were all strung with razor wire. The decks forward of where the OC grenades were detonated were likewise fouled with razor wire.

At this point the pirates had nowhere to go except to jump over the side, which is exactly what they chose to do. All five men threw themselves over the rail into the ship's frothing wake. One of the boats went to recover them, while the other two boats immediately began firing AK-47s and rocket propelled grenades into the Pearl Lady's side and superstructure. Boucher and his men were ready.

Boucher watched as the men standing in the boats who were firing on the ship began to fall one at a time. Three were knocked violently over the side of their boats as the back of their heads exploded like watermelons before the others realized what was happening. Curiously, there was no sound of gunfire coming from the Pearl Lady – the pirates still had no clue they were under lethal counterattack. Then the boats themselves began to erupt in fire and smoke. Their outboard engines each systematically disintegrating into pieces and flames.

Even so, one more pirate stood, aiming an RPG at the ship. His chest suddenly exploded back through his spine, spewing blood, bone and flesh over his fellow pirates as he was violently flung into the sea across the opposing side of the boat.

Watching through his binoculars, Boucher saw the panic on their faces as the remaining pirates jumped into the sea to escape the mayhem. The boat that had rescued the five pirates who jumped overboard from the Pearl Lady approached the other two floundering boats. All at once its twin outboard engines exploded in flames.

Boucher observed the pirates frantically scoop water from the sea with cupped hands and splash it on the burning engines in a desperate attempt to put the fire out. He clicked his radio mic open.

"Cease fire, cease fire."

He heard a series of three double clicks of static over his radio, which were his three fire teams acknowledging his order using typical SEAL radio brevity – clicks instead of words.

Captain Palmer lightly squeezed Boucher's arm to get his attention.

"Shall I go back and recover the survivors?" he asked.

Boucher walked out onto the open bridge wing and raised his binoculars, studying the scene now playing out behind the ship. Two of the three boats were in the process of sinking. The pirates in the last boat were madly bailing water to keep it afloat.

The scene reminded him of the North Korean patrol boats he and his men had blown up to make good their escape from the Spratly Island outpost several years ago. Just like these pirates, his North Korean pursuers went from hunters to the hunted in a fraction of a few heartbeats. The element of surprise and overwhelming violence worked then the same as it did today. Boucher learned years ago that men always react the same way when surprised with circumstances they don't expect - especially when those circumstances result in violent death and unrestrained destruction. He took comfort knowing that again, he had won and, again, the bad guys had lost. Boucher's face softened as he turned toward Captain Palmer.

"No, Captain, they have a mother ship out there somewhere and their friends will find them sooner or later. None of the survivors are wounded and the ones we shot are very dead. I want them to go home and tell all their sorry-ass pirate buddies what's gonna happen if they mess with a U.S. flagged vessel again."

"But what about Admiralty Law, Jake? It's my duty to recover survivors."

"These punks aren't signatory to Admiralty Law or any other kind of law for that matter. They've been stealing air that decent people could be breathing and getting away with it for too damn long. Besides, it's impossible to win the hearts and minds of people who possess neither."

Palmer shook his head ruefully. "It sounds like you've elected yourself judge and jury because you're certainly passing judgment on these people."

Boucher considered Palmer's words before responding. He turned and faced Palmer with a consoling look on his face.

"Judgment is always a compromise between mercy and justice. No, Captain," he said softly, "they just got all the mercy we're going to give them. We could have easily killed them all, but we didn't." He turned back towards the floundering boat, now almost out of sight behind the ship, "They don't deserve protection under the rule of law. This is justice, nothing more - nothing less."

Boucher momentarily contemplated his own words. It was justice but it couldn't justify his losing Sandra. That would have to wait. He blankly stared at the horizon, subconsciously taking pleasure in what had just happened, knowing he was back in the game.

Chapter 2

U.S. Military Forward Operating Base (FOB), Afghanistan, night

Behind sandbagged, guard positions and a reinforced barbed-wire outer perimeter U.S. Navy SEALs, Special Operations Marines, Army Rangers and Air Force 8th Special Operations Squadron pilots and crews had gathered in a dimly lit makeshift conference room for a joint mission briefing. Powdery dust coated the table tops and maps hanging on the unpainted plywood walls. Highlighted satellite imagery and topographical maps identified their target and the suspected danger areas surrounding it. Ingress and egress routes were marked along with the CV-22 landing zones. A whiteboard had the timeline written on it in blue marker.

Navy SEAL Lt. Morgan and his platoon of eighteen SEALs had been deployed to Afghanistan for the past ten months. This was their last combat mission before leaving for home at the end of the week. Morgan, a veteran of both the Iraq and Afghanistan Wars, felt almost giddy at the thought of going home but he had to focus. He and his men would be patrolling deep in bad guy country in a few hours. He knew a lack of focus would mean certain death, if not his, perhaps some of his men. Focus.

Like Lt. Morgan, many of the men sat on makeshift wooden benches but some benignly stood in the rear. At age 32, most of them were younger than Morgan. Some had regulation "high and tight" haircuts while others, like Morgan and his fellow SEALs, wore full beards to better blend into the indigenous population in their area of operations. Their facial expressions sported a mix ranging from nervous anticipation to terminal boredom.

Only the briefer, a clean cut boyish-looking Army major standing in the front of the room, spoke as he traced the route the blocking forces would take to get into position without being detected by the enemy. He ran his pointer across the imagery, pausing to highlight several small villages, through deep, poppy field-strewn valleys, stopping his pointer on a rectangular patch of poppy fields that had a circle in the center with the symbol "LZ Red" drawn on it in red wax crayon. Then he traced the route the ground assault forces would follow from the landing zone to this night's objective.

Morgan recognized it as a key transit area for drugs and al Qaeda fighters and the Taliban and he knew the enemy was in firm control of it. He thought about the previous week when the Taliban had stopped a busload of local villagers not far from this night's target area and beheaded them, leaving twenty-one headless bodies sprawled beside the road. It was all about intimidation and the locals knew the Afghan government couldn't protect them. The local tribes were all at the mercy of the Taliban but perhaps tonight, he and his men could make a difference.

Morgan's mind drifted momentarily away from the briefing as he considered this war. The U.S. had been waging this war in Afghanistan for nearly ten years and it had not gone well. The Taliban and al Qaeda had made an unholy alliance aimed at weakening and dividing the more powerful tribes, thereby upsetting the traditional balance of power within the country. Destabilization allowed them to set up a shadow Taliban government which only served to intensify the struggle between the corrupt Afghan government and the common Afghan citizen.

Morgan recognized that strategy also drove the U.S. into a parallel war with the Taliban and al Qaeda, while marginalizing the U.S.-supported Afghan government. Further complicating the situation, President Banner's foreign policies had alienated most all the allies whose support the U.S. once enjoyed. Morgan realized the old approaches and worn out strategies were a losing and costly combination . Nonetheless, he and his SEALs would follow orders. After all, this was their last combat mission for this ten month deployment. He refocused on the briefer.

"Tonight's mission," the major explained, "is the first in a new bold initiative to capture the enemy's top leadership rather than directly engage the enemy on the ground with U.S. forces."

Morgan replied in his mind, *Yeah sure, but we all know direct engagement takes a lot of troops which, because of the president's troop reductions, the U.S. simply doesn't have to spare. Secondly, direct engagements almost always resulted in casualties, both U.S. and local civilian, that generated an undesirable media feeding frenzy negatively branding U.S. operations.*

Morgan had also heard the rumors that General Wayne, the Marine Corps general commanding the U.S. Central Command, didn't like special operations forces for a variety of personal and professional reasons and avoided using them every chance he got.

Tonight's operation was different, Morgan contemplated. *Capturing Saif Al-Adel from the midst of one of his strongholds seems crazy, but it might just work and what a prize he would be. Besides, Operation Brave Night had been directed by the Secretary of Defense – end of discussion. Game on.*

A picture of Al-Adel flashed on the flat screen for all to see. He was a bearded, round-faced man in his early forties who wore wire rimmed glasses. The briefer continued, "This is our man. He's on the FBI's Most Wanted list. He's an up-and-comer, Egyptian-born, Muslim by the name of Saif Al-Adel. His known aliases are: Al-Fatima, Al-Abdullah, Al-Mohamed, Nur, Ustaz and The Soldier."

Morgan glanced around the small room at his comrades. Many of them smiled as the briefer read through all Al-Adel's aliases.

"He has thousands of radical al Qaeda followers throughout the world who are known to operate in sixty-eight countries. During the last ten years he has overseen the training of between ten to twenty thousand Muslim terrorists in al Qaeda camps here in Afghanistan. Since December, 2001, when U.S. troops and aircraft pounded Tora Bora there were numerous times Al-Adel acted as al Qaeda's spokesman. We believe there are links between his statements and subsequent al Qaeda attacks and that his statements probably constitute "go" signals for several of those attacks.

"His modus operandi seems to involve lengthy target surveillance. We believe some of these surveillance operations have lasted for up to five years. He usually takes another four to six months to do his target planning and the cells he uses for the planning are not the same as those he uses to execute the operation. So he's patient, he's thorough, and he's operationally disciplined.

"I won't bore you by reading his complete history with al Qaeda and how he ended up here in Afghanistan. Just suffice it to say he joined the Egyptian Islamic Jihad in 1979 and, like Bin Laden, he quickly moved to Afghanistan to aid in the fight against the Soviet occupation. Over the next few years, Al-Adel's role included plotting numerous assassinations, murderous attacks against both civilian and state targets, and traveling to raise money to cement the Islamic Jihad's ties with other militant groups. In December 1996, he went to Chechnya to see about setting up a base there but was arrested in Dagestan and sentenced in April, 1997 to six months for illegal entry. He was released almost immediately after Bin Laden paid to bail him out. Finally, in August, 1998, Al-Adel merged his Egyptian-based Islamic Jihad into Bin Laden's al Qaeda and became one of Bin Laden's deputies and a trusted Islamic ideologist. Most recently, he has been linked to drugs for arms deals with Communist-backed factions in Colombia and Venezuela. He has established an international network with tentacles leading to places we are only now becoming aware of." The briefer paused and momentarily stared at his audience, "Now you know why he's so important to us and why we need him alive. Good luck tonight, gentlemen and good hunting. So BOHICA, gentlemen!"

Morgan smiled, *BOHICA. Bend over here it comes again. What an understatement.*

Following the briefing, the assault force departed in silence and scurried to prep their weapons, night vision devices, assault equipment and to conduct communications checks. Air Force pilots and flight crews carefully conducted pre-operation flight checks on their special operations-equipped variant of the CV-22 tilt-rotor aircraft and suited up. It was show time.

Inside a thirty-man general purpose tent, Lt. Morgan huddled with his men around a topographical map he had spread out on top of a stack of wooden pallets they used for a makeshift table. They used red lights for illumination so their night vision wouldn't be affected. Morgan reviewed the rules of engagement and their mission plans a final time.

Standing next to the makeshift table, Morgan switched on his red lens flashlight, holding it above the map. He unconsciously adjusted his body armor to ride higher on his torso and squirmed slightly as its weight settled again against his shoulders and chest.

"Okay, boys," he said confidently smiling, "this is our last mission before we return to the states so let's make this a good one. As you know, we're going in to snatch Al-Adel. The Admiral wants him alive, repeat, we want to take him alive. Collateral damage must be kept to a bare minimum. If we have the opportunity to spare any non-combatants – do so. Otherwise, we rock and roll the rest. See the target and shoot it – you all know the drill. I want the grenadiers to take an extra twenty rounds each. Mk-46 and -48 machine gunners, each take an extra three hundred rounds."

"We'll split our eighteen-man platoon evenly between two, Air Force 8th Special Operations Squadron CV-22's. The 8th is sending a third CV-22 along with us as a spare – just in case we have a problem. The CV-22s will stay below ten thousand feet on the inbound leg. Whenever they need to follow the terrain through the mountain passes they'll drop down to the necessary altitude. Staying low will mask our engine noise plus we won't have to be pressurized, so we have no supplemental oxygen requirement. Our insertion altitude is above nine thousand feet, so we are intentionally going in with a minimal fuel load. That way our gross weight will be down so the CV-22s can safely hover before they set us down."

"We got room for two of those birds on the LZ?" one of the older SEALs asked.

Morgan put his finger on the map and tapped it twice, "Yes. We'll be inserted here on this gravel wash at an altitude of about nine thousand three hundred feet. It's the only somewhat flat place they can both safely touchdown. Once we're on the ground, the CV-22s will depart and loiter about ten minutes away in case we need them in a hurry for an emergency extraction. When we extract, our aircraft will obviously be low on fuel because of the load, altitude, range numbers and the requirement to hover for landing, so don't poke around or we'll be walking home."

"Do we have a Spooky?" one of the men asked.

Morgan nodded. "We'll have a Spooky flying a race track close by keeping an eye on us in case we need covering fire." Morgan ran his finger on the map and again pressed his finger on a point marked with an orange X. "We'll patrol through this web of ravines to this point. It should provide excellent concealment all the way in and give us ample cover." Moving his index finger a couple of inches to the left, he tapped the map. "We'll set our ambush here, about a hundred yards from the camp."

Morgan put two high-resolution 8x11 aerial photos of the village camp on the table. There were a dozen small mud-rock huts with arching doorways surrounded by high, mud-rock walls. A well, surrounded by mulberry trees, was central to the village. It all looked mysterious and medieval like something out of a Hollywood movie set.

Morgan pressed his finger on one of the pictures which showed the rugged terrain detail surrounding the village camp. "We'll wait here for our target to arrive. We'll open the assault on my order by simultaneously firing a spread of six Claymore mines aimed at the hard structures. We'll immediately follow the Claymore detonation by each firing a LAW rocket into each of the structures. I want you to put'm through the doors. Then I want the grenadiers to begin lobbing forty mike-mikes into any center of mass that threatens us. Machine gunners, you boys hose down everything else. Once we suppress fire, we'll assault forward, and take advantage of the element of surprise. We'll grab Al-Adel and extract back to the LZ along the same path we came in on."

Morgan threw a third picture on the table which was a frontal of Al-Adel's face.

"Al-Adel always wears his glasses. He stands about five nine and weighs about one-seventy. You've seen lots of pictures of him in the target folder so I'm sure you'll recognize him when you see him. Don't shoot the son-of-a-bitch. Questions?"

Morgan's senior enlisted SEAL and assistant, Chief Springer, always liked clarification, if not to satisfy his own curiosity, he would ask to ensure his fellow SEALs went into battle with complete clarity. He leaned his imposing six-foot, two-inch, two hundred pound frame toward the table and raised his gloved hand.

"Yes, Sir. What if Al-Adel slips through?"

"Good question, Chief. As you know, the Rangers will be the blocking force on our west side. The Marines will block on the east side. If he runs either direction, they'll grab him. If he runs north, he'll be caught between a steep mountain face and our assault with no place to go," he explained pointing to the terrain picture again. "Just try not to kill the son-of-a-bitch. Anything else?"

"Sir, what if Al-Adel is wounded in the action?" the SEAL corpsman asked.

"Well, Doc, we want him alive. I really don't give a rat's ass if he's got some holes in him. Just don't let him bleed out - keep him alive."

"L.T., intel says the odds against us are six to one, maybe more. What's the plan if they counterattack?" one of the SEAL machine-gunners asked.

"What's not to like about those odds?" Morgan laughed. "It just means we'll have a target-rich environment. You guys all know the drill - we project maximum violence on the objective and don't let up. If we start running low on ammo and it starts getting really dicey, we'll have a 4th SOS AC-130 gunship close by to cover our extraction."

"How close, Lieutenant?" the machine-gunner soberly asked.

"We can have Spooky overhead and in range to fire inside of five minutes. Anything else?"

Morgan glanced around, making direct eye contact with each of his men in silent affirmation. As they had done countless times before, they would all go in together and they would come out together. No one would ever be left behind, dead or alive. It was the Navy SEAL creed.

Over the past year, the blond-haired, blue-eyed, boyish-looking Morgan had matured into a fine SEAL officer and seasoned, combat-hardened leader. His men loved him and would follow him to hell and back if that's what he asked them to do. He would now lead them on a high risk mission which probably had as much chance of failure as it did of success. He knew it and so did his men, but it didn't matter, they would attempt the impossible. If it was easy, anybody could do the mission. That was the SEAL Team way.

He again adjusted his body armor and casually slung his Mk-17 Special Operations Combat Assault Rifle, or SCAR as it was called, over his shoulder. "Okay boys, keep your heads down and your muzzles up. I want you all coming back out in the vertical position. Let's go get in the fight." Morgan set his jaw forward, "Follow me."

Chapter 3

Afghanistan, Kandahar Providence, mountain road, the same time

In Afghanistan, farming does not produce surpluses and industry is nonexistent. Lacking navigable rivers or access to the sea, Afghanistan's bleak, mountainous, arid terrain is inhospitable to population centers, making it a perfect environment for the Taliban to carry out its guerrilla war. The infrastructure, for anything other than the illegal sale of opium, is completely absent. This translates to a drastic lack of taxable commodities as a source of revenue to fund meaningful local and national government, and sustain a military capable of rooting out the Taliban and securing the country. Without a gross national product, smuggling of nearly everything one can think of is how people get what they need and the Taliban control the smuggling, which, in-turn, provides a perfect source of funding for their guerrilla operations. This is the nature of the conflict itself and American strategy to reshape the country falls pathetically short of measurably influencing this reality.

With lights off, two open trucks filled with heavily armed men slowly negotiated a steep, dirt road running along a narrow mountain pass on their way to a training camp located near the Afghan–Pakistan border. The sound of the trucks' straining engines was muffled by the surrounding rugged terrain and steep mountains. A cruise missile streaked above and disappeared from view behind a high mountain. Like distant lightning on a hot summer's night, a bright flash illuminated the horizon moments later. The men riding in the trucks showed no alarm. Most of them were in their own backyard and they knew the terrain like the back of their hand. They had roamed this area since childhood and were confidently secure believing no one else would dare confront them there.

Unbeknownst to them, a U.S. Air Force MQ-9 Reaper drone was observing their progress toward the camp from high above. So high above, in fact, that the sound of the drone's powerful turboprop engine could not be heard from the ground. The real-time imagery it was relaying via satellite back to the battle staff was spectacular. Over the past several years U.S. reliance on high tech unmanned drones to locate and observe potential targets had grown to near habit. Compared to manned reconnaissance aircraft that were expensive to operate and put the pilot's life at risk, the drones were cheap to operate and could remain aloft for hours. Some could even refuel in-flight which significantly extended their range and time aloft far exceeding that of any manned aircraft.

Afghan mountain village, Sinkay Kalay, several hours later

The SEALs observed from their camouflaged ambush position on a rugged hillside close to the target camp. Morgan and his men had been working closely with the Tajiks, Uzbeks, and Turkmen and even a couple of Pushtuns, for over a month-and-a-half in what they all understood was a futile attempt to win the Tribes' hearts and minds.

All he could say for sure was all the tribes were like actual present day living Huns; they loved to fight and they lived to fight and he knew it's what they did and it was all they did. He saw fathers forcing their five-year-old sons into human cockfights to defend their family honor and playing polo with dead calves was their least violent means of conflict resolution. Morgan couldn't compare their culture to any other on the planet. They had no respect for anything, not for themselves, not for their families, not for each other.

They were little more than tribal savages who roamed in packs. They were like cavemen with AK-47s and it pissed Morgan off when the news media referred to them as smart. Hell, most of them were still figuring out how to work the safety on their assault rifle. They were definitely not smart. No, Morgan saw them as cunning, like lions and wolves and like their animal counterparts, they were persistently ruthless and cruel without conscience. And when individually confronted, they were cowardly like jackals and hyenas. Most of all, they were hateful, malevolent parasites who created nothing and destroyed everything else. Fighting one another was their way of life and now they had an enemy they all could fight - the Americans. They didn't know why and it didn't matter - just fight.

Lt. Morgan peered through his night vision goggles at the encampment a short distance to his front. Two trucks loaded with armed men, slowly made their way into the camp. Illuminated by campfires, men dressed in dingy shalwar kameez mobilized, grabbing weapons from adobe huts and three-sided, lean-to tents. More men emerged from caves, hidden by large rock formations and scrub foliage on the rocky hillside behind the camp. These were the kinds of places they spent their entire lives reading only one book; the Koran, and considered hygiene and indoor plumbing to be products of the devil.

The SEALs all knew talking to a Taliban or al Qaeda warrior about improving his quality of life was like trying to teach a monkey how to hold a pencil: eventually he would just get frustrated and stick you in the eye with it.

Morgan noted the caves on the rocky wall behind the camp with concern. They hadn't shown on the imagery for some reason and intelligence had not reported their presence. He glanced around for scorpions, then slowly shifted his position. Absently, he touched his BDU shoulder pocket, where he carried three anti-venom vials. He had suffered two scorpion stings over the past few months, and that was enough for him. Nothing like a wasp or bee sting, it was more like getting hit with a lightning bolt.

The first time it had happened, Morgan had been up close and dirty with the enemy and it was all he could do to control his autonomic reflex to jump up and cry out when the pain lanced through him. But his SEAL training had held. Still motionless against the rocks they were using for cover, he'd shut off the pain of the scorpion sting and calmly, swiftly self-injected the anti-venom that prevented anaphylactic shock.

Morgan saw a man exit the lead truck as the others with him stood around him. The others fell in behind him as he casually walked toward the campfire. Camp leaders assembled in a gravel wash around the encampment's central campfire. The man was greeted and kissed by his officers. Following the euphoric greeting ritual, they all sat around the fire and began to talk.

Morgan whispered into his radio throat mic, "Standby, on my mark."

He studied the men around the campfire using the color night vision scope mounted on his assault rifle's top Picatinny rail. As sparks suddenly erupted into the sky, he saw Al-Adel's face clearly illuminated by the newly stoked campfire. His glasses reflected the orange flames, making his face momentarily look like a Halloween jack o' lantern.

Morgan keyed his squad radio, "Listen up," he whispered. "He's there, fourth from the left, facing us. You guys all got that? I repeat, Saif Al-Adel is the fourth guy from the left, facing us."

Morgan heard three distinct double clicks over his earpiece. At that moment Al-Adel stood gesturing toward the cave area behind him. Morgan realized it was now or never.

"Commence fire!" he said aloud into his radio mic. "Repeat, commence fire!"

The SEALs initiated the ambush by detonating multiple Claymore mines that ripped through the encampment, each slicing and dicing people and equipment in a deadly hundred yard swath. One Claymore luckily scored a direct hit on Al-Adel's lead truck which had been parked in front of a nearby hut. Morgan saw Al-Adel dive face first into the dirt behind the campfire. Following the Claymores, the SEALs fired their LAW rockets into the adobe huts and cave entrances. The grenadiers followed, lobbing their deadly 40mm grenades as fast as they could reload, flinging high-velocity fragmentation into every fleshy mass they could find. Bright flashes from all the exploding warheads illuminated the surrounding area in strobe-like surrealism.

Morgan crouched behind a large rock watching the battle unfold. At this point the enemy still had no idea where the attack was coming from. Although highly aware of his surroundings, it reminded him of a similar battle he was in about a year earlier in Iraq when his former platoon commander, Lt. Moran, was killed in action. They projected maximum violence on the objective that night too, but when Moran led his men forward in the assault, the enemy scored a lucky hit that killed him instantly.

The sharp smell of burning cordite and high explosives wafted over Morgan, slicing into his lungs and burning his eyes. It was a unique and familiar smell. On one level, he knew it meant death and destruction. At another level it was euphoric. He watched startled men run wildly about the camp, frantically trying to find both their weapons and cover from the murderous explosions and machinegun fire. He watched many of them fall and not get back up. It was like a front row seat in an IMAX theater, but the air was thick with death and smoke. His body hummed with energy, ready for anything.

A few seconds later, the SEAL machine gunners opened up and began raking the camp, mowing down anything that moved. Morgan stood in a low crouch and, with his men flanking his sides, charged forward assaulting directly toward a stunned Al-Adel still sprawled on his stomach behind the camp fire. They were forty yards from the campfire when Al-Adel saw them. He attempted to get up but couldn't get his feet under him. One of his men stepped in to help lift Al-Adel to his feet just as one of Morgan's men fired. The man went down on top of Al-Adel, his dead weight momentarily pinning Al-Adel to the ground.

Morgan charged at him, now less than twenty-five yards away. Morgan was now out in front of his men, a dangerous place to be in the middle of a firefight especially at night, loping towards Al-Adel in the line of friendly fire. The scene looked more like a defensive team in a football game trying to recover a loose ball than it did a disciplined SEAL assault force.

Al-Adel raised up on one elbow heaving his dead comrade to the side. He peered directly at the fast approaching, Morgan who was hell bent on capturing him alive. Morgan dove towards him. Al-Adel eyes widened as he rolled to the side. Morgan crashed down just behind him frantically grabbing at Al-Adel who was now just beyond his reach. On hands and knees he scurried into the darkness behind a hut a few yards away.

Morgan's men stitched the hut with automatic weapons fire coming dangerously close to Morgan. Fortunately, Morgan had the presence of mind to not continue his pursuit of Al-Adel lest he be accidentally shot by his own men.

As his men joined him, Morgan led his fire team in the same direction Al-Adel had gone but it was too late. They arrived behind the hut in time to glimpse Al-Adel headed in the direction of the mountain caves. Several followers opened fire on the SEALs, heroically defending Al-Adel's rear. The SEAL machine gunners and grenadiers returned fire cutting most of them down where they stood.

The SEALs relentlessly pursued Al-Adel but ran into a wall of murderous enemy fire coming from the direction of the heavily fortified caves. Two heavy and four light machine guns opened up, sharply stopping the SEALs advance.

Morgan was surprised. *Where the hell did those guns come from? Why didn't INTEL know they had them and warn us they were there?*

The SEALs immediately took cover and returned fire, but the momentum of their assault had been stopped and they were now out-gunned from fortified positions above. Al-Adel's men quickly regrouped and began raining mortars along with withering counter-fire back at the SEALs. Morgan realized Al-Adel had escaped into the caves and that carrying the assault further would be costly. It was time to go.

"Break contact! Repeat, break contact! Extract. Extract!" Morgan switched his radio to a different frequency and called the AC-130U gunship high above. "Spooky, Spooky, this is Timberjack, we're on target and taking heavy fire, breaking enemy contact. Request immediate covering fire for exfil to LZ Red, over."

Morgan and his men directed their combined fire toward the caves in an attempt to suppress the enemy fire as they withdrew. As Morgan passed by the place where he tried to tackle Al-Adel he noticed a satchel. He snatched it up hanging its strap over his left arm. Without compromising their volley of fire, the SEALs quickly fell back to the safety of the mountain ravine where they'd begun the attack. There they would wait for Spooky's arrival above.

The AC-130U gunship was the latest variant the Air Force had. It was equipped with a 25mm trainable Gatling gun that fired at eighteen hundred rounds a minute, a single barrel 40mm L60 Bofors cannon, and a M102 105 Howitzer. It was no less than a virtual flying fire support base. The U model also had dual target attack capability which allowed it to detect and simultaneously engage two targets up to one kilometer apart. It could also see and fire through clouds, using the same radar target acquisition system installed in the Air Force's F-15E Strike Eagle fighter jets. It was easy to understand why the Air Force's 4th Special Operations Squadron's nickname was "Ghostriders" and their slogan was, "You can run, but you'll just die tired."

Typical procedure for the AC-130s was to orbit several miles away from the target at an altitude of twenty-five thousand feet or more so their engine noise would not be heard from the target location. As a means to ensure their ready availability to provide close air support for the ground forces, they would begin their depressurizing descent toward the target area the moment enemy contact was made, or in this case, upon initiation of the ambush. In the absence of any anti-aircraft artillery (triple-A) threat they would most often take station directly over the target, flying a racetrack pattern at an altitude of five to ten thousand feet above ground level.

Morgan's radio crackled with the cool voice of the AC-130's co-pilot.

"Timberjack, this is Spooky, we hold your position, over."

"Roger, Spooky, request immediate suppressing fire on cave area located approximately two-five-zero yards directly north of our position."

"Roger, Timberjack, we have target area sighted. Firing now."

A stream of tracers, immediately followed by a horrendous roar came from the cloud-obscured night sky above. A shaft of fire covered every inch of an area the size of a football field. In return, a stream of machinegun tracers leapt skyward from one of the cave entrances in the direction of the AC-130. It was immediately extinguished by six well-placed rapid fire shots from the gunship's 40mm Bofors cannon.

Morgan moved his men back and melted into the darkness of the surrounding terrain. There, he took a head count to ensure they were all there. He then assembled them into patrol formation for the dangerous trek back to the CV-22 landing zone, which was located about two miles away on the only patch of level ground in the vicinity.

The SEALs patrolled along a mountain trail that led to the landing zone without incident. They were not being pursued. They remained vigilant and all breathed a relaxing sigh of relief.

The point man suddenly stopped the patrol and crouched to the side of the steep trail. The SEALs stepped off the narrow trail and took defensive positions crouching beside large rock outcrops or other terrain features that made them difficult to spot. Morgan cautiously moved up to his point man to see what the problem was. Then he saw why the patrol had been halted. A goat herder and his young apprentice were herding their goats along the trail dead ahead.

Over the past forty minutes the SEALs had been climbing as fast as possible and the altitude was beginning to take its toll. Morgan checked his GPS. The landing zone was located just a thousand yards further over the hilltop.

Morgan knew he had a decision to make and he only had two options to choose from. He could kill the old man and the boy and move on up the trail, or he could take them prisoner. Taking them prisoner was a liability because at some point he would either have to let them go, risking obvious compromise, or take them back to the forward operating base in the CV-22s for later turnover to the Afghan forces. He knew from experience that turning them over to Afghan forces was essentially a death warrant.

"We have two goat herders just ahead. Move up and take them," he ordered over his squad radio.

The SEALs quietly advanced in the darkness catching the old man and the boy by complete surprise. Using nylon ties like handcuffs, they secured both of their hands.

As the patrol reformed all hell broke loose around them. The enemy began dropping mortars on them from the other side of the opposing mountain. The first round exploded on the hillside above the SEALs, the second exploded below them in an effort to bracket their position. Panicked goats bolted in all directions. The old man crouched next to a rock outcropping about twenty feet away and the boy stood on the trail, jaw gaping and eyes glazed with fear as hot shell fragments whizzed by.

Morgan's point man darted from cover and hauled the boy off the trail, pulling him down beside him. A third mortar exploded nearby killing several goats and wounding some others. They lay on their sides, aimlessly kicking frayed limbs in a feeble attempt to stand. The scene was turning chaotic. Morgan knew the next rounds would be even closer until the enemy found their mark.

"Spooky, Spooky, this is Timberjack. We're taking mortar fire from our northwest. Our current position is one-thousand yards southeast of LZ Red. Request immediate fire suppression, over. Break, break, Racer, Racer, this is Timberjack, prepare for extraction at LZ Red in two zero mikes. LZ may be hot. Coordinate your approach with Spooky, over," Morgan barked into his radio mic.

Once again the cool voice of the AC-130's co-pilot crackled over Morgan's earpiece.

"Roger, your last, Timberjack. We got that mortar position in sights, firing."

Three flashes in rapid succession occurred high above as the gunship fired its 105 Howitzer, followed by three horrific explosions on the hillside about five hundred yards to the northwest. A second later the 40mm Bofors cannon opened fire, targeting an area about one hundred yards to the left of the first target. Silence reigned as the SEALs huddled in the darkness to the side of the steep mountain trail.

"Let's get out'a here," Morgan told his men over his squad radio.

"What about the kid and the old man?" Chief Springer asked.

"Bring'm along for their own safety. We'll release them when we get to the LZ."

The SEALs re-formed their patrol and hurried up the steep trail toward the landing zone. About twenty minutes later they arrived at the edge of Landing Zone Red.

Morgan clicked open his radio, "Racer, Racer, this is Timberjack, request immediate extraction at LZ Red, over."

The sound of approaching tilt-rotor CV-22 aircraft slowly intensified to the deafening sound of rotors beating the air into submission and jet engine whine as the two completely darkened aircraft touched down precisely in front of the waiting SEALs.

Morgan cut the ties on the hands of the old man and the boy. He reached into his cargo pocket and pulled out a handful of chocolate-coated energy bars. He put them into the boy's hand and smiled. He pointed back down the trail and gestured for the old man and boy to leave the area, then scurried over the open tail ramp into the closest CV-22s.

Inside, he was given a headcount to ensure they had everyone. Morgan gave a thumbs-up to the crew chief. The aircraft lifted off, climbing near vertically several hundred feet to get above the surrounding hilltops before transitioning into forward flight.

Strapping into a bulkhead-mounted jump seat, his mind shifted to his return state-side. his had been a long deployment for him and his men. Five days from now they would return home – return to the world – as they often referred to it. They would all take some well deserved leave and then be reassigned elsewhere for three to six months of pre-deployment training and work-ups until their next deployment rotation came around about six to ten months from now. Morgan stared into the plane's dark interior wondering where he would be assigned next. Wherever it was, he hoped it would be a wet place with lots of green foliage.

As the two planes transitioned into forward flight, the enemy again opened fire with a heavy machine gun from a nearby hillside, spewing orange tracers across Morgan's lead aircraft. Both planes had a pedestal-mounted .50 caliber machinegun on their tail ramps and the tail gunners in both aircraft returned fire but the enemy position was out of their effective field of fire. Morgan's CV-22 took several enemy rounds through its nose, belly and left wing. The ground fire knocked out the plane's forward-looking infrared. Fortunately, none of its other critical mechanical or electronic systems were damaged. Miraculously, no one inside was hit.

The AC-130 gunship opened fire on the enemy machinegun position completely covering the location with a blanket of tracers, totally destroying it. Morgan's damaged CV-22 was able to limp back to the forward operating base and land safely.

During the flight, Morgan rummaged through the satchel he found at the ambush site. It contained a number of documents and a map. The documents were written in Arabic. But he carefully examined the map which showed several Taliban supply routes. The safe houses they used were marked as were the major Afghan Army locations. He rummaged a third pocket and found a flash drive inside a Ziploc baggie. He held it between his fingers trying to imagine what information it might contain.

Chapter 4

Desert mountain camp - first light

On foot, Al-Adel and his lieutenants cautiously returned to the camp. Pausing on a ridge above in the pre-dawn light, they carefully studied their still-smoldering camp. After detecting no movement or enemy activity, he sent a two-man scout party down to the camp just to be sure. His scouts stopped short of entering the camp and waited there for several minutes before warily signaling the all clear.

Al-Adel and the rest of his men guardedly patrolled down to the camp. He cautiously walked through his camp, stepping over bodies, body parts and rubble. Dozens of his dead loyalists lay about the smoldering camp. His heavily armed guards checked the dead followers for signs of life. They found none. The stench of burned flesh and human carnage was overwhelming. He was outraged. He knelt down on one knee and angrily threw a handful of gravel in the direction the SEALs had retreated hours earlier.

"The devil has invaded my home," he hoarsely proclaimed.

His lieutenants flocked around their troubled leader.

"Thirty-six dead," a lieutenant reported. "The Americans also bombed our border factory in Sharif. It is still burning," he grunted in a low voice while kicking at the gravel.

"Our other camps were destroyed by American missiles. Many are dead," another lieutenant offered.

Al-Adel grabbed another handful of gravel and threw it in the same direction he threw the first.

"They seek to kill us and return power to our Taliban brothers. They think this will defeat al Qaeda. But the Taliban do not need to negotiate with the Americans and they will never keep their word even if they do. Our lines of supply into our Pakistani bases are secure and the Americans can never deny us or our Taliban brothers a sanctuary. The Taliban have many intelligence agents within the Afghan and Pakistani forces."

Al-Adel paused and scooped up another handful of gravel.

"That is why we will always know what they intend. The Russians learned the hard way, the Americans still have not learned." Al-Adel let the gravel slowly strain through his fingers as he emptied his hand. "We shall see if the American president will stake his presidency on success in Afghanistan and Pakistan. I think he will not."

What Al-Adel didn't share with his men was that he had another far more credible source of intelligence about American worldwide operations; even British, French, Russian and Chinese operations. It was a source outside al Qaeda and the Taliban. It was a source that existed outside the realm of any single government. His handlers would provide the means – they always did – in return for his total allegiance to them. He had secretly worked for this powerful shadow group for nearly ten years and was handsomely rewarded for doing their bidding. Even Bin Laden didn't know about Al-Adel's extracurricular activities and now that he was dead and gone, he never would. Al-Adel felt joy knowing the whole Middle Eastern conflict was contrived and manipulated by this shadow group. As incredible as it seemed, he knew first-hand that they had the power to control more than just nations.

Al-Adel stood and defiantly emptied his AK-47 in the air.

"For every believer who shed his blood for Allah last night, a thousand American infidels will die."

"God is great!" they all chanted firing their AK-47s into the air, "Death to infidels! Death to America! Praise be to Allah!"

Chapter 5

Jakarta, Indonesia

The steamy streets of Jakarta continually buzz with people and traffic. The clogged sidewalks look like the confused mass migration of a school of fish, with no clear direction. A beat-up taxi slowed outside of Energy International Shipping Corporation's (EISC) Indonesia field office and pulled over to the curb. A passenger in the back seat handed the driver a brown envelope stuffed with a wad of cash. The driver opened the envelope, checked the money and smiled, then nodded approvingly back at his passenger. The passenger pulled a photo from his pocket and showed it to the cabbie, then exited without comment. He sauntered through stopped traffic to a sidewalk across the street where he lit a cigarette. Leaning back against a shaded wall he watched the EISC entrance across the street. He took a long relaxing inhalation, slowly exhaling the smoke skyward. Several cigarettes later he recognized the man in the photo, Bill Hart, a licensed merchant fleet officer, exiting the front of the EISC building. He nodded over to the waiting cab driver. The cabbie moved his taxi up next to Hart and signaled he was vacant. Hart got into the back seat. Even though all the windows were down, the first thing the cabbie noticed about his new passenger was that he smelled like a brewery.

"Where to, sir?

"Airport," Hart simultaneously said, slapping the back of the cabbie's vinyl covered seat with a pop.

"No problem. Where you headed, sir?"

"Sunda Kelapa."

"Yes, sir. Big ships there. Are you a captain?"

Oblivious to the cabbie's question, Hart removed an inch thick booklet containing engineering check lists from his briefcase and began running his finger down the marked items on its pages.

"Are you a seaman?"

"What? No, no, I'm a Chief Engineer."

As the taxi disappeared down the busy street, the passenger who got out of the cab earlier, dialed his cell phone.

Thirty minutes later, along the road to Jakarta airport, the taxi proceeded slowly through jammed traffic. The cab driver again checked the envelope he was given and smiled before turning onto a side road that quickly narrowed into little more than a jungle trail. Hart suddenly found himself choking from the stench of rotting jungle. He looked up and realized the cab had pulled off the highway.

"Is there a problem?"

The driver glanced at Hart in his rearview mirror and smiled. Hart was completely distracted from his surroundings as he studied his engineering notebook.

"Please excuse, sir. I must relieve myself. I will only take a moment."

The driver stopped the cab and disappeared into some thick foliage in front of the cab. Hart continued to study his check sheets, penciling notes in their margins.

Moments later a motorcyclist pulled up beside the taxi on the passenger side. Hart looked up in horror realizing he had no escape. The man emptied a pistol through the open window into the back seat. Hart slumped onto the seat, his blood slowly pooling on its vinyl cover.

The motorcyclist dismounted and quickly reloaded a fresh magazine into his pistol. He then opened the cab door and pulled Hart's lifeless body onto the ground. He took everything from Hart's coat pockets along with his notebook and briefcase. As the cab driver emerged from the bushes unafraid, the motorcyclist drew his pistol and shot him dead, too. The motorcyclist grabbed the envelope with the money from the driver's shirt pocket and sped away.

U.S. Department of State, Washington, DC

Secretary of State Cummings was sitting in her 7th floor office when the phone on her desk rang. She had been closely following Iran's belligerent policy regarding their nuclear weapon development program. Shortly after leaving office, her husband, the former President of the United States, had worked a deal with the United Arab Emirates (UAE) to build upwards of twenty nuclear power plants throughout the UAE, Saudi Arabia and Kuwait. Their intention was to share the power grid, thereby weaning them off the use of their own fossil fuel for the generation of electricity. Of course, she and President Banner publicly opposed this initiative because of the nuclear weapon proliferation issues involving the potential for reactor dual use in plutonium production.

Behind closed doors she was delighted, because it would ultimately result in her and her husband becoming filthy rich from all the UAE and Saudi "consulting" payoffs. Kept from general public knowledge was the fact that, by default, the former president's involvement in jamming this deal through the approval process essentially sanctioned Iran to go forward with the construction of their nuclear reactor program.

She knew full well that Iran had sinister ulterior motives involving their own nuclear reactor construction, but by approving the neighboring Arab countries' nuclear power initiatives, U.S. leverage to prevent Iran from doing the same had been significantly diminished.

She and her husband had been involved in other get rich schemes previously, some of which were at the expense of the U.S. taxpayer. One more didn't challenge either's conscience. Besides, they both thought Banner was an idiot and they would have to close this deal under his watch lest the opportunity would never again present itself. Her desk phone intercom suddenly chirped to life with the voice of her secretary.

"Madam Secretary, Ambassador Mahmoud Zayid of Egypt wishes to speak with you on line two."

She sighed as she clicked the speaker phone intercom button, "Thank you, Shawna, I'll take the call."

She pressed the flashing button labeled Line 2.

"Secretary Cummings," she softly announced.

"Madam Secretary, I hope you are well today."

She instantly recognized the voice on the other end as Egyptian Ambassador Zayid.

"Yes, I am well, Ambassador Zayid, thank you."

"Madam Secretary, I am calling you to personally remind you that Egypt will not tolerate armed merchant vessels transiting our territorial water. We have received some very disturbing reports that a U.S.-flagged merchant vessel recently fired on some suspected pirates in the Gulf of Aden and that this ship had transited the Suez Canal and Red Sea only days earlier. Is it necessary that we now search every U.S. flagged merchant vessel that enters our waters?"

Cummings knew Egypt's rules regarding armed merchant vessels and she knew all about Boucher's encounter with the pirates.

"Ambassador Zayid, I don't know the details to which you refer, but I will certainly look into it and get back to you. I can assure you that the United States has the highest respect for Egypt's rule of law and we value your friendship and support. I hope this alleged incident can be overlooked and that the trust which we share between one another has not been endangered."

"Madam Secretary, I knew you would understand. It has also come to my attention that President Cummings should talk to us about nuclear power plants. We have heard that he has been instrumental in clearing the path for U.S. government support to build a number of these plants throughout several Middle Eastern nations."

Cummings now knew the real purpose of Zayid's office call and had to be very careful how she responded to his feeler.

"Ambassador Zayid, you know that I cannot use my office for such matters."

"Of course, Madam Secretary, I am not suggesting that you abuse your office. I am only informally wishing that you might mention it to your husband, perhaps over dinner at my residence sometime soon. It would be worth a great deal to have him involved."

Cummings saw dollar signs surrounding the ambassador's request.

"My husband and I would be most honored to have dinner with you at your residence. I'm sure he will contact you soon."

"Thank you, Madam Secretary. I am sure Egypt will not have any interest in searching U.S. flagged vessels transiting our territorial waters. And, since President Banner has announced that the Global War on Terrorism is over, I am also sure that my country is now anxious to talk with you about supporting some of your regional military basing requirements. Your continued friendship is very important to us. Good day, Madam Secretary."

Cummings hung up the phone and leaned back in her chair. She glanced up at the ceiling smiling the back at the phone. "Yes!" she exclaimed, throwing her pen across the room at the credenza where her husband's picture stood.

Indonesian Port, Sunda Kelapa, three days later

An EISC-owned liquefied natural gas (LNG) supertanker was moored to an offshore loading terminal. VIRGO, the ship's name, was painted in three foot high black letters on each side of the ship's bow and across her stern. Supertankers like the Virgo were so large that they typically on loaded and discharged their explosively hazardous cargo of liquefied natural gas at a pier-like terminal located well offshore. This lessened the requirement for the ship to enter harbor areas of restricted maneuverability while increasing safety, should a spill or fire occur while pierside.

Inside Virgo's pilothouse, high above the ship's weather deck, a middle age, no nonsense captain, by the name of Bakke, examined his navigation charts. His short white beard, sun-baked skin and leathery hands contrasted against his starched and pressed khaki shirt and trousers. He carefully ran his finger over the planned route already plotted on the navigation chart that he would be sailing from Indonesia to New Jersey. Apparently satisfied, he grunted to himself and departed for the weather deck five levels below.

On the weather deck, Jon Deeds, the Virgo's new Chief Engineer, called Chief, for short, was checking on his two-man engineering team to ensure they had properly secured the pumps and valve manifolds for sea, following the cargo on-loading of liquefied natural gas. Captain Bakke approached him from behind.

"Chief, how soon?" Bakke demanded, startling him.

Deeds wheeled to face the voice and recognized his captain with a smile.

"We're fully loaded, Captain. Pumps and tanks are secure and ready for sea. Main engineering is standing by for your order."

Bakke carefully inspected the valve manifold where Deeds was standing.

"Lousy timing for Hart to go AWOL," Bakke commented.

"Yeah, licensed in steam, motor and gas turbines, he can pretty much do it all – he's a fine chief engineer."

"No, he isn't," Bakke countered. "He's a womanizing drunkard. I'm glad you happened to be in country and were available to fill in. I'll only excuse Hart's disappearance if he's dead. It's nearly impossible to replace a qualified chief engineer on one of these tankers at the last minute." Bakke raised his handheld radio. "Chief Mate, prepare for departure."

On Virgo's bridge, Samantha Hill, the first female chief mate in the entire merchant tanker fleet, walked out of the pilothouse onto the open bridge wing. She was an attractive woman in a man's world and went by Sam. A tough-as-nails, forties-something blond, with a toned figure and sexy long legs, she grabbed her radio and responded to Bakke's order.

"Preparing to get underway, Captain."

"I never used the word 'underway.' I said, 'prepare for departure,'" Bakke scolded. "There is a difference and you should know what it is. Don't do anything until I get there."

An hour later, the nearly four football field long Virgo, maneuvered out of shallow waters to a calm blue water sea. Giant swells gently kissed the side of the mammoth ship rolling her so slightly it was as if she was responding to a gentle caress. Walking on an elevated catwalk spanning the top of the LNG storage tanks, Deeds thoughtfully inspected the piping running along the globe-shaped tanks. He wiped the sweat from his forehead with his handkerchief, and then replaced his sunglasses and ball cap. Using his hand to shade his eyes, he carefully scrutinized the ship's masts protruding seventy five feet skyward from the main deck. It was as if he was studying their relationship to the globe piping manifolds below.

Bakke observed his new chief engineer from the forward bridge windows and liked what he saw. He liked Deeds' attention to detail and his obvious engineering competence. He turned to see Sam checking the navigation plot on the chart against the ship's GPS position.

"Chief Mate, you see our new Chief out there on deck inspecting the auxiliaries?"

"No, Captain, I hadn't noticed."

"That's your problem. If you ever expect to have your own ship someday you need to 'notice' everything."

"Sorry, Captain, I've been kind of busy making sure we don't run this tub aground or hit another ship during our seaward track. I'll try to pay better attention to the deck and the distribution manifolds next time around."

Office of the Coordinator for Counterterrorism, U.S. Department of State, Washington, DC.

The Office of the Coordinator for Counterterrorism, or S/CT as it was abbreviated at the State Department, was abuzz with activity. S/CT had activated their emergency operations center (EOC) along with the other major agencies of the Executive Branch, shortly after the Department of Homeland Security raised the threat level to Red. This increase in threat level was predicated on intelligence that pointed to an imminent terrorist attack on a major U.S. city that was expected to occur within the next seventy-two hours, using a weapon of mass destruction, or WMD. The problem was the intelligence community neither knew which city was targeted or what kind of WMD, chemical, biological or nuclear weapon; the terrorists had at their disposal or would likely use.

Unbeknownst to the American public, this very sort of threat level elevation happened several times a year, usually around Islamic holidays or whenever the President's chief of staff read a new Vince Flynn novel with a scenario that he believed plausible and kept him awake at night. Regardless of the driving motivator, the entire U.S. government intelligence, counterterrorism, law enforcement and emergency response communities would go to full alert, activate their emergency operations centers, or EOCs, and man them with full twenty-four hour-a-day watch sections until the threat was mitigated or otherwise proven to be invalid.

Sitting at his desk in the S/CT's EOC, retired Navy SEAL Captain Dean Blackburn, mindlessly sipped his coffee while he carefully read through a hodgepodge stack of classified intelligence cables that had been arranged in date-time group chronological order by the watch section's duty officer.

"Hey, Captain," a familiar voice said from behind. The voice belonged to his former Navy subordinate, Lieutenant Jimmy Bruce, who was, in Blackburn's opinion, the smartest operational intelligence analyst he had ever worked with. Blackburn had retired from the Navy under a cloud of unproven controversy involving a frivolous sexual harassment charge brought against him by a young woman while he was the Commanding Officer of the Kennedy Irregular Warfare Center at the Office of Naval Intelligence. Bruce became so disgusted with the way the Navy allowed Blackburn, a man with a thirty-eight year flawless career, to be thrown under the bus because of political correctness, he resigned his commission and left the Navy in protest. Both Blackburn and Bruce were immediately hired by the U.S. Department of State at the personal direction of Secretary of State Cummings. They were now both reporting directly to Aldridge McKenna, the Ambassador at Large for Counterterrorism in S/CT.

"Jimmy, how many times do I have to tell you to call me by my first name?" Blackburn replied pushing back from his desk. "We're not in the Navy anymore."

Bruce held the greatest respect and admiration for his former Commanding Officer, current boss and mentor, and he insisted on maintaining military protocol even though it was otherwise unnecessary.

"I thought I did, Captain."

"Okay, suit yourself Jimmy," Blackburn chuckled, "but one of these days you gotta let that shit go. We're both civilians now. What'cha got?"

"I invite your attention to this cable," Bruce said as he passed a clipboard to Blackburn.

Blackburn flipped up the orange-colored, Top Secret cover sheet and began to read the three-page intelligence report. Finishing the executive summary on the first page of the intelligence report, he stopped and put the clipboard down on his desk.

"Tell me, Jimmy, do you agree with this analysis regarding the 'color' revolution?"

"You want my opinion or the party line?" he replied already knowing what the answer would be.

"Your opinion - if you please."

"Well, Sir, as you know, it's a convoluted issue. Iran is experiencing tremendous internal political turmoil largely brought on by two powerful factions within Iran. Ahmadinejad is on the one side and Rafsanjani is on the other.

"Ahmadinejad is blaming the CIA for trying to topple his government. If you recall, after his election there were protests against his regime, claiming that the election was fraudulent and that he stole the election. These protesters used the Iranian national colors as their symbol for revolution. The Western media reported on it like it was a full scale challenge by pro-Western protesters to delegitimize the ruling regime. In contrast, Moscow reported it was an attempt by the U.S. to repudiate the election and install a pro-Western government by encouraging a color revolution. Naturally, Ahmadinejad sided with Russia in claiming the demonstrators were puppets of the CIA and the Islamic republic had come under threat. This strategy worked to cleverly discredit anything the protesters said."

"The Russians?" Blackburn asked in surprise.

"Yes, Sir, the Russians. If you recall, right in the middle of all the protests Ahmadinejad attended a multinational Shanghai Cooperation Organization conference in Moscow, arriving a day after it had begun. I thought that was kind of peculiar since he left Iran during a period of significant unrest, and at the time we didn't see Russian involvement. Since then, Rafsanjani's more moderate side has accused Russia of encouraging the color revolution and providing 'advisors' who directly helped Ahmadinejad quell the post-election unrest by cutting all forms of electronic communications like cell phones, land lines and radios and restricting travel. It also appears the Russians provided some pretty significant intelligence support to Ahmadinejad as well."

"Geez, Jimmy, I had no idea the Russians were players to that extent."

"Yes, Sir, they're players alright and I think it's getting worse. The Russians are surging even further into Iran's political landscape and that explains why the Russians have denied the U.S. any meaningful assistance on matters that involve Iran."

"So how do you think we should deal with it?"

"We should continue to encourage Rafsanjani supporters to position the Ahmadinejad regime as pro-Russian and paint Ahmadinejad as a very wealthy elitist who has lost touch with his people and the Islamic republic cause that

Ayatollah Ruhollah Khomeini founded when he took power during the Iranian Revolution in 1979."

"Do you think this will bring Ahmadinejad down?"

"It's hard to say, Sir. He has lots of enemies, but it appears the Russians are keeping him fully advised and amply warned of potential threats well in advance. Most importantly, they have clandestinely provided him with Russian military special operations help to safeguard his regime. That makes him frightening, both politically and militarily, to those who oppose him. We think the Russians are close to providing Tehran with their ultra-sophisticated S-300 strategic air defense systems. The S-300 is formidable to everything we have except our F-35 stealth bombers. As you know, our influence in Iran was already suffering, but when President Banner refused to even so much as comment on Ahmadinejad's post-election protests we lost what little influence we had left. In my opinion, Russia is playing its hand masterfully and has succeeded in developing a true Russian-Iranian entente. And, it is the strength of that entente that has now resulted in our strategic problems throughout the entire region."

Blackburn flipped back a page in the report and read it aloud. "It says here Israel may feel threatened enough to attack Iran's nuclear weapon development facilities."

"That's right, Sir, and I concur. The one thing that both Ahmadinejad and Rafsanjani agree upon is Iran's ambitions to become a nuclear power. Once they have the bomb, they'll be working from a position of strength as a member of the Nuclear Club. That will give them a strong political platform from which to ultimately expand their Islamic extreme fundamentalist objectives throughout the region and abroad. I don't know about you, Sir, but that scares the hell out of me. President Banner has made it publicly clear that we will not take any military action toward Iran so we no longer have that bargaining chip to use either. The president has also unsuccessfully tried to force Israel into committing to join his 'world community' position but they won't ever do that nor in my opinion, should they."

"Agreed, but what do you think they'll do?"

"The Israelis have already deployed two of their submarines and three of their corvettes through the Suez Canal into the Red Sea. My guess is they'll slowly work their way to Karachi and base out of there. That will keep them close enough to Iran's southern border and the Persian Gulf to threaten Iran's shipping in the event Israel bombs Iran's nuclear development facilities and Tehran retaliates. We also need to keep an eye on North Korea. They're providing shiploads of nuclear bomb making materials to Iran in open defiance of the United Nations Security Council resolutions demanding they stop."

"It sounds to me like President Banner needs to reconsider our policy with regard to Iran, Israel and North Korea and put our military option back on the table."

"Yes Sir. Exactly."

"One more thing, Jimmy. What do you know about former President Cummings' visit to North Korea to get those three American journalists released? President Banner must have conceded something to North Korea to buy their release, but no one knows what it cost us. It's been bugging the hell out of me."

"Are you asking me for my opinion, Sir, or the party line?"

"Damn it, Jimmy, your opinion."

Bruce chuckled.

"Sir, you may recall when Cummings was president he facilitated the sharing of our nuclear reactor technology for peaceful uses with North Korea. Of course North Korea never abided by their promise to keep their technology peaceful so they ended up with some nuclear reactors that China and Russia sold them and an unchecked means to make plutonium."

"Yeah, but didn't the United Nations' International Atomic Energy Agency ride herd on their progress?"

"Well, Sir, they were supposed to, but North Korea refused to fully cooperate and took their program underground - literally."

"Just like Iran has done."

"Yes Sir, and since Russia and China both have seats at the UN's Security Council table, the UN was unable to vote any consequential sanctions into place against North Korea."

"So if I understand what you're saying accurately, you think Cummings went to North Korea with President Banner's full approval and offered them a deal involving nuclear power plants?"

"That's right. He was also the mover and shaker for the nuclear power plant deal with the UAE last year and I'll bet he cut a similar deal with North Korea. There's no doubt that Secretary of State Cummings is in on it as well. She'll probably run for president again. And North Korea would love to see that happen because of their relationship with her husband, former President Cummings."

"Yeah, scary thought. So Jimmy, what is the status of North Korea's nuclear weapons program?"

"They seem to be in the process of simultaneously taking two closely-related directions towards acquiring a nuclear arsenal of their own. First, they have no intention of quitting their own development of an atomic bomb. They have a number of deep underground nuclear weapon development facilities, some of which are cleverly located beneath major population areas. This makes bombing them politically impossible because of the civilian casualties that would result. Their second thrust is to develop and expand the depth of their experienced nuclear weapon scientists, engineers and technicians. Since their own program is comparably small in terms of state-supported nuclear weapon development, they are selling their technology to Myanmar and providing them with North Korean scientists and engineering personnel to run the programs. This allows them to expand their cadre of experienced personnel while keeping them gainfully employed and disbursed in another country. It also gives them an opportunity to leverage a dual effort for their nuclear weapon development program. It's no less than brilliant and there isn't a damn thing we can do about it short of military action."

"But if we know this is going on, why would President Banner authorize former President Cummings to cut any deals with them?"

"All I can say is I hope both Banner and Cummings are stopped before it's too late. Can you imagine two radical regimes like North Korea and Myanmar both armed with nukes? I mean, if they have them you can bet your sweet ass al Qaeda won't be far behind because North Korea and Myanmar will sell them to the other zealot loonies no matter who they are."

Blackburn threw his head back and snorted, "Now that's a concept – al Qaeda with nukes."

Chapter 6

Ocete, Antioquia Providence, Colombia, the same time.

The small B-105 helicopter hugged the terrain, masking its presence to radar. It followed a circuitous course flying low through deep valleys remaining at treetop level whenever it was forced to cross mountain ridges, only exposing itself momentarily at the peak, then quickly ducking down again into the next valley. Venezuelan Army General Perez was seated in the front right seat. He and a colleague had flown from Venezuela to a small airfield located close to Medellin earlier in the morning where they transferred to the waiting helicopter. It was no secret that the FARC rebel army controlled the entire region.

The Colombian Army, with the assistance of the U.S. Drug Enforcement Agency, had been running counter-drug operations in the area for years with little effect on the well-trained and equipped rebels who controlled the area. However, this day was exceptional because the DEA had solid intelligence that General Perez would be attending a 'drugs for arms' summit of FARC heads at his longtime friend's riverside villa hidden deep in the Andes Mountains along the sprawling Cauca River close to Ocete. The villa was only about forty-five kilometers northeast of Medellin and, while a treacherous drive by car, it was a relatively short trip by helicopter. This day also provided a rare opportunity for the DEA to capture or kill several FARC-related drug kingpins.

As Perez's green and black painted B-105 agilely skimmed above the mountainous terrain, a Florida National Guard Black Hawk helicopter, call sign, "Mallet Two-One", followed far behind. A second Black Hawk, call sign, "Grinder Six-Six", hovered out of sight behind a steep ridge, waiting in ambush for Perez's helicopter to appear. This was not unique, the Florida

National Guard regularly supported DEA counter-drug operations ranging from Nicaragua to Colombia with helicopters.

"Grinder Six-Six, this is Mallet Two-One, estimate target following terrain at altitude of one hundred fifty feet, range two miles from your position. He's heading straight for the mountain pass. We're going to close to about a half mile in case he turns and runs. How copy over?"

"Mallet Two-One, Grinder, copy all. We're ready. Out."

Moments later, as the B-105 entered the narrow mountain pass, the heavily armed Grinder Six-Six, intercepted it head on.

When the Black Hawk appeared, the B-105 pilot fired a short burst from his pylon-mounted machinegun in the direction of the Black Hawk and banked sharply to the left, diving to the tree tops. The Black Hawk's door gunner returned fire with his machinegun and the race was on.

"Grinder, Mallet, we have made contact and are in pursuit."

"Roger, Mallet, we're one half mile behind you on your eight o'clock, in pursuit."

The B-105 pilot was no stranger to this terrain and took full advantage of his detailed familiarity by staying so low he was actually clipping the treetops with the landing skids beneath the helicopter. The less nimble Black Hawks were forced to remain well above,making a kill shot at the small dodging and weaving helicopter below impossible. All they could do was follow and try to maintain visual contact. Fortunately for them, the sun was high in an otherwise blue sky so shadows on the ground were nonexistent.

Ahead, a small area of the steep mountain was devoid of foliage and looked unnaturally scarred. The B-105 approached a steep rock face and burbled to a hover. A gaping opening to a massive cave loomed directly ahead.

"Grinder, this is Mallet, you see the target?"

"Roger, take the shot."

The lead Black Hawk nosed toward the B-105 and fired two rockets which both detonated harmlessly to the right of the cave opening, showering rock and dirt onto the jungle below. The second Black Hawk slowed to a hover and took position to the left of the one that had just fired. The B-105 pilot had a trick up his sleeve which the National Guard Black Hawk pilots could not have expected. As the Black Hawks slowly approached the B-105 in an effort to force it to land, the small B-105 disappeared inside the cave opening.

"Mallet, did you just see that?"

"Roger, Grinder, we need to close this opening and trap him inside. I'll come around and fire from your seven o'clock."

Moments later the two Black Hawk helicopters fired a battery of missiles into the area above the cave opening, sealing it with rubble.

"Mallet, this is Grinder, I'm going to land and check it out."

"Roger, Grinder, I'll remain above and cover."

The second Black Hawk landed a short distance from the smoking cave opening. Four armed DEA agents ran from the helicopter to the cave and cautiously surveyed the damage. They turned and held a thumbs-up for those in the helicopters to see, then returned to their waiting Black Hawk.

"Mallet, this is Grinder. Looks like we nailed him in the cave. Scratch one corrupt general and a FARC drug kingpin."

"Good work, Grinder. Let's get out of here before his friends come looking."

The two Black Hawks gained altitude and headed away from the cave in the direction of Medellin. About a mile away, a streak of smoke rose from the jungle below marking the launch of a shoulder fired surface to air missile. It streaked straight toward the two Black Hawks high above.

"Mallet, Grinder, SAM launch, deploying counter-measures."

The two Black Hawks turned away from one another and dove while they launched chaff and flares to decoy the missile's guidance system. The counter-measures worked. The missile harmlessly streaked by, heading toward the sun.

"Grinder, Mallet, where the hell did that come from? They weren't reported to have anything like that."

"Mallet, Grinder, I guess they do now. Stay sharp."

On the other side of the mountain, the B-105 emerged from a cave opening partially hidden behind a high waterfall. The B-105 followed the river flying just above the water for several miles downstream before banking sharply right and landing beneath some tall trees in the front yard of a sprawling riverside villa. Heavily armed men were defensively positioned in every direction. Perez and his colleague stepped from the helicopter and were escorted into the villa.

Inside, they were greeted by its owner, a former Colombian Army colonel, now a FARC boss.

"Hola General, Es bueno verte de nuevo."

"Sí, Coronel, siempre es bueno verte. Permítame presentar, Al Sr. Rajakovics, nuestro amigo Ruso. Habla Inglés."

The FARC boss offered his hand to Rajakovics and studied him for a moment as their hands clasped. Rajakovics had a ruddy complexion and dark features. He was powerfully built and very fit. He projected a creepy aura, an aura that the FARC boss liked. It was a look that suggested he was a killer. *Perfecto*, the cartel boss thought smiling.

"It is my pleasure to finally meet you. How was your flight?" the FARC boss asked in near perfect English.

Virgo's Bridge, eight days later

Bakke snatched the weather forecast from the printer tray and read it. He didn't like what he saw. He studied Virgo's intended course on the chart table and realized they were heading directly into a tropical depression forming in the Southern Atlantic. He quickly plotted a new heading and drew a pencil line on the chart marking the new course.

"Come right to new heading," Bakke ordered the Virgo's helmsman. "Steer course two seven five degrees. I want to skirt the north side of that storm developing to our south-west."

"New course, two seven five, Captain," the mate repeated as he turned the ship's wheel to the right.

Turning a ship the size of the Virgo took a period of time along with some distance. It just didn't happen fast. The mate watched the gyrocompass slowly arrive at 275 degrees as he centered the ship's wheel, skillfully bringing the massive ship onto its new heading.

Three decks below in the Crew's Lounge, six off-duty crew members bitched to one another as they played poker in the smoke-filled room.

A crewman slugged back his lukewarm coffee, "Added duties, longer hours, less time off. Shit, they've whittled our thirty-two man crew down to..."

"Twenty-five men and a...," the guy on the other end of the table said, almost finishing the sentence.

The crewmen slowly turned toward Sam, who was sitting by herself a few tables away reading a technical manual, and quickly turned away again without her noticing.

"Remember the good ol' days - wooden ships and iron men?" a third crewman blurted.

"Yeah," the guy on the other end of the table replied, "not silicone maidens."

Garth, the youngest of the bunch held up his Playboy magazine with the top half of the centerfold partially open for all to see.

"Worst of all, our Chief Mate is a split-tail blond."

The men all whistled and gave cat-calls, then chanted in unison, "S-a-m-a-n-t-h-a?"

Sam slammed down her coffee cup, launching a vertical column of the black colored liquid upward like a miniature volcanic geyser.

"That's it! I've had it with you assholes! You guys call me Samantha again and I'll kick your asses from here down to the bilge keel. Give me that!" she demanded, ripping the dog-eared Playboy from Garth's hand.

She flipped the centerfold completely out and held it up in front of the young crew member.

"You have something you've been wanting to tell her, don't you?"

"Well I...I..."

"Oh, it's okay, I'll speak to her for you." In her best, bad soap opera acting voice Sam continued, "Dear Miss September - I'm sorry, I mean, Stacy. You're the greatest. You've meant everything to me this month. You've been my reason to live - my very world. Every time I see you it's been like dying and going to heaven. But the time has come. It's over between us. No, no, it's not Miss October. Oh, oh, oh, please don't cry." Sam grabbed a paper napkin off the table and dabbed Stacy's glossy paper eyes. "It...it's not you, it's me." Sam came eye to eye with a crew member sitting at the card table. "Why, you ask? It's because life is complicated. Oh baby, you're such a young chick, so innocent. I'm sooo sorry. I didn't want to hurt you, but, I've found someone else. She's what I've been waiting for, she's real, she's 3-D and she's got no staples in her ass. Best of all she's right here on this floating shit bucket I call home. I hope we can still be friends? Bye!" Sam chucked the Playboy on the table in front of Garth. "I'll call you," she said smirking down at Garth. "You limp dick excuses for real men sit here on your brains think'n this chick-o-the-sea ain't half bad. Her tits? Amazing how they defy gravity. They must be silicone. And her ass? Best I've ever seen on a chief mate. All that and she can drive a supertanker too! Bet I could do her."

Some of the crewmen became uneasy and nervously looked away. Sam knew she had them where she wanted them. She took no joy in acting like this but it was a necessary evil, and a survival skill she had perfected. She continued her poker face rant even more animated than she was before.

"But then, reality smacks you upside the head and you ask yourself, can I pony-up for this ride? Just like a supertanker, she's most definitely high maintenance. What would it take? Pop open a bottle of expensive bubbly? Dinner and dancing at the Rainbow Room? Maybe a box of chocolates from the Duty Free shop will do it. Is she worth a box of chocolates?" Sam said in her best Forrest Gump voice imitation. "Nah, forget the dinner and the chocolates. I'm so suave and debonair I can sweet-talk my way into her Victoria's Secrets."

Some of the crewmen hooted as Sam ominously stomped her foot down on the table top next to Garth a little more than a foot away from his face. He stared at the crease between her legs silhouetted beneath her tightly stretched khaki slacks.

"Okay shipmate, you look like a card-carrying member of the Iron Dick Club, sweet-talk me! Let's hear it! Come on Captain Universe, talk! Catfish got your tongue?"

The crewmen hooted again. They knew she was a competent professional and an excellent Merchant Fleet officer but she was still the only woman on their ship. Hell, she was the only female chief mate in the entire tanker fleet and she didn't make it all the way to that position from her good looks. And at some level, Sam knew her crew saw her as such. Nonetheless, she wasn't going to take any bullshit from them. She shoved Garth's hungry face away and took two steps backward.

"You boys have my word, the only erection you seamen stains will ever share with this chick is...," she slowly raised her middle finger and lovingly said, "screw you all very much!"

The lounge erupted in laughter. As she briskly turned her back on them, Sam was among the laughing, but she didn't let them see her face. She hurried to the door without turning to look back and headed for the bridge.

Office of the Coordinator for Counterterrorism, U.S. Department of State, Washington, DC, the same time.

Jimmy Bruce knocked on the open door as he entered Blackburn's office.

"Sir, did you read this morning's intelligence summary?"

Jimmy, why don't just save me the pain and brief me?"

Blackburn gestured for Bruce to sit in the chair beside his desk.

"Sir, yesterday morning the Jakarta police discovered two male bodies in the jungle about twenty miles outside the city. They were badly decomposed and their bodies had been ravaged by animals. The authorities thought one might be a Caucasian, the other looked like a local. Both were shot multiple times in what looked like an assassination or execution style murder. There was no ID on either man. The bodies were too decomposed to identify."

Oh, wow, Jimmy, two assholes are found dead. That's some really unique intelligence. Why do we care?" he pointedly asked.

"The FBI liaison agent from our embassy in Jakarta was able to remove the forefinger tip pads and thumb pads from the Caucasian's putrefied fingers and press reasonably good prints by putting the flesh over his own gloved finger."

"He did what?"

"He cut the flesh off the dead Caucasian's fingers and put it over his own finger and pressed the dead guy's fingerprints. It's done all the time, Sir. Anyway, the FBI database positively identified the prints as those belonging to a U.S. citizen by the name of William Franklin Hart. He was born in Norfolk, Virginia in 1960. His parents divorced in 1972. His father was an oil exploration geologist who worked for Chevron, primarily in and around Venezuela. After the divorce, Hart stayed in Caracas, living there with his father until he was sixteen. Then he moved back to the states and lived with his mother who remarried a Venezuelan national by the name of Alvaro Alfonso Perez. Perez had a son, Miguel Arvelo Perez, from a previous marriage. Miguel Perez remained in Venezuela and is now a Lieutenant General serving in the Venezuelan Army."

"Damn it, Jimmy, you're babbling about a bunch of extraneous bullshit and you're confusing the shit out of me. Get to the point. Who is Hart and why do I care?"

"Please bear with me on this, Sir." Blackburn waved at him to proceed. "After high school, Hart attended and graduated from the Merchant Marine Academy in 1983. He went into the merchant fleet after that as a career engineer. He has no record of arrest and seems to have been an upstanding citizen in all respects. He has been a chief engineer employed by the Energy International Shipping Corporation headquartered in New York City for the past four years. EISC has a fleet of U.S. flagged supertankers that primarily haul liquefied natural gas and liquefied propane from Indonesia to Japan and New Jersey. EISC confirmed Hart's employment and said that he had reported into their field office in Jakarta two weeks ago and was supposed to sail from Sunda Kelapa onboard one of their supertankers by the name of Virgo. They said he never reported to the ship and they assumed he found a bar and a woman somewhere along the way there. He apparently had a reputation of being a heavy drinker and liked chasing skirts."

Blackburn laughed, "He probably got capped by some jealous husband."

Maybe, Sir, but the National Police in Jakarta are investigating it as a homicide. So far they don't believe there are any jealous husbands or Tanzim Qaedat al-Jihad ties to the murders. Maybe it's just a simple case of robbery gone bad for the victims. Our embassy is shipping Hart's remains back to the States tomorrow. Besides his stepbrother in Venezuela, the only living blood relative he has is his eighty-eight-year old mother who is still living in Norfolk and she's accepting the body."

"That's a pretty extensive file on a guy who's never been arrested."

"The only reason we have this info on him is because Hart participated on a Maritime Administration task force a few years ago and he held a security clearance."

"So I ask you again, Jimmy, why do I give a shit about this guy Hart?"

"Because, Sir, Venezuelan Lieutenant General Miguel Arvelo Perez is Hart's stepbrother."

"That name rings a bell but I ask again, so what?"

"General Perez reports directly to Venezuelan dictator-president Hugo Chavez and has links to al-Qaeda on the Arabian Peninsula."

Blackburn sat forward straightening his back. "You have my attention, Jimmy," he said smiling proudly at his young protégé.

Chapter 7

Bay Ridge, New York City, morning

A city taxi pulled up to the Anchors Away Bar and carelessly parked, partially invading one of the handicap spots by the front door. The driver, Tommy Thompson, got out and went inside. Joey Hoy, a captain on the Staten Island Ferry and Denny Burns, a deckhand, had just come off the early morning shift and were seated at a corner table. Thompson joined his two old friends at a table and ordered coffee. Shortly they were laughing loudly and joking about sex, sports and the mayor trying to enforce jaywalking in New York City.

"If I had me a fuck'n time machine I'd wanna start all over again, 'cept I wouldn't give the fuck'n Indians the sweat off my balls for Manhattan," Hoy declared. "I myself would turn Manhattan into the biggest fuck'n casino you ever did see and fuck Atlantic City and da fuck'n Jersey horse they rode in on!"

The wall-mounted big screen TV showed a special report on U.S. troops in Afghanistan. The three of them stopped talking for a moment while they watched.

Turning away from the TV report, Thompson swallowed hard, "President Banner's fuck'n war? Our guys over dere are now peacekeepers...? Banner is gonna give us a world without war...? Ha! I ain't buy'n dat horshit for one New York minute. I see myself makin' love to all dhem Spice Girls at once while Martha Stewart makes an arrangement with my family jewels before dat ever happens!"

Burns looked puzzled. "Martha Stewart?" he quizzically asked his friend Thompson.

"Denny, you are such a dumbass. You dunno who dat bitch Martha Stewart is?"

"Ahh Tommy, I know where my balls are. You want for me to put'm on your chin and show you?"

The three men laughed as they gulped their morning coffee and packed jelly-filled donuts in their mouths. A heavily tattooed black man with his hair in dreadlocks entered the front door and ominously approached their table. Except for his dirty-white Kufi skull hat, he was cleanly dressed. He was carrying a red and green-colored backpack slung over his left shoulder. He stopped a few feet short of the table and scrutinized the three men as they joked with one another.

"Hey," he interrupted in a thick Harlem accent, "whose drivin' dah cab outside?"

"Who dah fuck wants to know?" Hoy demanded as he rose up from his chair to face the man.

The startled man stumbled backward, obviously intimidated by Hoy's sudden challenge.

"Ahh, I do."

"You got a frick'n name, buddy?"

"Jones. My name is Jones. I need to hire a cab."

"Why you need a cab, Jonesy?" Thompson demanded.

"The courier service did not come when he promised me." The man slipped his backpack off and yanked a plastic wrapped cardboard box about the size of a shoebox from it, putting the box on the table. "I need this part delivered to Milan Tadic. He's the Third Engineer on the MS Royal Norwegian Empress. He's waiting for this box at Pier 88 by the cruise ship terminal on the Westside where the cruise ship Empress is moored. I must get this part to him before they sail today at twelve noon."

"Not this hack, comrade," Thompson replied. "Some of us never drive to Harlem, me, I never set foot in Manhattan."

The man pulled out two crisp C-notes and held them up in front of Thompson. His two friends looked at him in disbelief. "Never?" both Hoy and Burns chided in unison.

Thompson looked at the money. "Another hundred and I'll audition for amateur night at the Apollo wear'n my wife's pink-laced skivvies."

His friends laughed as he grabbed the bills and bolted out the door with the box under his arm.

Old Waterside Warehouse, Fells Point, Baltimore, the same time

Rusting bollards and mooring cleats stood like monuments around the edge of a weathered dock. Severely damaged propellers of all shapes and sizes adorned the outer wall of an aging red brick warehouse across the street from a dilapidated dock. Inside the door, a corrugated tin hut-like office housed a 1950's vintage old wooden desk and some dented gray metal file cabinets. Vietnam, Lebanon, Panama and Desert Storm military honors and plaques covered the office walls from ceiling to floor. Behind the desk, a large, gold-colored Navy SEAL Team insignia plaque, engraved with the slogan, "Dirty Deeds Done Dirt Cheap," hung like an ominous warning to those who entered.

Jake Boucher, unshaven and dressed in worn out pants and shirt like a homeless person, dozed on a worn brown leather sofa nearby. A small TV rested on an unpainted wooden box in the room's far corner, blaring a History Channel narration about Alexander the Great's campaign into Afghanistan. The phone began to ring and ring and ring. Boucher rolled toward the back of the couch and yawned, but didn't wake up.

Jack Doyle, one of Boucher's helpers and former SEAL Team platoon member, yelled from the other side of the warehouse, "Hey Jake, you gonna get that phone or just let it ring off the hook forever?"

Boucher finally snatched the phone on the eighth ring.

"Prop Shop, Jake," he said in a disinterested growl. Suddenly he sat up. "Hey, Deb. Do you a favor? What is it? Uh-huh," he said as he began to perk up. "Seriously…?" Of course I'll do it. I'll be there to pick them up before dinner. I'll call you when I land, bye. Hoo-yah!" he shouted as he hung up the phone. "Hey, Jackie," he shouted, "that was Deb, Pat's ex. She asked me to take Pat's kids for the weekend. I'm gonna fly out to San Diego right now. Please ask Mossman to get the Gulfstream fueled up and ready to go ASAP. I need you guys to fly me out to San Diego."

Doyle walked into the office smiling. He knew how important Leon "Pat" Patterson was to Boucher. Patterson was nearly killed by an assassination attempt against Boucher nine months earlier and sustained severe brain trauma from a bomb blast meant for Boucher. He had been in and out of Baltimore's Johns Hopkins Hospital neurology clinic and rehab facility several times since his injury, but never improved enough to go home. Boucher had blamed himself for Patterson's injury. In fact, Boucher sold his house in Laytonsville, Maryland, where the attack occurred, and moved onboard his yacht which he kept in Baltimore's Inner Harbor just so he could be closer to Patterson. Ever since the incident, he had devoted himself to making sure Patterson was taken care of, and because Patterson could no longer be there for them, Boucher tried to provide a father image for Pat's two teenage kids.

"Pat's ex got herself a boyfriend," Doyle off-handedly commented.

"What makes you say that?"

"Cause I saw her swapping spit with some dickhead at the Babcock & Story Bar in the Hotel Del last week when I was out in Coronado visiting my son."

"You think?"

"Yup, she can't find a sitter. Why else would she call you?"

"Boy, you sure got her number."

"Not really, just been there myself. My ex used to do that to me all the time. The bitch fought me for custody and never gave a shit about giving the kids to me beyond what the court ordered until she got a boyfriend. Then she tried to unload them on me for weeks at a time so she could go play. With her whoring around and all, it's a damn wonder they both grew up with good attitudes."

Boucher stopped packing his bag and looked over at Doyle, "Pisses me off with Pat still in a coma and all."

"Yeah, I guess it's probably a good thing Pat doesn't know about her new boyfriend cause I know he'd try to warn that poor, dumb bastard about what he's getting into. Let's pray the dumbass marries her before Pat comes out of his coma."

Boucher's mind was already on Pat's kids and the weekend.

"What do you think I should do with the kids? They're both teenagers you know."

"Why don't you ask them? Maybe take'm camping to someplace special or something like that."

"Yeah, good plan. That's what I'll do, I'll ask'm and then take'm camping. I know just the place too." Boucher chuckled at his longtime friend, "You know something, Jackie? I don't pay you enough."

"Been telling you that for years, Jake. Lucky for you I don't need no more money."

Twenty minutes later Boucher and Doyle threw his camping equipment into his Ford F-350 dually and headed to the Baltimore-Washington International Airport where they kept their G-4 Gulfstream corporate jet.

Three Blocks from Boucher's Warehouse, Fells Point, Baltimore, Maryland, same time

A telephone linemen's truck was parked in the Safeway parking lot. Its antennas were concealed in its roof rack which carried several ladders. Its bucket lift was secured in the truck's roof storage rack. It looked like any other telephone linemen's truck common in a city environment. Inside, however, it was very different. It was cram packed with state-of-the-art electronic eavesdropping monitoring equipment.Two men dressed in linemen's work clothes sat at a digital console that had three flat screen monitors, computer keyboards and a control panel containing a variety of switches, knobs and digital meters.

"Tafasta?"

"Yes, good copy. Got it all on audio and video live feed."

"Okay, upload the files and relay them to headquarters. He still doesn't know. Kach aw Kak, Chaverim shelanu chayavim Liheyout moochanim."

"Yes, our operatives must be ready. This information will help them."

"We will wait until Boucher and his people are in their plane before we go back to the warehouse and remove our technical collection devices. Anachnu lo yicholim lihistakaim psharah."

"Agreed, we must be careful they do not detect us. I'll tell Unit Two to stand by. They must be followed when they leave the warehouse. We must ensure he conducts the mission."

"Sasbatzar is close and knows about everything they intend. We must be careful."

"Agreed."

New York City, Westside Manhattan, Pier 88

A man, dressed in the MS Empress blue coveralls engineering uniform, waited in the shadows at the head of Pier 88 puffing a cigarette. Pier 88 is New York City's Hudson River cruise ship terminal and pier. A huge cruise ship, the Royal Norwegian Empress was moored portside to the pier with her bow-in. Several large forklifts busily unloaded truckloads of fresh vegetables, frozen meat, dry goods, wine and beer, positioning the pallets on the pier close to the ship's provisioning gangway. Smaller forklifts took the plastic-wrapped pallets up a heavy-duty steel ramp from the pier into the ship's storage lockers and massive refrigerators.

Fuel and freshwater hoses the diameter of a man's thigh ran from pier station manifolds into special receiving ports on the ship's side where engineers monitored the gauges on the manifolds, ensuring that the pressures remained within acceptable pumping tolerance. It was a well-orchestrated provisioning process with multiple moving parts that was practiced every time the ship readied itself for its next cruise and this day was no different. It was all a process that the passengers never saw and one for which they had no appreciation in its direct relationship and importance to their comfort.

A steady stream of passengers boarded through a glass-enclosed, air-conditioned gangway that ran high above the pier. The passenger gangway was well isolated from the scurry of replenishment activities taking place on the pier below. The cruise line even made passenger-boarding fun with live music and free cocktails as they ushered people from the terminal's third floor check-in area across the gangway to the double wide passenger entrance on the ship's main deck. A uniformed off-duty New York City cop stood at the ship's entrance, joking with arriving passengers. He occasionally spot-checked passengers' carry-on luggage, being careful to not jam up the flow of boarding passengers. His role there was more feel good than functional, but it provided the illusion of security.

Escorted by police cars front and back, a black stretch limo arrived at the VIP drop-off area in the front of the passenger terminal. News crews surged forward, surrounding the car as the Governor of New York, his wife and daughter stepped out. A reporter pushed his way to the front of the pack and shoved his mic in front of the Governor for an impromptu interview.

"Governor! Governor! Are you going to announce? Governor! Are you going to run for president?"

The Governor put his hand up, gesturing in a weak wave toward the reporter and the others surrounding him.

"I'll make an announcement by the end of the week," he said smiling widely. "Right now I'd like some private time if you don't mind. I'd like to wish bon voyage to my wife and daughter. Thank you."

Several uniformed New York City police officers stepped in between the governor and the reporters and formed a human barrier. In full view of the press, the governor kissed his wife and daughter as camera shutters clicked and flashes strobed.

Unnoticed, down at the head of the pier, a New York City yellow cab pulled up and stopped. Hoy exited his cab with the cardboard box and placed it in plain view on the cab's roof.

Milan casually smashed out the cigarette he had been smoking and emerged from the shadows next to the cab.

"This box is for me."

Thompson checked the name written on the box, "You Milan Tadic?"

"Yes," he replied turning the ID badge that was clipped to his shirt pocket toward Hoy. "I'm the Third Engineer on the Empress."

Thompson handed him the box and returned to his cab without further adieu. Before getting back inside, he put his right hand down deep into his front pants pocket. Smiling, he felt the crisp C-notes he had folded over his other cash.

Milan casually strolled down the pier beside the Empress being careful to remain clear of the busy forklifts loading the ship with stores. He went to the refueling station and put the box inside a worn canvas tool bag. Milan checked the gauge pressures on the manifold then keyed his radio and notified the engineers onboard the ship that he was going to secure from pumping. Next, he turned the valves off to the refueling hoses leading over to the ship and unhooked the hoses one at a time so they could be pulled back into the ship's fueling bunker onboard. Upon completion of this task he grabbed his tool bag and climbed the crew's gangway. At the crew entrance door he showed his crew ID to the ship's security officer and disappeared inside the ship. Minutes later, Empress's horn blasted a deep throaty tone, signaling its pending departure.

Thirty minutes later a crane removed all the gangways. The ship's mooring lines were thrown off the cleats and bollards on the pier and hauled aboard the Empress. The ship blasted its horn three more times in rapid succession as its Norwegian captain skillfully thrusted the ship away from the pier and began to slowly back it out into the Hudson River.

Virgo at sea, the same time

Far at sea, the Virgo sailed northwest under partially cloudy skies on choppy blue water. On the bridge, Sam reviewed the new heading on the chart table. Puzzled, she checked it against the GPS plot and suddenly realized where the new course would take them.

"Captain?"

"What?" Bakke impatiently replied.

"Our course, Captain - you've changed it. We're headed directly into prime fishing waters and this ship won't have net cutters installed on its screw until its next yard period."

"And why do you have a problem with that?"

"Sir, I wasn't questioning your order, I was just trying to point out..."

"Yes, you were. You've been Chief Mate on this tanker for how long?"

"Four and a half months."

"Singles cruises to Cancun, that's where you belong, not here on a tanker."

"You personally cleared my assignment, Captain. I'm more qualified than any XY chromosome you could find and you know it. I belong here, damn it!"

"You are qualified on paper but..."

"But what?"

"Off the record, I thought you were a man."

"On the record, my father was a United States Marine Corps Gunny

Sergeant and wanted a son. I grew up in on-base government housing at Camp Pendleton and Camp Lejeune. I could have gone to the Naval Academy on a full ride but I chose the Merchant Marine Academy instead because I wanted to drive ships, big ships, just like this one. Sorry you're disappointed, Captain, but this is what you got. Sam I am."

Bakke became flustered. "Oh, yes. Well, I'm sure your father was a good man. Your name...I thought... I'm going below. You have my ship. Call me the moment you have any question."

Sam quietly watched Bakke as he left the bridge, then slowly raised her binoculars and scanned the horizon ahead for contacts.

Chapter 8

Coronado, California, Joint Expeditionary Base

Driving a SUV rental car, Boucher approached the traffic light at the intersection of BUD/S Alley and Silver Strand Boulevard at the Joint Expeditionary Base that previously went by the name, Naval Amphibious Base, Coronado. Off to his right he noticed SEAL trainees in the obstacle course negotiating the "slide for life." Then, eight trainee boat crews emerged from the BUD/S training compound carrying large inflatable Zodiac-style boats on their heads. He stopped at the red light as the trainees began crossing the road from the SEAL training area off to his right, to the opposite Naval Amphibious Base side of the street. *Probably going to lunch*, he mentally surmised. A BUD/S instructor barked insults at the wet, shivering, sand-covered, zombie-like men.

An instructor recognized Boucher sitting in his rental with the windows rolled down.

"Hey, Commander, how you doing?" the instructor asked, trotting up to Boucher's open driver's-side car window and saluting him.

"Not bad for a Monday, Senior Chief. Hell week?"

"Sure is, Sir. You miss it?"

"Hell week? Hell no," he flatly replied, returning the salute.

The instructor smiled, then turned and yelled, "Boat crews, halt," stopping them in the middle of the street. "Left face. I want you pieces of whale shit to meet Commander Boucher. He's a real Navy SEAL. I served with him in SEAL Team One back in the 80s. We've been all over the world killing bad guys together. You frog turds will never work with an officer like him because you're a bunch of pussies who think being a Navy SEAL is glamorous. So, glamour girls, up boats, extended arm carry! Lunch will have to wait until one of you losers quits."

Another instructor paced around the trainees as they painfully pushed the heavy boats above their heads on outstretched arms.

"Come on, I know one of you sweet peas wants to go ring that bell and end the pain," the instructor pleaded. "Just think, a warm shower, a soft rack, sleep... whack'n-off non-stop, watch'n Demi Moore in G.I. Jane. All you gotta do is ring that bell."

Some trainees sagged, others shook from the strain, but none yielded.

The Chief looked back at Boucher and loudly asked, "See any SEALS in this sorry ass bunch of pussy-boys, Commander?"

"One or two, maybe," Boucher replied loud enough to be heard.

The Chief lowered his voice and bent down close to the open window, "I wish you were still with us, Jake. Two Dogs and I still laugh about that last operation we all did together in Haiti."

"It wasn't funny at the time."

"Yeah, I know. It was scary as hell."

"I was lucky."

The Chief considerately observed his trainees who were now all showing serious fatigue.

"Yeah, I guess we were all lucky."

"Where is Two Dogs these days?"

"Ahhh...he's an assistant platoon officer at SEAL Team Two. You know he's in zone this year for selection to LDO."

"Wow, he deserves it. Good on'm."

"Scuttlebutt has it that his platoon is do'n some kind of special operations suitability checks onboard the Navy's newest experimental littoral combat ship somewhere in the Atlantic. I think the ship's name is the Independence. They're riding onboard and running their operations from the ship - counterdrug stuff last I heard. Good to see ya, Commander, I gotta keep'em moving before one of'm decides to quit."

The Chief saluted and Boucher returned the salute.

As he drove away he could hear the Chief yelling at the trainees, "Pick up the pace girls! If you wanted it to be easy you would'a joined the Air Force. But we're not about easy here, we're about pain. And remember, ladies, pain is good - it builds character. Now pick up the pace or we'll head back through the surf zone."

Boucher smiled to himself. He hadn't thought about his old friend, Glenn "Two Dogs" Hardy, in a long while. Hardy got the nickname, Two Dogs, because of an old joke that he told over and over and it was the only joke he ever told. It was about the young son of an Indian chief who was not happy with his name and asked his father how the Indians named their children. The Indian chief replied, "After our children are born we walk from the teepee and the first thing we see is what we name our newborn after. That's why I named your older brother, 'Screaming Eagle' and your sister was named, 'Running Brook.' So you see, Two Dogs Fucking, I do not understand the nature of your complaint."

Boucher smiled again at the thought of his old friend, Two Dogs. He casually checked his rear view mirror and noticed a rusted-out, primer-gray pickup following far behind and vaguely dismissed it. After turning into Deb's neighborhood he saw the same van was sill following him. He was now concerned. He turned into a parking lot and waited for the van but the van turned onto another street before the parking lot. He sat there for a moment and waited. Nothing. As he pulled back out onto the street he unconsciously relaxed.

Fish factory ship, three hundred miles S.E. of Bermuda, the same time

The gill nets had been soaking for nearly nine hours and the fish factory ship had returned to haul them in and claim the bounty they held. The ship's powerful winches drew in the mile-long net across its specially designed stern, dumping tons of flapping fish onto the deck. Deckhands rapidly sorted through the fish and shoveled the keepers down a special shoot sending them to the factory below for processing. There, the fish were immediately cleaned, packaged and frozen by Asian and Hispanic workers on a production line that rivaled any land-based meat processing factory.

The workers all wore yellow knee-high boots and white vinyl aprons as they filleted, trimmed, packaged and flash froze the fish. In a different line the fish heads were pressed for their oil and then, along with the entrails, the remains were processed into cat food and plant fertilizer. There was little waste and what was, was jettisoned overboard. A frenzy of feeding seagulls following the ship's wake fought over the parts and parcels.

A deck-mounted crane was used to hoist the massive, now-empty net to the ship's stern, precisely positioning it so it wouldn't tangle. A flurry of deckhands slowly released the mile-long net back into the sea behind the ship, allowing it to pay out into the ship's wake as the ship drove slowly forward. The nets were typically suspended just below the water's surface along their entire length by small floatation buoys about the size of basketballs. The deckhands were careful to ensure that these buoys, and the net they held below, were not tangled. Both ends of the nets were anchored to the seafloor to prevent them from drifting out of the designated fishing area. The anchored ends were marked with radar reflectors atop larger buoys to make them easier for the ship to locate and retrieve.

Commercial fishing ships like these commonly set and tended several nets spread over a several thousand square mile area of prime offshore fishing grounds. This was just another day for them in a fishing year that had seen their harvest numbers significantly drop below those of previous years. Some people believed it was from over fishing, others claimed it was the result of global warming, but no one really understood the real reason the fish population seemed to be dwindling. Competition was also very keen.

The Russian and Japanese fishing fleets regularly hunted the rich fishing grounds off the U.S. east coast with little regard to species, quantity, propagation or conservation, further negatively impacting the fish population. The crew of the fish factory ship only knew they were working twice as hard for less money and that translated into setting more nets, more often, for more extended periods at sea.

Imperial Beach, California

Pat's fifteen year old twins, Jake and Jacqueline, finished loading their camping gear and climbed into Boucher's rental. They had been patiently waiting for him on the front porch for over an hour. He stood nearby supervising them.

"Put your sleeping bags on the top, kids."

"Uncle Jake," young Jake asked, "is it a long drive to the campground?"

"Nahh, Mossman and Jackie leased a helicopter and they're going fly us to an airport close by. We'll be there well before dark and have plenty of time to set up our camp."

Boucher closed the SUV's rear doors. Pat's chilly ex-wife, Deb, watched from her doorway. She was a fit fifties-something ebony black woman with the looks to turn any man's head her way. She was wearing a black skin tight workout leotard that accented every curve and crevice on her body. Smiling, Boucher approached her.

"Hey, Deb, I hear you met somebody?" he artfully asked.

"Don't you worry about it, Jake, just be sure those alimony checks come on time."

Boucher acknowledged her with a nod and a smile.

"You ever gonna let the kids visit Pat in the hospital? I'll come get'm in my Gulfstream. It won't cost you a dime."

"He's a vegetable. He wouldn't know them even if I did let you take them to visit him. But then, he's always been brain-dead when it came to putting his family first," she sarcastically replied.

Boucher stared into her cold brown eyes with a frown. "You're right, maybe he wouldn't recognize them, but the kids would surely recognize him. Come on, Deb, he's their father. It couldn't hurt to let them visit him."

Deb waved her hand at the kids in the rental SUV and forced a smile their direction.

"And you're their adopted uncle. By the way, where you taken' them?"

"We're flying to Farmington, New Mexico in my plane. Then we're going by car to Shiprock on the Navajo reservation. I got a campsite and horses standing by and ready to go."

"When you bringing them back?"

"I suppose we'll be back late Sunday evening if that works for you."

"Uh-huh... Just don't surprise me like you did the last time, Jake."

"But, Deb, surprise is the story of my life."

"Yeah right."

Boucher returned to the SUV and started the engine. He fumbled with the digital buttons, attempting to crank up the radio volume for an "oldies" station playing 60's music. He loved his best friend's two children like they were his own. After all, Pat had named his son after Jake. And with no children of his own to spoil and cherish, Boucher wanted them raised right.

"Damn, digital crap," he complained. "What ever happened to knobs and dials?"

Suddenly the radio blared. Looking over at Jacqueline and then back at Jake through the rearview mirror he yelled over the music, "Okay, you guys ready to rock and roll?"

Both kids silently shrugged as he pulled away from the curb without first checking the passenger side mirror, almost causing a collision with a car coming down the street. The car blew its horn as it screeched to a stop inches from the passenger side door where Jacqueline was sitting. She screamed. Boucher swerved back to the left and jammed on the brakes, barely averting an accident.

The woman driving the car leaned out of her window and began yelling a tirade of four letter insults aimed at Boucher. He sat unemotionally taking her verbal abuse without reply. As she drove away he shook his head.

"Women drivers," he growled beneath his breath.

Chapter 9

Shiprock, New Mexico, sunset

Boucher stirred the pot of water he was boiling over the Coleman gas camp stove while keeping an eye on the sun. It was now low in the west. He gathered the empty plastic and foil wrappers from the MREs they had eaten for dinner and put them into a trash bag. He made himself a cup of instant coffee and hurriedly gulped it down burning the tip of his tongue in the process. He judged the sun would disappear below the horizon in about forty-five minutes. It was time.

"Saddle up, gang," he cheerily announced, "we're heading over to Shiprock."

On horseback, Boucher led young Jacqueline and Jake to a huge, naturally-sculpted rock formation, protruding 1,700 feet above the desert floor. They stopped about a quarter mile away.

"A hundred and fifty years ago white men came through here." he explained, pointing at the odd rock formation jutting proudly from the otherwise flat terrain. "They said at sunset that big rock formation over there looked like a windjammer – you know, an old sailing ship, so they called it Shiprock. The Navajos believed the rock was once a giant prehistoric bird. They called it Tse Bi dahi, 'the rock with wings.' Even today they still believe it has a magical power that can lift the human soul above the problems of our daily existence."

"Have you ever climbed it?" young Jake asked.

"When we came home from Vietnam in 1969 your Dad and I climbed to the top and camped out overnight up there, but these days you're not allowed to go up there because it's considered a Native American sacred site. We can only admire it from here."

"What did you and Dad do up there?" Jacqueline asked.

"Oh, lots of things."

"Did you talk about the war?"

"Yes, Jacqueline, and we talked about our friends and those we left behind."

Jacqueline smiled.

"Uncle Jake," young Jake soberly asked, "what did you and Dad find on the top?"

"I guess you could say we found each other. We took a poison promise to always do what's right."

"What's a poison promise?" Jake asked.

"It's a promise that means more than your life. We promised each other to stand up for what's right or die trying. There was a lot of racial tension back in the 60's. Your Dad and I never saw each other as a black man and white man. Instead, we equally saw right and wrong. We swore eternal hostility to the corrupt, the unprincipled, the incompetent and the foolish who endeavor to lead the people and corrupt our liberty. I guess you could say we promised to believe in each other. In fact, I think it was then, on the top of that rock, when we both knew we would be brothers for the rest of our lives. And you guys know what – we have been. Your Dad is my brother from a different mother and I love you guys big time."

Jacqueline smiled contentedly. "Uncle Jake, did Dad ever tell you why he got out of the Navy?"

"Well, as you know, he was a fighter pilot who got shot down and captured by the enemy. We were lucky to rescue him. I think he knew not to push his luck so he got out and became an FBI agent."

"Why didn't you get out of the SEALs, Uncle Jake?"

"I guess because the Teams were my family and I knew I belonged with them. Besides, what would a guy like me do if there weren't bad guys to fight?"

"What about the giant bird?" young Jake injected.

Boucher smiled and nodded, pointing up at the rock mountain.

"The Navajos believed it lived up there on top," he said glancing into the captivated faces of both kids. After a short pause he continued, "and it would swoop down and devour their young children. But you're both too old for that nonsense – right? And Jake, you're probably too tough for that poor old bird to eat anyway."

At that moment Jacqueline's horse spooked.

"Whoa, boy!" she cautioned, patting her horse's neck to calm him.

As the light changed, Shiprock magically transformed into a windjammer sailing on an ocean of heat waves rising up from the desert floor.

Jacqueline was awed. "Look, Uncle Jake...it's a sailing ship just like you said."

"Awesome," young Jake commented in child-like amazement.

A large eagle suddenly appeared soaring high above. Boucher studied the expressions on the faces of his best friend's two children and smiled. *I wish Pat could be here to see this*, he thought to himself. *God I love these two kids more than life itself.*

Virgo's pilothouse, Atlantic Ocean, night

Virgo's blunt bow rammed through the sea like the back of a giant soupspoon being pushed through an ocean-size dish of custard. Creating a four-foot high bow wake as it displaced tons of water that pressed equally against all sides of the ship's steel hull, the ship's powerful diesel-electric engines easily drove the mammoth ship forward. Luminous microscopic sea creatures sparkled beneath the sea's black surface as the ship rumbled by. In the pilothouse located eight stories above the waterline, the dull glow of red bridge lights illuminated the concern on Sam's face where she carefully checked the radar scope for contacts in the direction of the ship's heading. She knew full well the string of bobbing floats that suspended the hazardous fishing nets were too small to be detected by the ship's surface search radar in choppy seas like those outside. She also knew that the radar reflectors marking the anchored ends of the net were small and nearly impossible to see under conditions like this unless you had a GPS position for them and knew exactly where to look. They were now sailing through prime fishing waters and even though things were going fine so far, she had a gut feeling something bad was going to happen.

She again checked the radar scope then stepped outside the pilothouse onto the ship's open bridge wing. She strained through her binoculars to detect anything ahead of the ship that resembled fishnet floats or buoys, but her search was in vain. It was too dark to see anything but the ship's frothing bow wake and an occasional white wave top as it spilled in her direction.

Suddenly, the deep draft tanker's propeller snagged a fish net. As the net spooled around the spinning propeller shaft, the net's anchors were drawn into the giant propeller and pounded violently against the hull and rudder.

"All stop!" she yelled through the open door at the mate manning the ship's control panel and helm. "Damn, I must be psychic," she mumbled aloud.

Bakke burst onto the bridge moments later as she was returning back inside. Deeds followed close behind.

"What the hell just happened?" Bakke yelled.

"Fishing nets," Sam replied in a monotone. "We're fouled in a damn fishing net."

Deeds cussed and kicked the chart table chair in obvious frustration. He had daggers in his eyes as he fixed his gaze at Sam.

Bakke let loose a tirade aimed at Sam, "Damn it! I thought I could trust you!"

"Captain, you..."

"Doing your nails again?"

"My nails?"

"If you'd been checking radar you wouldn't have missed the marker buoys!"

"Wait a minute, Captain," she insisted. "You knew the risk when you altered our course. Buoys that small hide in the sea clutter and there's a shit load of clutter out there from the storm-driven surface chop. Look," she said pointing at the digital radar screen.

The radar screen looked like a million fireflies flashing against a black glass plate every time the radar's cursor swept the screen.

"I don't need to look. Experienced seamanship; that's what I'm talking about."

"We're dead in the water, Captain," she stated as a matter of fact. "All we have are thrusters to hold our position and maybe they're damaged as well - I'm not sure."

Deeds tore a weather printout fresh off the printer and quickly reviewed it before handing it to Bakke.

"The storm is coming our way fast, Captain," Deeds said while glaring at Sam. "We don't have much time to get this ship fixed."

Bakke read the printout.

"That damn tropical depression is intensifying. My ship is a sitting duck here. Chief Mate, get somebody out here to fix this now."

"Yes, Sir."

Sam went to the radio room to compose a cable to EISC corporate headquarters, alerting them of the situation and requesting emergency repair assistance.

Bakke pointed at Deeds, "We've got to hold our position to the sea. Check the thrusters for damage."

"Yes, Captain, I'll have a damage report for you shortly."

Deeds hurried from the bridge for main engineering.

Office of the Coordinator for Counterterrorism, U.S. Department of State, Washington, DC, the same time.

Jimmy Bruce burst into Blackburn's office without knocking. He was clearly excited.

"Sir, there are strong indications the bad guys are going to try to hit one of our coastal cities along the Eastern Seaboard."

"Oh shit, not another La Palma tsunami scenario like last year?" Blackburn replied.

"No Sir. This time as I wade through the various intelligence sources, the target appears to be a single location. You may recall the SEALs failed to grab Al-Adel a few months ago in Afghanistan, but they did recover a flash drive."

"Yeah, I remember. What about it?" Blackburn asked disinterestedly reaching for his coffee cup.

Bruce smiled at his boss. He knew exactly how to get Blackburn to pay attention to him.

"The contents of that flash drive refer to something, or some big maritime operation, they call 'Green Lady.' Curiously, about two weeks ago Israeli intelligence also mentioned a plan called 'Green Lady' in one of their HUMINT reports which confirms there is something going on. I don't know what that means yet, but last year al Qaeda referred to an operation they called, 'Yellow Bird' and if you recall that attack involved the Canary Islands."

"But Green Lady, hmmm? You never cease to amaze me with your dot-connecting abilities, Jimmy. I don't know how you do it."

"It's not all that hard, Sir. First, you have to know where the dots are before you start connecting them. It's more like pulling the right thread when you're trying to unravel a sweater. And, it's helpful to understand how sweaters are woven before you try to unravel one. For example, the Afghan conflict of today is little different than the Afghan conflict that Alexander the Great faced. It's based upon tribal loyalty, custom, culture and law. We are not fighting a war in Afghanistan and I don't care what President Banner calls it."

"Oh really?" Blackburn asked, raising one eyebrow. "Then what the hell is it, Jimmy?"

"We're fighting an insurgency with counterinsurgency and I believe today's fight is not all that different than the fight Alexander the Great experienced two thousand years ago."

"Explain your thinking."

"You see, Sir, as counterinsurgents we're fighting in a foreign land against insurgents who were largely born and raised there. As such, enemy agents are undistinguishable from potential friendly citizens. So, since we can't tell them apart by their looks we must rely on intelligence. As you well know, available human intelligence is only as good as its sources. So when it's nearly impossible to tell the enemy agents from the friendly populous, it's equally difficult to separate valid intelligence from invalid intelligence with any degree of certainty."

"Agreed, so how do we win their hearts and minds?"

"In my opinion, Sir, that's a challenge we may never succeed in or accomplish. Unless we can achieve a concrete intelligence base, our counterinsurgent operations will never be secure and we will likely fail at our overall objectives of stabilizing the Afghan government and securing the country against insurgency. And, succeeding in those two objectives is necessary to disallow terrorist regimes like al Qaeda and the Taliban the use of Afghanistan as a sanctuary."

"So you're saying our intelligence pipeline is skewed because of the tribal thing and, therefore, the intelligence information we collect there is misleading at best and outright inaccurate at worst."

"Well, Sir, I'm not sure if that's how I would have worded it but, yes, that's essentially the bottom line."

Blackburn eased forward in his chair and momentarily studied his young protégé.

"How then do we see clearly enough to locate and effectively destroy the insurgent forces?"

"It's going to take some long-term patience plus a complete reanalysis and subsequent confirmation of our strategic rationale for being there. As far as I can tell, the only thing that makes Afghanistan critical to our strategic interest is the fact that al Qaeda and the Taliban operate from there and their intention is to widen their attacks against the U.S and our interests until we lose our resolve through our recognition that our fight against them is unsustainable. Remember what they did to the Soviets? The mujahidin kept the casualty count soaring to the point that the Soviets finally withdrew from a lack of political and popular support back home. And remember, the Soviets had twice as many troops there as we currently have and they still got their butts kicked."

"Oh yeah," Blackburn growled as he stood, "well that ain't going to happen on my watch, Lieutenant! We're going to kill the kingpins and deprive the enemy of his sanctuary and that asshole, Al-Adel, is who I want to see dead first."

Bruce smiled at the old warrior sitting before him, knowing he had just struck a nerve.

"Aye Sir, let me see what I can do to get him killed for you." Bruce clicked his heels together and braced to attention. "Is there anything else, Sir?"

"You close to anyone in the Israeli intelligence community?"

Blackburn loved to kid Bruce with off-the-wall comments because it was not only his leadership style but it kept the tension down.

"Ahh, well, Sir," Bruce shyly fumbled, "I've been dating a scary-smart Israeli student who's studying International Affairs at American University here in DC. She'll be doing her doctoral dissertation in a few months. Obviously, for OPSEC reasons I don't talk shop with her."

"Right, but if you get the opportunity you might want to feel her out and see what she knows about this subject."

Bruce laughed at Blackburn's choice of words and turned to leave.

"Hey, Jimmy," Blackburn called out, "I saw you two walking along 23rd street towards the Foggy Bottom metro stop last evening. She's an exceptionally nice looking chick – big tits and great ass. You get any last night or what?"

Bruce rolled his eyes and laughed. As he left the office he turned back toward Blackburn and held up two fingers, "Twice."

Blackburn sat back down and smiled. "Outstanding," he mumbled to himself.

Chapter 10

M.S. Royal Norwegian Empress

Cruising on gently rolling seas beneath a warm sun, the Empress crew went about their daily routine catering to their passengers and keeping their cruise ship clean, meticulously maintained, and running efficiently. Most all cruise ships have nightly entertainment themes in their main dining and ballrooms and their guests are encouraged to participate. Empress' theme this particular evening was a black tie, dinner-dance event in the ship's opulent ballroom. Everyone was wearing evening gowns and tuxes, many of which were rented from the ship's tailor shop just for the evening. On the stage above the dining area, the orchestra played soft dance music, as waiters wearing white dinner jackets and black bow ties served the passengers a lobster bisque appetizer and poured fine wine into crystal glasses. It was truly an experience in fine dining, elegance, and class.

Milan was working in the busy kitchen replacing a faulty hot water valve on a large stainless steel rinse sink. Even though the kitchen was well ventilated, the temperature easily hit one hundred degrees Fahrenheit during the crescendo of dinner preparation as the chefs worked their culinary magic. Milan finished tightening the hot water feed line connection and turned the water back on, checking for leaks. Satisfied there were none, he put the tools he used back into his canvas tool bag and casually strolled over to the open kitchen door, standing to one side out of the way. He felt the cool air from the ballroom soothe his sweaty face as it wafted into the kitchen. Busily arriving and departing, the waiters reminded him of worker bees at the entrance to their hive.

In Iraq where he grew up, his father had bee hives and so did his uncle. He spent hours observing nectar-laden worker bees arriving at the hive and dancing in circles at its silted entrance. He could still visualize how the incoming and outgoing bees' activities were organized. They obviously communicated, but how? His memory of the delightful smell and taste of the honey was so vivid he smiled. A loud shattering crash from the kitchen behind him again jolted his memories. The sound reminded him of the American bomb that killed his family. He could still see the mutilated bodies of his mother and brother staring lifelessly at him. The door next to him swung open. A waiter briskly entered the kitchen jolting him back to the present.

He curiously observed the guests in the ballroom, as they tried to impress one another with their formal-dinner, social skills. He marveled at the contrast – most of them were obviously average people who were role playing the elite. Even so he had no personal desire to ever join them, besides, it would be a sin. Watching from a distance was as close as he ever allowed himself to such a lifestyle. He was a devout Muslim, a true believer, and would remain untainted during this earthly life. He would prove himself worthy now and be rewarded in his next life for all eternity.

Checking his watch, he realized he had overstayed and was now behind schedule. Quickly departing, he hurried down the steel deck of the crew's private passageway running centrally through the interior of the ship and stopped at the Main Engineering access door. He hastily glanced up and down the passageway, ensuring he was alone, then used his master key and unlocked the door. Milan slipped inside the noisy engine room carefully closing the heavy steel door behind, once again securely locking it. He checked to ensure the door was secure and proceeded to the control room.

The Second Engineer was on duty inside the glass-enclosed air conditioned office-like space and paid no attention to Milan's presence. Milan took a clipboard check sheet off a bulkhead hook inside the control room and went back out into the main engine room. He methodically made his rounds through the main engine room recording lubrication pressures and temperatures on each of the main engines and the journal bearings that held the ship's massive drive shafts.

He stopped next at the main fire and flushing pump which supplied the majority of the non-potable seawater throughout the ship used for flushing toilets and fighting fires. It was a huge desk-size centrifuge pump powered by an equally large electric motor. He first checked to ensure the engineer on watch in the control room wasn't watching him. The man was sitting with his back to Milan reading a book and completely oblivious. Milan poured an acidic substance directly into the pump's powerful electric motor. The pungent smell of burning plastic insulation and hot wires rolled off the motor but Milan knew the engineer on watch inside the office was isolated from it. He would not know there was a problem until it was too late.

After completing his rounds, he left the noisy engine room, clipboard in hand, and made his way to the bridge, via the ship's top weather deck, to both cool off and get some fresh air along the way. This circuitous route to the bridge took him past the shuffleboard area and the sundeck lounge by the ship's pool.

Captain Dahl had just conducted a sunset marriage ceremony there and the post wedding celebration party was in full swing on the opposite side of the ship from Milan's path. Staying in the shadows, he slowed his pace watching the gala taking place on the opposite side. He saw a bouquet thrown by the bride, arc over her shoulder into the expectant hand of one of the bridesmaids. A loud cheer went up as the bride and groom kissed. A delighted Captain Dahl kissed the bride's cheek and shook the groom's hand, posing with them as cameras flashed.

Milan enjoyed seeing wedding celebrations. It made him remember the wife and two children he once had before an American-backed raid ended their lives as they sat in their home along with his mother, father, grandmother, sister, brother, two uncles and aunts and three cousins. They were celebrating the marriage of his sister when it happened. He would never forget the helicopters raining their deadly rockets and machinegun fire down on the unsuspecting wedding party as they relentlessly circled above. Only he escaped the carnage.

True, his family worked for a Taliban drug cartel, but they were made an offer they couldn't refuse. The Taliban offered them money and protection, two things they would never have raising a traditional crop of grain. The corrupt Afghan government controlled the price and where a farmer could sell his surpluses and that was always to a government agent. In contrast, all the Taliban asked was that they grow the opium poppy in the same fields - only now they would be paid well for their hard work. That didn't make them criminals. After all, they were still simple farmers and herdsmen. But then the Americans got involved. Milan cringed at the memory. The American president's war in Afghanistan against the Taliban and al Qaeda had cost him dearly and he would have his revenge against the Americans any way he could get it.

Arriving on Empress' bridge, Milan hung his clipboard bearing the checklist on the bulkhead hook beneath a placard marked "Engineering." He casually checked the ship's radar scope, ship's position, course and speed.

Milan rarely spoke to the navigator but this evening he went out of his way to strike up a friendly conversation.

"Looks like bad weather coming our way."

"Yeah, got a storm brewing to the southeast. The seas have picked up a bit so we're slowing down for a better ride. Our guests don't like being seasick."

"Slowing down? Won't that change our arrival time?"

"Maybe a little but it shouldn't change it much. I suspect it will hardly be noticeable to our guests. They'll still have plenty of time to go ashore."

"Well, I sure hope our schedule doesn't change. We wouldn't want to be late."

"Late?" the navigator repeated smiling. "No worries, mate, we won't be."

Milan returned the smile and departed for the ship's outside stern deck lounge area restricted to crew use only.

Arriving minutes later, he lit a cigarette and took a deep relaxing drag. On the well-lighted passenger stern deck above, a staff member was conducting skeet shooting for the guests. Milan always loved to watch people shoot.

"Pull!" the shooter yelled from the above deck.

Two clay birds were immediately launched into the air behind the ship. The forties-something man fired two shots in rapid succession missing both clay birds. He reloaded, fumbling slightly as he shoved two red shotgun shells into the bottom of the gun's receiver and again raised the shotgun to his shoulder.

"Pull!"

He fired twice again, cleanly missing both clay birds. The instructor interceded and patiently helped the shooter change his grip on the gun, then helped him reload.

"Pull!"

This time he chipped the edge of one clay bird with his second shot. Milan smiled admiring the auto-loading shotgun. He and his younger brother learned how to shoot AK-47s years earlier, but that was an assault rifle. Skeet shooting looked like fun as well as good eye-hand coordination marksmanship practice that could be applied to hitting any moving target, but al Qaeda training camps weren't interested in developing wing shooting skills.

He flicked his cigarette butt overboard and strolled to the forward end of the crew deck where the ship's gasoline storage area was located. The ship carried gasoline to fuel its recreational watercraft, outboard motors, diving compressors, and the portable fire and dewatering pumps used by the damage control teams in an emergency. He stopped short of the door to the inside the ship. There was no one else around. He looked up at a closed circuit video camera which was aimed aft. The camera was one of many positioned throughout the ship that fed into one of two twelve channel video recorders.

The cameras were not monitored real-time by the ship's security staff. Some of the cameras did have a feed to a monitor on the ship's bridge but it was not monitored by a dedicated watch stander. Rather, their recorded surveillance data was used as evidence should a crime occur within their field of vision. The cameras were more a deterrence than they were a useful tool for security alert and for this reason their maintenance was a very low priority.

Where he was standing was out of the camera's coverage. He pulled a pair of wire snips from his coverall's pocket. Using the dogs on the watertight door like a ladder he climbed up behind the camera and quickly snipped the coaxial cable a few feet behind the camera, rendering it useless.

Virgo's Bridge

On the tanker's bridge, Deeds stood flat-footed in front of the ship's maneuvering thruster control panel. Thrusters made maneuvering a modern ship the size of Virgo relatively easy because they provided a means to propel the ship through the water sideways. By design, Virgo's thrusters were nothing more than two eight-foot diameter propellers located fore and aft. They were powered by electric motors mounted in a shaft that ran perpendicular through the ship's hull both behind the bow and forward of the ship's stern deep below the ship's waterline. By running either propeller, forward or aft, or in tandem, the ship could be thrust sideways or pivoted in a circle if desired.

Making sure the auxiliary maneuvering function lights were all green, he revved-up the bow thruster for a full function test. Deeds breathed a sigh of relief as the ship's powerful bow thruster functioned flawlessly at full power. Next he tried the stern thruster. As he advanced the throttle a red warning light began to flash on the panel. *Damn*, he cussed to himself. Glancing over at Bakke, he saw that Bakke was also staring at the flashing warning light.

"The bow thruster works, but that's all, Captain. The stern thruster is spinning but it doesn't respond to directional commands, so it's unusable for maneuvering. Main propulsion is down hard," he reported. "We can't even jack the shaft over with the jacking gear, it's frozen. The propeller must be jammed in place. We'll keep trying it in both directions; maybe we can break it loose and get it to spin. I'm keeping the journal bearing lubrication pumps running at full pressure in case we get lucky."

Bakke nodded at Deeds, turning away sharply to address Sam.

"I know you can do this," he sarcastically said. "Use the bow thruster and hold us bow-on to the seas."

"Can do, Sir. As long as you're not..."

"Excuse me?" he loudly demanded.

"Bow-on to the seas, Captain."

Both glared at one another before Bakke left the bridge with Deeds in tow.

Shiprock, New Mexico, night

With a slumbering teenager on each side, Boucher threw a few pieces of wood on the campfire and watched the sparks explode into the night sky. He climbed into his sleeping bag and lay back studying the distant stars forming the galaxy that filled the night sky above. The Milky Way looked within arm's reach. A moist southwesterly breeze carried the faint smell of rain which wafted through the otherwise near still air at the campsite. Heat lightning flashed many miles away, dimly silhouetting the horizon but still so distant the rumble of its thunder couldn't be heard.

His mind drifted back to the 1968 Tet Offensive in the Vietnam War and the night ambush in Cambodia when he and his SEAL platoon rescued Patterson from the clutches of the North Vietnamese Army at the canal crossroad. It was raining that night and the stars were completely obscured by dense clouds.

Rolling on his side Boucher stared at the glowing orange embers beneath the low bluish flames of the campfire. It reminded him of the exploding Claymore mines the SEALs detonated at each end of the canal intersection bridge. He could still hear their ear-splitting blasts and see their instantaneously blinding white-orange flashes. He visualized Patterson being flung off the bamboo bridge by the Claymores' blast and splashing into the middle of the canal. He could still see Patterson disappearing beneath its black watery surface. Then the SEALs opened up from their ambush position across the canal with withering machinegun fire, killing every North Vietnamese soldier still standing.

Boucher looked away from the campfire. He had lost his night vision and now everything was pitch dark. He couldn't even see the stars anymore. The kids were sleeping soundly on the opposite side of the camp fire. He reached outside of his sleeping bag with one arm and threw another piece of wood on the fire which exploded into sky-bound sparks.

That night at the canal intersection, he swam into the canal and found Patterson unconscious on the bottom. He pulled him to the surface, and under a hail of enemy counter-fire, half-swam, half-dragged him back to the opposite shore where his SEAL platoon was located.

He watched a large spark from the campfire climb into the air and burst into multiple sparks about six feet above the fire. He again saw enemy mortars exploding in the trees nearby and on the surface of the water as he pulled Patterson toward the shore. He cradled Patterson in front of him as he administered mouth-to-mouth resuscitation. He didn't stop; even when a sudden searing pain shot through his shoulder and he'd glanced down to see an enemy mortar fragment protruding from the flesh.

The only thing he saw in the sky that rainy cloud obscured night in Cambodia were machinegun tracers and a burning C-130 cargo plane that streaked above and crashed miles away.

His memory of that time ended as several shooting stars streaked across the clear night sky chasing one another into certain oblivion as they burned their way through the earth's upper atmosphere. He pulled his arm back inside his sleeping bag and checked his Novak custom built Special Operations model1911A1 .45 ACP pistol to ensure the hammer was fully cocked, the thumb safety was up and engaged, and it was next to his right hand inside his sleeping bag. He then pulled his sleeping bag up close to his chin and settled in. He felt its soft warmth glove around his body. Now relaxed and feeling secure in his surroundings, he slowly drifted off to a sound sleep.

He was awakened sometime later when his Blackberry chirped with a text message.

Damn, he thought to himself as he carefully read the screen. The message was from Mojo, his former SEAL teammate, longtime friend and assistant at the Prop Shop back in Baltimore.

Jake, urgent - call me. Offshore supertanker emergency. Return ASAP. Mojo.

He slowly crawled from his sleeping bag, slipped on his clothes, stuffed his Novak pistol inside his pants waistband and quietly walked a short distance away from the camp where he placed a call. Ten minutes later he returned to the camp and gently woke up the snoozing kids.

"Sorry kids, but I have to take you home. I just got an emergency request from one of my clients. They need me to fly far out to sea and rescue a ship with a fouled propeller."

Young Jake frowned and looked seconds away from tears. Boucher saw he was clearly disappointed.

"Uncle Jake," young Jake pleaded, "can't we just stay 'til tomorrow?"

"I'm sorry. I'm under contract and they need my help."

"What kind of help?" Jacqueline asked.

"There's a hurricane building and it's headed directly towards a ship that has lost its propulsion. Without propulsion the ship and her crew are helpless. The ship could break up and sink and a bunch of people could die in the process if we can't get them fixed and underway before the storm hits. I'll tell you what, I'll come back and visit you guys the first moment I get when I'm done with this job."

"How long is that going to be, Uncle Jake?" Jacqueline sighed reaching half-heartedly for her sleeping bag.

"Oh, just a fw days at most. I can probably be back to see you by next weekend. In fact, you tell me where you want to visit and I'll take you there – anywhere on the planet you like. Okay?"

Deb's home, Imperial Beach, California

It was 2:30 A.M. when Boucher and the kids pulled up along the curb in front of Deb's house. Except for an outside door light, the house was dark. He could see the faint flicker of a television shimmering against the front window curtains. *She must be home,* he thought. Standing on the front step with Jacqueline and young Jake behind him, Boucher hesitated a moment and counted to ten before he pressed the doorbell button for a third time. This time he heard commotion inside and an excited male voice faintly arguing with a female.

Finally, after more than a minute, Deb angrily yanked the door open. She was wearing a partially buttoned nightgown and her hair was a mess. She quickly pulled the top of her nightgown together and held it closed with one hand. The kids, laden with their backpacks and sleeping bags, crowded past her.

"Hey Mom," young Jake said in a husky tenor.

The look on her face was telling.

"Sorry, Deb, I tried calling you numerous times over the past several hours but there was no answer."

She was clearly pissed.

"That's because I had my phone ringer turned off for privacy. You understand privacy, right Jake? But, when I heard that doorbell somehow I knew it was you."

Her stare was mordant.

"Look, I'm sorry, Deb, but something has come up that requires my immediate return to the East Coast."

Boucher heard the back-door slam. Wearing only pants, with shirt and shoes in hand, a half naked man ran across the side yard to a car parked on the adjoining street. He started it up and sped away. Amused, Boucher watched him nearly lose control going down the street as he raced around the corner.

"Want me to catch him?" Boucher deviously chuckled in delight.

"Don't bother. *He could thread a needle with that thing.* I wouldn't have him back if he begged me."

"Oh, how disheartening - I'll tell Pat he spoiled you."

The door slammed shut in his face.

U.S. State Department, Washington, DC., morning

Blackburn was on the secure phone when Bruce appeared. He gestured for Bruce to sit down on the chair next to his desk.

"Thanks, Tom, I'll look into it. Out here," he casually concluded.

Blackburn returned the secure telephone to its hook and relaxed back into his chair.

"You ain't gonna believe this shit, Jimmy. That was Tom Zech, over at the Office of Naval Intelligence. He said they just finished translating a National Security Agency signal intercept from Al Zawahri, and it referenced our old friend Rajakovics. Remember him?" Bruce nodded affirmatively. "Apparently he's now working for al Qaeda as an operations planner and is the shaker and mover for some sort of a major attack plan against the U.S."

Bruce loved to kid his trusted boss by seeing how far he could run with one of Blackburn's statements before he realized he was being kidded.

"You're talking about, 'The Doctor'? The Egyptian-born rich guy turned terrorist?"

"Yeah, that's the one."

"And Rajakovics, the Kazakh-born former Russian Spetsnaz commando, is working for him?"

"Knock off the bullshit, Jimmy," he said smiling, "I'm on to your drama."

"Yes, Sir."

"You know, I sure wish Boucher and his guys would have killed that bastard in Dakar last year. Anyway, Tom thinks it's probably worth following since Rajakovics was the mastermind behind last year's Canary Island nuke attack. Man, if Boucher and his guys hadn't been on top of that one the whole Eastern Seaboard would still be sucking bilge water."

"I'll get my guys on it immediately, Sir."

Blackburn sat forward clasping both hands under his chin. "You know what I don't get, Jimmy? Why is that S.O.B. so damn hard to bag?"

"The thing that makes Rajakovics so elusive is the fact that he doesn't seem to have any ideological axe to grind with his victims. Unlike the late Bin Laden and his whole Islamic extremist gaggle, he's not trying to kill us because he hates us. He just seems to be in it for the money. For him it's just a matter of business, nothing more or less. Maybe there's a way to track him through his bank accounts or something."

"Maybe you're right," Blackburn replied deep in thought, "or maybe we can bait him by offering him a bigger payoff. You know, set up a plausible scenario through an unwitting third or fourth party that requires his services, make him an offer he can't refuse, or something along those lines. Put him in a position where he reveals some vulnerability and then kill the son-of-a-bitch."

"That would be very nice, Sir, but probably very hard to make happen because President Banner's new policies strictly forbid assassination at any level."

"Shit, Jimmy, I'm not talking assassination here, I'm talking about killing a son-of-a-bitch that desperately needs to be killed before he can murder more Americans. That's not assassination. What's illegal about killing the bad guys before they kill us?"

"Sir, let me see if I can peg his location. If I can nail that down we can go to Secretary Cummings and see what she might be willing to support. Maybe we should explore working with a friendly surrogate who also wants him dead."

"Like who?"

"Like the Israelis."

"Where did you come up with that?"

"My girlfriend might have mentioned him in general terms last evening. I think the Israelis might be after Rajakovics too."

"Now Jimmy, I don't care if you sleep with her but you got to be damn careful what you say around that chick."

"I am, Sir, don't worry. I just get the sense she's feeling me out in a roundabout way to see if we're aggressively pursuing him. She inadvertently referred to someone she called, Sasbatzar."

"Sasbatzar? That's a new one on me."

"Yes, Sir, me too. Sasbatzar means, 'keeper of the fire.' It goes back to the biblical days of King Solomon. Because fire was so hard to start, it was Sasbatzar's job to keep the fire burning."

"And she told you that?"

"No, Sir, I researched the name. I think she might be talking about an Israeli code name for some operation they're either conducting or surveilling. Maybe it's their codename for Rajakovics."

Blackburn rubbed his temples in painful relief and then blotted his sleeve across his right eye.

"Rajakovics…I just can't understand what the president is thinking when he gives murdering dickwads like Rajakovics a pass or releases those al Qaeda bastards we have in custody at Gitmo back into the world. And, then, at the same time, he won't let us go after the very assholes who are trying to cut our heads off and blow up our wives and kids because we don't believe the same Islamic extremism bullshit they believe. But if Rajakovics is different, he's a mercenary whose time has come and I'll betcha even God himself won't miss the son-of-a-bitch. It would be great if the Israelis would do the civilized world a favor and off that son-of-a-bitch."

Chapter 11

Above the Atlantic, sunset

The De Havilland Twin Otter cruised high above the dark sea. Frank "Mossman" Moss and Jack Doyle were at the controls. Moss was a Vietnam-vintage Navy Seawolf helicopter pilot who had saved Boucher and his SEAL platoon several times during the Vietnam War. He had a reputation of not only being a "hot stick" who could fly anything, he was known as a man who knew how to cheat death having miraculously survived numerous crashes. Doyle was a SEAL who, after retirement from the Navy, became a certified flight instructor in his second career. He too was a well experienced pilot who could fly nearly anything that had wings or rotors.

In the De Havilland's cargo compartment, Mojo meticulously checked Boucher's parachute harness and rigging that held the parachute pack closed. He carefully checked its static line link and slapped Boucher on the shoulder, "Okay, Jake, you're good to go."

Boucher zipped up the last six inches of his wet suit top. His equipment bundle was positioned next to the bulkhead by the plane's door. It contained his tools and diving equipment.

Mossman spoke into his intercom mic warning Mojo to get Boucher ready. "We're about five hundred miles off shore. I have the ship in sight. We'll begin our streamer approach in five mikes. Have Jake get ready."

Cold air blasted inside as Mojo opened the plane's side door and locked it against the interior bulkhead. Boucher hooked the equipment bundle's static line along with his own to a D-ring anchor point inside the airplane and crouched at the door. As they neared the ship he leaned out of the door on all fours, staring down at the dark water far below. Virgo's lights appeared ahead, first as small points of light in an otherwise bottomless black abyss, then as bright deck lights illuminating the topside decks and sides of a supertanker. He keyed his headphone mic.

"Okay boys; give me an eighty knot streamer pass directly over her at twenty five hundred feet."

Moss pushed his control yoke forward and pulled the engine throttles back, commanding the plane into a steep descent while dropping the plane's flaps at the same time. At twenty five hundred feet Mossman pulled the nose up and trimmed the plane for level flight, adjusting the speed to eighty knots. Boucher leaned out of the door over his equipment pack to get a full view of the ship below. He suddenly turned green and sat back inside the plane.

Mojo noticed Boucher's sudden repulsion.

"What's wrong? You sick or forget your tampons or something? You've done this same jump a hundred times."

Jake shook his head no, swallowed hard and forced himself to look back out of the door. Memories of a water jump gone wrong inundated his thoughts. It was at the beginning of the Granada operation when he and five other SEALs parachuted with their inflatable boat into the sea far offshore. The weather was marginal for a water drop and they probably would have aborted, but they needed to provide advanced reconnaissance to mark the Cubans' defensive positions prior to the U.S. invasion of the island. Despite the risk, Boucher and his men had made the jump wearing full combat equipment. Wind and highs seas had separated them and swept them away from the boat. Three of the men never made it to the safety of the boat. Although an exhaustive search was immediately launched by Navy surface ships in the vicinity, the men were never found.

Boucher could still feel the rough texture of his equipment pack brushing his fingertips as its weight drug him beneath the surface, eyes wild, one hand flailing at the water and the other clawing at the release clasp that held it to his body. He'd remember it for the rest of his life.

The tanker came into sight below jolting his thoughts back to the present. As they passed directly above the ship, he threw the wind streamers outside through the open door. Two fifteen foot long yellow crepe paper streamers gently floated down approximating the same rate of descent a parachute has and landed in the water about three hundred yards downwind of the ship's position. Boucher looked back at Mojo.

"I don't know how many jumps I have left in me."

"Ah, come on, Jake, you love this shit."

"The Canary Island operation last year changed that."

"Yeah, we're not exactly save'n the world here, are we? No presidential citations in this job."

"Nope, just a little excitement and a paycheck we don't need either."

Banking in a gentle two minute 360-degree turn, Mossman and Jack slowly brought the De Havilland back onto the wind line for the jump pass. Boucher checked his parachute harness quick releases and static line hook up one last time. Mojo readied the equipment bundle and positioned it in the open door in front of Boucher. The plane leveled off. Mojo, leaned over Boucher and gave him a thumbs-up, then slapped him on the shoulder.

"Now!" he shouted above the wind noise as he helped push the equipment bundle out of the open door.

"Go!" he shouted, smacking Boucher on the thigh with the palm of his open hand.

Boucher leapt outside and disappeared behind the plane. Mojo leaned out of the open door to see two open parachutes silhouetted against a golden sunset.

Boucher studied the large, glistening white, globe shapes protruding from the Virgo's main deck contrasted against the ship's overall mammoth size as he floated down. They looked like four monster eggs stuck halfway into the forward part of the ship all connected by elaborate pipes and valve manifolds. A few feet above the water he opened the quick release buckles holding him in his parachute harness and slipped free of it, splashing feet first into the chilly sea.

Virgo's bridge

On the radio from the ship's bridge wing, Sam directed the ship's twenty-four foot utility boat to Boucher's splashdown point several hundred yards off the ship's port side. "Come left twenty degrees," she advised. "He's about two hundred yards in front of you."

The utility boat motored up to Boucher, taking care to not get the boat's propeller tangled in his still partially-floating parachute lines. First, the boat crew wrestled his equipment bundle into the boat. Then they helped Boucher crawl aboard.

Bakke stood silently on Virgo's bridge wing, skeptically shaking his head as he watched from afar. Sam watched the action through her binoculars and reported what she was seeing.

"Sir, they've got him and his equipment in the boat."

"Bring him to my office the moment he arrives onboard," Bakke tersely replied.

Sam headed aft to the boat davits awaiting Boucher's arrival. The crew hooked the hoisting cable to the utility boat's lifting eyes and signaled to the deck crew above with a thumbs-up. The davit's winch was engaged, slowly reeling the boat up towards Virgo's main deck. Boucher was standing with one foot on its bow with his wet suit top unzipped down to his waist. He looked like a modern day Neptune as he slowly rose into full view above Virgo's gunwale.

Behind dark aviator-style sunglasses, Sam carefully studied him from head to toe. He was a tall, rugged-looking, square jawed, handsome man. His short cropped hair was thinning on top and the sides were silvery white – very professional and distinguished looking. He had a fresh purple scar on his forehead and some older ones on his cheek, jaw and right pectoral. She reasoned he had obviously been on the receiving end of something violent numerous times. She liked the smile lines that framed his penetrating steel blue eyes as he squinted into the sun. He had a sexy chest peppered with silver hairs and firm pecs bulging beneath broad shoulders.

She was glad he couldn't see her staring from behind her sunglasses. She unconsciously swept a wisp of loose hair behind her ear as she stepped towards him.

"Welcome aboard," she said, deliberately suppressing both her smile and fluster.

"Thanks," he softly replied.

"I'm Sam, the Chief Mate," she announced holding out her right hand.

He extended his hand grasping hers, "I'm Jake, the handyman."

She liked the firm squeeze he gave her hand that lingered for a moment longer than it should have – *unusual for a man shaking a woman's hand.*

"Right. The Captain wants to see you about our screw." She studied him. *He's probably like all the other jerks. No point getting all stirred up over some guy who isn't going to be here very long and is probably charming on the surface and a Neanderthal underneath. So…might as well just enjoy the view. Besides, I'm not going to fall apart the first time I meet a good-looking guy. Even a seriously good-looking guy.*

"Pardon me?"

"I mean…the Captain wants to see you in his office before you begin repairs on the screw," she stammered. "Please come with me. I…I mean, follow me."

Inside, Sam removed her sunglasses and led the way up through the massive ship's interior to Bakke's office located aft of the bridge. Boucher couldn't help but notice her slender, sexy figure and sparkling emerald green eyes which she seductively flashed his way as they walked. She had her natural straw blond hair twisted into a bun and neatly pinned up above her shoulders. He also noticed that she wore no rings on either hand.

He subconsciously wondered how she would look with her hair down. *No doubt damn beautiful.*

Sam opened the door to Bakke's office and led him inside. Deeds was sitting on a leather sofa across from Bakke's desk. Both he and Bakke were sipping coffee.

"Captain Bakke and Chief Deeds, I would like to introduce you to Jake Boucher. Mr. Boucher is here to conduct emergency underwater screw and shaft repairs."

The men shook hands.

"Please call me, Jake."

"What do you need to get my ship going again?" Bakke bluntly asked.

"I need the Chief Engineer to tag out the throttles and rudder motor. Nobody should touch anything that makes propellers spin or rudders wiggle while I'm down there."

"How about the after auxiliary intakes?" Sam suggested.

"Good call. Tag them out too," Jake added.

Deeds nodded his approval.

"You need anything else?" Sam asked. She held a small notebook in her hand where she had copied down everything that was requested and agreed upon.

"Please hang a Jacobs ladder over the stern for me."

"Done," Bakke replied.

"And it would speed things up if someone would help lower my equipment from the stern down to the water."

"I'll do it," Sam volunteered.

Bakke scowled at Sam.

"Get him a non-licensed seaman. Your place is on the bridge."

Boucher stood and smiled, "Okay, let's do it. The sooner I get to work, the sooner you get underway again."

As Jake turned to leave, Deeds stopped him with a grasping hand on his shoulder.

"How long?" he demanded.

Boucher glanced down at Deeds' hand. There weren't many things that instantly pissed Boucher off, but being slapped or being grabbed and held were two at the top of a very short list.

"How long what?" Boucher calmly replied lowering his voice. "How long until I rip your arm off? Or how long are you going be stupid enough to keep your hand on me?"

Deeds winced, "To finish your repair work, dim-wit!"

"Excuse me, Chief, but were we married once?"

"What?" Deeds replied, clearly repulsed by Boucher's response.

"I just wondered if in some past life if we, well you know..."

Homophobic, Deeds stepped back disgusted with the thought of it but still didn't release his grip.

"What the hell are you talking about?"

"Only my wife was authorized to call me a dim-wit. She lived with me for eight years and knew what she was talking about. You, on the other hand..."

"Go to Hell, Boucher. You're here to unfoul this ship's screw so we can get underway again. I don't have patience for this petty shit!"

Boucher stepped up in his face.

"Look, at this point I don't have a clue how much damage you did to your ship, but if you're in such a big friggin hurry, call Hertz and get a loaner. Meanwhile, there's a storm bearing down on us, I'm expensive, and time's a-wasting."

Deeds relaxed his grasp on Boucher's shoulder, but didn't release him. Boucher glanced back at Deeds' hand on his shoulder and smiled.

"So, I can stand here playing your game and answer your questions or I can go to work. Which is it?"

"Go to work," Bakke said waving Boucher and Sam out the door.

Outside in the passageway Boucher stopped Sam.

"What's up with him?"

"Xenophobia."

Fear of spiders? "Oh…, how unfortunate."

Arriving on Virgo's stern a few minutes later, Boucher saw two crewman finish rigging the Jacobs ladder next to the ship's lifeboat. They threw the rope ladder strung with wooden rungs over the stern railing, watching that it properly unrolled, finally dangling from the rail down to the angry sea twenty-five feet below. Boucher donned his SCUBA gear and selected several tools which he placed in a canvas bag. As he went to climb over the rail onto the ladder Sam stopped him. Staring into his eyes she gently placed her hand over his and gave him a slight squeeze.

"If you need anything just have your tenders let me know and I'll make it happen."

"Thanks," he replied smiling.

Without further ado, he descended the ladder into the water. A crewman lowered the tool bag down to him on a rope. Boucher tied off the bag and grabbed some tools, then disappeared underwater in a trail of bubbles.

Below, he followed the curvature of the ship's stern down to the rudder and from there to the propeller. Visibility was limited because the massive ship blocked the light. Using a flashlight, he inspected the huge propeller and shaft. Both were completely fouled with tightly wrapped fishing net and thick nylon anchor rope. A fishing net anchor was jammed between one of the propeller blades and the rudder post. Extensive damage to the propeller and rudder was obvious. Above him, the ship slowly pitched and rolled as the seas increased in strength from the approaching storm. Boucher returned to the ladder. He yelled up to a crewman on the deck.

"Tell the Captain there's a lot of damage and it's going be an all-day job."

The crewman gave Boucher a thumbs-up and disappeared inside the ship through a watertight door.

Boucher took a hacksaw from the bag and returned below. He laboriously sawed at the rope, slowly removing pieces and casting them adrift. Two hours passed. Exhausted and out of air, he surfaced and made the long climb up the ladder to the deck above. A crewman helped him remove his SCUBA tanks.

"I need to see the Captain."

The crewman led him to the Captain's bridge office. With his wet suit top unzipped, dripping and shivering, Boucher drew a diagram of the damage for Bakke and Deeds. Sam watched from the other side of the table.

"There's a lot of damage down there," he explained, "especially on the propeller."

"Oh, come on," Deeds challenged. "Other ships just cut the damn net off and they're underway again."

"If you get underway now, you won't get far. The propeller has gaping notches in it. The rudder has several severe dings in it and…"

Bakke cut him off. "How much time do you need?"

"Two, maybe three hours to finish cutting the net away. Then, I need to carefully inspect the rudder.

Deeds became irate, "Too long! Unacceptable!"

Bakke contemplated the situation aloud.

"This storm's bearing down on me and my cargo is boiling off, I haven't got an hour to waste." He looked at Sam, "Chief Mate, expedite this situation now!"

"What, he should use my nail file down there?"

Bakke glowered at Sam while Boucher smiled defiantly at Deeds.

"Go!" Bakke shouted, pointing to the door. "Get it done. I must get underway again as soon as possible."

On the way aft, Sam detoured Boucher into the crew's mess. He sat across from her chowing down on a couple of hot turkey sandwiches and several cups of hot java. She quietly studied him as he ate. They didn't speak until he was almost finished with his second sandwich.

"Thanks, I needed to get some carbs in me. It gets kind'a chilly down there after an hour or so," he blurted, breaking the ice.

"Let me apologize for their impatience. I've never seen them treat a non-crew member like that."

"No problem. I was harassed by professionals when I went through SEAL training, shit on by Ho Chi Min, married once, shot by terrorists, and damn near nuked twice. Compared to that, your captain and chief engineer are mere rookies."

"You were married?" Sam cautiously asked.

"Yeah, it was a long time ago. She died in a car accident."

"Oh…I'm sorry. Any children?"

"Had a son."

"Had?" she asked softly."

"He was an ichthyologist. He was working on a fishery project in Kuwait when Saddam invaded at the start of the first Gulf War. Never heard from him again. State Department reported him missing and believed dead. His name was Doug. We were never close." Sam moved her hand towards his but stopped short of contact. "I would have really liked to tell him about the stuff I've done over the years but it's too late." Boucher paused. "I named him Doug in honor of my brother who was killed trying to stop a terrorist attack against the American Embassy in Iran back in the seventies."

"That's terrible. Don't you have any family at all?"

"None."

"Oh my gosh, I'm so sorry."

Boucher slugged down a gulp of coffee. "Don't be. It was a long time ago," he softly responded stuffing the last bite of turkey sandwich in his mouth. "And you?"

"Oh," she replied, unconsciously sweeping a wisp of hair behind her ear, "never married. Thought I was in love a couple times but it never went anywhere."

He lifted his coffee mug as if he was going to take another swallow but set it back on the table. Their eyes met. There was undeniable chemistry between them. Both got the message without saying a word. Sam pulled her pocket notebook from her shirt pocket and opened it. She momentarily studied it. As she did, Boucher studied her. Her cotton khaki shirt stretched tightly over her breasts. He forced himself to look away before she caught him staring.

Boucher took a final chug of his coffee then wiped the back of his hand across his mouth.

"Well, it's best I get back to work," he said.

She touched his forearm and flashed him a flirtatious grin. "Don't you have to wait an hour before you swim?"

He shot her a dumb look, momentarily evaluating her comment, and then laughed aloud. "I'd like to," he softly replied as he turned away and headed for the stern.

Chapter 12

Diego Garcia, British Indian Ocean Territories, the same time

The briefing of the U.S. senior officers involved in the operation was about to begin. The only explanation given was that SECDEF wanted it that way. Air Force Brigadier General Pages, the head of DIA's Middle Eastern Affairs Section had flown to this God-forsaken island located about a thousand miles off the coast of Pakistan and India to personally attend the briefing his deputy, Colonel Wayne Grindle, would present on the situation. Though briefings like this were not unusual, the level of geopolitical detail was.

Over the past several weeks the U.S. had been secretly stockpiling special high tech bombs and missiles used in its stealth aircraft at their base in Diego Garcia, a secure island base the U.S. leases from the United Kingdom. There were about fifty British military and civilian personnel on the island and about three thousand U.S. military personnel -mostly Air Force and Navy, to support flight operations.

Colonel Grindle was standing at a small podium located at the front right side of the room. General Pages was seated behind. A large wall-mounted flat screen monitor was positioned centrally on the wall above him. There were over ninety senior officers and enlisted men present.

Grindle tapped on the microphone and the room became hushed.

"Ladies and Gentlemen, General Pages and I are here today to explain the dynamics of contingency operations for which we are preparing to run against Iran. The Secretary of Defense has personally directed this briefing which is at the secret – SPECAT level. I invite your questions as they come up so please feel free to interrupt me."

Grindle glanced down at his notes.

"During the course of this briefing we will review the special strategic relationship we have with Israel. We will discuss how that relationship may suffer as a result of an Israeli preemptive attack against Iran's nuclear development facilities and we will explore the realities which we may encounter as we are drawn into a larger conflict with Iran. But first, I want to review a little history and how it applies to our grand strategy in the Middle East and how Israel fits into that strategy. Again, I invite your questions as they arise."

Grindle paused a moment to scan his audience. He was a tall, powerfully built man who exuded strength, confidence and command presence.

"I think it's fair to say the Cold War was a colossal exercise in trying to maintain the global balance of power," he began. "The only two remaining superpowers, the U.S. and Soviet Union, both formed and supported opposing worldwide alliance systems. Both manipulated these opposing alliances to maintain regional balances of power by pitting one against the other so that any emerging regimes seeking to challenge them would be effectively neutralized by the alliance itself.

"At the end of the Cold War, United States strategy focused on the neutralization of three regional balances of power. They are the Arab-Israeli balance, the Iraq-Iran balance and the Indo-Pakistani balance of power. Having lost the Cold War and much of its superpower status, Russia was in disarray. Thus, we had an unrestricted open door to bolster these three regional power balances and that's exactly what we did.

"I want to briefly talk about the three balances in the order I listed them. As I mentioned, our policy objective in each of these was to achieve a balance of power but overarching to them all is a strategy I'll call, mutual neutralization of power. By this I mean the creation of circumstances that provide opportunity for local powers to neutralize other local powers which subsequently achieves a regional balance of power while we, more or less, remain out of the middle."

"Sir," an Air Force officer interrupted, "is the ultimate goal regional stability?"

"Good question, Major. Regional stability is certainly a desired byproduct resulting from a balance of power but it is not necessarily a lasting outcome. Here are a couple of examples. Of the three regional balances of power I mentioned, two of them are dangerously close to collapsing. Consider this if you will. After our 2003 invasion of Iraq we failed to put an anti-Iranian government in place. And look where we are now. Iran is having some success influencing Iraqi policy and the fledgling Iraqi government and it will only get worse without our troops there. We failed to successfully pit Iraq and its friends against Iran and of course, Russia is overtly fanning those flames to keep us occupied and the region's central balance of power destabilized. In turn, that has affected the Arab-Israeli balance of power to the point that if Israel bombs Iran's nuclear development facilities they will likely end up in a war with Hezbollah, perhaps even Syria and certainly Iran. That conflict will strain the peaceful relations they have with Jordan and Egypt and it could involve us having to take sides – maybe negative to Israeli interests. So, our strategic priority is to maintain the Arab-Israeli balance of power without getting directly involved."

A Navy captain raised his hand.

"Yes, Captain," Grindle said, pointing at him.

"Colonel, you mentioned an Indo-Pakistani balance of power. Would you please shed some light on the Afghan side of things?"

Grindle nodded his consent.

"We have an interesting dynamic there. Both the government of Afghanistan and Pakistan are corrupt and their leaders have recently increased anti-American rhetoric. The Afghan War has surely stressed our relationship between these two governments and I see Pakistan's government continue to weaken. That, in turn, is weakening the Indo-Pakistan balance of power by leaving a power vacuum that India will be driven to fill. That could leave India as the remaining unchallenged power on that sub-continent and completely inundate the Indo-Pakistan balance of power. I think it's fair to say we don't want to see India emerge as a regional superpower any more than we want to see Pakistan assume the same role. The result with all these failing balances of power will be a loss of regional stability which will ultimately involve U.S. interests and may well involve U.S. military action. Does that answer your question, captain?"

"A follow-on if you please, Colonel."

"Shoot."

"If I understand you correctly, the loss of any of these balances of power will cause a destabilizing ripple effect to the entire region so Israel is a key strategic asset in stabilizing the western balance of power. If we can keep the Arab-Israeli balance of power from collapsing, we have a chance at saving the other two. If the Arab-Israeli balance destabilizes there will be a domino effect we won't be able to prevent."

"Captain, you're spot on. Our policy is based on creating and maintaining stable relations with both sides of the power balance. President Banner is continually accused of trying to be friends with everyone but that is the policy basis for why he's shaking all those hands. Let's face it, our military is overstressed. We simply can't diverge from our strategic policy and take all these guys on. And, we must have a policy in place that will survive the current Heads of State in countries like Egypt and Jordan."

Grindle stopped and slowly looked around the room.

"As you know, shipments of laser-guided, deep-underground ordnance have been arriving here over the past several weeks. As I'm sure you have surmised, this ordnance is being pre-staged here in the event that it is needed for operations against Iran. Within the next five days a squadron of F-35 Lightnings and B-52s will arrive here and remain forward deployed here for the foreseeable future."

"Colonel," one of the senior enlisted NCOs in the second row interrupted, "why deploy them here? Why not Saudi Arabia?"

"If we forward deploy the ordnance and aircraft to Saudi, the cat will be out of the bag and every Arab nation in the region will know what we're doing. Bringing our assets here to Day-Gar is a matter of good OPSEC. There is another complication I suspect you may not be aware of."

Grindle glanced back at General Pages who nodded his okay.

"According to our sources, the Saudi base outside Tabuk has become an Israeli forward operating base for their combat assault helicopters and fighter bomber aircraft." There was a hush in the audience. "This is the most recent Israeli contingency preparation to counter Iran, quickly shifting large numbers of combat troops from the home guard, along with tanks, artillery and missile assets closer to the north-western border and into the Caspian region, in what is self described by the Iranian high command as a 'state of war'."

Hushed conversations immediately broke out among the audience. "But, Colonel," the NCO shouted over the noise, "you can't believe they're going to launch an attack against Iran from Saudi?"

Grindle tapped on the mic and held up his hand to quiet the audience.

"Consider this. Israel has recently added some other additions to its defensive and offensive capability. They launched a new secret reconnaissance satellite system into low earth orbit last month. The Israeli military's only comment was to say that the new satellite, Ofek 9, has unprecedented military capabilities. Ofek joins two other Israeli spy satellites presently in orbit and that has Tehran in a quandary." Grindle smiled. "We believe the imaging resolution from these satellites is less than a meter and that makes the Iranians very nervous because they know now they can't hide from the Israelis."

"But do you think the Israelis are going to attack Iran's nuclear weapon development facilities?" the NCO repeated.

Colonel Grindle's eyes twinkled. "Great question. Here's what we think. There can be no greater indication of the fear that Iran has caused among its Middle East Arab neighbors than the fact that none of them have muttered one negative word of invective against the 'Zionist occupiers', which is the Iranian catch-word they use for all things Israeli. So that tells us Israel has the green light as far as the Saudis are concerned, and probably, Iran's other neighbors as well."

"Don't you think Iran must realize its situation?" an officer wearing a flight suit asked. "Do you think they'll back down?"

"Well, let me put it like this. At this point I don't think the Mullahs could get off the hook if they rolled over and said they'd make nice. They're too far down the road to stop the momentum in their conquest towards realizing an operational Islamo-nuclear bomb. It's probably fair to say the Iranian government at large has lost control of the country's nuclear weapons program which has been taken over by the fanatical Revolutionary Guard."

"Colonel, can you tell us what forces we have close by?" a young pilot asked.

"Certainly. We have two naval carrier strike forces including an anti-submarine strike group along with an amphibious landing Expeditionary Strike Group, numbering some 8,000 Marines and sailors. With American, German, Israeli and Canadian Naval assets now in position and Israeli land, air and sea assets at the ready, it would seem that hostilities are imminent.

"Secondly, should the president decide to unilaterally strike, we can best launch a devastating surprise attack against Iran from here. Saudi Arabia has made it clear that they don't want us launching an attack on Iran from their soil probably because we would need to share the same corridor that has been created for the free passage of IAF combat assets on their way into Iran."

Another hand went up towards the rear of the room, "Sir, are we coordinating with the Israelis? I mean, do the Israelis know what we're up to?"

"Currently, we have no indication the Israelis know we are forward deploying our attack assets here to Day-Gar. The reason we need to keep this under wraps is twofold. First, maintaining the balance of power between the Israelis and their surrounding Arab neighbors is extremely important to our overall Middle East strategy. Second, we don't want the Israelis to believe we are prepared to take on Iran or mop up after their attack."

"What happens when Israel attacks Iran, Sir?"

"When? I think you meant 'if.' If Israel initiates an attack on Iran outside the framework of American planning, we will be immediately drawn into the conflict regardless of the outcome. We will need to take immediate military action against Iran to keep the Strait of Hormuz open and contain Iran from a potential retaliatory strike against Israel. While we're at it, we may well conduct air and cruise missile strikes to neutralize their defenses and eliminate their remaining nuclear development facilities. If we launch our operations from, say, Saudi Arabia, Kuwait or Turkey, for example, it would immediately make those countries a target by association. That is unacceptable to our overarching regional strategy because it would draw them into the conflict and force them to choose sides between their Arab neighbors and/or Israel. And the balance of power would undoubtedly go down the crapper in the process. Obviously, that would jeopardize our efforts to stabilize Iraq and Afghanistan and all our previous sacrifice there could go down with it."

"But what about Israel, sir?" a major asked.

"The one thing we want to see from Israel is for them to do nothing that could possibly destabilize the balance of power and make our already difficult task in the region more difficult. Does that answer your question, Major?"

"Yes, Sir, a quick follow-on if you would. Is it likely that we will run a pre-emptive strike against Iran's nuclear development facilities without Israel?"

Grindle glanced back at Pages. Pages nodded his okay.

"Let me answer your question like this, Major. That option is on the table for the president. We already have over a thousand targets identified on our target list. I suppose you could say that's why we're here."

Virgo, the same time

Storm-driven waves pounded Boucher as he descended the ladder. He again disappeared underwater and was momentarily caught in a whirlpool as the ship's stern slammed down from a large passing swell. Undaunted, he systematically cut and removed the net from the propeller.

Two hours had passed as he sawed the last piece of rope from the shaft. It had been a daunting task and in the resulting physical exertion he had used more air than he anticipated. He pulled down the lever on his SCUBA manifold switching to his five minute reserve air supply and swam back to the rudder. Using a hammer, he began to "sound out" the rudder. Beginning at the top, he systematically tapped its steel plating section by section, listening for the hollow sound of the rudder's void interior. He worked his way down past several deeply gashed areas where he heard only dull thuds. He knew they revealed a flooded interior section. At each one he used a white crayon and marked the section with a big easy-to-see circle surrounding an X that he put directly on the gash. Nearly out of air, he headed for the surface.

An exhausted Boucher slowly pulled himself up the ladder one rung at a time as the huge ship heaved in the stormy seas. Sam arrived at the stern just as he stepped on deck and began struggling to unzip his buoyancy compensator and remove heavy diving equipment. A deckhand held the weight of his tanks as he unbuckled the harness and set his equipment on deck. He was clearly dog-tired. He fumbled with his wet suit zipper and turned to notice Sam for the first time.

"Can you get the chest zipper for me?" he asked her. "My fingers are so numb I can't seem to hold on to it."

Trying to muzzle her libido, Sam worked the zipper down to his crotch where she fumbled to get the swivel locks unhooked and separated.

"How is it down there?"

"Huh?"

Embarrassed, she tried to clarify, "The shaft… The screw… Oh hell, you know what I mean."

"Oh, oh, the shaft. I got it unfouled and the screw is clear too, but the screw needs some additional work and the rudder needs a major band-aid. I figure one more dive should do it."

Sam radioed Bakke to advise him.

"Captain Bakke, Sam, over."

"Bakke here."

"Captain, our diver reports he has successfully cleared the shaft but he needs another dive to finish his repairs on the screw and rudder."

"Roger that. Tell him he'll have to wait. Prepare to get underway. Out."

Sam looked at Boucher, "I have no idea what he's thinking."

"We need to explain it to him."

Back in the pilothouse Bakke scanned a current weather forecast he had just printed. Handing it to Deeds, he explained his thinking.

"I can't sit here with this storm approaching. Look at the seas they're forecasting for this location. We're sitting ducks."

Deeds scanned the forecast.

"You're right, Captain. It's foolish to wait for another dive. If he has the net and line cut off we should be good to go."

Boucher and Sam burst onto the bridge as Bakke and his navigator plotted a new course. Boucher purposely walked up close to Bakke. Deeds handed him the weather forecast. Boucher read it and handed it to Sam.

"Are you crazy?" he challenged Bakke. "You can't run this ship through forty foot seas! Without further repair you'll cavitate the friggin' screw. It'll send vibrations from your keel to your bow. On any ship that's risky, but with the LNG load you're carrying, it could be catastrophic."

Deeds stepped up into Boucher's face.

"You're finished here. You better go to your quarters if you know what's good for you."

Unphased by Deeds' threat, Boucher sidestepped and pushed past him.

"Get outta' my way!"

An imposing Boucher towered next to Bakke.

"Captain, we're talking about my ass too. It might be your duty to go down with this bucket, but it's not mine."

Now red-faced, Bakke looked as though he was going to explode.

"Stop, you're just pissing him off," Sam cautioned but Boucher didn't hear her.

"Look, Captain, you're paying me big bucks to help you out. I think you should listen."

Bakke ignored him. Boucher tried again.

"Captain, you're either crazy or a damn fool if you don't let me finish the job."

Bakke reached his breaking point.

"Get off my bridge or I'll have you thrown off!" he angrily shouted. "Put as much ballast in her as she'll take," he ordered Deeds. "I want her as low in the water as we can safely put her." He sneered back at Boucher and Sam. "This cargo gets delivered, on time. Chief Deeds, power up the main engines. Chief Mate Hill, we're going to make best speed," he sternly ordered. "Do either of you two have a problem with that?"

Boucher glanced towards Sam in time to see her shake her head in frustration. Nonetheless, she obeyed the order. At that point, Boucher had enough of both Bakke and Deeds.

"If you're finished with my services, I want off this time bomb."

Both Bakke and Deeds ignored him as the ship began to power back up and get underway again.

Chapter 13

Royal Norwegian Empress

It was business as usual onboard an elegant cruise ship and just another typical night onstage in the ship's theater. The theater was located forward of the ship's main dining room and spanned the entire width of the ship's beam. It was large enough to comfortably accommodate three hundred. Small brown walnut-top cocktail tables adorned two sections of the theater. Waiters in tuxedoes busily served wine and elegantly decorated fruity-umbrella cocktails. Two comedians entered from the curtain to a resounding applause. It was eight o'clock and it was show time.

In his stateroom two decks below, Milan removed a shoebox from his locker and opened the lid. He pulled several fist-size balls of steel wool from the box along with plastic bags each full of fine silver-colored metal shavings and placed everything inside an old pillow sack. He stuffed the pillow sack into the front end of a worn canvas equipment bag beside some dirty rags. He checked his watch and nodded to himself, mentally confirming he was on schedule.

He exited the room with his equipment bag nonchalantly slung by its carrying strap over one shoulder and carelessly gave the door a shove with his foot, slamming it closed. He headed down the private, crew-only passageway on his way to do some repairs like any other member of the engineering crew routinely did on a near hourly basis every day of the week. Only this time he felt jubilant - *praise be to God*. His revenge, no, Allah's revenge against the infidels, would be triumphant and his reward would be eternal.

Virgo

Virgo plowed through twenty-five foot storm-generated waves occasionally shuddering as she buffeted into an abnormally steep swell. Asleep in his stateroom, Boucher awakened to an intermittent sound that resonated through the ship nearly each time it hit a wave.

He quickly threw on a shirt and trousers and stepped out into the passageway. He occasionally heard the sound but couldn't ascertain its source. He went down the passageway towards Sam's cabin. He hesitated at her door a moment and heard the sound again. It was the loudest he had heard it. He knocked on her door. She answered with her sea worthiness nearly exposed beneath a long, white T-shirt that glowed beneath the florescent white passageway lights. Her waist length blond hair shimmered with a ghostly sheen.

"Ah, it's Mr. Fix-it. Thanks for stopping by."

"Did you hear that noise?" he asked, straining to hear it again.

"Hear what?"

"Every time we plow through a wave I hear it. It resonated from somewhere here."

As the ship shuddered and rolled, he cocked his head to one side.

"There it is again. Hear it?"

She studied him momentarily like she thought he was joking.

"Un-huh, sure," she uneasily replied. "Do you come when you hear a dog whistle?"

She stepped backwards into the room. "Why don't you come in?" She beckoned with one hand while pulling the door fully open. "It's quieter in here."

Boucher took a step forward and stood in the open doorway. Sam sat down on the edge of her bed with considerable leg displayed. Boucher didn't seem to notice her and remained standing in the doorway with his head cocked sideways, listening.

"It's getting slightly louder every time I hear it."

Sam's desire quickly faded as Boucher strained to hear the noise again.

"Louder? Not harder?"

"Yes louder," he quizzically repeated, not getting Sam's overt suggestion.

She stood up from the bed and stepped toward him, "Look, you have to understand... I'm always very professional, but I find you..."

At that moment he heard the sound again and held up an index finger to quiet her as he listened. Her smile faded and she looked hurt.

"I'm starting to feel a little ridiculous," she said crossing her arms over her chest. "If you're not interested, no hard feelings, just don't come knocking on my door every time you..."

"Excuse me. What did you say?" he softly mumbled, clearly not paying any attention.

She realized Boucher hadn't heard a word she had said.

"Out! I said, get out and let me get some rack time before I go back on watch."

With both hands on his chest, she shoved him back out into the passageway and closed the door in his face. Still not realizing what had just transpired between them he slowly turned away, hesitating in the passageway, still trying to hear the sound and identify its source.

Office of the Coordinator for Counterterrorism, U.S. State Department, Washington, DC

"Captain," Bruce blurted as he burst into Blackburn's office, "I have a hot one I need to run by you."

"Shoot," Blackburn replied as he swiveled in his chair to face Bruce. "You have my undivided attention."

"My team has been following some developing intelligence that may link Rajakovics to a Venezuelan-backed, murder-for-drugs and oil conspiracy. This morning, the U.S. Immigration and Customs Enforcement Agency reported that one of their confidential informants claims a Venezuelan General by the name of Perez has a business relationship with our old friend Rajakovics. We dug up an old Israeli intel report about Venezuelan Army General Miguel Arvelo Perez that revealed Perez has been known for years to have a working relationship with the FARC. Apparently he's protected by his cronies at the top of the Venezuelan government who are sympathetic to the FARC's socialist agenda and reap huge payoffs to look the other way."

Blackburn impatiently raised his hand and stopped Bruce.

"Damn, that's interesting, Jimmy, but what's that have to do with the price of gas or counter-terrorism?"

"Actually, Sir," Bruce respectfully replied, "I think it probably has a lot to do with both. May I continue?"

"Jimmy, you're killing me with all this extraneous bullshit. What's your point?"

"Sorry, Sir, I just thought you needed to know the link. Apparently, Perez directed his FARC lieutenants to recruit teenage hit men from the barrios. The reason he is using relatively inexperienced teenagers is twofold. First, they're cheap and second, they're expendable. If they get caught they really don't know anything that can tie Perez's activities to sponsorship by the Venezuelan government of the FARC activities he supports."

"Now, Jimmy," Blackburn impatiently said, "where's the tie to the price of gas and counter-terrorism? You know I hate this kind of..."

"Please bear with me, Sir," Bruce pleaded, stopping his boss's scolding mid-sentence. "The tie to the price of gas is this: Venezuela is the sixth-largest oil producer on the planet and the third largest supplier to the U.S. They also produce natural gas. That means Venezuela is in direct competition with the other producers and it's that very competitive availability that controls the speculators and ultimately the price of energy. Better yet, al Qaeda appears to have direct drugs-for-arms links with both the FARC and Venezuela."

"No," Blackburn pronounced, shaking his head from side to side, "I don't see the link."

"Sir, it's easy. Perez used his FARC ties to cover his tracks and had his half-brother, William Hart, murdered."

"In Indonesia? There's no way his reach would extend that far."

"Rajakovics must have arranged for someone else to do the hit. That's the only way it could have gone down."

"But what impact could Hart's murder possibly have on the price of gas? And what of Rajakovics?"

"I don't know for sure, Sir, but I will find out."

"Yeah, good plan, Jimmy. While you're at it, find out where the counter-terrorism link fits into this too."

"I think I already have an idea about that part of it, Sir. You see, if Perez is providing Rajakovics with hit men like that ICE confidential informant suggests, then we can probably assume that the Government of Venezuela is probably involved in some sort of a terrorist conspiracy that will negatively impact U.S. energy resources and further weaken our economy through some form of intentional economic catastrophe."

Blackburn scratched his head and sat forward clasping his hands in front of his chin while keeping both elbows on his desk.

"You keep using the words, 'some sort.' Are you suggesting Perez and Rajakovics are in cahoots and either directly or indirectly Venezuela is involved in a conspiracy to negatively impact our imported energy supply line?" Bruce nodded, yes. "So by eliminating us as their competition, Venezuela will somehow gain both political and financial clout in the world's society of industrial nations? Jimmy, even if there's a shred of fact involved, do you have any idea what you're telling me here?"

Bruce nodded, put his hands in his pockets and rocked back on his heels.

"That's pretty much how I see it, Sir. It means we need to not only keep a close eye on Rajakovics and Perez, but on several of our esteemed senators who support Venezuela and who Perez has in his hip pocket. The thing that bothers me most is the FARC is not just a typical criminal gang of drug-dealing revolutionary thugs. It is an incredibly sophisticated, billion-dollar organization that has invested the time and resources to develop its own intelligence apparatuses which rivals most of the countries' intelligence services in the countries where they operate. They have heavily armed enforcers who possess state-of-the-art weapons and they don't think twice about using them. Wouldn't it be interesting if we could find a solid link between al Qaeda, the government of Venezuela and the FARC? "

"Yeah, it would, but nothing you've just told me sounds like you really have anything substantial enough to act on."

Bruce hung his head.

"That's true, my information is not actionable, but there's something about it that has a dark side I just haven't yet been able to nail down. I can't put my finger on it but I know it's going to bite us in the ass if we don't figure it out soon."

Blackburn nodded, "Okay, Jimmy, stay on it and keep me informed. I'm sure you'll get to the bottom of it sooner or later."

"There's one more thing, Sir."

"Shoot."

"You know that Russian freighter that mysteriously disappeared in the Atlantic a few months back?"

"Yeah, the Arctic Mist or something like that, wasn't it?"

"Yes, Sir, the Arctic Mist, that's the ship."

"As I recall it was carrying a load of timber from Finland to Syria, right?"

"Maybe not," Bruce countered.

"What the hell are you trying to tell me now, Jimmy?"

"There's a Russian maritime expert who has just gone public. He claims the ship was secretly carrying nuclear weapon precursor materials and extremely sophisticated, long range missile guidance and rocket motor parts to Iran. The timber they picked up in Finland was just a cover."

"I thought the reports said the Russians killed all the hijackers when they retook the ship. As I remember, they were all Sierra Leone radical Islamists."

That's what the Russians claimed, but it seems the Sierra Leonists they killed weren't the original hijackers."

"What?"

"We're pretty sure Israeli commandoes took control of that ship after it passed through the English Channel somewhere south of the French coast. Conventional thinking is the commandoes were probably delivered by submarine and boarded the ship underway from inflatable boats."

"But you don't think that?"

"No, Sir. I did a satellite review of all the ships in that general vicinity several days prior, during and after the time the Arctic Mist lost communications. I compared that visual to every available ships sailing record passing through that area."

Blackburn squirmed with nervous anticipation, "And?"

"Well, Sir, satellite imagery showed there was a Zim-owned container ship registered under the name, Shekou, loitering in that vicinity for about twenty-six hours. The company's official sailing log reported the ship had engine problems that were repaired underway."

"Big deal, Jimmy. So what's so unusual if a ship conducts repairs underway? All ships do that."

"Zim is the leading provider of global containerized shipping with major hubs in Haifa, Barcelona, Kingston, Shekou, Hong Kong, Singapore, Huand, and Kelang. And get this, Sir, Zim is owned by the Israeli Corporation. The Israeli Corporation is owned by the Israeli government and is the largest Israeli holding company and ranked number one of the top ten listed on the Israeli Stock Exchange."

Blackburn stared blankly at his young protégé.

"I think the commandoes who conducted that raid where using that Zim container ship as a mobile sea base of operations. It's a perfect cover."

"So convert a few cargo containers on the top stack to carry helicopters, maybe a few more for quarters and you have a stealth sea base. No one would ever suspect..."

"Exactly, Sir. Reportedly, the boarders wore black masks and didn't speak. They rounded up the ship's sixteen-man Russian crew and locked them in the crew's lounge. Then they must have dropped the cargo in question over the side because the timber the ship was carrying was left intact."

"How did they get it over the side while the ship was at sea?"

"The report mentioned that there were several gaping holes cut directly through the ship's side leading out from the cargo holds just above the water line. They must have thrown the cargo out through the holes."

"You're shit'n me?"

"No Sir, what else could it mean?"

"Okay, so how did the Sierra Leone pirates get onboard? You said the Russians retook the ship and found pirates onboard."

"We figure the Israelis sailed the ship to Sierra Leone waters and left it adrift there so the local pirates would board it. They must have figured when the Russian Navy caught up to it and boarded, the local pirates would be there in control of the ship. Oh, one more data point, the Shekou arrived in Barcelona a day and a half late. I think there's one thing we can be very sure of."

"What's that?"

"Those pirates the Russians killed didn't take that ship down off France and then sail it to Sierra Leone."

"Okay, this is all very interesting, but so what? Assuming it was the Israelis and it all went down as you say it did, so what?"

"Well, Sir, I just saw a HUMINT report from a Russian source that confirmed the Arctic Mist's cargo as Russian advanced rocket engines and guidance systems with the capability of accurately putting a payload into a specific high orbital path. I think the Israelis may know a lot more about this than they're sharing with us."

"High orbit? ICBM's are low…"

"Sir, what if the Iranians intend to target our satellites?"

"Our satellites? How so?"

"Our thinking on Iran's intentions to nuke Israel may be completely wrong, Sir. That might just be a cover they're using so we and the Israelis concentrate on the wrong thing. What if they intend to put the nukes they're developing into space and explode them up there where they'll toast the constellations of communications, intelligence and GPS navigation satellites?"

"EMP?"

Maybe, Sir. But most satellites are hardened against the effects of EMP unless it occurs right next to them and then the blast itself would get them. Besides, that would take a number of warheads to be effective."

"Gezz, Jimmy, that's a hell of a stretch. It would take too many nukes and Iran doesn't have that many."

"How about debris clouds, Sir? Just create clouds of high velocity fragments that the satellites would have to pass through? You know, kind of like trying to fly a plane through a cloud of nuts and bolts."

"Oh shit!"

Royal Norwegian Empress, the same time

Sailing a southerly course under a threatening night sky, the ship's lights dimly reflected off the dark tossing sea. In the theater, a miserable comedy act ended to the relief of the audience. The M.C. returned to the stage.

"Let's give a big hand to Hansel and Gretel, ladies and gentlemen. Who said Swiss comedy was dead? Now, straight from Broadway, the Empress is proud to present, CATS!"

As the orchestra began to play the introduction theme for the stage play CATS, the newly wedded bride and groom who were seated near the front of the theater responded to the clinking of glasses by the wedding party and passionately kissed. Milan watched them through an open stage door in amusement. He checked his watch and disappeared down a restricted, crew-only passageway that ran internally, bow to stern, amidships.

Five minutes later, and five decks above, he reappeared at the pool maintenance locker located around a corner passageway from the ship's pool and spa. Opening the locker, he removed three, one-pound buckets of chlorine granules. Taking a quick glance around the pool deck area to ensure he wasn't being observed, he stuffed the white plastic chlorine containers into his well-worn maintenance equipment bag. He carefully relocked the storage locker and departed.

Moments later he passed by the spa where a cigar-smoking, gold chain-wearing, sixty-five year old, Mr. Weinheim, was relaxing chest deep in the sudsy water. He was accompanied by two raspy-voiced, large-bosomed women who were drinking cocktails and smoking cigarettes.

"Beautiful evening, sir!" he commented, smiling at Weinheim.

"Beautiful is an understatement, son. I'm a lawyer. This is as close to heaven as I'll ever get."

The women all laughed and toasted Weinheim by holding their drinks up on outstretched arms. One of the women screamed in surprised delight as Weinheim pinched her bottom beneath the sudsy water. Milan glanced back at them smiling and continued past the trio without further comment. Approaching the glass safety wall ahead, he disappeared into the shadows beneath the overhang of the ship's forward observation deck.

Chapter 14

Virgo, the same time

The intermittent sound awakened Boucher again. It was louder now. He quickly threw on his pants and shirt, carelessly leaving it unbuttoned in his haste, and dashed around the corner to Sam's cabin. He knocked excitedly. The door opened and a hand yanked him into the room. He landed on her bed flat on his back and she pounced on top of him.

"Thank God!" she panted. *I was starting without you.*

Sam feverishly pulled his shirt fully open exposing his hairy chest. Still trying to hear the sound, he acted as though he was oblivious to her advance.

"There it is…again. Hear it?"

She stopped and sat straight up, "Are you sure you're single?"

He smiled at her calculatingly, "Nobody's sharing my bank account."

She quizzically stared at him.

Still smiling he raised up on one elbow, "Seriously, Sam, we need to find that noise."

Sam slid off him and stood beside the bed, still staring at him with puzzlement written all over her face.

"You're not…? You know…? You said you were a former Navy SEAL and were married once and all, but… I don't care which way you… Look, I just need to know," she asked nervously pushing a stray lock of long blond hair behind her ear.

For the first time Boucher realized what was going on. "Don't ask, don't tell." he said smiling.

"Don't ask, don't tell? That means you are? Right?"

"Right."

"Oh… You are?"

Boucher gave her a noncommittal grin."No, I'm not hearing that sound at the moment."

"Give me a second," she said as she slid her feet into her deck shoes and disappeared into her small adjoining office. "Why do I even give a shit?" she grumbled under her breath.

Moments later she reappeared with two flashlights and radios. Boucher was still trying to hear the sound and then it happened again, louder than before.

"There... hear it?" he said pointing aft. "It sounds like it starts somewhere back aft and promulgates forward. It's the opposite of what you would expect since we're bow-on to the seas."

"Ah, come on. Let's go find your noise."

She led him to the ship's aft steering compartment where they inspected the hydraulic rudder motor. It checked out okay. From there they headed to 'shaft alley.'

It was a narrow long hallway-like space that contained the ship's main drive shaft. Shaft alley ran from the engine room's aft bulkhead all the way back to the ship's stern where the shaft penetrated the hull below the waterline. The alignment and weight of the spinning massive shaft was secured by huge journal bearings the size of an office desk which surrounded the heavy shaft about every twenty feet along its entire length.

Boucher and Sam climbed down a long steel ladder inside an access trunk leading down to shaft alley. They inspected each of the main journal bearings that supported the spinning, eighteen-inch diameter, steel pipe-like shaft. Lubrication pressures were normal for each one. At the stern tub packing gland, where the shaft penetrated the ship's hull twelve feet below the waterline, water sprayed in from around the spinning shaft. The gland, as it was called, was designed to leak so sea water would provide a natural cooling lubricant to the 'lignin vita' wood that was used to surround the shaft inside the gland and provide an otherwise watertight seal.

Boucher scratched his head, pointing his flashlight beam at the spray, "I've seen a lot of these and that leakage looks excessive."

"Yeah, it's leaking more than it should. I'll let the Chief know so he can adjust it."

He grunted and turned back towards the way out. As they climbed back up the vertical escape trunk ladder, the ship pitched radically in the rough seas. On the ladder above Boucher, Sam momentarily lost her grip and fell backward, but he caught her. He pulled her in tightly against his chest. She looked up at him with wide green eyes, and a smile spread across her face. She relaxed against him, her body warm and soft against his. Then she frowned and cocked her head to one side.

"I just heard it," she whispered.

"What?"

"I just heard the noise. We need to go forward. I think I know where it might be coming from."

Smiling, Boucher helped her back onto the ladder. She realized his hand lingered at the small of her back a moment longer than necessary.

They raced forward to the access hatches leading to the void area crawl spaces beneath the four huge LNG storage globes.

"We need to split up. I'll go forward and check the voids beneath tank one and two. I'll start under tank one closest to the bow," Sam explained. "You check three and four. Keep your radio handy."

"Okay, since we're almost standing on it, I'll start with four. By the way, what specifically are we looking for, Sam?"

"Anything that doesn't look right. You'll know if you see it."

They separated and each entered their respective voids beneath the huge storage globe-like tanks. Sam crouched in the low crawl space as she went from section to section through the numerous baffled access openings beneath tank one. The voids were dark and eerie. The air inside was stale and smelled peculiar – kind of like a gymnasium locker room. She didn't like being inside the confined voids beneath the storage tanks and usually avoided going into them if she could. But tonight was the exception – the noise needed to be investigated.

She systematically ran her flashlight along the base of the globe being careful to check all the welds. She was looking for anything abnormal, but found nothing. As she carefully made her way back to the access hatch, Boucher's voice crackled over her radio.

"Sam, I got a tall frosty one here on the base of globe four and its in-line with the keel."

"I'll be right there," she responded. "Stay where you are."

Moments later she joined him in the dark, cramped void beneath storage globe four. Using his flashlight beam as a pointer, Boucher showed her the damage.

"Check out these hairline fractures here and here," he pointed with his flashlight. "They extend across to this welded seam that runs along the globe's bottom over here."

Numerous sparkling white frosted areas reflected off the flashlight beam. They ran several yards along the welded seams where the tank joined the supporting baffles in the void.

"Oh damn!" she said. "That doesn't look good. How bad do you think it is?"

"Well, Sam, unless you like fireworks I'd say it's real bad." Turning towards her in the cramped darkness he could see the concern on her face. "And, I'm sorry to say, I think we can expect these cracks to grow. As the weld fractures migrate further as a result of the vibration, the leaks will get worse. The liquefied natural gas will be exposed to atmospheric pressure and will boil off and return to its gaseous state." Boucher ran his flashlight from one side of the void to the other. "And this entire void will become an explosive bomb just waiting for an ignition source. Bakke needs to either vent this void outside or flood it with seawater to stop the LNG leak from boiling off and becoming gaseous."

Sam tugged at his arm. "We gotta let the Captain and the Chief know immediately."

They made their way back to the ladder and exited the void, closing the hatch and carefully ensuring it was tightly sealed.

Boucher took Sam by the hand and stopped her. "Sam, I just want to thank you," he said soberly. "This is real important."

"I know. Believe me, I know." She smiled.

"There's one more thing you need to know…" He tilted her chin up and looked into her eyes. "I'm not a complicated guy. I'm just composed of multiple layers of simplicity."

She laughed softly. "Right."

"One more thing…I'm not gay."

She squeezed his hand and pulled him a short distance down the passageway as they headed for the bridge to report their findings to Bakke.

The Pentagon, Office of the Secretary of Defense, the same time

"Secretary Hammond you have an urgent call from General Cline on line two," a woman's voice softly announced over the office intercom.

"Thank you, Janie. I'll take it here."

Hammond pushed the line-two button on his secure telephone and opened the speaker option so he could talk hands free. He really didn't know retired Army General Cline, the president's National Security Advisor, very well and at heart, didn't like him. After all, Hammond was himself a Harvard-schooled PhD constitutional law scholar like the president, and Cline was a West Point-trained, no nonsense, retired Army general who didn't seem to reflect the level of political sophistication the more elite members of the president's cabinet possessed. That's why Hammond insisted on using Cline's first name instead of calling him by his former military rank - General.

"Gregory, what's on your mind?"

Hammond knew Cline had an impressive resume of combat commands and was known throughout the military as a general's general. He also distrusted Cline across a variety of fronts. For that reason he always called him by his first name just to knock him down a notch or two.

"Secretary Hammond," Cline drawled, "the purpose of my call is to inform you of a potential issue that could bite you and President Banner squarely in the butt. As you already know, the operation our forces ran in northwestern Afghanistan failed to capture Al-Adel. However, during that raid our special operations forces recovered a flash drive from one of Al-Adel's dead lieutenants. That flash drive contained a treasure trove of actionable intelligence."

Hammond interrupted, "Gregory, I am already fully aware of this, so your review is unnecessary."

"What you are not aware of, Secretary Hammond is this: the captured al Qaeda flash drive revealed the names of a terrorist cell here in the U.S. This cell is composed of at least six, perhaps more, U.S. citizens who converted to radical Islam while they were doing prison time. Working closely with the CIA and the Department of State, the FBI has been able to link the cell's activities to conspiring to provide material support to terrorists and conspiracy to murder, kidnap and injure persons in a foreign country."

"So how does that affect my department, Gregory?"

"The cell leader's name is Jamal Jones. The FBI was able to hack into his computer files and phone logs and correlate that information to the information contained on the captured flash drive. It seems there are some common threads. First, Jones is a Muslim convert who lived in Pakistan and Afghanistan where he attended militant training camps from 1988 to 1992. In 1989 he fought against Soviet troops in Afghanistan and after the Soviet withdrawal, he fought with Islamist militants against the Soviet-backed Afghan forces during the Afghan civil war. In 1992, Islamic forces overthrew the Democratic Republic of Afghanistan and Jones returned to his home in New York to start his own terrorist cell."

"You got all this off a captured flash drive?"

"Yes, much of it, and there's more you need to know. Many in the Muslim community hold Islamic veterans of the Soviet's war in Afghanistan in reverence. They are romanticized as victorious mujahedin. They are looked on as 'holy warriors' who defeated the Soviets and their Afghan allies. The most troubling piece of information we have is that Jones had a handler who was known as 'Saifullah'. Saifullah is Arabic for 'the sword of Allah'. We have not been able to identify who Saifullah is."

"Okay, so has the FBI arrested Jones yet?"

"Not yet, but they have wire tapped him and that has led to this. Jones is involved in some kind of attack plot with a Kazak-born former Spetsnaz officer turned soldier-of-fortune. His name is Rajakovics."

"He's the guy who masterminded the Canary Island nuclear attack last year, isn't he?"

"Yes, one in the same. We believe he's up to something big again and Jones is helping him from this end. There are a large number of parallels between Jones, Rajakovics and al Qaeda's other plots and attacks. We think Rajakovics may be working for al Qaeda and we think there is a major attack on the way here. We just haven't been able to nail it down."

"Why not indict Jones and those in his terrorist cell?"

"If we did, that wouldn't stop Rajakovics. The CIA is doing their best to locate Rajakovics, but they seem to always just miss him. By not showing our hand, we may be able to use Jones to our advantage and hopefully, he'll reveal the way to Rajakovics."

"What does President Banner know about this?"

"He knows it all. He asked me to personally brief you."

"What does he want me to do?"

"At this point, nothing. We just don't know when, where, or what they'll use against us. However, the president may need to react very quickly so he wants you to ensure our military is ready to respond to anything from another 9/11 to a manmade disaster."

"Of course, Gregory. I'll share this with the Joint Chiefs?"

"No, this must remain at the Cabinet-level for now."

"Has DHS been briefed?"

"No. There are too many agencies, like ICE, ATF and DEA within the Department of Homeland Security that have been penetrated and compromised by foreign agents, drug cartels and organized crime syndicates. This must remain between the CIA, the FBI, State Department, you, me and the president until we have actionable intelligence from which we can develop a strategy to best deal with this threat."

Virgo

Arriving on the bridge, Sam and Boucher found Bakke and Deeds discussing the storm approaching from the south. Sam interrupted them to provide a detailed damage report.

"Captain, Jake and I just came from the void space beneath Number 4 storage tank."

Bakke raised a suspicious eyebrow like a father might if his daughter tells him she was alone in the bedroom with her boyfriend. "You did what?" he asked in a condescending voice.

Sam immediately picked up on what he was thinking.

"Captain, Jake and I heard a strange sound resonating from the stern that seemed to run forward along the ship's keel so we investigated. We checked all the void spaces beneath all four LNG storage tanks. Number 4 has a series of spider web cracks that cover a ten square foot area running above the main keel baffle. The cracks are frosty so there is definitely leakage. You need to either vent that void or flood it. I think flooding is the best and safest way to deal with this problem. Equally important, we also need to slow down and see if that will stop the vibrations. If that tank ruptures, the explosive hazard will be beyond anything we can deal with."

Bakke momentarily considered Sam's recommendations and cautions.

"Captain," Deeds appealed, "spider cracks aren't an issue and these so called vibrations - why don't we hear them or feel them?" Deeds shook his head in an air of doubt. "Captain, neither venting the void nor flooding it with seawater is a prudent option. Venting is ineffective and flooding it will add more stress to the welds from the added weight. We don't need another delay, especially an unnecessary one."

Boucher took issue with not taking preventive action.

"I disagree. Taking no action will result in catastrophe. I've seen the damage, Captain. The harmonic vibrations that caused this fracture are a result of the propeller damage you sustained from the fishing net anchors that clobbered you. I'm guessing the main shaft is out of alignment just enough to have stressed the keel all the way forward to storage tank four. You simply must not continue in this sea state without additional propeller repair to reduce the vibration on the shaft."

Deeds theatrically rolled his eyes at Bakke in an effort to discredit Boucher. Boucher scowled stepping aggressively toward Bakke. "Look, Captain, you need to secure that globe to keep it from rupturing. If I were you, I'd take my Chief Mate's advice and flood that void with sea water."

"And slow down, Captain," Sam added.

Bakke stared at Boucher and smiled.

"Alas, my presumptuous visitor from the deep, you are not me and neither are you my dear, blond Chief Mate. You don't tell me what to do on my ship, now or ever!"

Bakke grabbed Deeds' arm and snarled, "Vent the void beneath Number

4 and check out the damage for yourself. I want a qualified engineer's opinion."

Boucher stalked from the bridge without further comment and headed to his stateroom. As he entered, he slammed the door so hard it bounced back without latching and remained cracked open. Frustrated, he began writing his repair report sitting at a small fold-out desk next to his bed. Sam knocked lightly on the partially open door.

"Jake?" she softly queried.

"It's open," he said without looking back her direction.

She pushed her way in.

"I know you're right."

"Dead right and that sorry ass excuse for a Chief Engineer you have knows it too."

He stood, reached behind Sam, gently shoved the door closed and looked into her piercing green eyes.

She laid her hand on the back of his neck and said, "So, what are we going to do about it?"

"Find Deeds and try to get him to understand we're riding on a time bomb."

Boucher led Sam out of the room where they chance encountered Deeds coming toward them in the passageway.

"I need to talk to you," Boucher demanded.

"No you don't."

Boucher blocked his path with his massive frame.

"Do you understand how dangerous that tank fracture is? If this thing blows near land it'll be just like Hiroshima."

"I've personally inspected the tank," Deeds said trying to push by. "You're not an engineer and you're overreacting."

"In this storm that fracture will grow. You need to flood that void."

"Easy my friend," Deeds warned. "I did the calculations. If I add water to the void the additional weight will slow us down and create even more stress on the ship's structure. And that means the tank will rupture more, not less."

"Look," Boucher insisted, "I might not be an M.I.T. Naval Architecture graduate, but I know bullshit when I hear it."

Sam stepped up in Deeds' face, "We're all going to die if you don't flood that void."

"Nonsense!" Deeds objected. "You're showing your lack of practical experience, my dear and you're both overreacting," he said staring directly at her breasts.

"I'm logging this conversation," Sam declared, seething at the insult.

"Be my guest. You may be the Chief Mate, but I'm the Chief Engineer and when it comes to anything engineering-related on this ship, what I say goes."

Chapter 14

Milan cautiously approached the paint locker and stopped short to survey the area for other people. After checking that no one else was around, he stepped up to the paint locker's sheet metal door. Its numerous successive coats of white paint accumulated over a number of years made it look more like it had been plastered than painted. The door had large yellow placards mounted on the outside that read, FLAMMABLE LIQUIDS. NO SMOKING WITHIN 25 FEET.

Milan set his equipment bag down being careful to ensure the chlorine buckets inside the bag were all sitting right side up, flat on the deck. He then unlocked and opened the paint locker door and removed a gallon container of glycol from a shelf in front of him. Without taking the chlorine buckets out of his bag, he carefully removed the lids on all three. He opened the box containing the plastic bags of magnesium shavings, and then mixed a bag of the shavings into the chlorine granules in each bucket. Milan meticulously tore the steel wool mitts into small pieces and worked the pieces into the mixture, ensuring the steel wool pieces, magnesium shavings and chlorine granules were uniformly distributed throughout the mixture. He then poured about a pint of glycol evenly over the mixture in each bucket and quickly replaced the lids.

Milan placed one bucket on the shelf in the paint locker next to several five gallon cans of volatile paint thinner and locked the door. He then departed for the stern with the other two buckets concealed in his equipment bag.

Minutes later Milan arrived at the door leading outside to the ship's stern crew deck area. As he passed through the door he glanced upward at the security camera. The coaxial cable he cut previously had not been repaired.

He quickly proceeded to the dimly lit gasoline storage area. He took a quick look around to ensure he was alone. He quickly positioned the second bucket amongst the gasoline and oil storage cans, intentionally stacking several full gasoline cans around and on top of the bucket.

Milan put his hand on the side of the third bucket. It was getting hot. He knew he didn't have much time. He hurried up the crew's central passageway to the main engineering auxiliary switch panel that remotely controlled the ship's fire hydrants and flushing system. He opened the control panel doors and centered the third bucket in the middle of all the relay switches inside the panel. As he shut the doors he checked to make sure they were firmly latched and locked.

Virgo Bridge, same time

It was a dark night far at sea. The Virgo shuddered violently each time its propeller cavitated in the heavy seas. On the bridge, Bakke angrily threw his empty coffee cup across the pilothouse shattering it into porcelain shards against the opposing bulkhead.

"All stop!" he growled at Sam. "I can't go any further with my ship in this condition."

Sam retracted the engine control lever to the neutral position.

"All stop, Captain," she calmly reported.

"Okay, get that diver down on the screw again."

Deeds arrived on the bridge and checked his watch. He approached Bakke.

"We're less than five hundred miles off the coast of North Carolina and we have a storm running up our ass. We can make it, Captain."

"I'm going to give our diver enough time for a quick screw tune up and that's all."

Deeds cussed under his breath but showed no outward anger. "Yes, sir," he whispered just loud enough so Bakke would hear him.

Royal Norwegian Empress, the same time

The first incendiary Milan had put inside the paint locker began to smolder. Within minutes it started smoking. Then it burst into white-hot flames that simultaneously engulfed the volatile paint thinners and cleaning solutions immediately beside it. As those containers ruptured from the heat, their contents provided a source of burning liquid that rapidly spread throughout the rest of the paint locker. In no time the entire paint locker was ablaze and the fire had quickly widened into the passageway and several neighboring compartments.

On the bridge, Captain Dahl and Staff Captain Anderson observed fire warning sensor lights flash on the damage control panel display. Dahl studied the alarm display momentarily trying to make sense of the fire's magnitude.

"I think it could be a malfunctioning sensor," Anderson commented.

Anderson picked up the phone and dialed the deck office to get an accurate status. After a brief conversation he reported to Dahl.

"They tell me a fire party is on its way down to the paint locker to check it out. We'll know in a few minutes."

As Anderson hung up from his call, the phone rang again immediately.

"Bridge, Anderson," he tersely answered.

"Geez!" he exclaimed putting his free hand on his forehead. "Get the auxiliaries on line," he ordered. "I'll inform the Captain."

Dahl didn't need to ask how bad it was. The look on Anderson's face said it all.

"Captain, Engineering reports that the main fire and flushing pump motor just seized. The pump is down hard."

Virgo, the same time

Bakke impatiently paced the pilothouse watching the clock. On the stern, Boucher quickly suited up, thanks to the assistance of Sam and two unlicensed mates. Boucher was obviously irritated and Sam knew it.

"He's given me thirty minutes to finish repairs - that's a friggin' joke, right?"

"I wish it was, but unfortunately, it's not. I know you can do it," she smiled, gently touching his hand with hers. "Don't be long," she urged before turning away and heading for the bridge.

He checked his watch then descended the swaying Jacobs ladder. The deckhand lowered his tools down to him and watched as Boucher disappeared beneath Virgo's stern with his flashlight blazing through the water like a light saber in a Star Wars movie.

Below, Boucher positioned himself against one of the damaged propeller blades and manipulated a portable hydraulic press which was an underwater version of the Jaws of Life, to straighten the severely bent areas of the propeller blades. After straightening only one blade he checked his watch. His thirty minutes were up. He swam back up to the surface and grasped the ladder to keep from being swept away by the heavy seas. He yelled up to the mate on deck.

"Hey! Hey! Mate!"

The mate leaned over the rail, cupping his hand over his ear to hear over the surf pounding against the ship's hull.

"Yeah."

"Tell the Captain I can make this lady ride like a Rolls Royce if he'll give me another thirty minutes."

The mate gave Boucher a thumbs-up and clicked his handheld radio mic open.

On the bridge, Bakke's radio squawked with Boucher's request. Standing at the chart table with Deeds and Sam, Bakke nervously tapped his fingers contemplating his answer. He finally looked up at Sam.

"He wants thirty minutes more?" saying it more as a statement than a question.

Sam nodded affirmatively.

"Tell him to go ahead, but not a second longer."

"Thank you, Captain. I'll go aft and deliver the message myself."

"No you won't. This ship is in trouble; your place is here on the bridge. Chief, I want you to go aft and personally see to getting it finished in thirty minutes."

Sam immediately radioed the mate who was tending Boucher.

"The Captain is giving him thirty minutes more. Tell'm to get back down there now and work as fast as he can."

Deeds checked his watch again and left the bridge. On the way aft, Deeds went inside his state room and locked the door. He checked a chart on his desk and then his watch. He removed a pistol from a desk drawer and concealed it inside the front of his pants under his shirt.

Royal Norwegian Empress, the same time

Fire raged in the paint locker and two adjoining spaces. Toxic smoke seeped into a ventilation intake from under the door. The paint on the metal door began to sweat and slowly turn a brownish color as the paint melted off its face. Then it slowly deformed into a sagging, red hot metal sheet. Suddenly the door blew off. Thick black smoke voluminously poured out behind the ship. Captain Dahl glanced aft through the bridge windows and saw smoke trailing his ship. He quizzically surveyed the flashing alarm lights on the status board again.

"Status?" he calmly asked Anderson.

The Staff Captain listened to the chatter on his radio for a moment before reporting.

"The starboard paint locker is burning out of control. The sprinkler system is down hard! Two of our three diesel auxiliary pumps are down."

"What the hell is happening?"

Far aft, a bucket smoldered in the gasoline and recreational vehicle storage area, and then a bright flash erupted. More fire warning lights flashed on the damage control panel. Captain Dahl was dumbfounded.

"Sound the lifeboat alarm," Dahl ordered.

A mate opened the intercom mic and spoke.

"Fire, fire, fire, this is not a drill. Repeat, this is not a drill. All passengers immediately proceed to your lifeboat stations."

A third fire warning flashed.

Dahl froze as the Staff Captain yelled, "Fire in main engineering!"

Dahl winced, already knowing what the orders he was about to give meant.

"Close all flood doors from main engineering aft. Get damage control fire parties down there now. Clear all passengers and non-essential crew from the area. Ready all lifeboats."

Chapter 15

Virgo, same time

Deeds stopped in the passageway and zipped up his rain parka. He slowly opened the watertight door leading to the ship's stern weather deck and stepped outside. It had begun to rain. He quickly checked the position of his pistol hidden beneath his outer garments. Distant lightning illuminated the stormy sea surface frothing to and fro against Virgo's hull. Rumbling thunder crept closer with every threatening flash on the horizon. Gusting rain pelted the two crew members tending Boucher. They leaned over Virgo's stern safety rail eagerly anticipating his appearance on the surface. Deeds appeared behind the two crewmen.

"How's our diver doing?" he inquired, startling the two men.

They reeled around recognizing their Chief Engineer.

"He's bustn' ass down there, Chief."

A faint beam of light from underwater gradually grew brighter. Telltale shafts of expanding air bubbles rising from below marked Boucher's ascending location. His head suddenly popped above the surface illuminated by the ship's security lights the crewmen had aimed down at the water. He rummaged through the canvas tool bag the workers had suspended next to the Jacobs ladder and selected another tool.

"Hurry up!" Deeds yelled down to him over the sound of the surf. "This storm is closing on us faster than we expected. We need to get underway."

"I'm working as fast as I can," Boucher shouted back, his voice barely audible over the noise of the surf pounding against the ship's hull.

"Good, okay," Deeds said giving Boucher a thumbs-up, "get it done as fast as you can!"

Before turning away, Deeds waited until Boucher looked his way and gave him a feeble salute. Boucher waved and again disappeared into the darkness beneath the massive ship's stern, his flashlight beam slowly disappearing into obscurity.

Deeds stared into the darkness of the abyss that had just swallowed Boucher. Distant lightning danced across the horizon like choreographed strobe lights on a sound stage, momentarily capturing his attention. They had to get the ship underway again and stay ahead of the storm. He checked his watch and cussed to himself. They were almost out of time.

Office of the Coordinator for Counterterrorism, U.S. State Department, Washington, DC

Blackburn was contemplating the ramifications of a Top Secret cable he was reading when Jimmy Bruce entered his office. Blackburn glanced up and nodded as though Bruce had been engaged in a discussion about the cable.

"You know, Jimmy, the three enemies of human progress are ignorance, ambition and fanaticism. These radical Islamist sons-of-bitches seek to keep their followers blindly stupid and fanatic because they're ambitious and want to impose their ideological bullshit on the rest of the planet."

Bruce chuckled, "I'm not sure if I would define them in quite the same way but that's pretty succinct. Do you know the Latin saying, 'Liberte' de Penser', Sir?"

"Yeah, it means freedom of thought or freedom of conscience, or some shit like that. Right?"

Bruce laughed again, "It's good to see you thinking along these lines, Sir."

Bruce had worked as Blackburn's assistant for almost five years at this point and knew him well. While retired SEAL Captain Blackburn came across as a knuckle dragger because of the four-letter vocabulary he regularly used, his analytical abilities were actually very sophisticated. He possessed the rare ability to verbalize extremely complex analysis using the simplest explanations and Bruce found his charismatic personality both fascinating and captivating.

"Stop blowing smoke up my ass, Jimmy." Blackburn threw the message clipboard down on his desk. "Everything I'm seeing makes my gut tell me there's something coming at us but I just can't put my finger on it."

"So far, neither can anyone else, Sir."

Blackburn thoughtfully stroked his chin with his thumb and forefinger, "What's your gut telling you, Jimmy?"

"I think whatever it is, we're in the crosshairs and it's headed our way."

Royal Norwegian Empress, same time

On the Empress's bridge, Captain Dahl's radio chirped with very excited unintelligible voices. The paint locker fire raged out of control and had spread to the surrounding area.

"This is Fire Team Alpha," the bridge intercom radio crackled with a status report. "We've tried everything we can. The fire is out of control. We're pulling back."

Fire crews were overwhelmed and retreated in chaos. Captain Dahl monitored more reports of the spreading fires.

"This is Team Bravo. We're backing out of the crew passageway. We'll try to cool it down as long as we can but it's a lost cause. I ain't never seen no fire burn this hot," the Bravo team leader reported.

"What's our position?" Dahl asked the navigator.

"We're five hundred and forty-one miles due east of Moorhead City, North Carolina, Captain."

"Keep her headed into the wind. Slow to five knots."

Dahl opened the intercom to his communications officer, "Send an S.O.S."

The Empress now bellowed smoke from sixty-five percent of its outside openings. Hysterical passengers grabbed life jackets and ran through the choking smoke to the lifeboats, crowding onto them without regard to their individually assigned boats. The ship's crew struggled to prevent panic as the situation began to deteriorate. Suddenly, muffled explosions were felt deep inside the ship as far forward as the bridge. The Empress shuddered like a dying beast. Her main engines wound down and stopped. Lights throughout the ship flickered and slowly dimmed to obscurity. Battery powered emergency lights immediately flashed on, illuminating the critical escape passageways. The Empress was now helplessly adrift without engines or electrical power.

Turning to his First Mate, Captain Dahl finally gave the order no sea captain ever wants to give.

"Sound the alarm, abandon ship. I want every space searched and every single person accounted for. Once you have everyone outside, close all watertight doors and seal the main spaces. Maybe we'll get lucky."

The First Mate sounded the alarm and repeated Dahl's order over the intercom.

"Abandon ship, abandon ship. This is not a drill. I repeat, abandon ship, this is not a drill."

Ten minutes later, Milan was helping with the room checks to ensure no passengers were left behind. He pounded on Mr. Weinheim's locked cabin door without any response from the inside. Finally, opening it with his master key, he found Mr. Weinheim and the two women from the spa in bed unfolding from a compromising position.

"Didn't you hear the alarms? The ship is on fire. We must abandon ship!" he warned. "Go to your lifeboat station immediately! Come with me immediately, you have to move it. Everyone on deck now!"

"Huh? What alarm?"

Milan grabbed two robes from the bathroom and threw one to each of the scantily clad women. "You don't have time to dress. Put on these robes and slip on your shoes. Weinheim, still dressed in his tux, rolled out of bed and slipped on his shoes. Milan pulled them out into the smoky passageway.

"Take that stairway up one level," he said pointing. "Turn left at the top and go through the door to the main deck. Find your lifeboat station. Hurry, we don't have much time."

Under Milan's watchful eye, Weinheim and the two women frantically scurried up the stairs. The women were carrying their clothes in one hand and holding onto Weinheim's coat tails with the other. Milan turned away with a faint smile. The smoke permeated his nostrils. It reminded him of the odor he smelled right after the American attack that consumed his home and family. He dutifully continued the room check knowing he would soon have his revenge.

Chapter 16

Virgo, same time

Deeds again checked his watch. The time was 12:57 A.M. He shone his flashlight down on the sea's surface below, marking Boucher's stream of air bubbles. He casually looked over at the two mates leaning over the rail beside him and lit a cigarette, offering each of the seamen a smoke from his pack. They both obliged, carefully cupping their hands over their smokes to keep them dry.

"Lucky he was still on board," Deeds commented as he flipped his lighter top open and lit each man's cigarette. "This old girl's been shakin' like a one-legged tap dancer."

"She sure has," one of the soaking wet mates replied, noticeably fighting off a shiver.

"Say, why don't you guys go inside and warm up? I'll tend to our diver."

"That's okay, Chief, I don't mind staying," the other mate replied. "That guy's been down there a long time. He's gonna be tired when he comes up and will probably need our help getting back onboard."

"Go on, you've been up all night freezing your asses off!"

The mate stared down at the water.

"You sure, Chief?"

Deeds checked his watch again; it turned to 12:59 A.M. He casually checked to see if anyone else was around as he slowly reached under his parka for his gun. Lightning flashed in the distance, momentarily illuminating the men like a strobe light in a night club. The other mate grabbed his friend by the arm and motioned to Deeds that he was chilly.

"I wouldn't mind a warm up and a hot cup of java. What do ya say?"

The other mate peered over the side again beaming his flashlight down on the water surface straining to locate Boucher's air bubbles.

"Okay, a cup of coffee would be nice about now. You sure you can handle this by yourself?" he asked Deeds.

"No problem, you guys go warm up. I'll take care of the diver."

The two mates headed for the warmth of the crew's mess without further comment.

On the bridge, the printer chirped to life and buzzed out a short message.

Sam read the printout and called Bakke in his stateroom, "Captain, we just received an S.O.S."

Moments later Bakke appeared on the bridge. Sam handed him the message. He mumbled through it aloud.

"The cruise ship Royal Norwegian Empress, on fire, abandoning ship. Two thousand, one hundred and thirty-one passengers and crew. Fire raging out of control..." Bakke looked up in astonishment. "God save them, they're on fire."

Bakke and Sam quickly plotted Empress's reported position on the navigation chart and were astonished how close they were.

"They're just over the horizon, Captain. We can be there in about an hour if we get underway now. We need to recover our diver immediately."

Bakke checked his watch.

"You tell the Empress we have a diver in the water. We will proceed to assist as soon as he is recovered. ETA is approximately zero two three zero hours local time. I'll have the Chief Engineer see to the diver."

Beneath the ship's stern, Boucher tapped the rudder from the top down. The sound changed from a hollow drum to a dull thud. He found a deep gash in the rudder's metal skin that had allowed water to flood into its void interior. He immediately swam to the surface and grabbed a cofferdam from the tool bag.

Cofferdams come in many sizes and shapes but they all work the same way. They are nothing more than a box which is open on one side. A rubber gasket is fixed around the contact edge on the open side to seal it against the ship's hull. The cofferdam is fastened open side in against the hull area that is to be sealed. The water is blown out of the box using a compressed air source – usually from a diver's SCUBA bottle. Once it's clear of water, hydrostatic pressure presses the box tightly against the previously leaking area. This seals the leak until the hole can be welded shut with a permanent patch from either the inside or outside.

Deeds checked his watch. It was now 1:30 A.M. The lightning flashes were getting closer as thunder rumbled louder after every flash.

Boucher yelled up at Deeds, "Your rudder is partially flooded. I'll put a cofferdam over it, then blow the water out. Twenty minutes, max!"

Deeds waved down at him, "Okay, do whatever it takes."

Lightning flashed again, dangerously close. An instantaneous thunder clap resounded. Deeds gave Boucher a thumbs-up. Boucher waved back and again disappeared beneath the surface. Deeds wasted no time and immediately pulled Boucher's tool bag up on deck. He then pulled up the Jacobs ladder. Just as he finished piling it on deck, Bakke unexpectedly showed up.

"Is he finished?" Bakke asked.

Startled, Deeds checked to see that Boucher was still underwater and his flashlight wasn't visible from above.

"Yes, he's finished."

"Good, we have a ship close by that needs our help."

"So I hear on the radio. I was just leaving for main engineering. My Second Engineer says we're good to go."

Bakke raised his radio. "Chief Mate, the diver is finished and the repairs are completed. Get underway immediately. Make best speed. Advise Empress our ETA is approximately one hour. I am going to Main Control with our Chief Engineer, then I'm on my way to bridge."

"Roger your last, Captain. Getting underway momentarily."

"Good, make best speed."

Sam called the engine room and ordered the removal of the red lockout tags and directed them to make preparations to get underway without delay. The engineers were already aware of the reason for the urgency and were standing by to immediately execute the order. The idling main engine was immediately powered up and the auxiliary systems were brought on line. Within a few minutes, the engine room reported full readiness to the bridge. Sam ordered the mate at the helm to advance the engine throttles and turn the ship's wheel to a rendezvous heading with the burning Empress.

The propeller began spinning, tumbling Boucher helplessly through the swirling water. One of the large blades stuck his SCUBA tank and nearly decapitated Boucher. He fought his way through fizzing bubbles reaching the surface in time to see Captain Bakke and Deeds leave the stern deck. Straining against the giant propeller's thrust, he ditched his diving gear and pulled himself hand over hand along his tether line, barely reaching the ship's hull.

The rudder turned again, driving the propeller's thrust away from Boucher, giving him a chance. Half-drowned, he attempted to catch hold of a pad eye but he missed. Twenty foot swells slammed him into Virgo's stern. As the ship came about on its new heading it plunged through a huge wave. The wave washed over the forward deck and ran aft past the LNG globes, slamming into the superstructure like a storm wave hitting a seawall.

Bakke and Deeds entered the bridge and saw Sam was smiling widely.

"Damn! That diver is as good as he looks," Sam cheerfully reported to Bakke. "He got this girl purrin' like the Caddie my daddy always dreamed of. But don't get me wrong, she still drives like a tanker."

Bakke gave her a wincing glare.

"How's he doing?" she asked.

"Who is 'He'?" Bakke asked as he adjusted the radar screen to its maximum range.

"Tired and cold," Deeds replied. "He wanted to take a hot shower and hit the rack."

"Understandable," Sam said nonchalantly, "he's had a long day."

Bakke now held the cruise ship on radar as Virgo quickly closed the distance. A faint red glow appeared on the horizon.

Deeds studied the scene ahead through binoculars.

"So what have we got here?" he mumbled aloud.

Bakke raised his binoculars, sweeping the dark horizon and stopped, focusing on the red glow emanating from the horizon miles ahead.

"A burning cruise ship," he gasped. "My God, she's almost fully engulfed."

"I guess there's no one else closer?" Deeds questioned.

"We're three hours closer than anyone else," Sam said, turning to face Bakke. "Captain, with Number 4 tank leaking, don't you think it's risky going too close to that burning ship?"

Bakke seemed irritated by her warning.

"Samantha, you wouldn't be here if you didn't want responsibility, right?"

"Yes, Sir."

"You want your own ship someday, right?"

"There is nothing in the world that I want more."

"You realize that being Captain makes one ultimately responsible. There's no buck to pass when you're in the Captain's shoes." Bakke put down his binoculars and casually polished the compass face glass in front of the helm with his shirt sleeve. "Here's a hypothetical...a tanker has a fractured tank filled with liquefied natural gas - it's leaking. As the liquid boils off it becomes a volatile gas. The more gas that accumulates onboard the ship, the greater the possibility it could find an ignition source. We all know what happens then."

"A big bang!" she said.

Not seeming to hear her, Bakke quizzically stared through the bridge windows towards the red glow of the burning cruise liner.

"Right now, two thousand men, women and children are abandoning that burning ship. They're scared to death and praying that we get there in time. Am I crazy to stay onboard a tanker that could detonate any second? Am I even crazier to bring two thousand people onboard my ship?"

"Captain, I only meant..."

"Don't interrupt! If I ignore this S.O.S., those lifeboats will drift across a hundred square miles of storm-driven sea before they're found, then maybe, just maybe, with a little luck, a couple of hundred people will make it. What would you do?"

"It's a no-brainer," Deeds responded, "we gotta go and rescue them."

"Sir, I would make the same decision as you have but I thought with Number 4 tank leaking it would be prudent to stay well outside of the downwind line and avoid any burning embers that could potentially ignite our leaking tank."

Bakke was perplexed. "Oh. Well. Of course," he said, uncomfortably glancing at the clock on the bulkhead. "Chief Mate, why don't you go ahead and take your break now. I'm sure I'll need you fully alert and ready when we arrive."

Sam left the bridge without speaking another word and went directly to Boucher's stateroom. She knocked softly, listening for a response or sounds of movement inside. She knocked again, louder this time, but still heard nothing. Concerned, she opened the lock using her master key and cracked the door open a few inches.

"Hello," she said peeking inside the dark room, "you cheat'n on me sailor?"

There was still no response. Sam reached inside and switched on the room light and cautiously entered. She glanced around the small cabin. His bed was made. She checked the shower and felt the towels. Everything was dry and unused. She was puzzled.

As she left she relocked his cabin door and headed for the stern. There, Sam found the coiled ladder and tool bag on the deck. The rain pelted her face. She walked over to the rail and beamed her flashlight down at the frothing wake behind the ship, but still nothing.

"Jake?" she whispered.

Dumbfounded, she checked her watch and headed for the crew's lounge.

The storm was now raging. Lightning illuminated Boucher dangling by a short tether from a stern pad eye just above the waterline beneath the curvature of the ship's hull. He showed little sign of life. Like Moby Dick dragged Ahab, the Virgo now dragged Boucher beneath the heavy swells and windswept waves.

At the void beneath storage tank Number 4, Deeds opened the access hatch and climbed down inside.

Chapter 17

Royal Norwegian Empress

Milan courageously led a group of passengers to a lifeboat, carefully ensuring they stayed together and didn't panic.

"Be careful everyone, you're going to be just fine," he said calmly. "There's room for everyone." Stopping by one of the boats, he turned back to the passengers in his care, "This is our lifeboat."

Milan caringly assisted an older woman into the lifeboat.

"Take your time and watch your step, ma'am. I won't let you fall. Careful now…"

"Thank you honey, you're very sweet," she said in a raspy smoker's voice.

Milan smiled reassuringly. "No problem, ma'am. Just sit right here," he said helping her into a seat. "Please let me know if I can be of further assistance."

Suddenly there was a problem at the next lifeboat station aft. A crew member shouted over to Milan.

"Hey! I need help over here."

Milan headed for the lifeboat. There, he and the other crewman helped lift a very pregnant woman into the lifeboat. The woman's husband remained by her side trying to comfort her. Milan then helped the governor's wife and daughter climb into the lifeboat and got them seated. The young bride and groom Captain Dahl had wed earlier were seated across from the governor's wife and daughter clutching one another.

"It's coming!" the pregnant woman screamed to her husband who was a nervous wreck.

"Damn. Where's that rescue ship?" the lifeboat coxswain asked.

"I don't know," Milan replied. "I'll stay with her in this boat. You take my boat."

Milan tenderly eased the woman into a prone position on her husband's lap and secured her seat belt around her pregnant belly. He gently covered her with a rain poncho.

Looking at her husband, Milan tried to calm him down, "She's going to be fine. Help is on the way. Keep her covered with this poncho." Milan momentarily cradled the woman's head in his hands. "Relax, you're going to be okay."

She painfully smiled at Milan as the boat was lowered into the water below. Moments later, Milan started the boat's engine and skillfully maneuvered the lifeboat away from the burning cruise ship. He noticed a young girl with her life vest improperly buckled. It was the governor's daughter. He gave her a beguiling look as he made his way to her.

"This isn't safe young lady," he gently warned as he straightened out the nylon webbing and properly buckled her life vest, readjusting the length of the straps.

"Are we going to die?" she asked? Her mouth quivered.

"No, no... not yet," he replied with a wry smile.

As the little girl's mother hugged her, she pointed to the Virgo.

"There! Look Mommy! It's a ship."

A cheer went up from every lifeboat as the mammoth tanker appeared out of the stormy darkness like a giant ghost, illuminated by lightning flashes and the glowing orange flames of the burning cruise ship. Milan checked his watch and smiled.

Virgo

Outside on the bridge wing, Sam pulled her binoculars away from her eyes and pointed. "My God, Captain!" she said. "They're out there, lifeboats — dozens of lifeboats."

Sam and Bakke observed what looked like a D-day landing of fleeing lifeboats as red and orange flames violently devoured the Empress behind them. Deeds checked his watch and grinned.

Bakke snapped his binoculars down from his eyes and stared into the darkness at the burning ship. He turned towards Sam and nodded, confirming to himself what he knew he must do next. "Okay, we're not too late. Reduce speed and bring her about on heading three two zero. Give me a port leeside a quarter of a mile upwind and hold her there with the thrusters."

Sam made a sweeping turn to position the ship for survivor recovery.

"We're in position, Captain."

"Very well." Bakke began barking orders over his handheld radio to his deck crew. "Get those nets and ladders over the port side. Lower the accommodation ladder. Standby to recover survivors."

Royal Norwegian Empress

Below deck, the Empress crew completed a final passenger check as fire blew through a bulkhead close by, singeing them as they fled topside to the remaining lifeboats. Captain Dahl stood on deck as the last members of his crew embarked the only remaining lifeboat. He hesitated momentarily before boarding the boat as if he was contemplating another course of action.

"Captain?" a mate asked. "We need to go now or never."

Dahl turned and nodded at the crewman and stepped aboard. They cast off the lines and had barely cleared the ship's side when several explosions rocked the ship deep below the waterline. The small lifeboat motored away at full speed. Moments later there was a single horrendous explosion. The top of the ship's superstructure vanished into the rainy blackness above, and burning embers swirled high into the stormy sky. A few moments later, a chunk of debris that looked like the lid of a grand piano splashed down beside the ship. It was followed by more debris, various sizes and materials, some nearly the same size as the fleeing lifeboats.

People in the lifeboats instinctively covered their heads with their hands, huddling low in an attempt to escape the wrath of the falling debris. Milan's boat, carrying the pregnant woman and the governor's wife and daughter, was well inside the area where debris was raining down. Without warning, a huge piece from the Empress splashed into the sea only missing the boat by a few feet. The boat heaved up violently and pitched over on its side, nearly capsizing from the impact-generated wave. The governor's wife began screaming and pointing. Her daughter had been hurled through an open section of the boat's canopy into the sea.

Milan reacted immediately, thrusting the boat's engine into reverse, stopping its forward motion. He spotted the little girl helplessly bobbing ten feet away and heroically dove into the churning sea. He swam to her side and grabbed her lifejacket

"It's okay, little one. I have you. You're going to be fine."

He towed her back to the boat where passengers assisted pulling the girl and Milan back into the lifeboat. The governor's wife hugged her daughter, crying hysterically.

"Thank you for rescuing her. You are a hero and I will never forget what you did tonight. All I want to do is get back to our home in New York."

Milan smiled and patted the girl on the shoulder. "We must all return to New York. It is our destiny."

The governor's wife smiled wiping her tears as Milan returned to his coxswain duties. Revving up the engine, he resumed the boat's heading toward Virgo's port side.

At this point, all the lifeboats had cleared the umbrella of falling debris. Miraculously, no one had been injured. Nonetheless, the sight of the once beautiful cruise ship burning to the water as pieces of it rained down from the sky was terrifying.

Virgo

The first lifeboat reached Virgo's side. Bakke had the ship's accommodation ladder lowered to the water, providing a narrow set of stairs from the water up to the ship's main deck. The problem with using the accommodation ladder was that only one lifeboat at a time could pull alongside it, and then only a single file of survivors could climb the narrow stairs. The process of unloading a fully loaded lifeboat was excruciatingly time consuming. To speed up recovery, the crew had also rigged nylon cargo nets fore and aft of the accommodation ladder. These nets hung down twenty feet from the main deck's gunwale to the water below providing a rope-like ladder for people to climb up Virgo's side. It was less than safe because it took strength to make the climb and not fall off the net back onto the waiting lifeboat below. In an attempt to make the climb safer, Virgo's crew employed makeshift safety lines which they tied to individuals making the climb.

Boucher still dangled unconscious at the ship's stern waterline far from the passenger recovery area. He seemed to be more dead than alive.

On the bridge, Bakke nodded his approval to Sam, "Hold her right here, Samantha. Bow thruster only. We must keep our port side in the lee to protect those lifeboats as they offload."

"Will do, Captain."

Bakke broadcast on the ship-wide intercom.

"Attention all hands, this is your captain! We will hold our position and not leave until we have rescued every single one of them. Do what you can to make our guests comfortable. Good luck."

The Virgo droned ominously as Empress' lifeboats made the massive ship's side, their coxswains fighting to keep the boats positioned so survivors could grab onto and climb up the cargo nets to safety. The rescue process was slow and tedious. Hours passed.

At the stern waterline Boucher awakened, coughed and spit out a mouthful of saltwater and blood.

"Ooo....," he moaned.

Exhausted, bleeding, cold and in pain, he attempted to unhook his carabineer and climb up to the next pad eye but he was too weak. He dangled helplessly against the ship's hull.

Like penguins on an Arctic ice sheet, hundreds of shivering Empress survivors now huddled together on Virgo's exposed weather deck above. Except for occasional coughing, they were eerily quiet and orderly.

Sam was trying to organize small groups of survivors and take them inside the ship where they would be out of the weather and could warm up but her task was daunting as more and more survivors arrived onboard faster than she and the crew could get them off the weather deck. The second problem she faced was the fact that Virgo wasn't designed with crew space to accommodate over two thousand people. Virgo was designed to accommodate a crew of thirty, max. She finally grabbed Virgo's Third Mate and put him in charge of finding space below so she could return to the bridge and assist Bakke.

Chapter 18

Coast Guard Search and Rescue C-130, above

The orange and white Coast Guard C-130, call sign Niner-two Delta, had been airborne for almost two hours on a heading aimed to take it to the disaster unfolding far out at sea. The plane's co-pilot held two ships on its surface search radar as the pilot cautiously descended in an effort to get beneath the storm clouds. Clipping the cloud bottoms at an airspeed of two hundred and fifty knots and altitude of four hundred and fifty feet, the co-pilot looked up from his radar screen and peered out through his cockpit windshield.

"There," he said to the pilot as he pointed at the horizon, "Eleven o'clock."

The pilot strained a moment and suddenly sat forward in his seat, "Holy shit! I never thought I'd see something like that. I'm going to hold this heading and slow us down to one hundred and fifty knots."

The pilot rapidly pulled the four engine throttles back to flight idle to slow its speed and trimmed the truculent plane for level flight. The gear warning horn immediately began squawking its alarm. The co-pilot silenced the horn and reached down next to gear handle where he started tracking-in flaps, little by little, as the plane slowed. The storm-driven turbulence pummeled the plane making the crew's ride extremely rough. Sheets of rain loudly buffeted the windshield. It was indeed dangerous to fly this low in a storm so menacing but the entire Coast Guard crew knew the risk and rescue was their mission. Just before the plane arrived at one hundred and fifty knots airspeed, the pilot pushed all four engine throttles forward to a low power setting that provided just enough power to hold the plane in level flight and still maintain the desired airspeed.

The co-pilot adjusted his helmet mic closer to his lips to make his voice more easily heard over the noisy cockpit. Using binoculars, he strained to see through the rain soaked windshield as the wipers struggled to keep up. A trail of windblown black smoke was billowing from what was left of Empress's burning hull. Yellow flames leapt high into the sky above her. The Virgo was positioned about a quarter of a mile upwind, safely outside the burning ship's wind line. Lifeboats helplessly bobbed up and down as they rode from wave top to wave trough waiting to transfer their precious cargo to the Virgo.

"Geez, you see all those lifeboats?"

"Yeah, it's an incredible sight. Raise Virgo on the radio and get their status. We'll relay their stats and position back to HQ."

"Roger." The co-pilot opened the emergency radio frequency and transmitted, "Virgo, Virgo, Virgo, this is United States Coast Guard rescue aircraft Niner-two Delta. We have you in sight. Say status, over."

Virgo bridge

Sam grabbed the radio mic and replied.

"Coast Guard Niner-two Delta, this is Virgo, over."

"Ahh...roger, Virgo. Interrogative rescue status, over."

"Coast Guard Niner-two, the cruise ship Royal Norwegian Empress is abandoned, on fire and sinking. High sea state is hampering operations - Rescue is proceeding slowly. So far we think everyone is accounted for. No casualties reported at this time, over."

"Roger, Virgo. We will remain in orbit above as long as possible and provide command and control if additional help is required. Good luck. Niner-two Delta, out."

Sam and Bakke watched as the C-130 banked left and began circling above them just beneath the cloud bottoms. The rescue was proceeding slowly and now somewhat disorderly. Sam realized a senior officer was needed on deck to direct and organize it.

"I'll be on deck. They need some supervision down there," she advised Bakke as she shoved her portable radio into her belt pouch and slid on her yellow rain suit.

Jake gathered his strength. He unhooked his carabineer from the pad eye and began the treacherous climb up to the ship's deck. About half way up, a wave smashed him against the hull and he lost his grip, plunging backward into the sea.

The governor's wife was in a lifeboat loitering behind the Virgo waiting its turn to come along side the ship's accommodation ladder. She noticed a splash at the stern of the tanker and pointed at the spot.

"Did you see that?"

"What?" Milan asked straining into the darkness.

"Head over there!" she yelled, pointing at Virgo's stern. "I think somebody fell overboard. There," she said pointing, "I see somebody."

Milan turned the lifeboat and headed over to Boucher. Milan and several others pulled him into the lifeboat.

Suddenly a loud metallic groan came from the Empress. It was if the burning ship was calling out in pain. Virgo's crew and the Empress survivors all watched in awe. The cruise ship had burned to the waterline and it was now in the throes of death. First, the ship's bow slowly submerged. Loud hissing sounds were followed by geysers of steamy water which shot skyward and gradually subsided. Lightning flashed and rain pelted the survivors on Virgo's open deck like an ominous demon's curse to the dying ship.

No one spoke as they watched the burning cruise ship sluggishly roll on its starboard side. The scene was spellbinding. Waves pounded along its now exposed portside bilge keel. After several minutes, the once elegant ship leisurely righted itself as if the hand of God was at work. Only now, what was left of the ship's main deck was completely awash and the angry sea showed no mercy. The last of the ship's emergency lights flickered, then dimmed and extinguished. The Empress had lost her fight.

Marked only by geysers of steam and gushes of bubbles, the Empress was slowly swallowed by the sea. Then she was gone. The sea surface where she had been again became one with its surroundings. Floating debris littered the storm-whipped sea, temporarily marking the spot where the majestic ship had last been. Suddenly, it was very dark. Only the sounds of lifeboat motors and the windblown surf crashing against their hulls could be heard. In the stormy darkness, Virgo's well lighted deck contrasted her colossal size. All attention was now on her. She was the only salvation.

After wrestling her stretcher up the accommodation ladder, a crewman and her husband lifted the pregnant woman onto Virgo. Her stretcher teeter-tottered on Virgo's safety railing. Sam rushed over to help, grabbing the stretcher to prevent it from sliding over the side.

"I have it!" she yelled. She spotted a nearby crewman and waved him over. "Give me a hand here!"

Sam stared at the pregnant lady on the stretcher. The woman cringed, occasionally crying out in pain. Her husband held the woman's hand tightly.

"Is she in labor?" Sam asked him.

"She's having occasional contractions but she isn't due for another six weeks. I mean, we only went on this cruise to celebrate my new job. The doctor said she wouldn't have a problem."

"Yeah, but who would'a thought your ship would catch fire and sink." Sam stepped back and looked around, "I need a doctor here. Anyone here a doctor?"

A geeky-looking passenger wearing a soiled white shirt and thick lens glasses stepped up to Sam.

"I'm a doctor."

Sam gave him a once over. "You are?" she asked skeptically.

"Yes, I have a PhD in Sociology."

Sam pushed past him. "Thanks, but I need a real doctor."

A second older gentleman stepped forward. He was wearing an Empress officer's uniform.

"I'm the Empress's doctor."

"Great, Doc. I think this baby is ready to pop."

The doctor examined the woman, gently feeling her tummy and the area above her pelvic bone trying to locate the position of the baby's head, back and extremities. Suddenly his face fell ashen and he cringed.

"I think this is a breech baby," he warily reported to her husband who was kneeling next to his wife with her hand in his. "Of course I'll need to examine her more closely to be sure. But if that's the case, she'll need an OB Doc and a hospital STAT. All my medical equipment went down with the ship."

Sam collected her thoughts for a second, then shouted at the doctor.

"You got it! Let's get her below to my cabin."

In Sam's cabin, the doctor resumed his exam. He began palpating her uterus. Sam and the woman's husband watched nearby.

"I need an ultrasound to confirm the baby's position," the doctor commented.

"Let me see what I can do," Sam replied as she squeezed between the pregnant woman and the doctor to get back to the door. She clawed her way through the door between the wet and cold passengers, Mr. Weinheim and the bride and groom, while attempting to contact Bakke on her hand held radio.

"Captain Bakke, Sam, do you copy, Captain?"

A dripping wet lady interrupted her.

"Do you have any towels? I need a towel." Sam ignored her.

Sam's radio crackled to life. "What you got, Chief Mate?"

"Captain, I'm at my state room with a very pregnant woman and the doctor from the Empress. Here, I'll let the doc tell you himself."

Sam passed the radio back inside to the doctor's hand.

"Well, Captain, we urgently need an OB/GYN doctor here as soon as possible, along with a portable ultrasound. This baby is breech and without a C-section they both may not make it."

"Okay, doctor, I'll call the Coast Guard and see what they can do."

"I told you I need a towel," the lady again demanded as she pushed her way into Sam's stateroom.

"Sorry, we had enough towels for twenty five, not two thousand. You'll have to share."

The wet lady angrily got in Sam's face. "But I don't want to share."

"Then I guess I'll just have to run your fat ass up the flag halyard to let it air dry. Now get the fuck out of my stateroom, lady!"

The wet lady stepped back and huffed, "Well, I never!"

Sam followed her into the passageway heading for the ship's first aid locker where they stored a small quantity of emergency medical supplies. A short distance from the locker she encountered the bride and groom. She was still in her tattered and soiled wedding dress.

"How you kids doing?"

"Some honeymoon," the bride said rolling her eyes at her new husband.

Sam smiled. "You're alive and safe so savor the time you have together."

"There must be some place on this ship where we can be alone," the groom asked.

At a time like this? Sam grinned at them. "Look below deck forward."

"Come-on," he said taking his bride by the hand, "we'll find a place."

Chapter 19

Scott Air Force Base, St. Louis, Rescue Coordination Center

An Air Force colonel and major entered the operations room and studied a wall chart. The Virgo's position was marked with a red circle. The major put his finger on Virgo's plotted position.

"Virgo's current location rules out Coast Guard rescue helos. The ship is three hundred miles beyond their range."

"I concur, Major. Only an Air Force HH-60 Pave Hawk can make it out that far. What's the status of the Coast Guard's C-130 rescue plane they have on-scene?"

"It's still on station overhead. They advise they have about another hour of fuel before they'll have to return. They can't help anyway. We need to send a Pave Hawk out there with a flight surgeon."

"Okay, let's bring the Coast Guard's C-130 home. What about the weather?"

"The tropical storm is building to hurricane strength. It's now tracking towards the Dominican Republic. It's expected to continue on a northwesterly track toward the Gulf and then swing north toward New Orleans. If it continues on its current track we should be fine."

"Got it. Where's our closest Pave Hawk?"

"We have one at Fort Bragg participating in a joint training exercise. We can FRAG them along with an MC-130P tanker for in-flight refueling. I did some checking already. There's a trauma doctor-flight surgeon already at Bragg and he's available."

"Alright, FRAG the Pave and the tanker and get the flight surgeon assigned to the mission. We need to get'm out to the ship ASAP. One more thing, Major. The Navy advises that they have one of their experimental littoral combat ships headed to the vicinity from the south. It's the USS Independence. She's reportedly several hours away. She had to reduce speed because of the storm, ETA unknown. Make sure the Pave has their call sign and frequencies."

"Will do, Sir."

The major started to leave but stopped and turned back to the Colonel.

"Sir, the Pave pilot is my twin brother. Just thought you'd like to know."

"What's his name?"

"Jeremy. Major Jeremy Murphy."

"Thanks, Major, I'm sure you're very proud of him."

"Yes, Sir, my entire family is."

Ft. Bragg, North Carolina, one hour prior to first light

A U.S. Air Force HH-60G Pave Hawk sat idling on the helicopter pad, its red, green and white marker lights colorfully strobed intermittently. Low blue taxiway lights ringed a portion of the pad, making the scene look more like something out of a science fiction movie than a rescue mission in the process of launching. Air Force Major Jeremy Murphy sat at the controls completing his preflight engine starting check list with his co-pilot Captain Todd Zech. He did a final visual check of the engine and transmission instruments on the vertical instrument display panel located on the dash before him and was satisfied with what he saw. All the strips were in the green range.

Murphy had nearly two thousand hours at the stick flying this highly-modified search and rescue version of the Sikorsky-built UH-60 Black Hawk helicopter and knew its capabilities like the back of his hand. He also knew he would be relying on the aircraft's upgraded communications and navigations suite to get him to and from his operating area far at sea.

He methodically checked the integrated navigational system, ensuring the inertial navigation, global positioning and Doppler navigation systems were synchronized. Zech tweaked the forward-looking infrared system, and then checked the engine/rotor blade anti-ice system ensuring the all-weather flight capabilities were functioning properly. Satisfied, their helicopter was mission-ready; Murphy turned backward slightly to get eye contact and gave a thumbs-up to his flight engineer who was kneeling between him and Zech.

"We're green and mean," he said into his intercom mic.

"Roger, sir. Our doc should be here momentarily."

The Flight Surgeon he was referring to was one of the Joint Special Operations Command's trauma doctors and arguably one of the finest, most highly trained and experienced doctors in the military today, if not in all of medicine.

A crew chief was standing in front of the helicopter just outside the rotor swath. He was wearing a headset with hardwired communications to the pilot and was there to marshal the helicopter while it readied for takeoff.

A van pulled up beside the helicopter being careful to remain outside the helicopter's rotor swath. The flight surgeon got out carrying a large waterproof bag with a medical symbol on its flap along with a soft aircrew-style drab-colored, folded, clothing bag. Two Air Force Pararescuemen, nicknamed PJs, got out of the van and carried a suitcase-size waterproof container over to the helicopter and loaded it into the open side cargo door.

Next, the flight surgeon and PJs boarded the helicopter and the van departed. A PJ assisted strapping the flight surgeon into his seat. The crew chief returned to the helicopter, coiling his headset wire as he approached, and handed his headset and wire inside to one of the PJs. He then slid the side cargo door closed from the outside and returned to the front of the helicopter where Murphy and Zech could both see him.

Murphy opened his intercom mic, "Pilot to crew, everybody ready?"

He heard three abbreviated replies.

"Roger all, we're good to go. We have an emergency delivery to make far at sea."

He pushed the engine throttles forward commanding the Pave Hawk's powerful twin GE- T700 jet engines to spool up to full power. Zech switched the helicopter's landing lights on brightly illuminating the surrounding area. As the rotor blades increased their RPMs, they whipped the surrounding air into a frenzy. Murphy checked his controls and slowly pulled up the collective. The sleek helicopter lifted ten feet into the air and hung there like a giant dragonfly above a watery bog while Zech checked the engine pressures, electronic navigation systems and automatic flight control system. Zech gave a thumbs-up gesture to the crew chief that was still standing in front of the helicopter who returned the gesture transitioning his hand into a snappy salute.

While maintaining his altitude a few feet above the ground, Murphy skillfully pivoted the helicopter onto an easterly heading. Satisfied everything was operating within parameters, he carefully air taxied toward the active runway gaining altitude and speed as he proceeded east into a dark stormy sky.

Virgo, Sam's stateroom, same time

Sam's phone rang. Mr. Weinheim picked it up on the second ring.

"Yello," he answered in a thick Hebrew accent.

Sam grabbed the phone from Weinheim and plugged her other ear with her finger so she could hear over the noise in the crowded cabin.

"Hello. Who? Damn. Hold on a second." Sam yelled above the noise, "Quiet please." She singled out the loudest talker, "Hey! You! Quiet! Thank you." She returned to the phone, "Who? Oh, it's you." Her eyebrows lifted in surprise. "Look, it's probably none of my business, but where the hell have you been? I looked for you. You weren't in your room." Sam listened to Boucher's explanation. "He what? No way! I'll be right there."

Sam bolted from her room.

Chapter 20

Turboprop news plane, early morning

A reporter was in the middle of broadcasting the rescue that was playing out below live from the plane. His flat screen monitor showed the ship's location marked on a map of the Atlantic accompanied by pierside pictures of the Empress and Virgo. As the screen switched to a live picture from above, the reporter began.

"As fire swept through the cruise ship, Royal Norwegian Empress last night, this eerie looking ship named Virgo came to the rescue of what could otherwise have been a disaster of Titanic proportions."

The screen flashed to prerecorded footage of empty lifeboats adrift, then to a live overhead close-up of Virgo's bridge wing.

"I have the Captain of the Royal Norwegian Empress, Captain Dahl, and Captain Bakke, the Captain of the rescue ship, Virgo, on the radio. Let's talk with Captain Dahl first. Can you hear me, Captain Dahl?"

"Ya-ya, Dahl here."

"Captain, can you tell us what caused the fire?"

"No, vee could not tell vhat started dhem. Da fires broke out simultaneously in different areas of da sheep. My crew could not contain dhem."

"Are there any casualties, Captain Dahl?"

"Da people in da last lifeboat iz still unaccounted for but vee can zee dhem heading our vay. Da good news iss, ve have a baby about to be born. I am tolt da Air Force iz flying a specialist to us out here right now."

"Thank you, Captain Dahl. Captain Bakke, you and your crew are heroes.

"We did what any able seafarer would do. We had our problems getting here but we made it. I am just glad we were in time to help them out."

"Captain, how would you describe having two thousand people onboard your ship?"

"Cozy."

The camera returned to the reporter on the plane.

"A remarkable rescue; we all wish them well. This is Leonard Bowes, Fox News. Back to you, Callie in the news room."

The picture switched to a frontal of her seated at the anchor's desk in the news studio. Callie Oettinger was a blond bombshell who could easily be a cover girl for any glamour magazine. Flirtatiously smiling into the camera, she took the lead.

"They're heroes all. Great job out there, Lenny."

Pausing, she turned slightly to a different camera and sobered her expression, agonizingly pressing her lips together.

"In another breaking story we have just received word that Poland's President, Marek Zuhoski and his wife, along with eighty-eight members of Poland's foreign ministry died when their plane crashed while coming in for a landing in thick fog in western Russia's Smolensk region. Among the dead were the deputy foreign minister, the national bank president, head of the National Security Office, deputy parliament speaker, civil rights commissioner, chief of staff of the Polish army, chief army chaplain, and at least two presidential aides and three senior lawmakers. They were reportedly on their way there to mark the 70th anniversary of the Katyn massacre, where Soviet secret police murdered thousands of Polish prisoners who had surrendered to Soviet forces at the end of World War II."

The picture switched to local media footage of the crash scene showing firemen dramatically spraying numerous arches of water on the plane's vertical tail fin with Poland's white and red flag colors the only thing recognizable in the smoldering wreckage-strewn area.

"There is no word yet on what caused the crash or whether there was foul play involved. The presidential plane was a twenty year old Soviet-built Tupolev TU154M."

A flat screen located behind Oettinger sitting at her desk in the studio switched to a file picture of a TU-154 parked on a runway. She continued the report.

"Fox News has learned that the exact plane involved in today's crash was fully overhauled last December receiving repairs to its three engines and the updating of its navigation instruments. The Polish aviation director who supervised the overhaul told Russian TV he had no doubt that the plane was flight worthy."

The picture narrowed to a frontal on the attractive blond anchor.

"According to the Aviation Safety Network, there have been sixty-six crashes involving TU-154s, including six in the past five years. Russia recently announced that it intends to withdraw its entire TU-154 fleet from service. Polish officials have long considered replacing their fleet of TU-154s, but said they lacked a sufficient replacement."

The screen behind Oettinger switched again ,this time showing the picture of a Polish government official standing at a microphone.

"We now go to Warsaw and Fox News associate Hans Rinker who is at Poland's Foreign Ministry. Hans what can you tell us?"

"Callie, in a press announcement just made a few minutes ago, Poland's Foreign Ministry spokesman, Waldemar Sniadek, told reporters that the scope of this tragedy cannot be fully understood and what it may mean to the future of Poland. He said we can assume with great certainty that all persons on board the plane have been killed."

Oettinger interrupted, "Hans, do you have any information on what caused the crash?"

"Not at this time, Callie, but the spokesman said that even at this preliminary stage they do not suspect foul play. That said, Sniadek claimed the plane's black box flight recorders have been located but their condition is unknown at this time. Regardless, Sniadek says the cause of the crash will be fully investigated."

"Okay, Hans, thank you for the report. In other news today, the Israeli Defense Force shelled two locations inside Syria after a Hezbollah-fired rocket barrage rocked an Israeli settlement killing three Israelis, two of whom were school children…"

Caracas, Venezuela, the same time

Rajakovics was seated in a swanky downtown restaurant. He was sipping his second cocktail while he waited. He was there for a dinner meeting to work out some final details for a follow-on operation he would be coordinating. It was a unique operation that he had been hired to plan and direct. He took great pride in his ability to discretely run very sophisticated and complex operations that required precise timing of seemingly unrelated events which resulted in a grand finale of devastating effects. While he took great pride in the success of his work he never became emotionally tied to the political agendas of his employers. It was just what he did and he was paid very well to do it.

An attractive woman strolled into the lounge area close to his table. Her tight blouse and short, fitted skirt accented her every curve. He couldn't help but stare. She had a dark complexion and judging from her features, he judged her to be of Middle Eastern descent. She caught him staring and smiled. He stood and rolled his arm toward the vacant chair at his table inviting her to join him. She graciously obliged and sat down carefully crossing her legs as her short skirt rode up nearly exposing her lace bikini undies.

"May I offer you a drink?" he asked, forcefully trying to avoid staring at the point where her skirt ended and her legs crossed.

"Yes, thank you," she replied in near perfect English, "perhaps a glass of Chablis."

At that moment his phone buzzed, alerting him to an incoming call.

"Excuse me one moment."

He hit the 'answer' button on his Blackberry.

"Yeah," he said tersely.

He listened for a few moments and became increasingly irritated.

"You must not fail," he flatly stated. "I will leave tonight."

He angrily pressed on the 'End Call' button and immediately replaced the phone in its belt clip. He returned his full attention to the woman.

"Sounds like you need to leave," she said in a sexy low voice. "How unfortunate."

"Yes, I am sorry but I must catch a flight to Paris."

"Will I see you here again?"

"Perhaps in two weeks I will return. Then we will get to know each other."

He stood and kissed her hand.

"May I know your name?" he asked slightly bowing while still holding her hand.

"Nicole," she replied smiling. "Nicole Maalouf."

"Ahh, you are Palestinian?"

"No Lebanese. And you?"

"Claude Baudelaire. I live in Paris and I must return tonight - business."

After he had departed she joined a man at the bar.

"That's him. He's on his way to Paris," she said just loud enough for the man to hear.

"Tachbūlōt," he replied in Hebrew. "I will let Metsada know. Our katsas will track him upon his arrival there."

The White House, Oval Office, the same time

Ever since President Banner announced his decision to abandon the plan to base ballistic missile defense (BMD) installations in the Czech Republic and Poland, Russia had repositioned itself to apply gripping political and military pressure on the nations that formerly composed the Soviet Union. Cline understood that Russia saw this as a necessary strategy to maintain a security buffer zone. Cline knew this resurgence by Russia as a major regional power was a clear attempt to regain its former superpower status and catch the Banner Administration flatfooted and largely unprepared. Timing was everything and he knew Russia was playing its foreign policy hand masterfully.

"So, General Cline, where are we on the BMD backlash?" Banner asked.

"Mr. President," Cline patiently replied, "your recent announcement to base the BMD afloat, onboard upgraded U.S. Navy Aegis guided missile cruisers deployed in the Eastern Mediterranean Sea, the North Sea and the Baltic Sea, has raised serious concerns from our German and Polish friends as well as several other NATO allies."

"Perhaps so, but I think we can work through those concerns. Besides, their concerns are largely baseless and Russia likes my decision."

Cline's face showed a glint of disappointment. "I respectfully disagree, Sir. If you recall, the original BMD system was designed as a ground-based midcourse defense interceptor system with the capability to shoot down a missile originating in Iran, aimed at Central and Western Europe." Cline knew Banner had zero military experience or understanding of its tradecraft. Hell, the president was a Harvard Law School professor not a political-military strategist. Remaining professional, he unwearyingly took the opportunity to once again educate his boss. "BMD is the system the news media analogously describes as hitting a bullet with a bullet. Curiously, the system is actually irrelevant to the security of both the Czech Republic and Poland as they are probably not within the hostile missile engagement envelope themselves. Moreover, while the BMD doesn't threaten Russia's security, Russia's negative obsession with the U.S. putting bases inside Poland is completely understandable if viewed in a historical context."

"How so?" Holiday challenged.

Cline didn't much like Holiday because he was a Chicago political hack who always insisted on the last word, right or wrong. He had no military strategic planning expertise himself but for some reason, always seemed to challenge those who had and that irked Cline down to his military core. On the other hand, Cline, a retired Army four star, was a veteran of numerous combat campaigns who had also been a European theater commander in charge of NATO forces and held a Harvard PhD in Political Science to boot.

Cline unemotionally sized up Holiday and shifted his full attention back to the president. "Since recorded history, Poland has been the route used for all major invasions into Russia. That's why Russia won't allow the U.S. or any other military power to establish bases there for any purpose, missile defense-related or otherwise. Additionally, Russia sees Germany as a potential threat and mistrusts post-Cold War reunified Germany's intentions – more historical baggage from Russia's past. On the other hand, Russia has positioned itself as Germany's major supplier of natural gas and petroleum vital to fuel their rapid industrial expansion. This gives Russia a non-military economic stranglehold on Germany. Russia feels it must utilize Poland as a neutral buffer zone for a variety of defensive and historically-valid security reasons. Worse yet, Russia is backing Iran who is going forward with its secret nuclear development program in spite of the United Nations demand for open inspections and threat of additional economic sanctions. All I can say is, Israel beware."

"Oh come, come, General." Banner smirked. "Iran's quest to build a nuclear arsenal and intermediate range missile delivery systems is no secret. Their threat to wipe Israel off the map through nuclear annihilation can't be taken seriously."

"On the contrary, Mr. President. Iran's repeated threats against Israel must be taken seriously," Cline responded curtly. "I guarantee Israel takes Iran seriously."

Banner leaned back in his seat and threw his chin up defiantly. "I have made it clear to Israel that we will not support a preemptive attack against Iran. I mean, they need our support. Besides, they know where their bread is buttered."

"Mr. President, I don't think your threat to withdraw U.S. support has a whole lot of meaning to Israel," Cline countered. "They don't need U.S. support or our permission. There are three triggers that will drive an Israeli strike against Iran. First, if Israel learns that Iran has enriched a sufficient quantity of weapon grade uranium or is near to obtaining enough weapon grade uranium to build a bomb, they will attack and attempt to destroy the enrichment and weapon development facilities. This will be no small task because Iran's weapon development facilities are many, they're housed in hardened deep underground facilities and they are well disbursed throughout Iran's ruggedly vast territory."

"Second," Holiday interrupted, "if Russia sells its ground-based, ultra-sophisticated S-300 air defense system to Iran, Israel will feel threatened enough to strike Iran before the missile defense system can be delivered and made operational."

"Correct," Cline replied. "That particular Russian-built anti-aircraft missile system is the only one advanced enough to reliably shoot down the Israeli F-16s and those planes will be strategically key for Israel to conduct the attack."

"And third?" Banner asked Cline.

"Iran already demonstrated it has medium range missile delivery systems that are capable of reaching Israel with a conventional or nuclear warhead, but they've not yet deployed these systems operationally. Should Israeli intelligence detect a push to operationally deploy these missile systems aimed at Israel, I have no doubt they will conduct an immediate preemptive strike to take out these systems along with their supporting elements."

"But Gregory," Holiday objected, "do you really believe Israel has the wherewithal to successfully take on a country like Iran?"

"In all cases, Israel will rely on the use of its air force and navy to conduct a combined attack on Iran's key coastal and inland targets. And in all cases, we can expect Iran to immediately mine the Strait of Hormuz and effectively close all maritime access to and from the Persian Gulf. This will immediately stop the flow of oil from the Middle East's oil-producing nations to the U.S. and other Western industrial nations, and cripple the economies of those nations, most of who are still slowly recovering from the world-wide economic recession. In short, Mr. President, an Israeli attack on Iran will be economically devastating to the West whether they're successful or not."

"Well," Banner replied, turning his attention outside the window toward the Reflecting Basin across the National Mall, "the National Intelligence Estimate I was briefed on said differently, General."

"Mr. President, I'm sorry, but I've carefully read every single NIE for the last thirty five years and I've never seen anything that even remotely suggested anything different. In fact, immediately following an Israeli attack we can expect the Iranians will mine the Strait of Hormuz. When that happens we will be immediately forced into military involvement because only the U.S. Navy has the capability to secure the area from further Iranian mining and sweep the mines."

"What about the Brits and the French?" Holiday asked. "They have mine sweeping capabilities, right?"

"Regrettably, Mr. Holiday, I think we can expect to go it alone and we'll have other worries as well. Iranian Naval bases that can support mining activities and ship attacks utilizing swarms of small high-speed boats loaded with explosives in suicide attacks will also need to be targeted and destroyed. We will also need to neutralize Iran's somewhat formidable land-based anti-ship missile batteries which they will undoubtedly target against any vessels for which they can acquire a sight picture."

Banner pressed his lips tightly together. His cheek muscles strained. "How do you think Russia might react to an Israeli attack against Iran's nuclear reactor and weapon development facilities?"

"Russia is the wild card in all of this," Holiday quickly inserted.

Cline smiled while keeping his eyes on the president. "I suspect Russia will withdraw its consent for the U.S. to cross its territory in support of your Afghan Campaign." Cline was observant in his choice of words emphasizing 'your Afghan Campaign.' "No matter how Russia plays its cards, our recourse in this conflict will be very limited and thus, will be largely ineffective."

"Really, Gregory?" Holiday challenged. "Do you know Iran imports over forty percent of their gasoline? Are you telling us we don't have alternatives like gasoline sanctions against Iran?"

"If memory serves me, it's more like they import forty three percent," Cline shot back. "And no, Mr. Holiday, I'm telling you none of the available alternatives are favorable to us and none of them will work without Russia's cooperation. Russia has ample gasoline and other refined petroleum reserves to supply Iran indefinitely. Between trains and trucks they can easily sustain Iran's production demands and we certainly can't attack Russian supply efforts without a direct confrontation with Russia. Furthermore, we simply can't allow Russia to redraw the map of present day Europe and reassert itself in today's independent states that once formed the Former Soviet Union. That would essentially give Russia the green light to achieve its national security goals through regional pre-eminence and Pandora will have left her box."

Banner leaned forward staring at Cline. "What if we just allow Iran to develop its nuclear power program for peaceful purposes, General? I see no issues with that."

"Mr. President, Iran doesn't know the definition of 'peaceful.' They hate us. They hate Israel even more and they want us both dead."

Banner held up his open hand interrupting his National Security Advisor like a teacher gestures to his class to quiet them down. "Perhaps, General, but wouldn't you agree that one country's hatred is another's well-reasoned argument?"

Cline subtly shook his head no. "That philosophical argument might work in a university classroom but not in the real-world, Mr. President. Allowing Iran into the Nuclear Club is not something that most nations in the Free World would like to see, including Russia." Banner opened his mouth to speak but Cline continued. "Consciously allowing them into the Club is a course of action that may temporarily result in the least problems for everyone, but it will require continued pressure on the Israelis to not attack Iran's nuclear weapon development facilities."

Banner glanced at Holiday, then at Cline. "So you're telling me that waiting to see what they do is not an acceptable strategy?"

"Sir, the obvious drawback to the strategy of waiting to see what happens before taking any action is that we may likely be drawn into a broader conflict we have no stomach to deal with. We must guard against being thrust into a reactionary response rather than dealing with the key issues upfront from a position of strength. A 'none decision' is still a decision, Mr. President."

Banner sighed and stared through the office window. "Let me be clear," he said sternly. "I have already announced my decision to not put our ballistic missile defense in Poland and the Czech Republic and that decision also serves as a gesture of good will toward Russia. I think we can live with an Iranian nuclear program and I think Russia sees my decision as a symbolic gesture in support of our mutual goal of world peace and recognition that the U.S. is not the only power on this planet."

Cline felt a throbbing behind his eyes. "Frankly, Mr. President, I don't think the Russians see any concession we make related to ballistic missile defense basing, or Iran's nuclear development program, as a symbolic gesture. I think they're betting you'll panic over Iran and you'll back off."

Holiday butted in. "They misjudged John F. Kennedy during the Cuban Missile Crisis thinking he would be weak and indecisive. Now didn't they, Gregory?"

Cline winced at Holiday, and then peered out the window with Banner. "Sir, you cannot allow the Russians or the Iranians to have their way with you," he said in a low voice.

Chapter 21

Virgo Bridge, same time

Sam checked the navigation charts and instruments. Glancing at the ship's control panel she noticed the ballast indicator light for Number 4 storage tank was on "Flood." Water gushed into the nearly full void beneath storage tank Number 4.

Sam was confused. "Now he's flooding it?" she whispered to herself.

Sam opened the mic to the ship's intercom. "Chief Engineer Deeds, please call the bridge."

Deeds was in his stateroom. A large map of Manhattan lay open on his stateroom room table. A circle radiating from pier 88 was drawn around much of downtown New York City. Deeds pushed the map aside and called the bridge.

"Deeds, here. What do you want?"

"Are you flooding Number 4?" Sam asked.

"Yes, what of it?"

"Why now?"

"Your diver friend was right. We need the added stability. With all these passengers onboard I decided to flood it."

Sam sensed something was amiss, but she wasn't sure what it was.

"Does the Captain know?"

"Ask him," Deeds snapped and slammed the phone down. Milan stood beside him studying the map.

Sam left the bridge and weaved through a long line of women waiting to use the restroom as she headed toward aft steering. A lady with an errant false eyelash and heavy make-up exited the restroom and collided with Sam.

"Excuse me, do you know where I can find the concierge?"

"Concierge?" Sam repeated completely dumbfounded by the question.

A second lady exited coming face to face with Sam, "There's no toilet paper!"

Sam actually found the situation humorous but forced herself to remain professional. "I'll alert housekeeping."

Sam pushed past the two ladies, paying them no further attention, and headed for the aft steering compartment. She carefully opened the watertight door and looked for Jake. The light inside was already on and nothing was out of place. The emergency tiller was neatly stowed in its rack on the bulkhead. She finally found him still in his wet suit, sleeping in a fetal position on an open bail of rags. He looked like hell. She nudged him with the toe of her shoe.

"Hey fella, I'm the one who needs the beauty sleep, not you."

His eyes partially opened. She helped wrestle him up to a sitting position.

"Jake, while you're slackin' here, Deeds flooded the void under Number 4 storage tank."

He popped up fully alert. "No way."

"Way."

"Something's wrong. I'm gonna' take a look inside Number 4 void."

"What for?"

"It's just a hunch. I hope I'm wrong."

Sam watched as Jake painfully stood up and limped to the door.

"Hey! You really think he tried to kill you?"

"He all but pureed me down there when that propeller began spinning, then he tried to strand me in the middle of the frickin' ocean. If he wasn't trying to kill me he sure is one rude son-of-a-bitch!" Jake unzipped his wet suit top and slid it off. "I need to find him. Got anything dry I can change into?"

"Wait here," she said.

Sam returned to her stateroom and rummaged through her locker finding a pink silk robe. She then spotted Mr. Weinheim in her outer office in his tux.

"You, take off your tux," she ordered.

Surprised by her demand, Weinheim, looked around to see if she really was talking to him.

"Me?" he asked, pointing at himself with both hands.

"Yes, you!" She pointed a straight finger directly at him. "Strip!"

Weinheim's eyes widened and a smile spread across his face, as if his fantasy had finally come true. "Are you going to watch?"

Sam became impatient.

"Do it now," she demanded. With one hand on her hip, she held her pink robe up in front of him hooked over one finger of her other hand. "Don't make me explain."

He ripped his clothes off without further question, and then turned towards her, standing flatfooted in a full frontal view. Sam winced slightly in disgust as she threw him her pink silk robe.

"Here, put it on."

"Ohhhh God, I love the sea!" he sighed. He slipped into the shimmering robe and inhaled deeply, as if savoring the faint aroma of Sam's shower gel.

Sam grabbed his clothes and disappeared into the passageway before he realized she was gone.

Back in aft steering, Jake struggled to put on Weinheim's tux.

"The pants are too short and the waist is too big," he protested. He slipped on the XXL shirt. "Where did you get this shirt? Omar the tent maker?"

Sam stood gazing at his predicament with a faint smile.

"Son-of-a-bitch, Sam, couldn't you find any damn work clothes or coveralls or something? I look like some kind of a debutante yuppie-scum dickhead on my first date."

"I borrowed this ensemble from one of our distinguished guests."

Sam held up the black tux dinner jacket and helped him slide into it, smoothing the shoulders and back with her hands. Boucher snorted loudly. "Geez, you smell the fufu juice aftershave on this jacket?"

"Yeah, I think it's Old Spice. Smells good."

"You're shittin me, Sam. It smells like a French whore house."

"And how would you know what that smells like?"

Boucher hesitated and frowned. "Damn it, Sam, will you just stop taking everything I say at face value?"

"Okay, you're in dry clothes and look fine so stop complaining. Besides, it's the best I could do on short notice so suck it up. I could have given you my pink silk robe to wear."

The look on Boucher's face was telling. *It will be a cold day in hell when I wear a pink silk robe,* he thought.

"I'm gonna look for Deeds. Then I'm going to Number 4 void and check it out. Meet me there as soon as you can."

Now on a mission Boucher tried to push by her. As he approached the door, Sam stepped in front of him blocking his path.

"Hey, sailor," she said smiling, "you're certainly no Daniel Craig, but you look kinda cute in that monkey suit."

"Yeah, monkey suit for sure," he grumbled forcing a pained smile. *Daniel Craig? Who the hell is Daniel Craig?* Without asking, he left the stateroom and headed down the people-congested passageway in search of Deeds. He passed a smiling Mr. Weinheim waiting in line to use the bathroom. Several women stroked his silk robe. A few yards further he encountered a yelling match between two senior citizen passengers.

"Hey, I was sitting there!" one old geezer said to the other.

"Was," the other replied sarcastically.

"I had a first class cabin."

"Had!"

A scuffle broke out between the two passengers then spread through the corridor.

Boucher was caught in the middle of all the shoving. He was whacked by a senior with a cane when a Richard Simmons look-alike cruise director came down the passageway talking into a megaphone.

"Ladies and gentleman, please! Please, stop! Can't everyone just get along? Everyone calm down! Stop the fighting! We need to all relax, people."

As the scuffle spread, a plastic medicine bottle jettisoned from one of the flailing bodies. The cruise director picked it up and read the label.

"Whose Viagra?" he boomed through his megaphone.

As if on cue, everyone stopped. As they turned toward the cruise director, several hands went up.

The cruise director put his hand on his hips canting one hip outward. "Oh my Gawd! No wonder the boat was a rock'n last night."

Boucher was out of patience and tried to leave the corridor but the cruise director grabbed him as he attempted to pass by.

"Come here, you ruggedly handsome man. I don't remember seeing you before. You look like Daniel Craig."

"Who?"

"You know, the actor who plays James Bond."

"James Bond?"

What's your name, big fella?"

Blood filled Boucher's face as he resisted the compulsion to grab the SOB by the throat and choke him to death

"Look, I'm busy, I can't do this now," Boucher pulled away from the hand that clutched his arm.

"Ah come on!" the perky cruise director urged.

"If you put your mind to it, you can do anything!" Looking around at the other passengers he flailed his arms out in front of him and loudly asked, "Right people?"

"Right!" they replied in unison.

The cruise director now redirected his attention to Boucher.

"You're gonna be great! Tell us your name big fella?

"Jake," he muttered despairingly, completely dumbfounded by his predicament.

The cruise director threw his hands limply in the air and began clapping for all to see.

"Let's give Jake a big hand, people?"

A short-lived applause ensued as Boucher stood there in utter disbelief.

"Yeah, that's the way, people! I love every single one of you! And I bet our new friend, Jake, loves you too. Right, Jake?"

Boucher grunted, wondering how the little maggot had lived as long as he had.

"See, I told you so. Now come on everyone, line up. It's Hokey-Pokey time. Here we go…, Jake, you follow me. Put your hands on my hips. Here we go, anda' one, anda' two, anda' three, anda' four…"

The cruise director began singing and leading the Hokey-Pokey down the hallway. Deeds appeared at the front of the crowded hall unnoticed by Boucher. But he saw Boucher and quickly vanished into an intersecting passageway. The cruise director was insistent in his one-man crusade to ensure everyone's happiness and continued singing gleefully into his bullhorn.

"You put your left foot in, you take your left foot out, you put your left foot in and you shake it all about…"

On deck, sea spray filled the air as an enraged Deeds connected with Milan, motioning for him to follow him aft. Milan and Deeds slowly drifted together on the stern deck. As they leaned over the rail, Milan casually lit a cigarette. Deeds snatched it away flicking it overboard.

"Hey! No smoking! You'll blow us to hell and back before we even finish this job."

"What are you talking about?" a confused Milan asked.

Realizing Milan didn't know, Deeds leaned close to his ear and explained, "She's leaking gas from a ruptured storage tank forward."

"Leaking gas?"

"Yeah, but we've got a bigger problem."

"What?"

"That diver?"

"Yeah?"

"How the hell he got back on board I'll never know."

Milan checked his watch, "Twelve hours to go, the boss man is on the move now." "Yeah, I need you to take care of the problem. Get rid of that diver."

Milan turned away and nonchalantly disappeared in the crowded deck.

Chapter 22

Montreal, Trudeau International Airport, the same time

Air France flight 342 had flown all night nonstop from Paris to Montreal. It routinely landed and taxied to the gate. As the plane's door opened, passengers jockeyed for position in their race with one another to disembark. A well-groomed man with a ruddy complexion who was seated in the front bulkhead passenger row behind the first class section, casually left the plane smiling cheerily at the flight attendants and walked down the ramp into the Immigration and Customs check area. There, he patiently waited with the other passengers on the flight and claimed the two bags of luggage he had checked in Paris the previous evening. He proceeded to Immigration, showed his French passport and was passed through without question. He entered the Customs area and handed his declaration form to a waiting Customs officer.

"Rien à déclarer," he said in French while cocking his head slightly and shrugging his shoulders. The Customs inspector nodded and passed him through without the slightest question.

He made his way to the security area exit gate where he was met by a man holding a cardboard sign with a name written on it in black marker. He silently acknowledged the man with a nod and followed him to the parking garage where the man stopped beside an older model car and passed a set of car keys to him. The man departed without speaking.

He unlocked the car and slid his bags into the back seat ensuring they were in full view. He then got into the driver's seat, inserted the keys into the ignition and started the car. He adjusted the mirrors and ensured the windshield-mounted portable GPS navigation system was turned on and his destination data was entered. As he drove out of the garage he watched the

GPS acquire the satellites high above and update its position. The GPS screen finally flickered to life showing him exactly how to leave the airport with an end destination in New Jersey.

The man cracked the driver's side window and lit a Montecristo Habana cigar he had brought with him. He turned the car's radio to a country station. He liked American country music and the stories the songs always seemed to tell about trucks, drinking and lost lovers. He settled back into his seat knowing he would soon pass through a U.S. border check point as he crossed from Quebec into New York. His passport was in order and he had nothing to hide, plus his purpose was business and it would be brief.

A black car followed far behind.

Virgo, day

Pushing his way through the crowded passageway, Boucher finally exited through an outside watertight door leading onto the main deck. He drew in a deep breath of moist fresh air and slammed the door behind him with a loud metallic clank. Before continuing his search for Deeds, he stood outside momentarily, feeling the relief of escaping the idiocy inside. The rain had slowed to a drizzle but the storm remained ominously present. Windblown wave tops regularly erupted above the angry sea. He climbed an outside stairs that led him up five levels above. Arriving at the top he inhaled a lungful of salt-laden air and exhaled it through his nose. Its moist coolness cleansed his lungs and soothed his mind. He unwittingly hummed the Hokey-Pokey and suddenly realized it.

"Damn stupid-ass song," he murmured aloud.

Inside his stateroom, Deeds checked his pistol to ensure it was ready. Satisfied, he again concealed it in his belt beneath his shirt and left the room.

Boucher made his way to the bridge and entered. The mate on watch did a double take.

"Hey, look at you; a tux? You look like, like..."

"Daniel Craig?" Boucher blurted.

"No."

"Bond?"

"Bond who?" the mate asked dumbfounded.

"James Bond."

"No, no, no, no, you look like my cousin, Victor. He's head waiter at Sardi's."

Bakke came through the door onto the bridge and was likewise surprised to see Boucher standing there, much less wearing a tux.

"I thought you were burned out after your last dive and hit the rack for some deserved rest and recuperation."

"Had a wet dream," Boucher snarled.

The two men walked out on the bridge wing and looked down at the crowded deck. Bakke turned and put his hand out to shake Boucher's hand.

"You did a fine job on the propeller. I am grateful to you for that."

"Thanks," Boucher replied trying to figure out where Bakke was coming from.

"I wouldn't have been able to save those cruise ship folks down there without your help."

"I still have an hour's work to do on the rudder. Have you seen Deeds?"

"Not lately, why?"

"I want to give him something."

Boucher stepped further out on the bridge wing and looked for Deeds on the crowded deck below. Bakke followed and uncharacteristically made a friendly gesture.

"Can I give it to him for you?"

"Nah, it's kinda' personal."

"This hasn't been a normal job for you has it?"

"Spend twenty five years as a career Navy SEAL and everything is normal."

"I didn't realize you still have an hour's work left."

"I think it would be a wise precaution."

"Deeds said you were finished."

"Yeah, I thought so too."

"What's left to do?"

"I should secure a cofferdam patch over a gaping gash about a third of the way down the port side of the rudder and then blow the water out. You can't count on its reliability when you carry that much water weight in it."

"I didn't know it was flooded that badly. The ship seems to be handling just fine. Besides, we can't take the time now to stop for repairs. I need to get these poor people we rescued to New York before this damn storm catches up with us. Every hour counts."

"Yeah, so tell Sam... ah, your Chief Mate to go easy maneuvering into

New York harbor or she'll burn out the rudder motor. If we lose steering in a channel of restricted maneuverability we'll be up shit creek without a..."

"Rudder?" Bakke awkwardly offered finishing Boucher's sentence.

They almost laughed but neither wanted to be the first. Boucher sensed that Bakke hadn't known Deeds for very long and decided to ask.

"I saw you talking to Deeds on the stern when we got underway. You guys must go way back."

"Why would you think that?"

"I thought tankers contracted regular crews."

"No, we change out crew members in nearly every port. In fact, we scrambled to find Deeds just before we got underway after loading in Indonesia. He is a last minute replacement for my regular Chief Engineer."

"What happened to your regular Chief Engineer?"

Sam entered the bridge wing unbeknownst to Bakke or Boucher and approached them from behind.

"Probably a woman," Bakke smiled, "always is."

"I hear you, Captain, been there myself."

Bakke lowered his voice, "In Shanghai there was this girl..."

Sam placed her hands on the back of their shoulders, surprising them both. As they turned she wiped a fake tear from her eye, "A girl? You guys make me wanna' cry."

Bakke, speechless and embarrassed, cleared his throat. A mate urgently approached, breaking the spell.

"Captain, we just got a message from the USS Independence. They'll rendezvous with us shortly."

"What kind of ship is the Independence? Do they have a doctor onboard?"

"Ahh, I don't know," the crewman replied scratching his head.

Boucher interrupted, "The Independence is a gas turbine - diesel powered U.S. Navy littoral combat ship and it's fast – fifty knots or faster. As I recall it's over four hundred feet long and has a weird looking silhouette about it. It only has a crew of twenty six so they won't have a doctor onboard. It's very small by Navy ship standards. The LCSs were built to support SEALs and other special operations forces in littoral special operations. Providing there's a SEAL platoon embarked, they will have a SEAL corpsman as a member of the platoon. SEAL corpsmen are damn fine medics but unfortunately they aren't trained or equipped to do breech deliveries." Boucher nodded affirmatively to Bakke and Sam, "They were probably doing counter-drug ops somewhere in the area and are running from the storm the same as we are."

Chapter 23

Virgo, bridge

Peering through his binoculars, Bakke studied a speck growing on the horizon. As it approached Virgo it grew into the USS Independence. It was an odd dart-shaped ship with a long slim bow that gradually expanded into a sleek ninety-three foot wide beam. The stern area behind the angular-shaped superstructure supported a wide flight deck. A deck-mounted 57mm Bofors naval gun protruded about halfway back along the bow deck with a Rolling Airframe Missile launcher internally installed below deck behind the gun. Nulka Decoy launchers adorned the superstructure. The ship had such an unconventional look to it that Bakke didn't realize he was standing there spellbound completely captivated by its futuristic appearance.

White water occasionally covered the small ship's entire forward bow as it knifed through the steep storm-generated seas. As it pierced through the larger waves, seawater surged all the way back to the superstructure where it blasted upward in a geyser that covered the entire after half of the ship in a veil of spray.

The bridge radio crackled next to Bakke startling him, "Virgo, this is the USS Independence, interrogative your medical emergency. Please state the nature of your medical emergency? Over."

Bakke grabbed the mic and replied.

"Independence, this is Virgo, Captain Bakke here, we have a woman in the early stages of labor and the baby is breech. Over."

"Roger, Captain. At current speed, you are twenty-three hours from New York. Be advised a U.S. Air Force Pave Hawk long range rescue helicopter is air refueling one hundred and fifty miles to your west. They're coming to deliver a flight surgeon and surgical equipment to your deck. Pave Hawk call sign is 'Jolly Three Three.' How copy? Over."

"I copy all, Independence. Tell Jolly Three Three to hurry. The baby isn't going to wait. Over"

"Roger, Virgo, we'll continue to match your course and speed and track beside you in case we're needed. Out."

Bakke hung up the radio mic and again studied the approaching ship. He was impressed at how fast the Independence closed the distance from the horizon to the Virgo. They did it in about twenty minutes in spite of the sea state. Boucher was right; this sleek looking littoral combat ship was the fastest ship he had ever seen. The Independence made a graceful sweeping turn onto a parallel course maintaining about a five hundred yard spacing from Virgo's port side. Bakke couldn't help but envy its captain and imagine how much fun it would be to drive a ship like that.

MC-130P Airborne Refueling Tanker

Below the storm clouds, one hundred fifty miles due east of the Virgo's position, a U.S. Air Force MC-130P aerial tanker, call sign "Kingbird," was in the process of refueling a Pave Hawk long range rescue helicopter. The MC-130P was flying straight and level ahead of the Pave Hawk maintaining one hundred ten knots air speed. The Pave Hawk, call sign, "Jolly Three Three," buffeted slightly in some clear air turbulence as Major Murphy skillfully moved his helicopter to the left observation position flying approximately forty-five degrees from the tanker's centerline, slightly above and behind the tanker's drogue refueling station trailing from its left wing pylon.

"Jolly Three Three, Kingbird, you are clear for contact."

"Roger, Kingbird," Murphy reported into his helmet-mounted radio mic.

At the same time Murphy noted a visual light signal coming from the MC-130's paratroop door confirming that he was cleared for drogue contact. He slowly maneuvered his helicopter down and right to the pre-contact position.

The pre-contact position for drogue and probe refueling, as it is known to pilots and their aircrews, is located aft of the refueling drogue, with the helicopter's refueling probe tip in line with and behind the drogue receptacle which trails on a hose behind the transferring tanker aircraft. Once the receiving aircraft is in this position, the pilot moves his aircraft forward with a positive closure rate that assures his probe nozzle contacts the drogue with approximately one hundred forty pounds of force. That is the minimum force required to properly seat the probe nozzle in the drogue receptacle. Too small a closure rate will result in a soft contact, and the drogue will not seat properly on the probe nozzle.

After contact, the receiving aircraft moves to the left refueling position to transfer fuel. This position is aft of the left wing tip of the C-130. The C-130's fuel transfer hose is designed to automatically retract and extend as the receiver aircraft moves fore and aft as it flies in close formation to the tanker aircraft.

Fuel can only be transferred when the refueling hose is extended between fifty-six feet and seventy-six feet from the tanker's refueling pod. These distances are marked by white bands painted every five feet on the refueling hose. When fuel transfer is complete, the receiver moves right and down, then straight back to disconnect. Approximately four hundred twenty pounds of force is required to unseat the nozzle from the drogue receptacle. The disconnect is always made five to ten feet above the contact position so that the drogue drops away from the receiving aircraft's refueling probe. The receiving aircraft then moves back to the left observation position or peels off to continue its mission. Aerial refueling is always tricky, but when doing it in a storm where air turbulence and visibility factors are marginal, it is extremely dangerous.

Major Murphy held his Pave Hawk steady on the MC-130's left refueling station with the helicopter's extended nose probe in the drogue basket taking on hundreds of gallons of fuel by the minute, but it was getting more difficult to safely maintain position as every second ticked off. Storm turbulence began to radically buffet both the MC-130 and the Pave Hawk. Murphy knew he could no longer safely remain in the refueling station in such close proximity to the MC-130.

"Kingbird, Jolly Three Three, we're heavy. I can't hold it any longer in this turbulence," Murphy reported. "Breaking away!"

The Pave Hawk broke away from the refueling basket, banked left to clear the MC-130 and immediately descended. The refueling hose trailing behind the MC-130's left side wing was immediately retracted back into its storage pod beneath the wing pylon.

In the Pave Hawk's cockpit, the co-pilot touched the digital fuel gauge drawing Murphy's attention to it - it read half full.

Murphy opened his radio to the MC-130P.

"Kingbird, Jolly Three Three, we have enough fuel to reach the objective plus thirty minutes. We'll hit you for another drink upon leaving the objective."

"Roger, Jolly Three Three. We show one thousand pounds transferred. We'll establish a track ten miles south of the objective. We'll be there when you need us."

"Roger, Kingbird. We're going for it. Out. Break, Break, USS Independence, Jolly Three Three, did you copy my last? Over."

The 170-foot Independence littoral patrol ship submarined through the windblown wave crests and disappeared in the troughs as it paralleled Virgo's side. White spray occasionally engulfed the small ship's entire weather deck and superstructure all the way back to the stern. On its bridge, SEAL Warrant Officer "Two Dogs" Hardy replied to the radio call from Jolly Three Three.

"Roger, Jolly Three Three. Copy all. Independence at objective and standing by if needed."

The Independence held station three hundred yards off Virgo's port side skillfully matching Virgo's course and speed.

Bakke radioed the Independence.

"USS Independence this is Virgo. Do we have a blueprint?"

"Roger, Virgo," Two Dogs responded. "The flight surgeon is onboard Jolly Three Three. When they get here he will be hoisted down to your forward helicopter deck spot. Over."

Captain Bakke watched Independence nearly disappear in a wave as he replied over the radio. Sam listened attentively.

"Roger that, Independence. Virgo standing by."

Sam called Boucher's stateroom from the bridge phone.

"Jake, a search and rescue helicopter is on the way here with a flight surgeon to deliver that baby. They're going to hoist him down onto the forward helo spot."

"Great news. Wait! They can't do that! They'll kill us all!"

Sam wrinkled her nose and dropped her brow, "The glass is always half empty with you, Jake. What now?"

"Static - static electricity."

"Huh? I don't get it."

"We're leaking LNG from Number 4 tank, right?"

"Right."

The helicopter's rotors create an enormous static charge. A spark could..."

Sam interrupted before he could finish the sentence, "Okay, okay I get it. What else?"

"Has the Independence arrived?"

"She's three hundred yards off our port side. I talked to some SEAL by the name of Warrant Officer Hardy on the radio."

"Good, I know him. Have the helo hoist the doctor onboard the Independence and we'll highline him over to us. Relay this to Hardy, 'Two Dogs. Guerrë 'a' Mort.' You got that?"

"Two Dogs. Guerrë 'a' Mort. Got it."

"I'm on my way to the bridge."

The sound of the approaching helicopter's powerful jet engines could now be heard above over the beating noise of its rotor blades. Twenty years earlier, while receiving a vertical replenishment, Boucher had learned an important lesson about static electricity and helicopters lowering things to the deck of ships. One of his men accidently got between the cargo bundle being lowered and the ship's deck without first grounding it and was nearly killed by the static discharge. He knew what was about to happen and he had to stop it.

"Damn it!" Boucher shouted as he burst outside and raced forward along the main weather deck.

Major Murphy matched the Pave Hawk's course and speed next to Virgo's forward deck helicopter emergency evacuation spot. He then slowly moved sideways over to the spot hovering about forty feet directly above it in heavy rain. Two crewmen dressed in yellow foul weather gear were standing on Virgo's deck trying to look upward into the helicopter's eye-stinging rotor wash-driven rain.

The Pave Hawk's PJs slid his side cargo door open, hooked a container of medical supplies to the hoist cable and swung it outside the helicopter. The container spun slowly, swaying to and fro, as it descended on the winch's steel cable toward the deck below. The doctor sat to the side of the open door waiting his turn to be hoisted down. Boucher suddenly appeared on the deck below flailing his arms above his head frantically trying to wave off the helicopter.

Major Murphy and his co-pilot, Todd Zech, both responded to Boucher's frantic attempt in unison, "What the hell?"

Zech clicked open his bridge to bridge radio to Virgo.

"Virgo, Jolly Three Three, get that guy out of there!"

Bakke observed Boucher's antics, *Is he insane?* Bakke radioed the crewman on the forecastle, "Get that crazy son-of-a-bitch the hell outta' there!"

Grabbing her rain parka, Sam left the bridge and ran forward. Appearing moments later at the deck spot, she tried to pull Boucher away but he shrugged off her grasp and continued to frantically wave off the helicopter.

"The rotors! The static! We're leaking LNG!" he shouted up at the helicopter at the top of his lungs while waving madly. "Get outta' here! You'll blow us up!"

Boucher arrived at the touch down spot the same time the container arrived close to the deck. As Virgo rose up on a wave a powerful static flash discharged knocking him to the deck.

Still unaware of the leaking LNG, but recognizing the potential emergency, the PJ released the bundle while shouting into his intercom mic, "Pull up! Pull up! Pull up!"

Murphy immediately pulled up on the collective and pushed the control stick over to the right climbing his helicopter away and clear of the ship.

Chapter 24

Virgo

Everyone began to recover. Sam knelt down at Boucher's side and grabbed his lapel shaking him. His tux was smoldering. Boucher's face was pale and lacked color but he was conscious. He gave her a delusional wide eyed glance as she shook him. He slowly propped himself up on one arm and stared at Sam. His eyes seemed unfocused and his one eyelid was twitching uncontrollably.

"You okay?" she yelled.

He continued to stare at her.

"Jake, are you okay?" she asked again.

He sat up and crooked his head from side to side. "Yeah, I think so." Boucher sniffed his smoldering tux sleeve, "Damn, smells like my mother's cooking." His attention then went to the medical bundle laying on the deck close by. "We need to get this medical kit to the Empress doctor so he can prep for the surgeon."

Sam shouted over the surrounding noise and directed the two mates to take the bundle below to the doctor. Boucher tried to stand but fell backwards, still unsteady from the shock. Sam put her arms under his arm pits and helped lift Boucher to his feet.

Holding him steady from behind, she helped him stagger back inside the ship and to the doctor for a checkup.

She wasted no time returning to the bridge where she coolly picked up the bridge to bridge radio mic.

"USS Independence, this is Virgo, over."

The radio crackled..., "Roger, Virgo, this is Independence, over."

"Can you land the helicopter on your flight deck and take the flight surgeon onboard, over?"

"Negative, Virgo, the seas are too rough to safely conduct flight operations."

"Okay, understand, can the doctor be hoisted down to you, then you highline him over here?"

"We don't have a crew complement with enough manpower to rig and conduct highline operations in this sea state."

"You have a SEAL platoon currently embarked, right?"

"Affirmative, Virgo."

"Commander Boucher sends this message for Warrant Officer Hardy: Two Dogs. Guerrë 'a' Mort."

There was a momentary pause, then a man's voice boomed back over the radio.

"Roger, Virgo. This is Two Dogs. Tell that ol' meat eater we'll capture an island nation, or rig a highline for him, no charge. I've got sixteen hard dicks here with me beggin' to jump feet first into anything the Commander wants."

Sam smiled at the thought, "Just the highline today, thanks."

"Roger, Virgo, Independence out."

Sam hung up the radio mic and noticed Bakke was scrutinizing her competence from across the room.

"I'll be on deck supervising the highline operations if you need me, Captain."

USS Independence

Two Dogs watched the Pave Hawk make a flawless approach descending toward Independence's stern, slowing to match its course and speed with the ship. The Pave Hawk finally transitioned into a relative motion hover about ninety feet directly above the ship's stern and slowly descended to about forty feet. Its rotor blade downwash whipped the seawater into sudsy froth behind the pitching ship.

One of the Pave Hawk's PJs slid the helicopter's side cargo door open and pulled the hook on the rescue hoist cable inside. Two Dogs could see him clip it to the D-ring suspension point on the front of the flight surgeon's safety harness. The doctor was wearing his flight suit and flight helmet with the darkened visor down.

Then the flight surgeon scooted over to the edge of the door and swung outside using his feet against the helicopter's side to stabilize himself. He looked like a praying mantis poised against the side of an olive drab flower bud waiting to snag a hapless insect.

The Flight Engineer held his gloved hand on the hoist cable to steady it as he slowly began lowering the doctor toward the ship's tossing flight deck forty feet below.   Several members of the ship's crew waited below. The yellow raingear with orange lifejackets they were wearing made it look like a scene out of a comic book while in reality it was a deadly serious attempt to save the life of an expectant mother and baby none of the men at risk even knew.

As the doctor neared the ship's deck, crewmen safely grounded the hoist cable to discharge any static charge before the doctor touched down. Once on deck, the doctor was quickly detached from the hoist cable and hustled inside the ship.

With the flight surgeon's transfer safely completed, the Pave Hawk's hoist cable was retracted. It climbed to about one hundred fifty feet, and then dropped back in trail at a safe distance several hundred yards behind the ship.

Pave Hawk

Even though the windshield wipers were running at their highest speed, they were useless. Rain pelted the windshield so hard, forward visibility was impossible. Murphy and Zech were flying on instruments, which in itself was completely demanding of both pilots' full concentration. The low fuel warning light started flashing on the helicopter's digital vertical instrument display panel. It was a warning that had to be heeded but was not one that was immediately life threatening. Zech checked the fuel levels and reported to Murphy.

"Pilot, port and starboard tanks are down, we're on reserve," Zech reported. "We have twenty minutes of fuel remaining in main."

Murphy grunted and keyed open his radio mic, "Kingbird, Kingbird, this is Jolly Three Three. We're Bingo. We need that drink, now."

In the clouds above, the MC-130 buffeted in the storm turbulence. The pilot glared out through his rain-drenched windshield and cussed under his breath. He clicked open his radio mic.

"Roger, Jolly Three Three, conditions have deteriorated below minimums at my ARIP."

"Ah... roger Kingbird," Murphy coolly replied.

"We'll try a three hundred and twenty degree track north at three thousand and establish a new ARIP there in ten minutes."

"Roger," Zech replied, "track three two zero north at three thousand feet. See you there in ten minutes."

Murphy glanced over at Zech and clicked his mic open, "It's this way or no way. I really don't want to go swimming today."

"Yeah, we need to hit that tanker or we surely will."

"Yeah, I know. This is a bad place to run out of gas. That water looks cold down there."

The Pave Hawk began a steady climb and disappeared into the rain.

USS Independence

Matching their course and speed, the Independence and Virgo had closed to seventy-five yards apart and were now ready to pass the highline between the two ships. Highline transfers were relatively commonplace for most U.S. Navy ships but not for ships as small as the Independence. As for the merchant fleet, using a highline was almost never practiced if not unheard of. Both ships would have to jerry-rig the highline and tend it using men pulling on the lines to keep them taut.

Ten of Two Dogs' SEALs stood ready on the Independence's weather deck with ropes and a shot-line gun. Two Dogs was leading the charge.

"Okay boys, let's do it right. There's one of our own over there. Sherk," he yelled above the noise of the frothing ocean, "fire when ready."

The young SEAL nodded and took aim with a shot-line gun. The gun he held resembled a shotgun but it had a spool of light nylon red-colored line, called a messenger, protruding from its muzzle. The line was weighted with a lead slug that would carry the it the length of a football field as it unraveled. As the messenger arrived at the receiving ship, in this case the Virgo, it would be captured by the closest crewman on deck. The small line would then be tied to a larger line and hauled back across to the Independence where that line would be tied to a larger line and hauled back to the Virgo.

Once the lines between the two ships were adequately large enough in diameter to support the weight of the item to be transferred, the highline crew on Virgo would run the line through a block and tackle pulley configuration to maximize their mechanical advantage and hold the line taut by sheer manpower, pulling on the rope in a tug of war-like effort.

Sherk fired his shot line gun sending the fist-size weight arching high above the wave tops over to the Virgo. It smacked Virgo's weather deck just forward of the superstructure coming to a stop at the base of a piping manifold.

A cheer went up from both ships as two Virgo crewmen grabbed the line and rushed it aft to the ship's boatswain who immediately tied it to a larger line. The Independence's SEALs heaved the line back across to their deck and tied a larger line to its end. Now Virgo's crew began the arduous job of pulling the line back across where it was fastened to a tensioning block and tackle.

Surprisingly for both crews, it didn't take long to finish rigging the highline. The SEALs on the Independence held the line tight to prevent it from dragging across the wave tops. On the Independence's weather deck, the ship's Chief Boatswain argued with Two Dogs.

"Hey, sir, this highline ain't even close to regulation. The Old Man will pull the plug when he sees this clusterfuck. The book says…"

Two Dogs cut him off in mid-sentence.

"If Commander Boucher ran his Persian Gulf operations by the book, I'd already be dead nine times, so let it go, Boats. I owe this old swim buddy big time and I'm not going to turn my back on him now because somebody wrote some dumbass regulation about how to rig a highline."

"Well, okay, sir, but I don't like it."

"Let it go, Boats, we'll be fine."

Two Dogs could see Boucher rigging the highline to Virgo's port side bulkhead cleat then hanging on it to test its strength. Two Dogs did the same on his end and gave Boucher a thumbs-up.

The Air Force flight surgeon reluctantly approached the highline escorted by several SEALs. He had obviously never been "highlined" before. In fact, he found the whole idea of sending a man across a nylon line stretched between two underway ships dangerously outlandish if not outright foolhardy.

"Don't push," he protested, "I'm going, I'm going."

The SEALs strapped the flight surgeon into a mountain climber's Swiss Seat harness. They faced him toward the Virgo and lifted him up to the now taut highline. Two Dogs hooked the harness to the highline with a carabineer and did a quick safety check to ensure his harness was properly tightened.

"Whoa," the flight surgeon questioned, "you sure this is safe?"

"Safer than an iron dick whack'n off in a thunderstorm," one of the younger SEALs shouted, followed by laughter from his fellow SEALs.

Two Dogs scowled at his men, quieting the laughter. "No sweat, Doc. The Navy's been doing this sort of stuff ever since they invented wooden ships and manned them with iron men. You're gonna be fine."

The flight surgeon was still dubious and had a white knuckle death grip on the ship's gunwale lifeline. Two Dogs checked the doctor's harness one more time to ensure it was rigged and fastened properly then reported into his handheld radio.

"Virgo, he's good to go. Retrieve when ready."

Boucher double checked the highline rigging and nodded approval to Sam.

"Okay Independence," she said into her radio mic, "let's do it."

"Roger that, Virgo."

Two Dogs confidently gave the flight surgeon a thumbs-up. As he returned a feeble salute, Sam, Boucher and several Virgo crewmen began pulling in the line. The doctor slowly slid up the highline from the undersized Independence toward the mammoth tanker suspended fifteen feet above the Atlantic on a line by a carabineer.

Windblown waves licked at the flight surgeon's heels as Virgo's crew slavishly pulled him over. Approximately half way between the two ships, an abnormally large wave reached up between the two ships and soaked the flight surgeon. Boucher yelled over his shoulder to the crewman pulling behind him.

"Pull harder! Harder! Harder!"

Suddenly, a large rogue wave savagely smacked the doctor. Its force spun and twisted him around the highline, fouling the rigging. The flight surgeon now dangled helplessly, two thirds of the way across.

"Oh my God! Jake, look!" Sam yelled above the noise of the surf.

The crews on both ends of the highline worked feverishly to untwist the lines but couldn't react fast enough. The doctor was hit again by an even more powerful wave that nearly ripped him from his harness. He now hung upside down. The two ships slowly begin converging, slacking the highline to the point that the doctor was being drug through the waves between the two ships.

"Hurry, pull the line taut! Get tension on the highline!" Sam screamed to the crewmen on the line behind her. "Keep him above the water!" But, it was an impossible task as the two ships continued to slowly converge.

The slackened highline now began whipping across the wave crests as the two ships rode the swells. The panicked flight surgeon was being drug uncontrollably through the frothing surf between the two ships becoming ever more entangled in the rigging lines.

"We're going to lose him!" Sam warned at the top of her lungs.

Using a short piece of rope, Boucher quickly tied a loop-shaped sling. Sam watched him but didn't understand.

"What the hell are you doing?" she demanded, shouting at him above the noise.

He attached the sling to the now slack highline and climbed over the safety rail, holding himself by one hand, as he stood poised to mount the line.

"After I reach him I'll hook up to him. I'm gonna cut him away from the tangle. When I give you the signal, pull us in."

Sam was clearly flustered. "I don't know what to say."

Boucher smiled, "How about, you're out of your mind, or you're too old for this shit." He threw one leg over the side, then stopped and turned back to Sam. "Now don't go try'n to talk me out of it, do'ya hear me, Sam? I said don't try and..."

Sam smiled and gave him a quick hug. Boucher momentarily savored her closeness and the warmth of her cheek against his own.

"Be careful, Jake. The doctor's waiting," she yelled above the noise.

"He's in my office now, let him wait."

Sam saw the flight surgeon take the full force of another wave and helplessly sprawl in his fouled harness no longer able to hold his head above the water.

"He's drowning, Jake."

"Now you're making me feel guilty."

Standing beside Bakke on the bridge wing above, Deeds observed Boucher clip his sling to the retrieving line with a carabineer and then slip it over his shoulder. As Boucher turned back towards Sam, he noticed Deeds watching him from the bridge wing above. Their eyes met. Deeds nervously checked his wristwatch and disappeared from sight.

Boucher pulled himself out on top of the highline. He was lying face down on the line with his arms outstretched. He dangled one leg below and had his other leg hooked over the line behind him. By pulling with his arms and pushing with the one foot he had hooked over the line from behind, he could control his foot by foot progress as he pulled himself down along the line.

While no one onboard the Virgo had ever seen anything done like this before, Boucher was no stranger to this technique. Throughout his SEAL career he had regularly trained for this maneuver and was very familiar with the risks involved. It was used by the SEALs to cross things like deep ravines, fast flowing streams, or even from roof to roof. The SEALs onboard the Independence immediately recognized Boucher's technique as "the slide for life."

Chapter 25

Pave Hawk and MC-130P

The key factor for the MC-130P tanker was acquiring the Pave Hawk at the Air Refueling Control Point. This required precise timing to slow the C-130's air speed from 210 knots as to arrive at the Air Refueling Initial Point, or ARIP, as it was known, at 110 knots, configured with flaps seventy percent down and the refueling hose extended, pressurized and ready to transfer fuel. This was accomplished by both the Pave Hawk and MC-130 arriving at the ARIP at the exact same time so neither had to play catch up or slow down.

Storm turbulence radically buffeted the Pave Hawk as Murphy skillfully positioned it behind the MC-130P so he could take on fuel. The MC-130P and Pave Hawk had difficulty maintaining close proximity because of the storm-generated air turbulence. Refueling under these conditions was too dangerous to attempt and both pilots knew it. The MC-130P pilot saw a possibility in a cloud opening ahead.

"Jolly Three Three, I'm climbing to that hole in the clouds ahead, we need calmer air."

Murphy saw the same hole in the clouds but knew he'd run out of fuel if he climbed and took the time to follow the MC-130.

"Negative Kingbird, I'm running on fumes, estimate one five minutes remaining. We'll never make it. It's gonna have to be now or never."

"Roger, Jolly. I'll try to hold it steady at five hundred."

Murphy inched the Pave Hawk's extended probe closer to the drogue basket dragging sixty feet behind the MC-130P.

"Kingbird, I'm almost there," Murphy calmly reported. "Hold what you got."

The Pave Hawk's probe pushed into the drogue basket but it didn't have enough force to properly seat. Gallons of jet fuel spewed from the pressurized drogue over the windshield of the helicopter instantly eliminating what little visibility Murphy had. The helicopter's windshield wipers smeared the fuel and rain across the glass in a blur of masses without detail.

Suddenly, turbulence threw the Pave Hawk toward the MC-130P. Murphy instinctively threw the control stick over and broke left to avoid collision with the trailing drogue, but it was impossible to avoid. Although supposedly impossible, the helicopter's main rotor blade struck the drogue basket trailing behind the MC-130's left wing hacking a sizable piece out of its cloth skirt and deforming the rotor's blade tip.

Without the cloth skirt, the drogue basket no longer had the wind resistance to keep it extended behind the tanker aircraft and it automatically retracted back into the wing pylon no longer functional. Now out of aerodynamic balance, the rotor blade began to vibrate; violently shaking the Pave Hawk like it was driving down a bumpy dirt road.

"Breakoff! Breakoff! Shit! Kingbird, we're KO'd here. There's no way we can hit your right drogue in this shape. We're going to have to ditch," Murphy reported. "I guess we're gonna have a fine Navy day after all - down there in that soup."

"Roger, Jolly. We'll stay on station with you. Good luck."

The MC-130P slowly climbed and banked right as the Pave Hawk disappeared into the rain below.

Virgo Highline

The crews on both ships helplessly watched the unfolding drama as Boucher pulled himself along the highline knowing there was nothing more they could do. The doctor gasped for air, trying to keep his head above water, as waves pummeled him time and time again. Foot by treacherous foot, Boucher pulled himself closer down the line towards the doctor. He finally reached the floundering man and immediately began fastening a line beneath the doctor's arms around his chest.

The Pave Hawk suddenly appeared out of the rain about one hundred yards astern of the two ships flying about fifty feet above the wave tops. The Pave Hawk pilot radioed Independence.

"Independence, this is Jolly Three Three. Estimate one three minutes of fuel remaining. We'll hold as long as we can before we ditch."

Murphy spied Boucher still in his tux, attempting to rescue the semi-conscious doctor who was dragging through the sea on the fouled highline.

"What the hell?" he said into his intercom mic.

Murphy pointed at Boucher for his co-pilot to see.

"Take a look at that, Todd. Looks like...James Bond?"

Both Murphy and Zech glanced at each other with a dumb look on their faces.

"No... it can't be," they said in astonished unison.

Close to exhaustion, Boucher finally succeeded in securing his sling to the doctor's harness. Using the sling's carabineer, he clipped himself and the flight surgeon to the highline. He grabbed a folding knife clipped to his rear pants pocket and cut the fouled lines away that entangled the flight surgeon to the highline. He then signaled Sam to pull both of them back to the Virgo. Sam strained with all her might as she and the crew members pulled on the retrieving line.

"Come on, men," she yelled, "get your backs into it and pull! Together now, pull! Pull! Pull!"

On the deck above where the highline block and tackle was rigged, a sharp knife sliced through the nylon loop that anchored the highline to the ship's bulkhead cleat. All of a sudden the highline snapped, barely missing Sam's head as it whipped past her.

Hidden from view, Deeds watched as Boucher and the flight surgeon plunged back into the sea. Man overboard alarms sounded and chaos ensued on the decks of both ships as the two men disappeared beneath the frothing waves.

Pave Hawk

Chaotic chatter filled the radio waves.

"Holy shit! Did ya' see that, Todd?" Murphy said to his co-pilot.

Zech checked the remaining fuel level and pointed to the digital readout making sure Murphy saw the red digital numbers on its screen.

"Ten minutes of fuel left, Major."

Murphy and Zech looked at each other soberly and shrugged, knowing what they had to do.

Murphy opened his radio mic, "Independence, Jolly Three Three, continue on present course, we'll get'm."

Murphy jerked the control stick forward commanding the Pave Hawk to swoop low over the water bringing it to a hover above Boucher and the Doctor. The damaged rotor blade caused relentless vibration making control extremely difficult. Fortunately Major Murphy had over two thousand hours as a Pave

Hawk pilot and his experience made all the difference. The flight engineer knelt inside the open side door preparing the rescue collar and attached it to the hoist. A PJ had already donned his swim gear and was preparing to jump into the water with Boucher and the doctor.

Both Murphy and Zech knew putting a PJ into the water and hoisting them up would take too long. They didn't have enough fuel for that.

"Forget lowering the collar!" Murphy told his flight engineer and PJs over their headsets. "I'll get us as low into the water as I can without swamping the tail rotor. Drop the collar on top of them and drag'm in the open door."

Murphy brought the helicopter into a hovering descent and inched toward Boucher and the floundering doctor. Zech again tapped on the digital fuel gauge as if the tap would adjust an imaginary needle to accuracy.

"Six minutes fuel remaining," he coolly advised Murphy over the intercom.

The Pave Hawk's rotor down-wash caused huge swirling vortexes of windblown sea spray that enveloped the entire helicopter. As the two PJs hung out the open cargo door with outstretched arms motioning Boucher and the doctor closer, Boucher held up his hitchhiker's thumb in an attempt at misunderstood SEAL Team humor. Not finding Boucher the least bit funny, an angered PJ signaled Boucher to get in.

"Grab the collar!" a PJ inaudibly shouted, his voice overtaken by the jet engine noise.

Boucher pushed the doctor toward the PJs. Waves smacked upward toward the belly of the hovering helicopter making maintaining its control nearly impossible for the pilots.

"Five minutes of fuel left," Zech coolly reported over the helicopter's intercom.

A ten foot swell carried Boucher and the doctor close enough to grasp the rescue collar but receded before they could be grabbed by the PJs. Finally, a swell carried them to the PJs' grasp and they were pulled safely inside the open cargo door.

"Got'em! Go, go, go!!" the flight engineer shouted into his helmet mic.

Murphy clicked his intercom mic open to Zech and crew.

"Nice work, guys. We have about three minutes of fuel remaining. Prepare to ditch."

The Pave Hawk skimmed the wave tops as it caught up with the two ships. Inside, Boucher and the doctor shivered by the helicopter's open side door. Boucher grabbed the flight engineer by his flight suit and yelled above the engine noise.

"Thank you. You Air Force guys aren't so bad after all."

The flight engineer gave him a thumbs-up and a faint smile knowing they all would be back in the water in just a few more minutes. Boucher grabbed the doctor's shoulders.

"You okay, Doc?" he shouted.

The doctor gave him an uncertain thumbs-up. The flight engineer handed Boucher and the doctor an inflatable life vest shouting above the jet engine noise.

"Here, put this on! We're going to ditch."

Boucher gave him a quizzical stare, "Is this some kind'a joke?"

"Put it on," the man sternly instructed, "In a couple of minutes we're gonna ditch."

Boucher saw the PJs readying the helicopter's emergency inflatable life raft.

"This doctor has to get onboard that tanker," Boucher yelled into the flight engineer's helmet.

The flight engineer gave Boucher a thumbs-down, "Impossible! We're out of fuel. We're going to ditch."

Thinking for a moment, Boucher grabbed a radio headset and mic hanging on a hook by the open door.

"Sam? Virgo! Anyone listening out there?"

Boucher pointed to his mic and then to the Virgo.

"Switch me to the ship's bridge-to-bridge emergency channel!"

The flight engineer gave him a thumbs-up. Boucher tried to raise the Virgo.

"Virgo. Virgo. Virgo. This is Boucher, over."

"Two minutes to swim call," Zech reported over the intercom.

Sam's voice blared over radio, "Jake?"

"Sam, drop a lizard line midway down the port side. Tie some knots in it! Hang the Jacobs ladder over the side behind that!"

"Roger, Jake. But what...?"

"No time to explain," he interrupted. "Listen up everybody. Pilot, slow us down a bit," Boucher calmly asked Murphy keeping the ship-to-ship radio open with Sam. "Cast us just ahead of the ship. Sam, be ready."

Boucher threw off the headset and grabbed the flight engineer's hands shouting above the jet engine noise, "I need your gloves!"

Now several hundred yards ahead of Virgo, Murphy flared the Pave Hawk to a slow pace about twenty feet above the sea surface. Boucher gave the gloves to the doctor.

"Put these on!"

The shivering doctor yanked on the gloves. Boucher looked back at the oncoming Virgo, then at the doctor.

"Let's go," he shouted.

The doctor stared at Boucher in disbelief.

"No fucking way! I'm not moving!"

"If it's the last thing I do you're going to make this house call and deliver that baby."

"I'm going with you. The doc will need help with the delivery," one of the PJs yelled as he slipped on his fins and pulled his facemask down.

Boucher nodded and grabbed a handful of the doctor's flight suit pulling him out through the helicopter's open side door in a frantic tumbling leap into the sea.

"Shhhiiiiit!" both men yelled as they fell into the water. The PJ followed behind splashing into the water next to them.

They surfaced and saw the Pave Hawk bank slightly left as it rocketed ahead of the Independence. Now just above the wave tops, Murphy slowed his doomed helicopter. Both he and Zech jettisoned their side cockpit doors. The Flight Engineer and the remaining PJ threw an inflatable raft into the sea and jumped into the water. Murphy nodded at his friend and copilot. Zech unbuckled his seat harness and rolled out of his seat into the sea.

Boucher watched from afar as Murphy skillfully drifted his helicopter clear of his crew just as the engines sputtered and flamed out. Murphy was prepared for what was inevitably coming next. As his helicopter went down into the waiting grasp of the Atlantic, it immediately rolled onto its side. It's spinning rotors violently churned the water, before breaking off.

Murphy released his seat harness and swam out of his seat barely escaping as the open helicopter rapidly flooded with water and rolled upside down from the weight of its roof-mounted engines and transmission.

Boucher took some relief when he saw four inflated yellow life jackets bobbing on the surface, confirming the crew had all made it out of the sinking helicopter. Boucher turned back to see the Virgo bearing down on him.

"Swim! Follow me!" he yelled to the doctor and the PJ.

They swam toward Virgo's port side barely clearing the mammoth ship's bow as it plowed by dangerously close. Boucher pushed them away from the ship's rough barnacle-encrusted hull with his gloved hands.

"Hold on to me! Don't let go no matter what!" he warned the doctor. "Follow us and help the Doc," he shouted to the PJ.

The approaching lizard line danced through the water next to the ship's hull raising a seawater rooster tail a few feet in the air. Boucher was prepared and snatched on to it with both hands as it passed by. Now holding on with all his strength, both he and the doctor exploded from the water, skimming across the waves. Boucher strained as he pulled his way up several knots towards the dangling Jacobs ladder. Gathering his strength, he pulled the doctor's hand up onto a ladder rung.

"Climb!" he ordered.

The doctor hesitated. Boucher angrily shoved him onto the ladder.

"I said climb, damn it! Climb!"

Clinging to the ladder by one elbow bent around a rung to keep from being swept away, Boucher gave the doctor a boost to get his feet firmly seated on the trailing ladder rungs, then followed himself. The PJ pushed from below.

Above, Sam shouted encouragement as Boucher and the three men pulled themselves up the ladder toward the ship's main deck. With the help of the PJ, Boucher continued to push and shove the doctor all the way up. Finally, Sam was able to grab the shivering doctor's flight suit and help him over the safety rail. Sam wrapped a blanket around him aided by the PJ. The doctor had a blue cast to his face and hands and shivered uncontrollably.

"Hypothermia," the PJ commented to Sam and a crewman.

Sam nodded, "Take him below and warm his ass up, he's got a baby to deliver."

She then shifted her attention to Boucher who looked like a wet dog as he climbed over the rail onto the deck. Sam gave him a quick once over. He looked remarkably good considering what he had just been through. He wasn't shivering or really even breathing hard. He looked at Sam and smiled, straightening his posture. He put his hands on her shoulders and held her at arm's length.

"Thanks," he said, slightly squeezing her shoulders in his powerful grip.

She looked into his sparkling eyes.

"How you do'n sailor?"

"Not too bad for a Monday. How's the Love Boat?"

"Normal as it can be."

"Normal? Trust me Sam, this ship ain't even close to normal."

Boucher looked behind her and focused on the pad eye above where the highline rigging had been fastened.

"Give me a second. There's something I want to take a look at up there," he told Sam pointing at the pad eye above.

Boucher climbed the steel ladder that led up to the bulkhead pad eye. A piece of the rope fastening loop was still dangling from it. Not surprised, he saw the line had been cleanly cut.

"That's two," he mumbled to himself.

U.S. State Department, Washington, DC, the same time

Blackburn was sitting at his desk wearing head phones and listening to his drum part for a new tune he and his jazz ensemble would be performing at a Saturday evening gig in a swanky Georgetown jazz club. Ever since retiring from the Navy he devoted the majority of his free time to his obsession - playing jazz drums. Blackburn had a dichotomy of interests. He was arguably a hard-talking, hard-charging warrior, a patriot who would unquestionably sacrifice himself as necessary to see good triumph over evil and the rest of the time he loved listening to and playing jazz music. A self-admitted 'bull in the china shop' when it came to his SEAL-special operations career, he somehow looked like he had always been playing his drums professionally when he was on stage. If you didn't know his career history you wouldn't know he was one of the lynch pins in the U.S. counterterrorism intelligence community.

Bruce entered the office and sat down in the chair beside the desk, startling Blackburn.

"Damn it, Jimmy!" he scolded, ripping off his earphones and casting them on the desk in front of Bruce.

"Sorry, Sir, I didn't mean to surprise you. I just have some very interesting information you need to hear."

Blackburn smiled and sat back.

"Okay, shoot."

"Well, Sir, we've been racking our brains over two central issues. First, how can we defuse al Qaeda and the Taliban and second, identifying the primary target or targets within the continental U.S. or our interests overseas"

"Okay, tell me something I don't already know, Jimmy."

"Please bear with me as I walk through our thinking. We are currently in an intelligence battle against al Qaeda and the Taliban. I say that because their goal is to shift our forces' focus in the region from an offensive to a defensive position. As you know, a few days ago our SEALs failed to snatch Al-Adel. That failure was not a result of bad operational tactics or flawed execution on their part; it was a result of bad intelligence.

"They ran into a maze of extremely well-camouflaged, fortified caves that were being used as a central base camp and training headquarters. We're damn lucky we didn't take any casualties."

"But that operation is a prime example of us starting out on the offensive and leaving on the defensive. Why?" Blackburn asked.

"Because we didn't know we would be outnumbered and outgunned to the extent we were. We were working from bad intelligence. As you well know, Sir, we get the vast majority of our actionable intelligence from in-country indigenous human sources. These human sources, no matter who they are or what station they may hold within Afghan society, have tribal roots. Or, they have some form of tribal loyalty, and as such they can't be counted on to be reliable."

Blackburn held up his hand to stop Bruce in mid lecture, "So that leaves us where?"

"I started by saying their goal is to shift us from the offensive to the defensive. I think it's fair to say that they successfully achieved the same goal in Iraq. As both military and civilian casualties increased, political and popular support for the conflict decreased. With the election of President Banner our direction was changed. He decided that the war to fight was not in Iraq, but rather Afghanistan. We are now fighting a sophisticated, tribally-based enemy in Afghanistan and we must not lose sight of that. While we attempt to win the hearts and minds of the Afghan population in a massive counterinsurgency campaign, our enemy is more or less directly related to that population. That means when we fail in an offensive operation as we did last week in Southern Afghanistan, we lose credibility with that population and fail even more from a U.S. political perspective."

"Jimmy, get to the point, you're killing me with all this cerebral analysis horse shit."

"Well, Sir, I guess this all leads to one thing. Our enemy knows that if they successfully attack the U.S. homeland, they will strike a major blow to our counterinsurgency strategy in Afghanistan and our related areas of conflict because it will put us back on the defensive. You see, Sir, if they can shift our counterinsurgency timeline in their favor through a devastating attack against the U.S. homeland they will also undoubtedly shift President Banner's calculus as well."

"Okay, you're finally starting to make some sense. What attack?"

"Sir, if you recall, a couple of days ago I mentioned that we were seeing some intelligence derived from a flash drive the SEALs found on a man they killed during their failed raid attempt to capture Al-Adel."

"Yeah, you said it referenced a plan called 'Green Lady' or something like that, right?"

"Yes, Sir, it referenced a plan they called 'Green Lady.' We've since collaborated with other intelligence sources and distilled the intelligence we gleaned from the information contained on the captured flash drive. You see, Sir, I think we may have figured out what they were talking about."

Chapter 26

Downtown Manhattan, New York

New York City traffic was a mess. President Banner, along with five other heads of state, was there personally attending the historic opening of the P5+1 Summit at the United Nations in New York City. The United Nations Security Council, as fundamentally flawed as it was, provided the only internationally-recognized forum for an urgent meeting of its five permanent members, the U.S., United Kingdom, Russia, China, and France. For the purposes of this tedious negotiation with Iran, Germany was temporarily added to the Council and it was so nicknamed the P5+1 Summit.

Coincidentally, the first of the Guantanamo detainee trials began at the federal courthouse in downtown Manhattan. The world's media had invaded to cover both events. Between motorcades for the heads of state and the heavily armed U.S. Marshals' convoys transporting the Gitmo detainees to and from the courthouse, the normally dreadful traffic in Manhattan had become a virtual quagmire.

Worse yet, the city's subway system couldn't handle the overflow and it too was swamped. Even pedestrian movement was restricted when police closed multi-block sections of the city as motorcades and convoys passed through them. The city was completely snarled and its residents had lost what normally little patience they had for such things.

On top of that, most New Yorkers opposed the Gitmo detainee trials being held in their city. Most Americans opposed the fact that the Banner administration had given the Gitmo detainees who were captured on the battlefield, the same legal rights as U.S. citizens. The left-leaning media continued to cast the Islamists being tried as freedom fighters who were captured and imprisoned illegally by the evil U.S. military while the Islamists themselves only wanted religious martyrdom.

Compounding that mess, President Banner was staying at the President's Suite at the Waldorf and the Secret Service, with the assistance of the New York Police Department had restricted access to the surrounding streets. Russian President, Dmitry Anatolyevich Medvedev, was staying at the Russian Consulate downtown. Manhattan was a frenzy of special security details, blocked streets, armed VIP convoys and news media all competing for the right of way. The confused amalgam fueled every New Yorker's daily frustration and tempers throughout the Big Apple were at the breaking point.

Virgo's Bridge

Still thirty miles off the coast of New Jersey, Virgo turned west and approached the channel corridor leading to the Hudson River and New York Harbor. For the first time in several days the skies were clearing. The sun was shining down on the Virgo through a hole in the clouds, illuminating her in a white-hot shaft of light that looked like Divine awareness of the mighty ship's courageous rescue. A gentle breeze occasionally gusted from the south, warming the excited passengers who crammed Virgo's topside weather decks in anticipation. Bakke watched them from the bridge wing milling happily about on the deck below. He took comfort in the fact that he had successfully rescued them from the worst cruise ship disaster since the Titanic and he didn't lose a single person. He knew it was an accomplishment of historic proportions that would probably be written and talked about for the next fifty years. He was content knowing his legacy as a great sea captain was historically assured.

Inside the pilothouse, Sam was on the radio with New York Harbor Control trying to get clearance to enter and proceed up the Hudson River Channel to Pier 88, where the cruise ship terminal was located. There, they would offload all the rescued passengers.

"New York Port Control, this is Virgo, over."

"Roger, Virgo, this is Port Control, over."

"Port Control, request pilot transfer instructions and clearance to enter New York Harbor, over.

"Virgo, Port Control, stand by, out."

Below in his stateroom, Boucher awoke from a deep sleep and got dressed. He craved a cup of hot coffee. He hadn't seen Deeds since the highline incident and surmised that he was avoiding him for obvious reasons. He reasoned his evidence against Deeds was circumstantial at best and decided to give it a rest and let the air clear. There would be plenty of time to sort it out when they reached New York. Once law enforcement representatives were on-board they could investigate as appropriate.

Still groggy, Boucher left his stateroom for the Crew's Mess. As he walked the passageway he noticed how dingy it was for the first time. In fact, it was filthy. *Must be from all the cruise ship refugees.* Strangely, none of them were there now and it was eerily quiet.

As he rounded a corner intersection in a passageway, Deeds attacked Boucher from behind, wildly swinging a large pipe wrench in an attempt to hit his head. Boucher instinctively sidestepped and spun around meeting Deeds' attack face on. The heavy wrench glanced off the metal bulkhead with a clang. As Deeds followed through with the momentum of the swing, Boucher snatched the wrench from his hand and hurled him to the floor in one fluid motion. Boucher pushed him down using the wrench and pinned him in a stranglehold against the deck.

"What's your problem, Deeds?"

"Go to hell," Deeds snarled.

"You know, you're a very hostile guy and I'm really starting to get tired of your fucking bad attitude."

Deeds spat in Boucher's face. Boucher pushed the wrench down tighter against his throat.

"I'm asking nicely," he said calmly. "Why are you trying to kill me?"

Deeds strained toward the pistol he had tucked inside his trouser waist. Using his knee, Boucher pinned Deeds' hand to the deck and snatched the gun away.

"Either you find a different way to express your anger, or I'll have to..."

Deeds began to smile.

A large metal bar smashed Boucher from behind, dropping him on top of Deeds like a sack of potatoes. Milan menacingly stood over Boucher holding the bar at the ready. Deeds struggled out from under Boucher's limp body pushing him off to the side and got to his feet.

"You son-of-a-bitch!" he said in a low voice as he kicked Boucher's unconscious body in the ribs.

Then they heard approaching voices.

"In here," Milan said, opening a door off the main passageway that led into an auxiliary pump room.

They both took one of Boucher's arms and dragged him into the room. Deeds quickly latched the door. Two crew members passed by the room without the slightest suspicion anyone was hiding inside.

On Virgo's bridge, Captain Bakke was busy trying to get clearance to bring his ship into the harbor.

"Virgo. Virgo. This is New York Harbor Control, over."

Deeds entered the bridge rubbing his throat and neck. Bakke was on the radio. "Yes, this is Virgo. Go ahead Harbor Control."

"Permission to enter New York Harbor is denied. You are to proceed to anchorage twelve. Once anchored, ferries will rendezvous with you there and disembark your passengers.

"What? They can't," Deeds mumbled as he quickly left the bridge.

U.S. State Department, Washington, DC, the same time

Bruce hurried down the narrow hallway inside S/CT's main office area located on the second floor just above the Department of State's C Street reception area.

"Sir, I have a hot one," he blurted as he burst into Blackburn's office at the end of the hall.

Blackburn was in the middle of a secure phone call with his FBI counterpart, Supervisory Special Agent Wade Takemori, who headed the FBI's elite Critical Incident Response Group. Blackburn held up his open hand, stopping Bruce from further interruption and motioned him to sit down in the chair next to his desk.

"Wade, my principal analyst, Jimmy Bruce, just sat down next to me. Do you mind if I put you on speaker?"

Blackburn hit the speakerphone button so Bruce could hear the conversation.

"Let me get this straight, there are currently four heads of state already in New York City and by fourteen hundred today Germany will arrive."

"That's right, Dean, there will be six heads of state along with their senior representatives at the United Nations for the P5+1 U.N. Security Council summit later this afternoon. President Banner arrived here last evening and will be in attendance."

"So you're saying there's an LNG tanker about to enter New York Harbor and that poses a potential threat to the summit?"

"Yes, the ship's name is Virgo. I know it's a U.S. flagged vessel, but it should not be allowed into the harbor."

"Have you passed this info to DHS?"

"Of course. I personally called Under Secretary Dunkle over an hour ago. She said that she was in personal contact with Governor Giordano and she insisted that it wasn't a security issue from a DHS perspective. She said the Secret Service and DHS had everything under control regarding the summit and they didn't want or need any additional FBI assistance. Our New York Field Office Special Agent in Charge assures us the United Nations main campus along the East River and surrounding area is locked down hard."

"Where is that ship supposed to moor? Some place along the East River close to the UN or where?" Bruce was shaking his head no as he scribbled a note to Blackburn shoving it in front of him. "Ahh, Jimmy Bruce just informed me that they want to bring the ship up the Hudson to the cruise ship terminal. We think that's pier 88. That's where they will offload the two thousand passengers they rescued from the cruise liner that burned and sank off North Carolina yesterday. So, that means the ship would be a good distance away from the UN on the other side of Manhattan, right?"

"Yes, but according to our New York SAC, President Banner just informed the Secret Service that he intends to make an appearance at the terminal just after the ship's arrival to personally welcome the passengers home and praise the Virgo's crew for the miraculous rescue."

"Okay, what do you want me to do, Wade?"

"I want to get your boss to call for a Deputies Committee meeting ASAP. Between my boss and your boss maybe Dunkle will agree. We need to stop that ship from entering the harbor."

"Agreed."

Concluding the call, Blackburn sat back in his chair and gave Bruce his full attention.

"Whatcha got, Jimmy?"

"Sorry, Sir, I didn't mean to interrupt you."

Blackburn made a sour face as he took a sip of cold coffee.

"This coffee tastes like panther piss. Come on, Jimmy, I'll buy you a coffee. Ever since that coffee mess sexual harassment escapade I went through at ONI, I don't pour my coffee without a witness present."

Bruce nodded his consent and the two men headed towards the coffee pot located by a sink alcove halfway up the hall.

"You know what our problem is, Jimmy?"

"I'd love to hear it from you, Sir."

Blackburn smiled. "We've been conducting warfare-by-lawyers for so damn long we're now believing their bullshit."

"I'm not sure I follow you, Captain."

"We have lulled ourselves into believing that our enemies and potential enemies can be defeated through conventional military engagement bounded by rules of engagement that the lawyers dictate. We still see ourselves facing our enemy on a battlefield but now we have a bunch of dick-breath lawyers looking over our shoulders every step we take."

Bruce immediately recognized that his boss rarely offered his inner thoughts and when he did, he usually didn't expound on them. Bruce respected Blackburn's depth of knowledge and uncanny ability to see the forest for the trees. He wanted to learn more about where his boss was coming from but he knew he had to be careful so it wouldn't seem like an interrogation.

"Sir? I'm not sure I follow you. Are you saying we can't win on the battlefield?"

"You know, we throw our air power, ships and troops at them and overwhelm our enemy with superior firepower. The problem is we're fighting enemies who are so ideologically and religiously different from us that we overlook their underlying intention to kill us any way they can. Our think tank astrologers, news pundits and academic elitists have us in a state of denial and have conditioned us into believing our enemies' goal is something other than our destruction. This LNG ship thing is a perfect example."

"How do you mean, Sir?"

"Jimmy, these al Qaeda dicks aren't ever going to meet us head-on in a military engagement. They're going to sidestep us every chance they have and come in our back door while we're sleeping. While we continue to impose ever sterner restrictions upon ourselves on how we wage war against them, our mindset and modus operandi offers them ever-increasing opportunities to attack our military, financial and civil infrastructure."

Bruce considered Blackburn's words as they arrived at the coffee mess.

"So you're saying they're primarily targeting our infrastructure?"

"Yup, among other things. Their goal is to make every American's daily life so fucking miserable that we'll give up the fight against them. And you know what, Jimmy? We're only kidding ourselves if we think our infrastructure isn't fragile and very vulnerable. Think about it, Jimmy. All they need to do is create a tsunami that would wipe out most of the infrastructure along the Eastern Seaboard. Damn, unless my memory fails me, they tried that last year. Or, maybe take out some of our critical communications or GPS navigation satellites with crude nukes. Or, maybe even take out some of our larger cities like New York City and they're on their way to a strategic victory without ever confronting our military. We got some shitass countries like Iran, North Korea, and even little piss ants like Myanmar, building nuclear weapons. Jimmy, you gotta ask yourself, what for? Are we really naive enough to believe they won't use'm on us? The truth is they don't need to launch any nukes at us. All they need to do is explode some of those nukes in space to take out our critical communications and GPS satellites and it will bring our infrastructure to its knees. And that will open even further vulnerabilities that they can exploit and attack piecemeal on their terms."

"But if they nuke our satellites surely we'll retaliate?"

"Hell no! They know we won't retaliate. Hell, military retaliation would be politically incorrect. I mean innocent civilians might die if we retaliated and the fucking lawyers would have a field day putting our guys in jail. Besides, how do you retaliate against some nukes exploded in space? Our enemies all know we've lost our killer spirit. That's why our enemies see our home front as our weak front, and that's why they're going to keep attacking it over and over until we give up the fight. They know we've lost our will to take whatever measures are necessary to win and they know war is all about winning, not negotiating some pussy-ass political settlement. They know if you can't win playing by the rules, then win without the fucking rules. But win."

"Sir, this is good stuff. I like hearing it from you."

Blackburn made a face and raised his eyebrows.

"Jimmy, we got this huge fucking problem here in this country and I'm not sure if we just don't get it or we're in denial."

"How so, Sir?"

Blackburn scratched his head.

"The Islamists want us dead and are more than willing to die themselves, or even sacrifice their own people, to accomplish that goal. Our old friends, the Russians and the Chinese, have an emerging war fighting doctrine that employs an all-inclusive strategy. They will attack an enemy anywhere, in any way, and do whatever it takes to win. That means everything is on the table from cyber warfare to infrastructure sabotage, from global nuclear exchange to using third party surrogates to first weaken and then paralyze us until they can position themselves to nail us with the death blow. Make no mistake; our enemies are coming after us in ways we haven't even thought of because we're too fucking sensitive that we might offend somebody's religion, or afraid we might get sued because we violated some dickwad terrorist's civil rights."

"But the Russians and Chinese lack the military might to…"

"To do what?" Blackburn interrupted. "Think about this angle, Jimmy. The European Union is about ready to default the Euro and it will happen now that Greece, Italy, Portugal and Spain need EU bailouts. The only saving grace is if Germany shores up the Euro because they're the only European Union member state that still has a vibrant industrial economy. But Germany gets over eighty percent of its energy resources from Russia. Without energy like natural gas and petroleum, German industry goes tits up and their economy fails. So all Russia has to do is close the spigot a few turns. They don't even have to shut it off and the European Union implodes because Germany can't sustain keeping the EU's economy shored up."

"And a domino-effect ensues?"

"Yes, Jimmy. If the EU and the Euro fail, the U.S. economy will fail and we'll take Japan and a good percentage of China's economy with us. But none of that will affect Russia because they still use the ruble and essentially have a closed economy of their own. They'll revert to socialism and do just fine while the rest of us in the free market slowly die on the vine of capitalism."

"And Russia reemerges as a world superpower without ever firing a shot."

"Exactly."

"And what about China, Sir?"

"Those Commie socialist bastards own us now. When we default on all our loans, they'll revert to the pre-U.S. engagement and enlargement isolationist modus operandi. Hell, Jimmy, they lived just fine like that for three thousand years before we came along. They won't emerge as a superpower because they won't have to. China is the world according to China and without Europe and the U.S., they don't have a threat."

"But won't Russia see that as opportunity?"

"Russia and China have co-existed as neighbors for centuries. They both have always been closed societies in their own right. Their geography and the location of their population centers has always effectively separated them and prevented conflict. Unless some smart guy figures out how to remove the mountains physically separating them and move them closer together I think they'll continue peacefully coexisting much as they always have."

Blackburn poured two full cups of coffee and set them on the table beside the coffee pot. He grabbed an open, pint size container of creamer from the refrigerator and held it above Bruce's steaming coffee cup.

"You want some fucking creamer in this, Jimmy?"

New York State, Governor's limo

It was slow going. Even with a police escort, the governor's limo was caught in Manhattan's snarled uptown traffic. There just was no easy way or fast way to drive from one end of town to the other when heads of state were visiting Manhattan.

Governor Giordano's press secretary scribbled notes as he listened on his cell phone.

"Yeah, we're on our way there now." He listened for a few moments and became visibly nervous. "Hold on a moment, I need to run this by the governor," he interrupted, pushing the phone's mute button with his thumb. "Governor, the Coast Guard says the Port Captain ordered the tanker to anchor out in New York Bay between the Statue of Liberty and the Verrazano Narrows Bridge rather than allow it to come in and disembark the passengers at the cruise ship terminal. He says they're going to transfer the passengers off the ship onto the Staten Island Ferry and then use the ferries to take them to the cruise ship terminal."

Governor Giordano steamed, tightening every muscle in his face and jaw. He looked like he was going to explode any second. Then he began pointing at his press secretary. His voice was strained and his finger trembled as he spoke.

"You tell that son-of-a-bitch Port Captain if he wants to keep his job, or get any more port improvements funded during this lifetime, that ship with my wife and kids on it better be at the passenger terminal before I am! You tell that dumb bastard that President Banner, the Mayor and I are going to present that tanker captain with a key to the city and we're not riding a fucking ferry to some offshore anchorage to do it."

"Yes, Governor, I'll tell'm."

Verrazano Bridge, New York City

A white car pulled up to the bridge toll booth, paid, then proceeded onto the bridge. At mid-span, the car slowed, turned its four-way flashers on, and then stopped beside the guard rail in the far right lane. Traffic immediately began to back up. The driver waved traffic around from his open window. He got out, lifted the hood and opened a quart of oil. A New York-New Jersey Transit Authority cop pulled up with his blue lights flashing.

"Hey, what's da problem here?" he yelled from his open driver's side window. "You need for me to call you a tow or sump'n?"

"No, sir, officer," the man replied with a thick foreign accent. "She will start, just needs some oil to get me over the bridge. Thank you anyway."

The cop pulled alongside the stopped car and the cop rolled his passenger-side window down. The man began pouring the oil and looked over at the cop. "It's like my wife, needs a little lubrication once in awhile."

The cop laughed, "Yeah, I hear ya. Okay, buddy, get da oil in'er and get on your way."

The cop pulled out into the traffic stream and shut off his flashing lights. As he disappeared back in traffic, the man left his car and surreptitiously climbed up on the guard rail. He stared down at the water. He looked like he was going to jump but he stopped short and smiled widely. Other cars on the bridge slowed, jamming traffic as their drivers strained to see the river below. At that moment Virgo passed beneath the bridge on its way up the Hudson River toward the cruise ship terminal in Manhattan. The man watched the escorting fire boats and tugs salute Virgo in grand fashion by spraying geysers of patriotically-colored water high into the air around the massive ship.

The man looked up, shading his eyes from the bright sun with his open hand. A small plane circled above, towing a large banner that said, "Welcome Virgo – Heroes of the Sea."

Below, Virgo's decks were crowded with the rescued passengers who cheered and hugged each other with uncontrollable excitement. The sight of it all delighted the man. As he turned to step down and return to his car, a number of lengthy blasts from Virgo's throaty horn reverberated throughout the surrounding area in an obvious salute to the Statue of Liberty. He heard a long cheer go up from the passengers on deck after each blast.

Now back in his car, Virgo disappeared from his view. He stared blankly into the rear view mirror for a few moments before restarting his car. He removed his sunglasses and ball cap, and then straightened his wig slightly. He was a master of disguise and the one he was wearing had easily gotten him past the U.S. Immigration and Customs check point at the Canadian – New York entry point the day before. He had taken this contract without any apparent personal attachment to its cause or his employer. "God bless America," he mumbled to himself in English. It was just business as far as he was concerned and nothing more.

Three cars behind, a man and a woman watched him from a black Ford Taurus.

Chapter 27

Pier 88 passenger terminal, New York City

The Mayor of New York City eagerly awaited Virgo's arrival inside the Pier 88 passenger terminal. Bright lights illuminated several reporters who stood in front of their network's news camera promoting the heroic efforts of Virgo's captain and crew.

A band played as the ad hoc gala gained avalanche momentum. An aide approached the Mayor and spoke privately to him.

"Mr. Mayor, I've just been advised the president is on his way here. His aide asks that we hold our speeches and presentations until the president arrives."

"Great, first it's the governor, now President Banner. This is turning into a clusterfuck."

"Well, he did stump for you during your campaign. He just intends to make a short appearance. They're only asking for ten minutes."

"Yeah, right, ten minutes my ass. You know as well as I do there'll be a POTUS lockdown and the Secret Service will have to secure the area before they bring in the president and then everything will focus on him. It pisses me off!"

"Well, what do you want me to tell them?"

"How soon will the governor get here?"

"He's still about ten minutes away."

The mayor momentarily considered the situation before responding.

"Okay, call the president's aide back and tell him we'll hold the presentations and the speeches until he gets here."

Outside, tugs slowly prodded Virgo alongside Pier 88, the cruise ship pier, churning up muddy water from the river bottom as they strained to nudge the giant ship pierside. Bakke maneuvered Virgo remotely from the bridge wing control box using the ship's bow thruster to skillfully control the ship's parallel approach to the pier. Several narrow floating platforms called camels, made from heavy wooden planks, were pulled into place between the ship and the pier pilings to hold the ship's side about eight feet away from the pier's concrete curbside. Camels were used to protect both the ship's hull and the pier from rubbing and scraping.

Finally, the ship's movement ceased and the tugboats held Virgo against the camels and pier. Thick dirt-soiled white nylon mooring lines were passed methodically from the ship to the waiting longshoremen on the pier where they were secured to pier cleats and bollards. The lines were winched tight onboard the ship, securing the ship from all future motion. Shore personnel hooked auxiliary water hoses and electrical power cables to special shore power and auxiliary ports in Virgo's side allowing the ship to shut down its main engines and other auxiliary equipment that powered the ship. At the same time the passenger gangway was hoisted slowly from the passenger terminal onto Virgo's main deck. Emergency services personnel streamed aboard to help survivors down the gangway into the waiting arms of family and friends.

Several injured passengers were put in wheelchairs and taken to waiting ambulances. Governor Giordano's wife and kids stood in line to the side of the gangway waiting their turn to disembark. On the opposite side of the gangway, Sam cradled a newborn baby in her arms as a paramedic transported the new mother to the gangway in a wheelchair with her husband, the flight surgeon and PJ in tow.

Sam adjusted the blanket around the baby's face. "This is your millennium. Don't waste it," she whispered. Sam gently kissed the baby's forehead and handed it to the waiting mother.

"She's beautiful," Sam purred.

"Thank you for saving us," the new mother replied. "I'll never forget what you did."

Sam pointed at the flight surgeon, "Thank your doctor, not me."

"Goodbye," the new mother smiled.

The PJ guided the new mother's wheelchair onto the gangway with her husband following close behind. Sam raised an open hand as she shouted at the trio, "Goodbye... oh, in all the excitement I forgot to ask you. What are you going to name her?"

The husband turned and smiled, "Samantha. We're naming her Samantha."

Using her sleeve, Sam wiped away a tear as they descended the gangway ramp into the media frenzy inside the passenger terminal.

Two young couples approached Sam.

"Ma'am, we can't find our friends."

"Your friends?" she puzzled while at the same time thinking, *Ma'am, my ass!* She hated to be called Ma'am.

"Yes, they were married onboard the cruise ship a couple of days ago and we don't know where they are."

Sam recollected seeing the newlywed twenties-something couple shortly after the rescue. They were the ones looking for a private room who couldn't keep their hands off each other.

"Are you sure they haven't already disembarked?"

"No, we just can't find them anywhere onboard and they left their backpacks, passports, and wallets with us."

"They're probably already inside the terminal. Why don't you go check? If I see them, I'll tell them you're inside. Okay?"

"Yes, Ma'am."

Sam cringed again at the Ma'am word as she watched the two couples step onto the gangway and melt into the line of debarking passengers headed into the terminal.

From Virgo's bridge wing, Bakke and Deeds watched two well dressed men in dark suits cross the gangway from the terminal and approach Sam as she supervised the debarking frenzy. Sam's voice suddenly crackled over the hand held radio.

"Captain, I just spoke with a Secret Service agent. He said the president is expected inside the terminal within the next ten minutes and he, the governor, and the mayor want to personally thank you and present you and the crew with the key to the city. They would like you to come inside within the next five minutes."

Bakke smiled at the news cameras aimed at him from the terminal, "I love New York," he offhandedly commented as he turned towards Deeds. "I hear that it is a lot safer now, thanks to the mayor."

"Yeah...could be."

Bakke raised his radio. "Chief Mate?"

"Yes, Captain."

"You can handle my ship pierside, right?"

"Pierside? Oh, yes, sir, I can handle her pierside. Thank you, sir," she sarcastically replied.

Deeds casually checked his watch noting its stopwatch feature countdown.

"Chief Mate, you have my ship," Bakke declared. "Take care of her until I return. If you need me, call me on the radio."

"Yes, sir. I'm on my way to the bridge."

"Mind if I tag along with you, Captain?" Deeds asked Bakke.

"Of course not, after all, you are this ship's Chief Engineer. Without you this rescue would not have been possible. In fact, let's get all the crew over to the terminal. The ship isn't going anywhere in the next hour or two and I'm sure our Chief Mate can mind the store pierside without us."

After directing all the crew not assisting Sam in the debarkation process to leave the ship and go into the terminal, Bakke and Deeds left the bridge and headed for the gangway.

In Virgo's auxiliary pump room, Boucher came to his senses but didn't yet realize what had occurred. He sat on the deck not yet ready to try standing. His head hurt and his vision was blurry. He touched his fingers to the back of his head and felt the wet blood that had coagulated over the wound. Then his memory slowly returned. It was Deeds.

"That's three, you son-of-a-bitch," he mumbled aloud.

The bridge phone rang.

Sam answered it on the third ring, "Chief Mate...yeah, it's Sam...Jake? You don't sound so good."

She listened as Boucher told her what happened.

"You're shitting me, right?" She listened again. "No way. Okay, don't go anywhere. I'll be right there and let you out."

Sam rushed off the bridge to the room where Boucher was being held captive and unlocked the door. As she flung open the door, she saw Boucher slump backwards against the bulkhead and slide down to a sitting position on the deck.

"Ouch! How do you keep getting yourself into situations like this?" she mumbled in astonishment. "You look like hammered shit, Jake."

Boucher forced a weak smile, "That good, huh? We need to go to Deeds' stateroom."

"He's not onboard. He's with the Captain inside the cruise ship terminal."

"That doesn't matter. Give me a hand."

Sam helped Boucher to his feet and steadied him.

"You sure you're okay?"

Boucher straightened up shaking off his dizziness.

"Yeah, I think so, let's go."

Sam stayed by his side helping to keep him headed down the passageway as his strength slowly returned. Minutes later they arrived. Sam unlocked Deeds' stateroom door with a swift twist of the key and they entered. The lights inside were on. They quickly searched the room.

Sam located a navigation chart hidden beneath the mattress and bed fame.

"Jake, here."

She unfolded it and spread it across a small tabletop. It had two converging courses marked in pencil with time hacks, one labeled Empress, the other Virgo.

"Jake, take a look at this."

Sam continued to study the chart in amazement.

"Jake, the rescue was no accident."

Boucher seemed bewildered as he pieced the preceding day's events together in his mind. "Nope, it sure doesn't look like it was. The whole damn thing was planned."

Sam tapped on the chart and ran her index finger along Virgo's time line. "Jake, check out this timetable. We're still right on track."

The door abruptly opened and Milan stepped inside, startling Sam and Boucher. Boucher saw Milan's eyes flash down at the chart followed by a look of total shock. He had been compromised.

"Who the hell are you?" Boucher challenged.

Milan bolted from the room and headed down the passageway. Boucher was in hot pursuit and Sam a few yards behind him.

At the stairs leading up to the main deck, Boucher tackled him but was only able to hang onto Milan's one pant leg. Milan kicked Boucher with his other foot managing to break his grip. He raced up the stairs three steps at a time. Boucher was fast behind.

Milan burst outside onto the main deck. Darting toward the bow, he threw any objects he could grab back in Boucher's path. Closing the distance between them, Boucher dodged paint cans, buckets and tools as the objects clanked off the steel bulkheads and deck.

They finally cornered Milan between the life rail and the bulkhead near the ship's bow. Milan held a piece of pipe in his hands like a baseball bat at the ready. Boucher stopped short, remaining just outside the range of his swing.

Boucher saw Milan glance at him with a sly smile. Sweat was running down his face and he was panting breathlessly. It was the kind of reckless look that a crazed rapist gives his victim just before the act and it raised the hackles on the back of his neck.

Suddenly, he threw the pipe at Boucher and vaulted feet first over the ship's safety rail into the Hudson River thirty-five feet below. Boucher followed him over the side without hesitation. Both men frantically swam downriver toward Pier 87 where Milan disappeared into the darkness beneath the pier. In the shadowy darkness they played cat and mouse around the pier pilings.

"Give it up!" Boucher shouted.

"We will never give up! You Americans can't stop us."

"Stop who?"

"Without oil and drugs America is finished! You can't live without them!"

"What was that chart in Deeds' cabin all about?"

Milan laughed out loud as he answered, "As you call it in your football; a Hail Mary."

"Hail Mary?"

"A plan that had only one chance in hell to work. Believe me, everything that could go wrong, did, and we still got two thousand people off one ship and onboard another."

"You planned that?"

"You thought it was an act of God? That was just the end of the first half. We counted on America's predictability and your overwhelming need to save the world. You want to save everybody and everything; whales, trees, spotted owls. We knew you couldn't resist saving two thousand people. And now you'll get what you deserve!"

"Get what? What do you mean?"

"You and I know that that tanker should never be in this harbor. Fortunately for my side, somebody changed the Port Captain's mind."

"What about the tanker?"

"That tanker is pay back, it's one big Molotov designed especially for New York and there's nothing you can do to stop it!"

Milan laughed wildly, then there was silence. He quietly breast stroked behind another piling luring Boucher further under the pier.

Governor's motorcade - 42nd street, the same time

Governor Giordano and his press secretary sat in the back seat of their limo as their driver followed the siren-blaring police escort weaving through New York City's congested 42nd Street traffic.

"We'll be at the cruise terminal in about another ten minutes, Governor," his press secretary reported checking his watch. "Press coverage like this you can't buy no matter how many fund-raisers you attend. You need to give one of your famous patriotic speeches here."

"Fine. You got ten minutes to write one and I'll give it."

The press secretary dialed his cell phone.

"I'll have Ferguson come up with some talking points for you before we arrive. It doesn't have to be a long speech, just something appropriate and heartfelt. You know the deal."

"Okay, I just don't want to be upstaged by the Mayor. It's bad enough that he got to the terminal ahead of me. That Republican son-of-a-bitch will milk this with the media for months."

"Don't worry, Governor, I have the media under control. They'll hold him off presenting the tanker's Captain the key to the city until we get there so you can both be in the headline."

"The son-of-a-bitch better wait or I'll cut his nuts off."

"Maybe we can get some exclusive shots of you without him when you're reunited with your wife and kids. We'll get both of the ships' captains in the shot with you and your family. It will make a powerful headline."

"Yeah, make sure that's the way it works."

"No problem, Governor."

Giordano sat back watching people on the crowded sidewalk. Most of them didn't even turn to look at the police escorted limo.

"You know," Giordano said wistfully, "we need to come up with some gimmick like a 'key to the state' or something that trumps the Mayor."

Beneath Pier 87

Boucher lost Milan in the shadows. He stopped and listened but except for the gentle lapping sound of the water against the pilings it was otherwise quiet. He slowly breast stroked from one piling to the next pushing floating plastic bottles, cans and other trash from his path. As a former SEAL he had swum beneath numerous piers just like this one as a means to get close to a ship target unobserved. Trash always accumulated beneath piers trapped amongst the many pilings that held the pier. Even a pier in the fast flowing Hudson River had its share of trash.

As he advanced, he cautiously stopped by each piling keeping only his nose and eyes above the waterline while listening for any signs of Milan's movement. He heard nothing except the sound of his own slow breathing. Then, several pilings ahead, he heard a metallic creaking sound.

Behind a rotted piling, Milan slowly pried loose a foot long rusted bolt. He grabbed onto a hanging piece of steel reinforcing rod and stood on another piling bolt, extending from the piling beneath the water. He gradually eased himself upward, little by little, until he was waist high out of the water. Pressing his body against the piling, he held the bolt high and waited for Boucher in ambush.

As Boucher crossed by Milan's piling, he sprang down from behind, whacking Boucher with a glancing blow along his left shoulder. Boucher went under and didn't resurface. Milan frantically swam downriver toward the next pier where the submarine, USS Growler, and the famed World War II aircraft carrier, USS Intrepid, were moored on opposite sides of the pier as floating museums.

Boucher surfaced moments later bleeding from a gash on the top of his shoulder. "Son of a ...." he cursed to himself as he pursued Milan.

Milan now had a significant lead over Boucher and swam around the submarine Growler, beneath the pier to the Intrepid on the opposite side. Painters stood on scaffolds mounted on two floating rafts, painting the Intrepid's hull. A small flat-bottom Jon boat was tied to each raft. Milan climbed from the water onto a raft and jumped into one of the Jon boats. He threw off its mooring line, started the outboard and zoomed away, heading out into the Hudson River at full throttle.

Boucher painfully pulled himself up onto the raft by the second boat. Taking a wobbly run he jumped into the boat, landing with a thud on the far side. He barely caught himself from being thrown overboard as it tipped over from his weight. Blood flowed from his shoulder wound streaming down his arm. Exhausted, he glanced up at the surprised painters as he threw off the boat's mooring line and started its outboard motor.

"Sorry," he yelled to them before throttling up to pursue Milan out into the river. "I need to borrow your boat."

Now stranded on their raft scaffolds, the stunned painters shouted four-letter insults. Boucher continued the pursuit un-phased.

Chapter 28

Pier 88 - Passenger terminal

Governor Giordano's motorcade arrived at the passenger terminal. Surrounded by a flurry of reporters and police, Giordano was escorted inside the passenger terminal. There, he lovingly reunited with his wife and daughter. The scene he created was no less than heart touching and he made sure the news media captured every second of it. After the reporters had taken numerous pictures he turned away and shook hands with the mayor of New York City for an additional photo opportunity. Following that pose, he approached a podium, shaking hands with numerous well-wishing constituents along the way.

A few piers downriver, the Circle Line water taxi routinely departed the pier and headed out into the Hudson River channel on the way upriver to its next stop at Midtown 44th Street. Milan recklessly cut directly across the water taxi's bow barely avoiding a collision. The water taxi captain blasted the boat's horn in a belated warning as Milan zoomed back toward the piers. Boucher cut so close behind the water taxi's stern, his boat blasted chilly water on the surprised tourists who were standing on the taxi's open after deck admiring the Manhattan skyline. To no avail, the water taxi's captain again blasted his horn in warning this time stepping outside to shake his fist at Boucher's speeding boat.

Boucher cut the distance between the two boats by steering a straight line intersecting course ahead of Milan and began to overtake him. Milan turned sharply away from Boucher and aimed his boat directly at Pier 86. Boucher turned and followed.

Boucher saw Milan zoom under the pier, skillfully steering his boat between the support pilings beneath the pier. He followed him under the pier on a parallel course. Neck and neck, separated only by a single row of pilings, Boucher slowed and maneuvered through the pilings which put him only two boat lengths directly behind his foe.

They both frantically dodged cross beams and low-hanging debris as they raced toward a large, sunlit exit on the opposing side of the pier. Boucher's boat struck some floating log debris trapped beneath the pier nearly knocking him out of the boat. While he maneuvered around the debris, Milan's lead opened to eight boat lengths.

Boucher saw Milan turn to glance back at him. Just as he turned back to the front he was impaled through the chest on a steel reinforcing rod protruding down from the pier ceiling above. His unmanned boat aimlessly continued out into the Hudson.

Boucher slowed his boat to an idle and stared into Milan's lifeless eyes.

"You son-of-a-bitch." he growled as if Milan could still hear him. "Enjoy your 72 virgins."

Exiting from beneath the pier, Boucher sped out into the river. As he passed around Intrepid's stern, Virgo's Number 4 storage globe came into view with New York City's skyline in the background and he suddenly connected the dots. *Nah, they wouldn't,* he thought. *Hell yes, they would!*

Boucher zoomed back to Virgo's stern, grabbed onto the pad eyes welded to the hull and quickly climbed them up to the main deck. He looked up at the bridge wing and saw Sam standing there watching the gala inside the cruise ship terminal unaware he had boarded.

"Sam! Hey Sam!" he yelled up to her catching her attention. "Meet me below at Storage Tank Number 4 void hatch! Hurry!"

She gave him a thumbs-up and disappeared from the bridge wing. Boucher ran to his stateroom, hurriedly grabbed his face mask, swim fins and an underwater flashlight from his gear bag and raced to the Number 4 void hatch.

Arriving at the hatch before Sam, he decided to open it without her. The void was fully flooded and menacing. He spit in his mask, rubbed the spit around the glass lens and slipped it on. He switched on his flashlight, eased into the chilly dark water, took a deep breath and submerged into the void. His light revealed large circular partitioning baffles with man-size access holes running through them. Their shadows appeared like giant open-mouthed sea monsters waiting in line to gobble him up. He glided, through the access holes retracing the route he used days earlier when he and Sam discovered the fractures in the storage globe. He illuminated the fractured area with his flashlight beam. Like an aerator in a fish tank, small bubbles of boiling gas rose from numerous spider-like fractures beneath the steel globe.

Boucher swam through the next baffle keeping his flashlight beamed at the base of the storage globe. His eyes suddenly filled his face mask as his flashlight beam danced across a series of demolition charges connected by a sophisticated firing harness. He followed the wires with his beam when a red flash caught his eye. It was a detonator control box linked to the firing circuit. A digital clock was counting down from 63 minutes. The LNG storage tank was set to explode.

As he turned to swim back to the access hatch, he bumped face first into the wide-eyed, naked, drowned bride and groom. Their dead arms seemed to grab at him like they were trying to hold on.

Sam was nervously waiting at the hatch above the void in the dimly lit room. She occasionally saw a shaft of light beam by and strained into the watery darkness below, attempting to see movement of human form. Boucher suddenly popped up though the open hatch like a circus seal leaping from his pool for a fish treat, nearly hitting her. Sam jumped backward sprawling on her bottom.

"Damn it, Jake! You just scared the hell out of me! You look like you've seen a ghost! What's wrong now?"

He ripped off his mask, "I did! There's two of'm down there. She's rigged to blow!"

"Blow? Blow what?"

"Blow up! Explode! The tank is rigged to detonate! Come on, I gotta get you off this ship now. I'll take it out to sea!"

"Wrong! I'm the Chief Mate and this is my ship. We'll take her out to sea."

Boucher ran for the bridge, dripping a trail of water. Sam followed on his heels trying to get some answers.

"Are you sure there's a bomb down there?"

"If I wasn't sure, I'd be walking right now."

"Can't the bomb squad disarm it? I'll pump the water out of the void and call the New York bomb squad."

"No, Sam. I would have disarmed it myself but there's no time. It's got a clock timer and something that looked exactly like a hydrostatic switch connected to the firing circuit. If we drain the void, it's over."

"Why can't you just cut the red wire like they do in all the movies?"

"It has a very sophisticated firing circuit, Sam. Something like that has traps built into it so when you cut the red wire or any other one for that matter, the circuit collapses and it goes off. I would need to X-ray it and then do a complete assessment of the firing circuit before attempting a disablement procedure. Even then, the odds of success are not in our favor." He checked his watch. "There's no time. We gotta get this ship out to sea."

They continued their race toward the bridge.

"The president is on his way to the gala in the terminal," Sam yelled. "We need to stop him."

"Oh shit, President Banner?"

"Yeah! I'll drive," Sam directed, "you cut the mooring lines."

"What about the crew?"

Most of them are ashore with the Captain. We don't need'm anyway, the ship is automated. I can operate everything remotely from the bridge control console."

"I'll cut the lines." Boucher yanked a fire ax off a bulkhead damage control station and raced out onto the main deck.

Sam arrived on the bridge and sped outside onto the bridge wing. From there she could see through the terminal windows a short distance away and spied Bakke inundated by the news cameras, shaking hands with the mayor and governor.

She opened the ship's intercom and cranked up the volume, "Emergency, emergency, this is an emergency. All remaining passengers and crew please disembark the ship immediately!"

She watched several remaining passengers move slowly toward the gangway exit.

"I repeat, this is the Chief Mate," she now demanded, "all passengers and crew, disembark immediately. This is an emergency!"

Passengers continued to move slowly down the gangway.

"Get the hell off this ship now!" she yelled. "We have a bomb on board and it's set to blow up! This is an emergency!"

Bakke observed Boucher running along the main deck chopping the mooring lines off with the fire ax. He wielded the ax screaming like a lunatic at crew members and passengers and only stopped at the mooring lines long enough to sever them.

People panicked to get down the gangway. Some fell but were able to get back up and make it into the terminal.

Terrified passengers were screaming, "Let me off!" "A bomb!" "Hurry!" "Move it!" "There's a bomb!" as they stampeded into the terminal.

Bakke radioed Sam, "I leave you in charge and all hell breaks loose. What the hell is going on over there?"

"We have a bomb onboard, Captain, the entire ship is rigged to blow and there's no time to disable it! I'm getting underway and heading seaward. Tell the Secret Service to get the president as far away from here as they can as fast as they can."

Bakke and Deeds looked at each other. People were now being trampled as they ran through the terminal.

As Boucher cut the last line and it splashed down into the water, Sam blasted Virgo's throaty horn six long blasts. Virgo began to slowly inch away from the pier. At the helm, Sam worked the main engine throttle and maneuvering thruster. Boucher arrived on the bridge still carrying the ax.

"Jake, get on the emergency channel and tell the Coast Guard what's going on."

Boucher set the ax against the chart table and picked up the radio mic.

"Emergency, emergency, this is the LNG tanker Virgo, we have a bomb onboard. Repeat, we have a bomb onboard. We're underway at Pier 88. We're heading as far seaward as we can get before she blows. Remain clear. Repeat, this is an emergency, remain clear."

Old Executive Office Building, Washington, DC

Sitting at the head of the long walnut conference table in Room 203, Dunkle impatiently patted her hand on the table for all the attendees to see. DHS Under Secretary, Denise Dunkle was shunned by most of the other members of the inter-agency's counter-terrorism emergency operations community. She characteristically demonstrated a know-it-all elitist mentality which, when coupled with her short stature and disproportionately over-sized breasts, it was no wonder that her colleagues secretly called her "Double Ds."

"Let's get started," Dunkle declared in a loud voice. "H-e-l-l-o people," she shrilly blurted, "I said, let's get started."

The various conversations taking place around the table gradually quieted and everyone's attention turned to her.

"As you know, we have just gone to Threat Condition RED. About ten minutes ago, the Coast Guard notified DHS that the LNG supertanker Virgo has reportedly been rigged to detonate. They are attempting to move the ship down the Hudson River and out to sea as I speak. The Secret Service advises the president is in no danger. He has been taken to a New York City Police Department deep shelter for protection and will remain there until the threat is mitigated. As a matter of contingency, the vice-president is on his way to Andrews Air Force Base where he will board Air Force Two." Dunkle paused; throwing her head back as if to say, '*dig me.*' "So," she continued, chin in air, "the purpose of this emergency meeting is to come up with a recommendation for the president as to how the Administration should handle the potential detonation of a liquefied natural gas super tanker in New York Harbor. Jim, what does the intelligence community know about this situation?"

Jim Carmichael was a veteran CIA briefer and well-seasoned intelligence professional. He was particularly suited to issues involving the Taliban and al Qaeda because he was also an Army Reserve intelligence officer who had served two active duty tours in Iraq and recently returned from a deployment to Afghanistan supporting a Special Operations Task Force with targeting intelligence. He knew his stuff and the other members of the Inter-agency's Deputies Committee knew he did as well.

Carmichael stood and walked to the front of the room. The recessed ceiling lights were dimmed and a slide with the words, Top Secret Special Category – River Stone, in large bold red letters appeared on the digital flat screen on the wall behind him.

"Ladies and gentlemen, this briefing is SPECAT, and must be kept within River Stone codeword channels. Two days ago we intercepted a disturbing al Qaeda communication posted in an Arabic language forum that suggested a terrorist attack against New York is imminent. They urged all 'true believers' to leave Manhattan and its surrounding area."

Dunkle interrupted Carmichael in a loud voice.

"So it's true that the CIA was able to analyze the intercepted communication and as much as two days ago you knew that this was going to happen and you didn't notify DHS?"

Carmichael knew what she was implying and at that point he also knew she hadn't called this meeting to do anything but cover her own ass and lay blame. Carmichael took a deep breath and locked eyes with Dunkle.

"As you well know, intercepts like this one are commonplace. As you also know, your agency, as well as those other agencies represented around this table see the same intelligence we do. DHS has its own intelligence fusion center and this intelligence was passed to that center at the same time the rest of us received it. Should you take a moment to review the analysis trail related to this particular threat you will no doubt also see that the inter-agency team that analyzed and evaluated this particular threat deemed it not credible. DHS intelligence analysts were full participants throughout the entire process. Therefore, Madam Under Secretary, I strongly suggest that you look within your own department before you make groundless and potentially hurtful allegations against your sister agencies. Now, shall I proceed with my briefing or would you prefer to do the talking?"

Dunkle rolled her chair closer to the table and leaned forward. Her eyes rolled back as her eyelids fluttered. She looked like she was going to fly into a rage.

"Mr. Carmichael, I am an Under Secretary in the Department of Homeland Security. You are an intelligence analyst. You and those like you exist to provide answers to your customers within the inter-agency. Therefore, you will treat my office with the respect it deserves. Is that clear?"

Carmichael glanced around the table at his longtime colleagues in the counterterrorism community with the hint of a relaxed smile.

"Madam Under Secretary, you didn't answer my question," he stated, turning his entire body toward her. "Would you like me to proceed?"

Dunkle leaned back in her chair and limply flapped her hands at Carmichael like she was pushing bad air his direction. "Proceed," she mumbled.

Carmichael straightened his stance and pushed out his chest. He cleared his throat and continued.

"As Under Secretary Dunkle correctly noted, we currently have a fully loaded LNG supertanker making its way down the Hudson River. Reportedly, the tanker has been rigged to detonate as a fuel-air explosive. As some of you may already know, a fuel-air explosion, if properly designed and employed, can produce the same blast effects of a nuclear detonation minus the radiation. Obviously, the detonation must be sequenced exactly right and for something as large as an LNG tanker, that will require near perfect timing and some serious luck. Nonetheless, even a partially successful detonation of the LNG that ship is carrying could devastate Manhattan and cause thousands of casualties that could likely approach the six figure mark."

"Jim," Under Secretary of Defense Thomas Arnold asked, "do you know who's driving that ship?"

"Again, all we know is what's been monitored on the radio. Apparently the ship is being operated by its Chief Mate. And, I know you'll recognize this name; Jake Boucher, the man who stopped the terrorist nukes on the Island of La Palma last year. Lucky for us, as best we can determine, Boucher was onboard the ship trying to complete some underwater repairs when all this went down."

"Jim, we understand that if this ship is detonated we're likely going to experience a blast yield equivalency of between ten to fifteen kilotons – about the same as the nuke we dropped on Hiroshima."

"I know that's the estimate but who knows, there are many critical variables involved in detonating fuel-air explosives. Mr. Boucher reported that disabling the thing was impossible so all we can do is hope to put as much distance between Manhattan and that ship as possible before it detonates."

"So, Jim," Dunkle said sarcastically, "if the intel is so sketchy what makes you think al Qaeda is behind it?"

"I never said the intelligence was sketchy, Madam Under Secretary. I said it was the type of intelligence we see on a daily basis and that we were unable to confirm the validity of the source."

She huffed and waved him on. Carmichael nodded politely and continued the briefing.

"Yesterday, the Israelis informed us that they had uncovered an al Qaeda plot to bomb Manhattan. The timeline was sketchy as was the method of attack but they deemed it credible nonetheless. We were able to confirm this through our own collection efforts. Of course in hindsight, we now have an LNG tanker in New York Harbor that's rigged to detonate. While that in itself is alarming, about two hours ago we were able to confirm there is a second plot involving at least one, maybe two nuclear weapons. We believe these weapons may be in transit to the United States or may already be here."

"Are there any tippers on the likely targets?" Dunkle asked.

"Everything we're seeing leads us to believe they will be used against Washington, DC, sometime within the next three months."

Dunkle pointed at DOE's Under Secretary for Nuclear Security, Ron Vallee.

"Ron, can your Nuclear Emergency Support Teams detect such weapons?"

Vallee rocked back in his brown leather executive chair and frowned.

"Are you asking me if NEST can detect radiological sources or nuclear weapons? Didn't I answer this same question for you about six months ago?"

"Well, Mr. Vallee, perhaps if wouldn't be too much trouble, you could enlighten us once again."

Vallee kept a cool head and answered, "There is a distinct difference between detecting a radiation signature and unquestionably locating a working nuclear weapon and then being able to do something about it. Like I said before, the best thing we have going for us is intelligence. If Jim's guys can get us a specific location within a city block or so, we're prepared to deploy anywhere and deal with it. But without specific intel, finding a shielded nuke hidden in a city is like finding the proverbial needle in a haystack. We have everything from radiation detection-equipped aircraft to pager-size detectors that the law enforcement-types carry with them every day of the week. We have the major border check points and the major airports covered. We have NEST teams ready to deploy 24/7 but we must be very prudent when deploying our NEST capabilities because they're limited."

Dunkle interrupted, "How about using your special radiation detection-equipped airplanes?"

"Ms. Dunkle, we don't have the slightest idea where the nukes are or even if they're already here in the U.S.," Vallee countered, "so why would we deploy our limited NEST assets to some location someone thinks might be a target and begin a random search? A move like that would serve little more than to provide the illusion of threat mitigation when in reality it would be a misuse of our critical assets and make them readily unavailable to apply elsewhere should we get solid intelligence which requires our immediate action."

"DHS has jurisdictional responsibility for doing whatever it takes to protect the homeland and under that authority you will follow my direction."

Arnold always took personal joy in seeing Dunkle get spun up. He knew she had a standing directive to her staff to gather information from their interagency counterparts so her boss, the Secretary of Homeland Security, could "scoop" the President's other Cabinet Secretaries in the President's morning briefings. The other Secretaries and Undersecretaries knew that and took full advantage of her insecurity and nebulous standing as a Cabinet-level Under Secretary whenever they could.

This meeting was no different. DHS was chairing it, but from a protocol perspective, Dunkle should have asked the FBI to co-chair the meeting. Now she was in trouble and instead of yielding, she exposed her obvious inexperience in government and the emergency operations community. Dunkle's performance was the stuff Washington bureaucrats love to encourage and thrive upon.

Vallee subtly nodded toward his longtime political friend Arnold who returned the nod. He then returned his attention to Dunkle.

"If you really do believe that, Ms. Dunkle, you're intellectually unqualified to hold the position you hold," Arnold softly replied. "If you don't really believe that and you're just saying it to be politically correct, you're morally unqualified to hold the position you hold. Either way, you're wrong."

Chapter 29

Virgo

Bakke and Deeds leapt to Virgo's deck just as the gangway they were crossing ripped away and crashed down into the water between the ship and the pier. On the bridge, Sam thrust the ship away from the pier and engaged the powerful main engine. Virgo slowly moved backward toward the river channel. Boucher stood at the helm, steering as Sam directed.

"Give me ten degrees right rudder."

"Ten degrees right rudder," he repeated turning the ships wheel half a turn to the right.

Bakke and the Deeds arrived on the bridge.

"Chief Mate, you take the helm. I'll take her to sea."

Deeds drew a pistol he had concealed in his belt beneath his coat and pointed it at Bakke's chest while flipping open his cell phone in the other hand.

"This ship doesn't move!"

He pressed a speed dial button calling a programmed phone number. Bakke still didn't fully grasp what was transpiring even though it was happening before his eyes.

"Deeds, are you insane? Put that gun down."

Deeds menacingly motioned the gun at Bakke and then toward the pier.

"Run her back in!" he demanded.

Everyone stood frozen at gun point. Testing Deeds' resolve, Boucher took a step toward him.

"Don't move. I'm not afraid to shoot you."

Bakke reversed engines. The ship rumbled and shook as it strained to reverse direction. The ship finally inched ahead and slowly began to gain noticeable momentum but it was now angled at the pier on a collision course.

Moments later the Virgo's port forward quarter ripped into the pier jolting the bridge. Media reporters and news reporters stampeded, avoiding broken glass and splintered wood as Virgo's bridge wing invaded the second floor of the passenger terminal building.

Lincoln Harbor Yacht Club, New Jersey

Rajakovics screeched his car to a halt in the marina's parking lot. He peered through the windshield and spotted Virgo backing slowly away from the passenger terminal pier. He read a text message on his cell phone. He slammed his hands angrily on the steering wheel and cursed in Russian, "Blyadstvo!"

Rajakovics jumped from his car and madly searched the nearby boat slips for a boat with keys. He didn't notice the black Taurus pull up or the two men who got out and cautiously headed his way. He spied a high speed boat with two people crouching in the open cockpit snorting lines of cocaine. He headed toward the boat with angry purpose in his pace. He arrived at the foot of the small wooden-planked pier loudly striding toward the boat slip several dozen yards down its narrow length. When the boater and his friend saw him coming they tried to hide. Rajakovics pulled his gun and held it down by his pocket, out of sight.

"Good stuff, huh?" he asked, allowing them to see his gun.

"Yeah, uh-huh, yeah," the terrified boater answered.

"Oh, you want some?" the boater's companion asked.

"Never touch the stuff."

Rajakovics impatiently glanced around ensuring he wasn't being observed then brandished his gun as he jumped into the cockpit with the two boaters.

"Get off! Get off the boat! Off-off, I said off!"

The boaters leapt overboard and frantically swam for the nearby shallows.

It was then that Rajakovics saw the two men at the foot of the pier heading his way. Both were dressed in casual attire and both were carrying small day packs over one shoulder. They were out of place. They didn't fit and they must have seen him force the two boaters out of their boat.

Rajakovics started the boat. As he threw off the boat's mooring lines the two men started to run towards him. He pulled his pistol and emptied a fourteen round magazine in their direction as he roared out of the marina into the Hudson.

He turned back to see them running towards a black car that was parked close to his.

Office of the Coordinator for Counterterrorism, U.S. Department of State, Washington, DC, same time

"Sir," Bruce blurted as he entered Blackburn's office waving a Top Secret message in his hand. "We just got a Top Secret Flash message from American Embassy Moscow. They report that there have been three simultaneous suicide bomber attacks in the Moscow subway. Moments later a large vehicle bomb was exploded in front of the Russian Foreign Intelligence Service headquarters building. They report scores of dead and injured. The Russians say the attacks were the result of Islamist fundamentalists probably coming from Chechnya and Dagestan. This is some really bad shit, Sir."

"Yeah, it is and it seems like everything keeps getting worse instead of better. What's your gut feeling on the trend we're seeing?"

"Remember that South Korean merchant ship that was sunk last weekend? The one in the Sea of Japan? Well, now we have solid evidence that a sub torpedoed it; probably was the North Koreans. The North Koreans were running naval exercises with the Russians north of the area but they say they were on their side of the line and deny firing on the South Korean ship or having anything to do with its demise."

"That's just fucking great. We got some Russian mercenary working with the fucking FARC and some renegade Venezuelan general all trying to smuggle a nuke into the U.S. We got the North Koreans allegedly blowing a South Korean merchant ship out of the water and now the Islamists allegedly attacked Moscow. It's just too coincidental."

"What do you mean by allegedly, Sir?"

"I mean, how can we be sure it wasn't someone else just making it look like North Korea shot that torpedo or the Chechen Islamists were the perpetrators? Think about it, Jimmy. Boucher and his guys foiled the nuke attack in the Canaries last year. Israel is poised to attack Iran's nuclear weapon development facilities and we both know what that will mean to the U.S. North Korea is going forward with its own nuke weapon program while our president kisses their ass and apologizes for our previous negative policy toward them. Greece is close to default and the Euro will go tits up if Germany doesn't bail them out. But Russia controls Germany's energy resources and would love to see the whole European Union default if the Euro fails. Germany and Russia have more in common than do Germany and the rest of the EU so it's more likely that Germany and Russia will crawl into bed together."

"No argument, Sir, but North..."

Blackburn cut him off and continued. "Don't you think it's a bit peculiar that North Korea decides to torpedo a South Korean warship knowing it will probably escalate into war between North and South and we'll be pulled into the conflict? Now all of a sudden, Chechen Islamists blow up a bunch of Moscow targets and kill a bunch of Russians. The Russian Premier is one of the hardest dicks on the planet and the Islamists prove he can't protect his own capital city. It's a distraction, Jimmy. I'll bet you a blow job North Korea didn't fire that torpedo and Chechen Islamists didn't conduct the attacks in Moscow."

"I have a hunch, Sir."

"Jimmy, the one thing I have learned about you is your hunches are usually right. Let's hear it," Blackburn said motioning toward the chair beside his desk.

Bruce sat down and took a moment to order his thoughts.

"As you know, we are not publicizing our preparations to attack Iran. And, as you also know, U.S.-Israeli relations are at an all-time low. The Israelis are building houses in Jerusalem and President Banner is telling them not to. Most Americans think the strong anti-American sentiment towards the U.S. in the Middle East is brought on by our support for Israel. I think, if you look at history that couldn't be further from the truth."

"Now, Jimmy," Blackburn interrupted, "get to the point."

Bruce held up his hand to calm Blackburn. "You see, Sir, the truth of the matter is that Arab anti-American sentiment predates our open support to Israel. Prior to 1967 we provided almost no aid to Israel and then, what little aid we provided was almost all agriculturally oriented. Before that, France was the major arms supplier to Israel and our foreign policy was generally aligned with Egypt. In fact, when Israel invaded the Sinai in 1956 and France and Briton seized the Suez Canal, President Eisenhower intervened on the side of Egypt against Israel and pressured our two most powerful allies at the time, France and Briton, along with Israel, to withdraw from Egyptian turf."

"Yeah, then Nasser thanked Ike by becoming a Soviet ally."

"That's only partially right, Sir. Eisenhower was unwilling to give military aid to Egypt, probably because he saw the potential threat to Israel if he did. The Soviets jumped on that power vacuum and pumped massive military and economic aid into Egypt. In the process, Egypt became a Soviet ally and turned anti-American, so you see, its change in attitude had virtually nothing to do with Israel."

"When did France break off its support for Israel?"

"France pulled its support in 1967 in protest of the Arab-Israeli conflict. France apparently decided they would rather kiss Arab ass than remain supportive of an independent Israel and the only democracy in the region."

Blackburn started to laugh, "Damn, Jimmy, well stated...I must be rubbing off on you."

Bruce smiled and continued.

"I got a bit ahead of myself, Sir. I forgot to mention two key political coups which occurred in 1963. That's when the Islamic fundamentalist Baathist Party came to power in both Iraq and Syria. Both those governments instantly became pro-Soviet and anti-American and that alignment had nothing to do with a U.S.-Israeli relationship because at the time there still wasn't one."

"But if my memory serves me, didn't we give Egypt Hawk anti-aircraft missiles in 1964 in response to the coups in Iraq and Syria?" Blackburn interrupted.

"Yes, and we gave them to several other Arab nations in the region as well, like Saudi Arabia. The thinking was the Soviets would base fighter aircraft in Syria and Iran giving them air superiority and control over Israel and the Middle East's oil fields. Then, like I said, in 1967 we bolstered Israel in the Arab-Israeli War. France said good bye, and the United States became Israel's main benefactor. Later, in 1973, when Syria and Egypt attacked Israel we ramped up our Israeli assistance to massive proportions. So much so, U.S. aid accounted for around one quarter of the entire Israeli gross domestic product."

"Didn't Egypt join us around that time?"

"Yes, Sir. After the 1973 war, Egypt shifted to a pro-American alignment and we began aiding them. Jordan made peace with Israel and we joined with the Shah of Iran, the Government of Iraq, and the King of Saudi Arabia. We controlled the region and the vast oil fields they contained. Except for Syria and Afghanistan, the Russians lost their foothold in the region.

"Since Biblical times, the Arabs have always hated the Jews and have persecuted them. They refuse to acknowledge that Israel is a sovereign nation and has a right to exist. The Islamists take it much further. Today, we should refer to that conflict as an Islamist-Israeli conflict rather than an Arab-Israeli conflict. The Islamists hate us all, not just the Israelis, because we don't believe what they believe. They see Christians and Jews as a sub-human race much like they see animals. They don't want our land or our country, they just want us dead."

"Okay, Jimmy, that's a nice history lesson. When are you going to explain your hunch about who's behind the current clusterfuck over there?"

Bruce stood, again ordering his thoughts and slowly paced in front of Blackburn's desk.

"It's gotta be the Israelis, Sir."

"The Israelis?" Blackburn bellowed in complete surprise. "How so?"

"Let me answer you with some 'what ifs'. What if the Israelis have infiltrated the White House for the purpose of staying in front of us - to steer our foreign policy rather than waiting to see where it is taking them?"

"Steer U.S. foreign policy? There you go again, Jimmy, out into space. Are you sure you're not a Star Fleet Academy graduate instead of a Boat School graduate?"

Bruce laughed, "Yes, Sir, Boat School all the way, Sir. Here's my thinking. Surely Israel is every bit aware of the trump card Russia is holding with regard to keeping Germany under their thumb. Remember, Germany is the only EU country that can bail out the failing EU nations and keep the Euro from defaulting. We know the economic domino effect, if it happened, would result in a world economy default with the U.S. defaulting right behind the European Union. Russia controls Germany because they control Germany's energy resources. Therefore, they hold the trump card for the European Union. Russia is in the driver's seat right now and on a low risk path to emerge as the next superpower. What if the Israelis are trying to rein Russia in and keep that from happening? You know - by making sure Russia has a full plate of its own problems to keep them painfully occupied."

"You have my attention, Lieutenant."

Virgo, the same time

The ship jolted again as Virgo's bow rammed the quay wall at the foot of the pier. Deeds momentarily lost his balance and instinctively grabbed for the nearby chart table. Boucher was waiting for an opportunity and this was it. Before Deeds could recover his balance, Boucher kicked the gun from his hand. It hit the deck spinning under the chart table out of easy reach. Deeds retaliated with a swing that hit Boucher on his left cheek, knocking him backward momentarily, stunning him as his back hit the steel deck.

"Sam," Bakke yelled, "reverse engines! Back full!"

Deeds grabbed the fire ax and turned toward Sam holding it like a baseball bat ready to swing.

"You touch those throttles and you're dead."

Sam paused momentarily, staring into his eyes as she evaluated her options.

"Fuck you, Deeds," she growled and yanked the main engine throttle down into reverse.

Deeds swung the ax wildly. Sam jerked her hands clear, and the blade glanced off the top of the control panel. The entire ship shuddered as it changed direction towards the Hudson again. Boucher grabbed a metal stool by the chart table and held it out in front of him like a lion trainer in a circus ring. Deeds swung the ax again. It clanged against the stool seat with such force that it knocked the stool out of Boucher's hands and propelled him backward into the bulkhead.

Using the thrusters, Sam continued to maneuver the ship from the pier. Deeds swung again, this time at Bakke. Bakke stumbled backward, and the ax blade skimmed the buttons on his shirt, barely missing his flesh. Deeds threw down the ax and grabbed the pistol from the deck beneath the chart table. He pointed it at Boucher.

"Jake, look out!" Sam shrieked.

Boucher rolled away, groping for the stool, as Sam jumped Deeds from behind. Her long arms and legs snaked around his neck and torso and held fast. As Deeds thrashed to free himself, the gun fired. Bakke took a step back, staring dumbly at the spreading red stain in the center of his chest. Taking advantage of the moment, Deeds backed up, slamming Sam against the steel bulkhead with such force that it knocked the air out of her lungs. She fell, breathless, to the floor.

Frantically, Boucher cast about for a weapon as Deeds raised the gun to Sam's head.

"No. Not again," he yelled.

Boucher scooped up the ax and heaved it at Deeds. It spun toward him, and with a sickening thwack, embedded deeply beneath his left shoulder blade. His eyes bulged out. The gun discharged again, and Sam's body jerked with the impact of the bullet. She fell backward with a groan.

Deeds turned toward Boucher. Slowly, stiffly, like a zombie, Deeds approached with his gun pointed at Boucher's chest.

Boucher braced for the worst but kept his voice cool and resolute. "You better make your shot count because I'm gonna tear your head off and shit in your chest cavity if you don't."

Deeds hesitated and made an off balance grab for the chart table in an attempt to steady himself. Instead, he slowly collapsed, sprawling face down onto the deck. Boucher kicked the gun out of his hand and raced over to Sam. He lifted her gently, cradling her in his arms. Her eyes rolled back and she moaned. Memories of Sandra's death flooded through his mind.

He saw a blood soaked bullet hole in the left shoulder area of her shirt. Hurriedly, he ripped open the front of her shirt to check the severity of her wound. She began fighting him. With trembling fingers, he fumbled to open her bra.

"You okay, Sam?" he panted.

She grabbed a handful of his shirt.

"No, I'm not okay! I've never been shot before and it smarts like hell. Stop ripping my bra open!" she bellowed. "Here," she said pointing to her left shoulder.

Boucher pulled her shirt away from her shoulder so he could see the wound. Using his fore fingers, he gently probed the area around the wound and sighed in relief

"It's only a flesh wound," he assured. "You're not going to bleed to death."

"Easy for you to say. It's my flesh."

Boucher tore the sleeve off her shirt and used it like a compress over the wound. Even though it was relatively shallow it was bleeding like it was much worse.

"Here, press on this," he replied, placing her hand on top of it. "The bleeding will stop in a little bit. Give it a chance to clot."

Sam noticed Bakke move.

"Jake," she said pointing at Bakke.

He helped her over to him where she knelt down on her knees. His eyes slowly opened in a dull unfocused stare.

"Chief Mate?" he asked hoarsely.

"Yes, Captain."

He visibly relaxed and a glimpse of relief came over Bakke's weathered face as he apparently recognized her voice.

"You have my ship," he gasped, "take good care of her."

"I will, Captain."

"I know... I know...," he whispered comfortingly patting her hand.

A faint smile appeared on his face, he exhaled slowly and he died. Sam looked up and noticed Deeds painfully removing a small remote radio firing device from his jacket pocket. His eyes were glazed and his breathing shallow as he fumbled to get his finger on a small red button. Above the button was a small LED clock screen. Orange LED numbers were counting down from forty-eight minutes."

"Jake!" she shouted pointing at the device.

Boucher stomped on Deeds' hand and snatched the firing device away from him just before he could press the red detonation button.

"Not on my watch, you son-of-a-bitch!"

Deeds whispered, "You're a dead man, Boucher. Fey will finish you." He tried to laugh, but a choking wheeze cut it short."

"Wrong, you son-of-a-bitch. You're the dead man."

Boucher released his foot from Deed's wrist and stepped on his shoulder. As he pried the ax from Deeds' back, dark red blood pooled in the open wound. Deeds shuddered, groaned, and died with a final gurgling gasp. Boucher looked back at Sam.

"Can you still drive?" he asked.

She got to her feet. "Damn right! I can still do a lot of things."

"Come on, then, we need to get this ship as far seaward as we can."

She hurried outside on the bridge wing and quickly assessed the ship's relative position to the pier.

"All back one third! Hard right rudder," she shouted to Boucher. "I'm going to thrust the bow away from the pier."

"Aye, Captain."

As Virgo turned toward the channel its bow smashed along the end of the opposing pier ripping several pilings from their muddy sockets forty feet below the water's surface. A bow-damaged Virgo headed down the Hudson River toward the sea.

Boucher picked up the radio mic and called on the emergency channel.

"Coast Guard, Coast Guard, this is the LNG tanker Virgo. Emergency! Emergency!

"Roger Virgo."

"I need an F.A.E. blast radius calculation. Over."

"Ahh... an F.A.E. blast radius calculation? Standby."

"What's F.A.E.?" Sam nervously asked.

"F.A.E. is short for Fuel-Air-Explosive."

"Is that what he meant by, 'Fey will finish you'?"

"Yeah," Boucher replied pointing to the remote detonator he took from Deeds. "According to this, we have forty-six minutes to live. It's how Number 4 storage globe is configured to explode. Each charge is strategically placed beneath the globe so when they're fired simultaneously, they will burst the storage globe and project the liquefied natural gas upward. That's why he flooded it. The water will provide a tamping effect and help project the blast upward."

"Upward?"

"Yeah, it works something like this. The initial blast will burst the globe and form a cloud of atomized liquefied natural gas above and around the ship. The atomized gas then mixes with the oxygen in the air and the enriched fuel-air cloud engulfs the ship. Then a detonating charge goes off inside the cloud and the cloud detonates taking the other globes with it. You basically get the same relative blast damage of a nuke without the radiation."

"My God!" Sam gasped.

Old Executive Office Building, Washington, DC, the same time

Cline's executive assistant keyed the office intercom to his desk.

"General Cline, Captain Blackburn, State SC/T, is holding for you on secure line one, sir."

With an overall commanding appearance, he looked like a general from head to toe. Cline snatched the phone off its hook and pressed the secure button. He watched as the phone's LCD window displayed TOP SECRET, Dept. of State – SC/T.

"Dean, how are you doing?" he warmly asked, his voice resonating in a deep baritone.

Blackburn and Cline had served together on the Joint Staff shortly after Cline was promoted to general and put on his first star. Blackburn always liked Cline's no beating-around-the-bush direct manner and forthrightness. He was himself that way and liked others who practiced the same manner.

"Hello General, can we talk freely?"

"Of course."

"Thank you. I'm sure you're aware of what's presently playing out in New York City."

"Yes."

"Our analysis leads us to believe there is another attack headed our way. It is an attack that may have the gravest consequences should it succeed."

"What 'sources' are you referring to, Dean?"

"The sources are unimportant. The intelligence they provide is critical. Suffice it to say we regularly share intelligence with our friends."

"Friends that chase bad guys on boats in the Hudson River and maybe drive LNG tankers?"

Blackburn smiled, "It would appear they might occasionally participate in such evolutions especially if they shared mutual concerns over Iran's nuclear weapon development. And there could be third party involvement trying to help us stay out of trouble in the process."

Cline sat unemotionally and didn't immediately answer, then simply said, "Go on."

"You know, General, it would make a lot of sense to learn there is Israeli involvement. They have the most to lose in all of this and President Banner has disrespected them ever since he took office. You gotta ask yourself what the president is thinking when he puts more importance on Jews building houses in East Jerusalem, their capitol, than he does Islamists building nuclear weapons in Iran."

Cline smiled ever so slightly, "The Israelis?" he asked, "How so?"

"Yes, sir, the Israelis. We believe they have been in on this from the get-go."

"Dean, your powers of deduction are impressive, but remember," Cline warned, "I have not confirmed or denied your assumptions. Now back to your original statement. You say you believe there is another major attack on the way here in addition to this LNG tanker problem?"

"Yes, sir, it's a follow-on to the Canary Island attack last year – the one Jake Boucher stopped. But this time, instead of using nuclear bombs to generate a man-made tsunami like they intended by blasting the Cumbre Vieja Volcano's caldron into the sea, their plan is to outright nuke one or more of our major cities. We additionally believe they have already successfully delivered at least one nuke to our shores. The LNG ship attack may only be a diversion or maybe a precursor for several major follow-on attacks."

Cline showed no surprise as he sat there with the phone pressed to his ear.

"General, I am convinced that the reason we have been successful in stopping these attacks is because Boucher works outside of any government agency. It is no secret that inside the system our operations are often conflicted and, as a consequence, our response is slow and often misdirected. More troubling, it appears that we have a breach of security inside our own system."

Cline pushed up in his chair. "You mean a mole?"

"Yes, perhaps, and at the highest levels."

Cline leaned forward on his desk top, "What do you mean by, 'highest levels'?"

"I mean the president's closest senior staff," Blackburn said in a low voice.

"Do you know who?"

"Only a hunch."

"Who?"

"I think it's the president's Chief of Staff. I think it's Holiday."

Cline rubbed his chin between his thumb and fingers, "But who's he talking to?"

"He's talking to the Israelis and they're playing us like puppets."

"You're saying Holiday is a spy?"

"I'm suggesting that he is providing the Israelis intelligence so that they can stay ahead of us."

"What do you mean by, 'ahead of us'?"

"General, I think the Israelis have been covertly influencing world events and as such, influencing a strategy to prevent our political-military failure and shore up President Banner's lacking foreign policy. They have masterfully accomplished this by manipulating events to the point where we can only go one direction."

"And you think Holiday is feeding them critical policy information to make this possible?"

"Yes, sir, I do."

"And his motivation is?"

"He's a Jew, sir. In fact, he's an out-of-the-box Israeli flag-waving, open supporter. I bet if we were to surveil him, check out his bank accounts and phone records we'd find complicity."

"Dean, I've known you over twenty-five years. This is the first time you've ever sounded like a kook. Look, I gotta run."

Cline hung up and sat back in his chair. He scribbled Holiday on his notepad and grunted. Leaning forward he pressed the intercom button.

"Ms. Maguire, please get Mr. Holiday on the phone for me - secure."

Chapter 30

New York - New Jersey Port Authority Headquarters

The phone rang on Joe Jebeili's desk. He took a quick bite of his chocolate chip cookie and a sip of his Irish Cream latté before answering the phone on its fourth ring.

"Port Authority Engineering, Jebeili."

"Sir. This is Petty Officer Visbal from the U.S. Coast Guard. I have a request for an F.A.E. blast radius calculation.

"F.A.E.? A fuel air explosive blast calc?" he asked.

"Yes, Sir."

"Alright, I'll take it."

"Please hold, I'll patch you through. Virgo can you hear me?"

"This is Virgo, go ahead."

"Roger, Virgo, this is Coast Guard. I have patched Joe Jebeili from the New York Port Authority on channel 16. Go ahead, Virgo."

"Jake Boucher here, onboard the LNG tanker, Virgo."

"Hello. Joe Jebeili here at the New York - New Jersey Port Authority. What can I do for you?"

"Roger, Port Authority. We've got a supertanker with four storage globes, each filled with one hundred twenty-five thousand cubic meters of liquefied natural gas. One of the globes has been rigged as an F.A.E. and we only have about forty-three minutes to go before detonation."

"Forty-three minutes? You better leave now if you want to live."

"Yeah, I got that, Port Authority. That's why I need a blast radius calculation, now."

"Virgo, what is your location?"

"On the Hudson River heading seaward from Pier 88, the cruise ship terminal. We're at about 14th street."

"Geez! You're joking...right? Standby!" Jebeili leapt up from his desk to look out his office window. "Oh my God! Do you realize what's going to happen Virgo? Manhattan is screwed! You said four globes with one hundred twenty-five thousand cubic meters of liquefied natural gas each."

"That's affirmative."

"Standby a moment, I'll run the calculation."

Jebeili clicked his computer mouse on a screen icon and began to enter data. A GIS map popped up on his screen. He confirmed the tanker's approximate position and clicked a marker on the map. Red circles appeared radiating outward from Virgo's Hudson River position covering most of Manhattan.

"No good news, Virgo. With a fuel-air event of this magnitude at your current location, I estimate three quarters of a million people will probably die. I can't give you an estimate on the injured but it will be an astronomical number that exceeds those killed outright. Almost everything from the Battery to Central Park will be leveled. By my calculations, you've got the equivalent of a twelve kiloton nuke there. Hiroshima had about the same pop. Look, there's no time to evacuate above ground structures or get the population into deep shelter. If anyone in New York is going to have a chance in hell to survive, you've got to get way the hell out, beyond the Verrazano Bridge."

"Roger, Port Authority. Copy all. Virgo, out."

"Virgo, Virgo, this is Coast Guard, over."

"Roger, Coast Guard, this is Virgo, over."

"Virgo, we're clearing the channel in your path. Say number of souls onboard? Over."

Boucher paused and smiled reassuringly at Sam.

"Only two, over."

"Godspeed, Virgo."

At that moment Sam's and Boucher's eyes met. They both looked down at Deeds' digital timer. Forty-one minutes flashed across the screen.

"Forty-one minutes, Sam, you think we can we make it out far enough?" Boucher asked.

Weighing the gravity of the situation, Sam grabbed the radio mic.

"Emergency, emergency! Repeat, emergency! This is the LNG tanker, Virgo. We're rigged to explode. We're outbound mid-Hudson channel increasing speed. Remain clear. I say again, remain clear."

Boucher got a quizzical look over his face. "Sam, do you have a cell phone?"

"Yeah, it's on the charger in my stateroom."

"Who are you going to call?"

"An old friend. Give me your room key, I'll be right back."

"Wait, Captain Bakke usually carried his cell phone once we were in range. Check his pockets."

Boucher went through Bakke's clothes and found his cell in a shirt pocket. He quickly keyed in a familiar number and pushed the speaker button.

"Hello," a man's voice crackled after several rings.

Boucher recognized the voice of his longtime friend and mentor, Doctor Simon Barnhart. Barnhart was a retired Los Alamos nuclear physicist and nuclear weapon designer. Many years earlier, he had mentored Boucher when they were both members of the famed Nuclear Emergency Support Team. The previous year he and Boucher saved Amman, Jordan from nuclear destruction and stopped a series of terrorist nuclear bombs from detonating in the Canary Island of La Palma. Had those bombs gone off as the terrorists intended, it would have resulted in a manmade tsunami of Biblical proportions - a tsunami that would have devastated the entire east coast of the United States from Maine to Florida with a series of giant waves that would have ranged from ninety to twelve hundred feet high. Millions would have died, and the ensuing infrastructure devastation is incalculable.

"Si, this is Jake."

"Jake, I can't wait to show you the bells I've been making. I have them hanging in the trees in my back yard. You can hear them from the ski resort. Hey, how are.."

Boucher cut him off.

"Si, what do you know about the physics of fuel air explosives - you know, FAE?"

"A little, what do you need?"

"I don't have time to explain but I'm underway onboard an LNG tanker which has been rigged to go FAE. Disabling the burster charge is out of the question. How can I minimize the FAE detonation?"

"You said you're underway, right?"

"Yes, heading seaward in the Hudson River."

"Just go as fast as you can."

"What do you mean?"

"The burster charge will atomize the LNG which will form a cloud above the ship. There is a momentary delay as the cloud forms and mixes with the air and the detonation of the cloud. This delay is necessary to allow the fuel cloud to properly form and combine with the oxygen in the air. It must have adequate oxygen enrichment or it won't detonate at its full potential. The projection and positioning of the detonator charges within the cloud is also critical in getting a full blast yield. The detonator charges are obviously located somewhere above the ship's deck, perhaps on a mast or other high place, and there will be more than one. If you can move the ship under the cloud so the detonator charges are not properly placed within the cloud or so that some of them miss the cloud all together, you will significantly reduce the blast yield. So get your speed up as high as you can and keep it there prior to detonation."

"Got it, Si. Turn on Fox News and wish me luck. Out here," he said snapping closed the cell phone's lid.

Without saying anything, Sam advanced the ship's throttle to AHEAD FULL.

The Statue of Liberty loomed ahead. The Coast Guard was in the process of escorting a large container ship out of Virgo's path. Sam recognized they were on a collision heading.

"Son of a B...," she whispered to herself.

"Jake, give me five degrees right rudder. I'll pass astern of that container ship."

"Five right," he reported as he turned the ship's wheel and watched the gyrocompass gradually swing to a revised heading five degrees more to the right.

The ship's bow slowly came to a new heading taking it dangerously close to Liberty Island where the statue stood. Sam studied the green copper sheathed lady holding the torch of liberty above her head. Prior to her assignment onboard Virgo she had been in and out of this harbor and passed the Statue of Liberty dozens of times, but this time she saw it differently. She studied the beauty and the majesty of the statue for the first time. But they were closer than they should be and the reality of their situation overtook her longing to explore the statue more closely. Then Boucher's voice seemed to yank her back.

"Get'n a little too close to the Green Lady, aren't we, Sam?"

"Okay, Jake, bring us back to our original heading," she ordered.

Boucher worked the rudder control but it didn't respond. After several tries, the rudder slowly responded to Boucher. His attempt to bring them back to the original course failed as the rudder motor went dead before he could complete the maneuver.

"Sam, we're screwed. The rudder's not responding anymore. The motor's got to be shot. I told Bakke that was gonna happen if he didn't let me fix the rudder."

"That's just great! Mercury must be in feaking retrograde again," she cussed. "Listen, Jake, there's only one way. I need you to go to aft steering. You'll have to rig the emergency tiller and steer from back there. I'll try to steer as best I can using the bow thruster until you're ready. Here...," Sam threw Boucher a portable radio and placed a second radio next to the intercom. Boucher paused to question. Sam realized she needed to explain further.

"I'll give you the rudder orders over the intercom. Keep the mic open."

Boucher raced below to the aft steering room.

Sam peered through the forward bridge windows. Virgo was still on a collision course with the container ship.

"It's going to be ugly," she muttered to herself.

She grabbed the radio mic.

"Coast Guard, Coast Guard, this is Virgo. I have a main steering casualty and have lost steering. Repeat, I have lost steering. I'm on a collision course with the container ship crossing my bow to port. At my current speed I cannot slow and stop in time, over."

"Virgo, Coast Guard, we're moving her out of your way as quickly as possible, over."

"Roger, Coast Guard, I'm trying to steer using my bow thrusters but no promises. Out here."

In the aft steering room Boucher saw the engine speed indicator's needle reverse from AHEAD FULL to BACK FULL. Sam's voice boomed over the intercom.

"You ready, Jake?"

"I just got here, Sam. Give me a few minutes, would ya?"

"We don't have a few minutes."

Boucher wrestled the heavy tiller from the bulkhead and attached it on the top of the rudderpost. He then grabbed a block and tackle and hooked one end to a bulkhead cleat and the other to the tiller.

""Jake, I need steering now. I'm going to kick the engines ahead and try to maneuver."

"Almost ready, I still need to hook the other block and tackle to the tiller."

"Hurry, Jake."

He finished rigging the emergency tiller and had both block and tackles hooked to each side of the tiller's long arm. He stood centered in front of the tiller holding the two bitter ends of the lines running to the block and tackles.

"Okay, got it, Sam, I'm ready to go. Now what?"

Sam's voice echoed throughout the ship.

"Give me ten degrees right rudder, now!"

Straining, he grappled with the ropes and pulleys as he pulled the heavy tiller over to the right. At the same time the engine indicator returned to BACK FULL.

"Ten right," he reported.

"For a man, you catch on real good, Jake. You might even be trainable."

The Virgo slowly changed course but it was still heading for the container ship's stern.

"Jake! Jake! Give me another five degrees right rudder! Hurry, five right!"

Boucher gave the tiller a Herculean pull and moved it further right.

"Five right," he responded in a strained exhale.

Sam's voice was excited, "Quick, five more right. You got that? Right, five more!"

"Women drivers," he mumbled.

"I heard that!" she scolded, her voice echoing throughout the ship.

Virgo's bow rapidly approached the container ship's stern. The container ship was slowly maneuvering to the left to get out of the main channel and Virgo's way. Small Coast Guard boats astern of the container ship accelerated to avoid the impending collision between the two massive ships. Sam knew exactly what was about to happen. She blasted Virgo's horn six short blasts, and repeated the collision warning again. The container ship blasted the same warning but there was nothing more either could do to avoid the inevitable. Both ships were so massive everything seemed to be happening in slow motion. The two ships closed to yards, then feet and finally inches.

Virgo's bow barely missed the container ship's stern by inches. The worst was over but Sam realized Virgo would scrape her side along the other ship's stern as they passed at right angles to one another.

"Jake, we're go'n to hit another ship! Hold on!" she warned.

Virgo's port side ground like giant fingernails on a chalk board along the container ship's stern. Boucher took a tumble as Virgo lurched from the impact. The collision ripped steel debris and hull plating away from the impacted areas of both ships. Two Coast Guard sailors dove over the side of their small boat to avoid being caught in the middle of the crushing collision.

Sam ducked as the container ship's stern ground along the hull beneath her bridge wing. Then, as quickly as it happened, the two ships cleared one another. The container ship continued on its path away from the channel and Virgo continued outbound toward the sea.

Recovering from his fall, Boucher grabbed his radio.

"Damn it, Skipper, do you normally wait to the last second to tell your crew important collision shit like that?"

"You said it yourself - women drivers. What else can I say?" the intercom boomed back. "We're clear now but we still have to get through the anchorage before we pass under the Verrazano Bridge. Bring the rudder amidships and standby. I'm bringing our speed back up."

Boucher saw the engine speed indicator advance to AHEAD FULL and could feel the massive propeller deep beneath him vibrating as it increased its RPMs.

Sam studied the New York Bay anchorage area that lay ahead. The Verrazano-Narrows Bridge loomed in the distance marking the seaward mouth of the bay. The Verrazano-Narrows Bridge was once the world's longest suspension bridge. Its towers rise 693 feet above the water and are one and five-eighth inches farther apart at their tops than at their bases because the 4,260 foot distance between them made it necessary to compensate for the earth's curvature. The ends of the bridge connect Fort Hamilton in Brooklyn and Fort Wadsworth in Staten Island. The bridge not only connects Brooklyn with Staten Island but it's also a major link in the interstate highway system, providing the shortest route between the middle-Atlantic states and Long Island. Sam shuddered at the thought of what might happen if the Virgo detonated beneath the bridge. She knew no matter what, she couldn't allow that to happen.

The channel seaward beneath the bridge passed through the bay anchorage and there were a number of large ships anchored there. Using binoculars, she made a quick count of the anchored vessels in her path. There were seven ships anchored on the south side of the channel, three of them were fully-loaded petroleum tankers, the other four were container ships. There were five ships, all cargo ships, anchored on the north side of the channel. She quickly checked the navigation chart and estimated their position with reference to the channel markers and the Virgo. In another mile, she would have to turn due east to remain in the channel. She knew she would have to accomplish the turn at full speed and somehow avoid overshooting or shortcutting the channel. Either error in her navigation would surely result in a collision with one or more of the ships resting at anchor outside the channel.

She checked the detonation countdown clock. Thirty minutes remained. She reasoned she had enough time at full speed to safely clear the bridge and get the ship out to sea. If she slowed down she knew she wouldn't make it past the Verrazano-Narrows Bridge before it detonated. But navigating through the anchorage with a broken rudder at full speed would not only take superb seamanship, it would take a miracle.

"Jake, give me thirty degrees hard left rudder. We have twenty-nine minutes left. I'm going to try to make it through the Verrazano anchorage and head this tub out to sea. We don't have the time to slow down."

Tugging on the block and tackle, Boucher pulled the rudder tiller over to the left. "Thirty hard left rudder, aye. Let's go for it."

The mammoth ship slowly turned east and entered the anchorage. Sam kept a close watch on Virgo's position relative to the channel she was attempting to remain inside. The trick would be pulling the rudder back over at just the right moment so the ship wouldn't slip outside the channel after the turn. She was navigating by gut instinct and driving by the seat of her pants. She mentally calculated the ship's speed and closing distance in the turn. It was almost time to bring the rudder back – but not too soon and not too late.

"Standby, Jake. I'm almost ready."

"Standing by," he mumbled aloud. "Nothing else I'd rather do."

"Hold what you got, Jake. Just a little further."

Boucher was sweating like he'd just run a marathon in the cramped, poorly ventilated aft steering compartment. Pulling the heavy rudder tiller back and forth was a two-man job.

"Okay, Jake, bring the rudder slowly back to center."

"How slowly?"

"Count to twenty-five slowly as you pull the rudder back over. I need to line up with the seaward channel markers beyond the Verrazano."

"Okay, you got it. One…, two…, three…, four…," he began the count over the radio as he slowly pulled on the ropes attached to the tiller bringing rudder back to center.

Little by little, Boucher tried to meter the speed of the rudder's return to center as he pulled. Sam quickly checked the radar and mentally plotted her position relative to the outbound channel. The ship was responding too slowly. She would need to bring the bow around faster.

"Jake, center the rudder now. I'm going to use the bow thruster to line the ship up for the seaward run through the narrows."

"Roger, I'm centering it now."

Sam worked the bow thruster throttle, adjusting the ship's heading to perfectly line up on the outbound leg.

"Rudder is center."

"Okay, we're clear of the anchorage. I have the ship lined up to pass under the bridge. Secure the rudder. Meet you at the stern lifeboat. Hurry!"

Boucher tied off the block and tackle and checked the detonation countdown on his watch. Twenty-six minutes remained.

"Rudder is secure, Sam" he reported over the radio. "Let's get the hell off this firecracker!"

"Roger that. I have to make a radio broadcast first, then I'm on my way to the lifeboat. See you there."

Chapter 31

Virgo

Sam grabbed the radio mic, "This is the LNG tanker Virgo, outbound at the Verrazano-Narrows Bridge. Abandoning ship. Repeat, we are abandoning ship. Remain clear. Virgo, out."

Sam checked the throttle. It was set at AHEAD FULL. *Good,* she thought. She turned to leave the bridge and slammed face-on into a powerfully built man with a ruddy complexion who was blocking her path to the doorway. He forcefully shoved her backward with both his hands. Using his foot he poked at Deeds' body.

"Ah…who the hell are you?" Sam demanded.

The man kicked Deeds' body checking for signs of life.

"I'm his boss," he growled in a thick Russian accent.

"Boss?"

"Rajakovics," he said, as if she should recognize it. "Stop this ship now!"

"Like hell I will!"

Rajakovics drew a pistol from beneath his shirt and clicked the safety off with his thumb.

"You want to die young?"

Sam forced a laugh, "I'm way past young, dickhead!"

Sam's attention refocused on the Verrazano-Narrows Bridge approaching off the ship's bow.

Rajakovics glanced outside through the window and snorted disapprovingly.

"Move! Back away! Back, Back, Back!" he demanded waving his pistol at her.

Sam retreated as Rajakovics approached the console and reached for the throttle.

"Don't!" she pleaded. "The city…you'll kill everybody."

"It's nothing personal."

As Rajakovics reversed the engines a loud metallic clanking sound came over the radio.

"Sam," Boucher yelled, "the damn aft steering hatch is locked! I can't open it."

She tried to reply over the open mic laying on the control console, "Jake!"

"Shut up!" Rajakovics ordered threatening her again with his pistol.

"Jaaakkke…," she whispered.

Rajakovics grabbed Sam's radio from the control panel and threw it against the bulkhead breaking the battery pack off its back side. Then he yanked the throttle backward reversing the engine.

Sam grabbed a metal stool and swung it wildly at his head but he ducked. The momentum of her swing carried the heavy stool past Rajakovics and onto the control panel where it struck the throttle control lever. The handle snapped off, still in the BACK FULL position.

Sam bolted from the bridge. Rajakovics fired twice; missing her with both shots, and took off after her. The ship shook and vibrated as it strained to reverse its direction. The propeller churned the water and cavitated sending near earthquake-like tremors throughout the entire ship. Unbeknownst to any of them, the fractures in the flooded Number 4 storage globe lengthened and gas bubbles increased along all the fractures. The tank was now on the verge of catastrophic rupture.

Boucher heard Sam's frantic voice over intercom, "Jaaa…" and a demanding male voice, "Shut up!" echo through the ship. The man's voice and accent was strangely familiar. Boucher couldn't place it but he knew he had heard it before

Boucher saw the throttle indicator go from AHEAD FULL to BACK FULL and felt the ship shaking under him like a bus on a bumpy dirt road.

"What the…?" he mumbled to himself.

He picked up the radio.

"Sam, what's happening? Why are you backing down? Sam, are you there?"

Nothing but static was the reply. He tried to head out but the main access door was locked from the outside. He tried the emergency escape hatch above but it was sealed as well.

An acetylene torch stood in the corner of the small compartment. He checked the pressure gauges on the gas cylinders and found they were both nearly empty. There was an igniter hanging on the metal dolly that held them. The cutting nozzle seemed to be intact but time was running out. There was no time to spare. He grabbed the igniter and cracked open the acetylene gas flow to the cutting torch. He aimed the torch tip down and tried to ignite it. It popped several times but failed to ignite. He opened the acetylene valve a quarter of a turn more and added some oxygen, then tried again.

Sam headed for engine room, evading Rajakovics' bullets. She needed to find a way off the ship without getting shot in the process and she knew she was running out of time. Rajakovics was also aware of the countdown and had no intention of dying for a cause that was not his own. This was nothing more than a contract to him and like he told Sam, it wasn't personal.

In aft steering, sparks flew as Boucher clung to the escape ladder using the torch to cut open the jammed topside emergency escape hatch. He made it through the first hinge and started cutting the second one. Sparks and molten metal burned his bare hand as the torch cut along the hinge.

In main engineering, Sam entered and descended the metal stairs leading to the glass-enclosed main engineering control room. She hurriedly inserted her master key in the lock and pushed open the door slamming it closed behind. She had lost her pursuer somewhere on the deck level above. She rushed to the engine master control panel and knelt down next to it in an attempt to help conceal her presence.

Under the placard marked Main Engine Control, she pushed the lever to the AHEAD FULL position. She quickly glanced back through the control room's glass windows into the main engine room. There was still no movement but she knew she couldn't stay there. She had to get to the lifeboat and off this floating time bomb.

Still trapped in the aft steering compartment, Boucher methodically cut the hinge nuts off one at a time. Hot metal sparks burned his hands and arms but he continued the task knowing it was his only way out. The last hinge nut fell to the deck smoldering hot. Boucher pushed up on the hatch but it still wouldn't budge. He needed something he could use to pry it open. He glanced around the space and spied some exposed piping. Using the torch he cut a four foot piece. He extinguished the torch and cast it aside. Wrapping some rags around the hot end of the pipe to protect his hands he frantically pounded upward on the hatch in a last ditch attempt to pop it open but it still wouldn't budge.

Sam cautiously exited an amidships watertight door onto the ship's main weather deck. Standing along the bulkhead she took a quick look fore and aft for Rajakovics. She felt a moment of relief when he was nowhere to be found. She checked her watch and looked back toward the stern of the ship. She felt a momentary feeling of accomplishment when she saw the ship's frothing white wake. *Good,* she thought to herself, *the ship is moving ahead again.* She could see the Statue of Liberty in the distance behind the ship.

She raced to the stern where an orange, gravity-lifeboat, resembling a miniature submarine, was suspended at the ready on launch rails in a sharp bow-down angle, thirty feet above the water. She frantically opened the lifeboat's hatch. As she began climbing inside, the lifeboat's engine turned over then stalled.

"Wait, Jake, I'm not inside yet," she yelled over her shoulder. "Let me secure the hatch and strap in."

The motor turned over again and started. Sam scrambled inside and slammed the hatch closed behind, securely latching it from the inside.

"Just give me a few more seconds to get this harness on," she yelled as she threw herself into a seat and slipped the shoulder straps on and secured the chest buckle. "Let's go!" she yelled again as she completed belting herself in snapping the waist buckle closed.

She turned expecting to see Boucher at the controls but instead, it was Rajakovics. He put his hand on the boat launch release handle and began to pull it down just as Boucher arrived at the lifeboat.

Boucher heard the running engine and knew he had only one shot at surviving the ship's impending destruction. As the lifeboat began its launch slide down the launch rails, he leapt onto its fiberglass canopy and grabbed a safety line, riding atop of the now flying lifeboat all the way to the water below.

Sam felt momentarily weightless as the boat left its launch rails and fell toward the water thirty feet below. Then the boat hit the water and submarined beneath the surface dragging Boucher with it.

At impact, Rajakovics lost his pistol. As the boat righted itself, he and Sam unbuckled their seat harnesses and both frantically lunged for the gun. Rajakovics was a powerful man and had little problem overpowering Sam by grabbing a handful of her shirt right below her neck. But she was fighting for her life. She clawed at his face attempting to reach his eyes. He held on to her and was able to reach his pistol.

Stunned, Boucher lay splayed on top of the boat's canopy, tangled in the lifeline. Gunfire suddenly erupted from inside puncturing the canopy inches from Boucher's face, immediately bringing him to his senses.

Inside, Sam scratched, punched and kicked like an incensed wild animal. She was able to land the full force of a lucky kick directly on the hand which held the gun while at the same time scratching deep into his left eye. Rajakovics dropped the gun and it went spinning away. Sam lunged toward the gun but came up short. He and Sam struggled again to gain control of the gun. He got his arm around her neck from behind in a desperate struggle of life and death. She became panicked as her life-sustaining air was cut off.

The pain of being choked was miniscule compared to the burning sting she felt in her lungs as her reflexes commanded her to draw in a breath of air. Rajakovics pressed his full body weight down on her, squeezing what remaining air she had in her lungs out and tightened his choke hold pinching off her throat and jugular. As the carbon dioxide increased in her blood, her oxygen-starved brain throbbed and her vision began to narrow. Curiously, she felt a sudden calmness come over her.

She knew he was strangling the life out of her but for some reason she was at peace. She thought of her father. The only man she ever really loved and trusted. She could hear his calming voice. He was talking to her just like he did when she was a little girl, when she was afraid. He was telling her to be brave and face her fear. She could feel him hold her close to him and comfort her.

Her vision was narrowing even more. The inside of the lifeboat was cloudy and dark. Nothing was in focus. She was dying and she knew it. Then there was a bright light from above. The light was so intense and warm she knew it was God himself. *There is a God*, she dimly perceived and actually felt relieved it was true. *There is a God.* She saw a blurry hand reaching down to her - *God's hand*. As she felt the last bit of consciousness escape from her, she reluctantly surrendered to the afterlife.

From the hatch above, a strong hand gripped Rajakovics by his shirt collar and dragged him outside with one powerful yank.

Boucher and Rajakovics fought on top of the small boat's canopy and narrow deck, landing punishing blows upon each other. Rajakovics landed a lucky series of painful punches and an elbow into Boucher's face and was able to push him backward onto the canopy.

Boucher kneed Rajakovics in his solar plexus knocking him backward. Rajakovics grabbed for the lifeline and caught himself from going over the side. Boucher threw himself on top of Rajakovics, punching and gouging. They each had one hand on the other's throat and were using their free hand to counter the other's attack.

Boucher slammed the open palm of his free hand upward into Rajakovics' jaw breaking his strangle hold. As Rajakovics released his powerful grip on Boucher's throat, Boucher kneed him several times and shoved him with all his remaining strength.

Rajakovics tumbled forward again catching on to the lifeline and once again stopped his momentum. Boucher grabbed for his feet in attempt to pull him back. As Boucher leaned forward reaching for a better grip, Rajakovics kicked him in the face. Boucher sprawled backwards almost going overboard. Both men were nearly spent from the intensity of their struggle.

Rajakovics got up to a wobbly stand and pulled a snub nose revolver from an ankle holster. He straightened up and began to laugh as he slowly brought the gun up to bear on Boucher's chest.

"Pizdets tebe otmorozok obosraniy," he growled in Russian.

Sam slowly regained consciousness. She was disoriented and groggy. She heard a threatening voice outside and remembered Rajakovics. Not realizing why he was outside, she crawled to her feet and unsteadily made her way toward the throttle. She heard Rajakovics' threatening voice outside again. He was on the canopy above. Moving to the helm, she jammed the engine throttle to full and turned the wheel sharply, causing the boat to make a radical swerving turn.

Boucher heard the engine throttle up and braced himself. As the boat heeled over into a sharp turn he saw Rajakovics begin to lose his balance.

Rajakovics wildly fired a shot toward Boucher but he needed to grab on to something to keep from falling overboard. Boucher took advantage of his own stability and with a single blow, flipped Rajakovics over the side into the water.

Boucher lay back on the canopy gasping to catch his breath. It was then he realized the lifeboat was at full speed on a heading towards the Statue of Liberty.

"Sam?" he yelled.

Sam stuck her head out of the open hatch. "Get inside!" she screamed reaching toward Boucher in an attempt to grab his shirt sleeve.

"No," Boucher yelled, "turn around and go back so I can kill Rajakovics!"

"No, Jake, the ship's going to blow in few minutes! There isn't any time."

Boucher watched Rajakovics float on his back and raise his arm partially out of the water to check his watch.

Now a ghost ship in the distance, Virgo continued eerily seaward.

Boucher crawled inside the lifeboat and closed the hatch. He wiped his sleeve across his bloody face and pressed the back of his hand against his swelling eye, wincing from the pain. He spit some blood onto the deck and swallowed hard. His lower right side ribs throbbed and his knee was bleeding through a tear in his tux trousers.

Sam gave him a quick once over and checked her watch.

"Three minutes and fifty seconds," she said above the engine noise.

"Where you take'n me, Sam?"

"I'm heading the boat toward the Statue of Liberty. I think we can hide behind Liberty Island if I can get us there in time."

Sam glanced back at him and frowned. "You look like hell, Jake."

He dabbed his swollen eye again then lightly pressed on the area around his sore ribs and nodded, "Yeah."

"She checked her watch again."

"In about two and a half minutes there's gonna be a big bang."

Boucher peered back towards the Verrazano-Narrows Bridge through a canopy porthole trying to see the Virgo.

"Did we do it?" he asked, again pressing his sleeve against his bleeding face. "Is Virgo seaward of the bridge?"

"Yes, she should be well beyond it by now."

Boucher reached over to Sam and squeezed her hand. She winced in pain.

"Sorry," he said apologetically as he silently studied her. The knuckles on her hand were bleeding and raw. Her blouse was torn and stained with dried blood. She had a gash on her scalp and swollen bruise on her cheek. A dark bruise was forming along swollen areas on both sides of her slender neck. Her blond hair was knotted and caked with dried blood. Their eyes met. He nodded approvingly.

"You know what, Sam?"

"What?"

"You're okay for a girl."

She painfully rubbed her neck and checked her watch.

"We have two minutes," she said breaking the spell.

Outside, Lady Liberty loomed eerily in the distance. Her oxidized copper skin was green from exposure to the seawater environment.

Boucher had never been this close to the Green Lady before. Peering at her through a porthole he contemplated her meaning.

"I always wondered why they did it."

"Why who did what?"

"A gift from the French," he mumbled. "She was a gift from the French."

"The French? What do you mean?" Sam asked pushing up next to Boucher so she could peer out of the porthole at the famous statue.

He winced painfully as she bumped his cracked ribs but he didn't push her away.

"Just thinking about the Green Lady. You know, France is the only country we have never been at war with. Without the French we probably wouldn't have won the American Revolution. We'd have a king instead of a president. Sometimes I wonder if we're headed back that direction."

Sam gave him a weird look as she returned her attention back to steering the lifeboat toward the rear of Liberty Island. Boucher adjusted his seat position so he could continue to see the statue.

"Sam," he said glancing back toward her, "just in case this doesn't work out I want you to know I think you're one hell of a woman."

She stared at him. She just wanted to hug him and feel the warmth of his body pressed against hers but there was no time for that now. She quickly checked her watch.

"Thirty seconds," she reported sounding a bit like mission control during a missile launch. Straining to glance outside in the direction of the Virgo, "I think we should get down on the deck."

"Yeah, getting down low would probably be a wise thing to do about now."

Sam brought the boat's engine to an idle and turned the bow back toward the Virgo. She sat down on the deck. Boucher slid down behind her resting his back on the seat front. He slowly pulled her backward against his chest, cuddling her in his powerful arms.

"Jake, why do you do what you do? The cost . . . you've lost so much."

He gently squeezed her hands.

"The progress of man has always been measured by individual acts," he said carefully. "Throughout history, a few great men have sacrificed their comfort, wealth and even their lives in the case of good. At some point in our lives we have to decide whether we're going to be one of the few."

"Don't you ever get scared?"

Boucher smiled. "Of course I get scared. But a long time ago, my best friend, Pat Patterson and I took a poison promise to be the enemy of evil. I've tried to keep that promise. And I guess you could say it's helped me become master of myself."

She snuggled as close to him as she could. He gently kissed her forehead. They quietly waited for the inevitable.

"Be brave," he whispered.

"Oh Jake…"

Chapter 32

There was a moment of eerie quiet. Not knowing if they would survive or die, for Sam and Boucher it was surreal. Then they felt a muffled rumbling sound from the direction of the Virgo. It sounded like distant thunder on a hot summer evening. The rumbling quickly escalated into a colossal booming explosion resembling a small nuclear blast.

Boucher risked a quick peek through the lifeboat canopy's porthole and saw Virgo disappear in a fireball. The materials she was built from blew into fragments that rose upward and outward like a giant umbrella unfolding in slow motion. He quickly ducked back down and pulled Sam tightly into his chest in an attempt to shield her with his body. The blast's fast-moving shock wave raced over the small life boat as the blast-generated mushroom cloud penetrated the overcast sky above. Shock waves uniformly radiated outward in all directions.

The first shock wave hit Manhattan's waterfront, breaking windows. Fortunately, structural damage to the city's buildings was light because the blast occurred so far away, giving the overpressure space to dissipate. Second and third shock waves of lesser magnitude resonated back and forth over the city but caused no additional damage to the buildings facing the blast.

A blast-generated mini-tsunami wave splashed over the waterfront's low areas but caused minimal damage. Some people walking along the water front lost their footing in the frothing water as they were caught off guard but injury was light and there was no loss of life.

New York City had been spared.

As the water around the lifeboat calmed, an ominous black mushroom cloud towered high above. Various pieces of Virgo's debris splashed down randomly into the surrounding sea. Boucher and Sam slowly uncoiled from their embrace. Sam attempted to open the hatch but Boucher stopped her drawing her into a passionate kiss. They slowly moved back to the floor of the boat. They both lost track of time.

Suddenly, Sam pushed him away.

"I hear something," she whispered.

"Oh that's funny, Sam. That's real funny."

He pulled her closer and attempted to kiss her again.

"No, no I really do hear something."

Outside, the Staten Island Ferry pulled alongside the lifeboat. Tommy was leaning over the safety rail on the ferry's bow extending a long pole-like boathook toward the lifeboat. He tapped on the lifeboat's fiberglass canopy with his boathook. Joey Hoy was on a bull horn standing in the open door of the ferry's pilothouse.

"Aey, anybuddy in dere?" Hoy pointed to the boat. "Aey, Tommy, bang da boathook on da boat again. Maybe thems are sleep'n or sumt'n." Hoy ask again, "Anybuddy in dere?"

He finally heard muffled, annoyed, voices inside yell, "No!"

"Aaa, youz need any help anyways?"

Boucher and Sam both answered with a loud emphatic, "No!"

A confused Tommy and Joey shrugged at one another as they stared at the lifeboat.

Tommy yelled down at the boat, "Okey-dokey, youz don't want no help, we got other stuff to go do."

"Good," came a muffled reply from inside the boat, "go do it."

Chapter 33

U.S. Department of State, Washington, DC, four days later

Sam and Boucher were led into Secretary Cummings' private seventh floor conference room and seated beside each other at the central part of the long mahogany conference table. The leather-covered armchairs were soft and rocked back to a comfortable angle. Moments later, Cummings appeared and cordially greeted them. After dismissing all her bodyguards she sat down across from Sam and got down to business.

"May I call you Sam?" she asked accompanied by a charming smile.

Sam immediately felt uncomfortable. It wasn't that she was intimidated by Cummings; she just felt the power of her office and realized that she was seated on the other side of the conference table from one of the most powerful women on the planet.

"Of course, Madam Secretary," she replied forcing a nervous smile.

"Good," Cummings confirmed. "Before I tell you why I've asked you here to see me in person, I want to thank you and Jake for saving New York. That was a very courageous thing you did."

"Thank you," Sam said.

Boucher sat unmoved.

"Listen," Cummings blurted, "we still have a problem and I'd like your help resolving it."

"What is it?" Sam asked.

Cummings fixed her gaze on Boucher.

"Jake, you remember Rajakovics?"

"Yeah, I left him treading water at the Verrazano right before the ship detonated. I didn't have the time to finish him myself. He couldn't have survived the blast."

"I wish your assumption was true, but I'm afraid it's not."

Boucher sat up straight. "You have my attention."

Cummings clasped her hands tightly in front of her chin and dramatically lowered them to the tabletop.

"He not only somehow survived the blast but he made good his escape out of the country."

"No way!" Boucher protested. "How can you be sure of that?"

Cummings hesitated, momentarily glancing over at Sam.

"We know because he was positively identified in an international telephone conversation the NSA intercepted late last evening. They have his voice prints and the conversation he had was with a Venezuelan national who we've been watching because of his relationship with the FARC. The name of the man Rajakovics was talking to is Miguel Arvelo Perez. He's a general in the Venezuelan Army. Perez has close political ties to the very top of the Venezuelan government."

"Hugo Chavez?"

"Right," she nodded. "Rajakovics called Caracas from Montreal and spoke to Perez."

"So what do you want me to do, find him and kill him?"

Sam couldn't believe her ears. They were in a conversation with the U.S. Secretary of State and were talking about assassination and murder like it was completely legal and done every day. Cummings glanced at Sam and smiled disarmingly.

"Yes, that's pretty much what needs to be done but there's more you need to know. Our electronic intercepts have confirmed that Rajakovics and Perez were co-conspirators in LNG ship plot to bomb New York City – the attack you two stopped. And, we believe the conspiracy goes well beyond them. In a nutshell, we think al Qaeda hired Rajakovics to plan and carry out the attack. They funded it with drug money via their link to the FARC - that's the Perez connection. The Government of Venezuela either wittingly or unwittingly provided cover in the form of passports, safe houses and other logistic support so the operatives involved were able to be placed where needed without undue scrutiny."

Boucher interrupted, "So you're saying the bad guys who were involved in that very sophisticated attack against New York all worked for Rajakovics in one way or another?"

"Yes, it appears that was the case."

"So let me get this straight. Rajakovics took a contract from al Qaeda. Al Qaeda funded it through the FARC with opium money. Perez helped Rajakovics and his evil doers via Venezuelan embassies with fake documentation, passports and logistics support, maybe even some manpower?"

"It seems as though that's pretty much the way it worked but there's one more thing you need to know about. We think they're either in the process of transporting or already have a nuclear weapon in their possession."

"A nuke? Who is 'they' and where'd they get it from?"

"They are the same conspirators – Rajakovics, Perez and al Qaeda. We think the nuke is one of the several recovered from the seafloor over a year ago. I'm guessing it's probably one they didn't have ready for use in the Canary Islands attack last year."

"Do you know the nuke's estimated yield?"

"We don't know. All we have are multiple source intelligence bits and pieces that suggest they have a working nuke and they intend to use it against one of our cities as soon as they can get it here."

"And Rajakovics is involved?"

"Yes, according to the phone calls. So is Perez."

"So what do you need me to do?"

"Wait a minute, Jake," Sam interrupted, "I thought this involved the both of us?"

Cummings smiled at Boucher, "That's your call, Jake."

Boucher glanced at Sam and repeated his question, "What do you need us to do?"

"Get Rajakovics, Perez is optional, and put their network out of business. Use any means you want, just stay out of the news. And Jake, whatever you do, it must be non-attributable to the U.S. government, the president and me. Am I clear?"

Boucher sat back in his chair and exhaled as he clasped his hands behind his head.

"Does President Banner know?"

"Yes. He will give your operation top cover."

"What's the timeframe?"

"ASAP"

"Do you have a target folder with the specifics?"

Cummings picked up a TV remote control, pointed it at a large flat screen monitor on the wall located at the front of the conference room and clicked the remote. The screen flickered to life with the large bold words, TOP SECRET, displayed in bright red at the top of the screen. Beneath that were the words, 'Contains Quiet Storm material'.

"I'm going to read you both in to this operation." Cummings stated. "As you know, neither of you may ever discuss any of this information with anyone not cleared and directly involved in this operation. This is strictly need-to-know information."

"Wait a minute," Sam insisted, "I don't even have a security clearance."

"You do now, honey," Cummings tersely replied.

Boucher gave Sam a confident nod.

"Like I was saying," Cummings continued, "you may never discuss any of this information with anyone not directly involved and with a need to know, understood?"

Both Sam and Jake nodded their consent.

"Good, then I'll bring in my briefers. I believe you already know each other."

Cummings pressed a button on the edge of the table. Moments later the door opened and Dean Blackburn strolled in with Jimmy Bruce at his side. Boucher stood and reached across the table for a handshake.

"Dean, you old seadog, it's great to see you. Allow me to introduce my friend Sam. She's the…"

Blackburn interrupted, "First female chief mate in the supertanker fleet and was key in stopping the attack on New York City."

Boucher laughed, "Yup, that would be her."

Sam stood and gave Blackburn a firm handshake.

"I'm Jimmy Bruce, Captain Blackburn's assistant," Bruce bowed humbly as he shook hands with both Sam and Boucher. "Commander Boucher, I am honored to finally meet you. You're a living legend, sir."

"It's my pleasure, Jimmy. I don't know how you can stand working for a knuckle-dragging slipknot like Blackburn."

Bruce laughed, "He's not so bad, sir. In fact, he's way smarter than he looks and I kind of like him."

Cummings impatiently checked her watch and huffed, "Gentlemen, we need to get moving here."

"Yes, ma'am," Blackburn replied, repositioning himself at the head of the table next to the flat screen monitor.

"Sam, Jake, we believe Rajakovics is on his way to Caracas where he will link up with Perez. While we have some hunches, we are unsure exactly what the purpose of the meeting is. Here's a recent picture of both of them. Perez is the guy in the army uniform."

Pictures of both men appeared on the monitor.

"We believe you will have a window of opportunity five days from today. According to the intercepts, Rajakovics and Perez will helicopter from Caracas to a FARC safe house located on Margarita Island, Venezuela. The intercepts refer to a project they're working on located in the swampy jungle area located somewhere between Santa Marta and Barranquilla, Colombia. Interestingly, a few weeks ago some DEA bubbas ambushed them in Colombia about forty miles west of Medellin and chased their helicopter into a cave. They slammed a few rockets into the cave entrance sealing it with rubble. They thought they got him. Apparently they didn't."

"Dean, you're telling me they flew a helicopter into a cave and the DEA blasted the opening shut and he still got away?"

"Yeah, exactly, and we don't know how he did it. Anyway, it looks like we're going to get another shot at him five days from now in Venezuela. Interested?"

Boucher became animated with almost child-like mannerisms, "You betcha."

"Good," Cummings blurted as she again checked her watch. "I'll leave you to do the mission planning." Cummings stood and headed out. She stopped as she pulled the heavy wooden door partially open and turned back toward Boucher. "Good hunting, Mr. Boucher. Let me know if you need anything."

Chapter 34

The Prop Shop, Old Waterside Warehouse, Fells Point, Baltimore, the next morning

Boucher had assembled some of his old SEAL Team platoon members in his Fells Point warehouse. These men were all seasoned warriors of unquestionable loyalty. In attendance were Billy Reilly, Johnny Yellowhorse, Dick Llina, Mojo Lavender, Jack Doyle, and Frank Moss.

Boucher clapped his hands and, with an arm around her waist, gently pulled Sam over next to him, "Alright boys, listen up." The room became quiet. "For those of you who haven't yet had the opportunity to meet Samantha Hill, she goes by Sam."

Several muffled voices said, "Hi Sam." She smiled and nodded.

"She's the lady who saved me and saved New York City last week. I've asked her to assist us on this mission and she has agreed."

"Sam, I want you to meet Billy Reilly, he's our shaker and mover."

Reilly raised two fingers in a feeble wave towards Sam.

"Next to him is Johnny Yellowhorse. Johnny is the best point man I ever knew and he's probably forgotten more about ordnance than the rest of us have ever known combined."

Yellowhorse nodded without breaking a smile.

"Beside Johnny is Dick Llina who is the finest SEAL Team corpsman ever, plus he's a fine shot. Dick will be our medic."

Llina smiled and nodded acknowledging the introduction.

"And of course you already know Jackie and Mossman who are our air guys."

Doyle and Moss both nodded.

"And Mojo, who we always bring along on every mission for entertainment."

Mojo made a weird cockeyed face at everyone prompting a chuckle.

"I think most all of you already know, Dean Blackburn. Dean, and his assistant, Jimmy Bruce, standing next to Sam, will act as our home team and provide tactical intelligence support so we can locate our target and take him out."

Boucher paused and scanned the faces of his men. In the many years they had operated together he had never once given them a mission objective like this.

"This mission has only one objective," he doled. "I need your help to find Rajakovics and kill the son-of-a-bitch. If any of his friends get in the way, I'll kill them too. We're gonna be operating in Venezuela. Dean has some INTEL that reflects there's a window of target vulnerability opening five days from today. That doesn't give us much time to put this together. If any of you don't want to play, just say so, the rest of us will understand."

Boucher again glanced around the room at his men. No one budged.

After a pause he looked over at Blackburn, "Okay Dean, you and Jimmy are up."

Blackburn stood and went to the front of the room. He methodically unlocked, then unzipped, a canvas fabric document pouch. Reaching inside he pulled out a second, slightly smaller pouch constructed of the same fabric and unlocked it. Inside it he pulled out two over-stuffed folders containing papers and maps. Using push pins he hung some of the maps on the unpainted plywood wall behind him. He sorted through some of the papers and set a few aside on the table in front of him.

"Lady and gentlemen," he gruffly began, sounding a little bit like George C. Scott in the opening scene of the movie, Patton. "The U.S. has traditionally treated acts of terrorism as a law enforcement issue. We have generally been more interested in who done it, rather than how they did it. As such, we've been mostly focused on apprehending and prosecuting the bad actors instead of disrupting their plots and killing the dirty sons-of-bitches. Well, it's pretty damn clear to me that this rule-of-law horseshit tactic hasn't worked and never will." Blackburn quickly scanned his audience and noted everyone was nodding in agreement. "But this operation is different because, like Jake said, our primary objective is to find one of their masterminds and kill the son-of-a-bitch. The following target briefing is at the secret, special category level – code name, Quiet Storm. I know that giving you access to this information breaks every operations security rule in the book but then so does this mission. I'll now ask my partner, Jimmy Bruce, to give you the details."

Bruce stood and stepped up to the table. Blackburn sat down in Bruce's vacant seat and nodded to him.

"Like the Captain said, Rajakovics is our target."

Bruce tacked an 8x11 color photo of him on the wall and slapped it with the back of his hand.

"This is Rajakovics. I think most of you know he's the guy that masterminded the manmade tsunami attack against our Eastern Seaboard using nukes to blast the Cumbre Vieja Volcano's caldron on the Island of La Palma into the sea. Had you guys not foiled that attack last year we'd still be pumping bilge water. Based upon electronic intercepts we expect Rajakovics to head from Montreal to Caracas two days from today via Air Canada flight 235, arriving at twenty-thirty hours local time. He will be met at the airport gate by a Venezuelan Lieutenant General by the name of Miguel Arvelo Perez."

Bruce tacked a second picture on the wall.

"This is Perez. He has close ties to both Venezuela's dictator-president, Hugo Chavez, and to a FARC boss by the name of Rodrigo Guarnizo. Guarnizo is one of five Deputy Commanders for FARC's Central High Command and he heads FARC's North Eastern region of operations."

Bruce pinned a picture of Guarnizo up and pointed at it.

"This is Guarnizo."

"He's about an ugly sucker, ain't he?" Mojo blurted.

The men all chuckled. Smiling, Bruce pointed to a large jungle mangrove swamp located in the northeast corner of the map of Colombia that Blackburn had pinned to the wall.

"This is the area we believe he will be visiting. General Perez is a known FARC sympathizer and a weapons-for-drugs facilitator. We believe Perez also provides a direct link to al Qaeda and is the primary deal broker for Guarnizo and the FARC. He's the mover and shaker for the drug trade to FARC from Afghanistan via the Islamic community living on Margarita Island in Venezuela. "

Billy Reilly raised his hand interrupting Bruce, "This is interesting but it's so damn complicated you can't expect any normal asshole to remember it. I thought Rajakovics is our target. Where the hell does he fit into this mess, Jimmy? And refresh my memory on FARC. Shit, I can't even remember what the FARC is anymore."

"No problem, Sir" Bruce chuckled. "Let's start with FARC. FARC is the acronym for the Revolutionary Armed Forces of Colombia – People's Army.

In Spanish it's Fuerzas Armadas Revolucionarias de Colombia – Ejército del Pueblo, or FARC-EP. We shorten it to FARC. FARC is a Marxist-Leninist revolutionary guerrilla organization with somewhere between fourteen and eighteen thousand well-trained, well-equipped troops. They're basically the military wing of the Colombian Communist Party and they've been fighting the Colombian government in an attempt to overthrow it for over sixty years. They're considered a terrorist group by the Colombian government, the U.S., Canada and the European Union. Of course, as you might expect, Venezuelan President Hugo Chavez publicly rejected their classification as "terrorists" back in January, redefining them as 'real armies.' He even went so far as to call on the Colombian government and the international community to recognize these guerrilla terrorists as a legitimate force, arguing that this would then oblige them to renounce kidnappings and terror acts. Regardless of how you label it, the FARC is a bunch of very bad actors that kidnap, murder, trade weapons for drugs and vice versa, and most of all, hate democracies. They have a loose alliance with al Qaeda, sharing intelligence with them and providing manpower and arms for operations against their mutual enemies. Does that answer your question?"

Reilly nodded.

Mojo spit his chewing tobacco into his coffee cup and set it on the floor between his feet. "Geezzz, Jimmy, all we needed was a refresher not a dag-gum dissertation. What about Rajakovics?"

"Bear with me just a little longer, sir. I'm getting to Rajakovics, honest."

"Okay, but you're making my head hurt with all these names and places and stop call'n me, sir. I ain't no fucking officer, I work for a living."

Moss and Doyle chuckled at Lavender's frustration. Moss was sitting next to Lavender and gave him a playful elbow to the side.

"Okay, Sir, I mean, Mojo, where was I?" Bruce mumbled. "Oh yeah, here's how all these characters fit into the puzzle. Al Qaeda funds their operations against the Americas by selling drugs they get in Afghanistan to the FARC in Colombia. In turn, the FARC helps them do their dirty deeds against the U.S. homeland by providing manpower, logistics support and even intelligence. That's right, gentlemen, we believe they even share their intelligence. It's an unholy alliance that is both formidable and nearly impossible to infiltrate. Rajakovics is a mercenary plain and simple. The FARC bosses refer to him as "El Mas Loco.""

Sam interrupted, "The craziest one?"

"Exactly. He appears to serve as a sort of inspirational figure for them. And make no mistake, he's a talented and expert operations planner, coordinator and killing machine who works for anyone willing to hire him at the right price. For example, al Qaeda hired him to run the La Palma tsunami attack which you gentlemen foiled last year. And, they apparently hired him again to coordinate the New York City attack a few days ago which Commander Boucher and Sam prevented. As long as Rajakovics is alive I think it's fair to expect they will keep him on their pay roll and he'll keep trying until a catastrophic attack against our homeland succeeds."

Reilly interrupted, "If I may, Jimmy, please let me get this straight. By offing Rajakovics we are effectively reducing the al Qaeda threat against our homeland."

"Exactly."

"But we might have an opportunity to off Perez and that FARC dickwad, Guarnizo, too and that would count as a three-fer."

"For sure."

"So when and where do we find these assholes?" Mojo asked.

"According to our signals intercepts, Rajakovics is going to be meeting with Rodrigo Guarnizo and Perez this Wednesday and Thursday at a FARC safe house located on Margarita Island located off shore Venezuela."

"But Jimmy," Doyle asked, "you said Guarnizo's operation is located in the heart of a swampy mangrove jungle somewhere between Santa Marta and Barranquilla in Colombia. I mean, that area isn't exactly a great place to vacation. Do you know where his field headquarters is and why it's located in that area?"

Bruce pinned a poster-size blow-up of a satellite image of the area on the wall.

"We've done some serious analysis over the past several days and we believe it is located here." Bruce circled an area at the top of a canal-like finger that extended from the sea up into the swampy jungle. "We think it's here."

Doyle studied the imagery and shook his head.

"I don't see shit. All I see is a finger of water I'm guessing is about a half a mile long that winds into the mangrove jungle and dead ends – no camp."

"Exactly, Mr. Doyle. That's what you're supposed to see. The FARC are masters of camouflage. Now take a look at this infrared picture of the area which was taken from a U.S. Customs P-3 surveillance plane yesterday."

Bruce put the picture on the table in front of Doyle. It showed three brightly defined heat sources coming from the area where the canal finger ended.

"These heat sources are telling. We think they have three co-located areas here." Bruce circled a small area containing the three hot spots with a yellow highlighter. One is their temporary headquarters. It's separated from the other two hot spots by about one hundred yards. The heat source is likely a small generator to power their radios and maybe lights. The second spot next to the water is some sort of manufacturing facility. We're guessing it has a welder, maybe an engine of some sort. The third is about a hundred yards from the headquarters in a small cleared area, probably large enough for a helicopter to land in. All three are hidden beneath a false canopy. Notice the heat source at the clearing is almost negligible, probably a small gas cook stove. They probably do their cooking there to keep their IR signature down at the other two locations. Does that answer your question, Mr. Doyle?"

"Yup and I sure would appreciate it if you'd call me, Jack. This Mr. Doyle shit makes me nervous."

"Yes, Sir - I mean, Jack. Back to Rajakovics then. He's flying into Caracas Wednesday evening where he'll link up with General Perez. He and Perez will go from there to Margarita Island and remain overnight."

"Do you know exactly where he'll be staying while he's on Margarita?" Reilly asked.

"Yes. Based upon the intercepts, we're relatively sure he'll be staying at a FARC safe house located on the northeast shore of Margarita. Here, check out this imagery."

Bruce passed around several overhead pictures of a villa, airstrip, and surrounding jungle. The villa itself sat on a high bluff well above the sea. The house had a low rock wall surrounding its south side with an unobstructed ocean view from the house and surrounding grounds. The airstrip was located directly behind the villa and paralleled the bluff overlooking the sea. There were a number of sandbagged guard stations located around the perimeter of the airfield and along the road leading into the compound. Bruce had them all circled in red. Strangely, there was a vintage World War II-era Russian T-34 tank surrounded on three of its sides by sandbags in what appeared to be a fixed installation. It overlooked the sea directly behind the villa's back patio and commanded an impressive field of fire. The compound looked like a virtual fortified vacation villa for the rich and famous located someplace in a war zone.

Bruce continued, "The safe house is actually the villa you're looking at in these pictures. It sits on a hill overlooking the ocean at the end of a half mile long improved gravel road. It's very secluded and very private. It has an unpaved airstrip which is bordered by a cultivated coconut plantation on the south side and it's well guarded by sandbagged bunkers. I've circled them in red. It's otherwise surrounded by a natural jungle barrier that runs along the coast line on both its east and west sides. It's in a very isolated location compared to the rest of the island."

"What's with the tank?" Yellowhorse asked. "They got a VFW in that villa or some shit?"

Some chuckles briefly ensued. Even Bruce smiled.

"You're looking at a Russian T-34. The T-34 was Russia's main battle tank during most of World War II. All I can tell you is that according to our imagery records it has been sitting in exactly the same location for at least the last five years so I think we're safe in assuming it doesn't run."

Yellowhorse spit his chewing tobacco into his coffee cup. "How bout its gun? Does it work?"

"Doubtful. The turret and its gun have been pointing exactly the same way for the same period of time the tank has been there and to our knowledge the gun turret has never moved. It's probably rusted in place. We believe the tank is there more as a decoration than for its functional value."

Yellowhorse smiled looking over at his longtime friend, Mojo. "Yeah, reminds me of the dick on some people I know."

The men again all chuckled.

"But seriously," Doyle asked, "how's Rajakovics getting to the villa once he's on Margarita?"

"According to our signals intercepts, he and Perez will take a military helicopter from the airport in Caracas to the compound accompanied by an armed security detail."

Doyle scratched his head, "So why not just nail his ass in Canada before he goes to Caracas? Wouldn't that be a whole lot easier?"

"You can't kill him while he's on Canadian soil," Blackburn countered, "and if we issued an arrest warrant and rendition to bring him into the U.S. he would be given his Miranda Rights, lawyer up and stand trial in a civil court. That means the chance of compromising our previous successes in stopping his attacks would likely be made public and that disclosure would be devastating to our intelligence operations against al Qaeda. It's too risky. That's why we've been asked to take care of this problem elsewhere and outside the bounds of any official U.S. agency."

"Jimmy, do you know where Rajakovics is headed after his meeting with Perez and the FARC boss?" Sam asked.

"They'll helicopter to the FARC's mangrove swamp location I mentioned earlier in Colombia's Magdalena Province, sometime late Thursday. Rajakovics' best window of vulnerability will be while he's in the FARC safe house on Margarita Island."

Boucher interrupted, "Okay, you boys get the picture. We'll have an excellent window of opportunity while Rajakovics is on Margarita meeting with his pals. If we can take out 'The Crazy One', Perez, and the FARC boss all at the same time, we'll do it, no extra charge. Mossman and Jackie, we'll take the Gulfstream to Oranjestad, Aruba tonight. Line up a helicopter for us there. We'll need something with enough range to fly to Margarita, loiter for a couple of hours, and then make it back if need be."

Moss and Doyle nodded.

"Mojo, lease a high speed boat out of Oranjestad with enough deck space to accommodate our entire team and enough range to make it to Port of Spain."

"But, Jake, Port of Spain still ain't recovered from their earthquake yet."

"Exactly. It'll make a great place to get lost in if we have to run."

Sam interrupted, "I don't get it, Jake."

Boucher stopped and turned toward Sam, "You don't get what?"

"If you're going to take out the bad guys while they're on Margarita Island, I don't get why you don't support the operation out of Caracas. Instead of flying into Aruba and basing your operation from there, why not fly into Caracas, lease a boat and helicopter there and run your operation on Margarita? It's closer, faster and if you have to run you can still head to Haiti, Aruba, or even Trinidad and Tobago and there won't be any weather issues getting you to Margarita."

Boucher considered her idea then looked back at Bruce.

"Jimmy, do you have more imagery of the villa on Margarita?"

"Sure do, Sir."

Bruce spread several poster-size color satellite pictures on the table showing the villa and surrounding area.

"Here's the villa. Here's the landing strip and the access road leading to the villa. And here's the boathouse. The boathouse puzzles me because there isn't any pier. About ten years ago they built a makeshift breakwater jetty out of rock riprap on the north side. I'm guessing it extends about a hundred yards from the beach out into the water. It looks like they use a trolley-like system that rides on rails to launch and recover their boat. It sort'a reminds me of the kind used by rescue boats in the North Atlantic where the surf is too unpredictable to keep boats moored to a pier.

"See, the ramp that leads down to the water?" he said pointing at that part of the picture. "You can see the trolley rails. I'm guessing they must use that system because there's too much exposure to surf on the north side of the island."

"Or," Reilly interrupted, "they don't want anyone to see what they're launching and recovering from that boathouse."

Bruce nodded at Reilly, "Good point, sir" he replied, then continued. "Also note that the boathouse is built into the side of the cliff below the villa. There's only about ten feet of the visible roof extending out from the cliff. The rest of the building must extend underground back into the cliff; I can't give you an estimate how far. It looks like they cut a narrow access road along the cliff leading from the villa down to the boathouse. I'm guessing they built it when they built the boathouse as a means to get their equipment down to the construction site. Judging from the amount of overgrowth on it, I don't think it's in use."

Sam examined the pictures of the boathouse. She ran her index finger around the door frame, "From the approximate size of the boathouse doors and the trolley rail system, I'm guessing they probably can't get anything much bigger than a sixty-footer inside."

"You may be right, Sam," Boucher commented, "but I don't think the boathouse is a factor. I need to get inside the villa above. If that's a non-starter then I'll snipe Rajakovics when he arrives or departs from it." Boucher studied the pictures. "Okay, Sam, Caracas it is. We'll fly into Caracas and go from there. Billy, what have you come up with for the insertion point?"

Reilly had done an exhaustive LANDSAT imagery study on the target area prior to the meeting and knew nearly every detail about the area as well as Bruce did. He pushed Bruce's aerial photo towards Boucher.

"You'll launch from our boat seaward of the villa's boathouse and come in over the beach. There's a bunch of man-size boulders just to the northwest side of that jetty where the boathouse launch rails enter the water. That should give you adequate cover."

Sam placed her hand on Boucher's forearm and gently squeezed. "Jake, I'll drive the boat."

Boucher hesitated momentarily savoring the warmth of her touch. He saw his men nodding their approval.

"Sam, this is gonna be dangerous," he cautioned, turning towards her and covering her hand with his free hand. "We're dealing with a bunch of genuine bad actors that have a variety of motivations to commonly hate us and want to see us dead. And, as you well know, they don't give a shit about who they kill. No, Sam, I'm sorry, it's just too dangerous."

"Jake, I looked them in the eye and fought them on my ship. They killed Captain Bakke and blew up my ship, I owe them a payback," she insisted. "You need someone to drive and navigate your boat who can handle it and I'm that person. Besides, I'm fluent in Spanish and have all the right boat driver tickets. I can do the lease on that boat for us and no one will suspect a thing."

Boucher stared into her emerald green eyes as he thoughtfully contemplated her offer.

"Sam, I know you can probably drive a boat better than any of us and I don't doubt your courage, but…"

"But what, Jake?" she interrupted.

He saw the fire in her now squinted eyes and her facial expression change from one of the most traditionally beautiful women he ever met to the resolute look of one hundred percent determination. He had only ever seen a look like that on one other woman's face and that was Sandra. He knew he couldn't endure the heartache again if something happened to Sam. *Am I secretly falling for Sam? Is that why I am trying to protect her?*

"I don't know," he mumbled aloud.

Mojo stood, "Okay," he loudly boomed. "I want to see a show of hands from those who approve of Sam driving the boat."

Everyone raised their hands. Boucher didn't like it but he knew he was overruled.

"All right, Sam," he conceded, "you drive the boat. Mojo and Dick will crew for you. Okay?"

"That works for me."

American Embassy Caracas, Venezuela, same time

Joel Lopez, the Deputy Chief of Mission sat patiently at his desk as Nikolas Furner, the CIA's Chief of Station briefed him on some actionable intelligence. Notebook in hand, DEA's Country Representative from Bogota, David Castro, sat in a leather armchair across from Furner.

"It looks like we'll have another shot at General Perez in a couple of days," Furner stated. "When Dave and his guys chased Perez's helicopter into that cave outside of Medellin a few weeks ago we thought we got him, but somehow he escaped. Perez and Rodrigo Guarnizo, a Deputy Commander for the FARC Central High Command, will be meeting at a FARC safe house on Margarita Island this Thursday. It's a unique opportunity to nail both of them. Dave will now explain the plan."

"Thanks Nick. The mission is to apprehend Perez and Guarnizo and bring them back to the U.S. for trial. The Justice Department has issued warrants in Miami on both of them for drug trafficking, conspiracy to murder federal agents and murder of federal agents. They're bad people. We have a Mutual Legal Assistance Treaty in place with Venezuela for the capture of Guarnizo."

Lopez stopped him, "Dave, how do you know your MLAT won't compromise your mission?"

"We suspect it could. That's why we tried to keep the Venezuelan National Police on the purifier of this operation until the last possible moment."

"I don't like this. You better explain."

"We intend to conduct a coordinated covert combined operation. The DEA will be the lead federal agency. We will be supported by a detachment of Navy SEALs working from the Navy's littoral combat ship, the USS Independence.

Our plan is to run a two-pronged takedown against the villa and snatch both of these men and take them offshore to the Independence for return to Miami, where they will be formally charged."

Castro placed three 8x11 aerial photos of the villa in front of Lopez and pointed at the middle picture and gave Lopez a moment to study it.

"Just after midnight Thursday morning," he continued, "the SEALs will launch under the cover of darkness from the Independence which will be loitering twenty miles over the horizon."

He tapped his finger on a color aerial photo taken from high above showing a rocky beach line and surf zone. Lopez picked it up and closely assessed the imagery. Castro used a ballpoint pen like a small pointer.

"They'll land on the beach northwest of the villa," he said pointing to the rocky beach area shown on the photo, "and get as close as they can without making contact. They'll employ their snipers and act as our security and blocking force. Once they're in position, two Florida National Guard Black Hawk helicopters will arrive, seizing the element of surprise, and deliver a DEA assault team augmented by agents from the Venezuelan National Police to the villa. We'll grab our suspects and be out'a there before they know what hit'm. Ground time two minutes max."

Lopez straightened up, raising his brow in surprise. "So you intend to put U.S. armed forces ashore on Venezuelan sovereign territory?"

"Yes. Navy SEALs."

"Where the DEA intends to kidnap a Venezuelan citizen, who, incidentally, happens to be a general in their armed forces?"

"Yes, that's pretty much it but we have a federal warrant."

Lopez, a career diplomat, began shaking his head from side to side. "What you intend to do is an act of war no matter how you package it. It's out of the question, Mr. Castro. Besides, there is no way in hell the ambassador will approve this operation. Our relationship with Venezuela is already tenuous. It doesn't need further exacerbation."

Castro slyly smiled and sat back in his chair twirling his dark handlebar mustache between two nicotine-stained fingers. "Well," he said, "I'm not telling you this information because I'm seeking the ambassador's approval. As you know, the DEA conducts covert operations like this all the time. I can't speak for our political relationship with the Communist government of Venezuela or its corrupt dictator, but I can't imagine this operation will make it any worse."

"You do realize, Mr. Castro, I will brief the ambassador on this mission and he may put the brakes on your operation."

"I don't think so. This is coming from the top down,"

Chapter 35

Caracas, Venezuela, Wednesday, late afternoon

Moss and Doyle landed the Gulfstream uneventfully and taxied to the non-commercial aviation parking ramp located on the far side of the airport opposite of the commercial terminal. Customs was a breeze, facilitated by some solid gold South African Krugerrands which Boucher placed in the customs officials' hands.

Unbeknownst to Boucher and his team, two men dressed like locals observed from afar, photographing the plane and those on it through powerful telephoto lenses as they disembarked.

After securing the Gulfstream, Moss and Doyle immediately completed the rental paperwork for a Boeing 234 heavy-lift helicopter they leased from an oil exploration company and conducted a detailed preflight inspection of the aircraft. Reilly assisted them in preparing the helicopter for their needs.

The Boeing 234 is basically the civilian equivalent of the U.S. Army's twin rotor CH-47 Chinook heavy lift helicopter. It possesses a large cargo payload capability, long range to get to the objective and back again, and is ruggedly engineered to survive the punishment of combat operations. This particular helicopter had an auxiliary fuel tank installed inside on the cargo deck area that would extend its range by an additional two hours.

Sam and Mojo Lavender went by cab to the harbor where they boarded a thirty-six foot offshore fishing yacht they had pre-contracted via the internet. Boucher, Johnny Yellowhorse and Dick Llina followed behind in a small van with their equipment bags.

The two men from the airport followed in a non-descript pickup truck being careful to remain far enough behind so as not to be noticed.

Shortly after dark Sam eased the yacht away from its slip and headed seaward. As far as the locals went, it was just another charter boat taking wealthy Americans fishing and its departure went unnoticed. Boucher stood inside the pilothouse beside Sam who was seated at the controls. Mojo stood behind Sam holding onto her chair back. Yellowhorse and Llina flanked his sides.

Boucher took this opportunity to do some last minute contingency planning.

"Before I insert I want to go over our contingencies just so there is no confusion when the shit hits the fan." He opened his map of Margarita and spread it over the control panel, then placed several 8 x 11 aerial photos beside the map. "Sam, you're gonna put me off in this area," he said pushing his finger on the map seaward of the northwest side of the island. We have enough water under our keel there so you can get me relatively close to the beach. Mojo and I will take the yacht's dinghy to the shore in this area. I'll jump off here. The area is strewn with large boulders and rock slides. It should provide natural concealment in case anyone is looking."

"And, I'm bringing the dinghy back right away," Mojo interrupted, "and you're going ashore without me."

"Yes, Mojo, you're dropping me off and scooting." Boucher tapped his finger again on the picture. "The beach gradient is steep at our landing point. The beach only extends about five yards at low tide with no beach at high tide. There's a rock-shale cliff which rises up from the beach. The hinterland elevation behind the landing point rises up steeply to about one hundred and twenty feet. There are plenty of avenues up from the beach. None of them appear to be guarded. It will be a bit of a climb but nothing I can't handle."

"Jake," Mojo interrupted, "what's your plan if you run into a guard or sumthin?"

He held up a silenced FN P-90 sub-machinegun. "I'm carrying four extra fifty round magazines along with my favorite Novak custom 1911A1 forty-five pistol Wayne built for me. And, I'm packing six extra eight round 45 magazines."

Yellowhorse smiled and nodded; he had his answer. He knew the P-90's deadly 5.7 millimeter ammo would stop anyone Boucher hit with it and his Novak .45 pistol would mop up any hangers-on.

"I'll make my way up to the boathouse. From there I'll climb to the top of the cliff. Then, I'll make my way to the villa staying in the vegetation and using it for concealment. I'll take my time and do it quietly."

"Jake, tell me again about your plan once you reach the villa." Sam asked.

"Sam, once I'm close enough to the villa to put eyes on it, I'll look for the vulnerabilities and exploit them. We know the villa is heavily guarded but their weak side, according to these aerial photos, is the northwest end - the one I'm coming in from. Most of their guard positions are on the opposite side around the airfield and along the road leading in. Besides, they're looking outward, not inward. Rajakovics is supposed to arrive sometime before first light tomorrow morning. My initial goal is to figure a way to gain access into the villa without compromising my presence there. If access into the villa is too risky, I'll wait until Rajakovics shows himself and snipe him from outside. My primary target is Rajakovics, but if Perez or that FARC dickwad get in the field of fire, it's gonna suck being them."

Mojo loudly cleared his throat interrupting.

"Mojo," Boucher said hoarsely.

"Jake, how about we go over the emergency extraction plan again?"

"Sure. If I am compromised and can't make it back to you and the dinghy, I'll call Mossman and Jackie for an emergency helicopter extraction. Since I don't know where in reference to the villa that might occur, I can't tell you where the helicopter landing zone might be. All I can say is, if I call them to come get me, it's because I'm in deep shit and need a ride outa there in a hurry."

"You call, they'll be there," Mojo flatly stated.

"I know they will."

"We'll maintain comms with them from here and back you up just in case you can't get through to them."

"Good, Mojo." Turning his attention to Sam, Boucher again pointed to the chart. "After you drop me off, I want you to go seaward and loiter just over the horizon. Stay to the northwest. If it gets really nasty in there and for some reason I can't get a helicopter ride out, I'll find another way off the island. If that doesn't work I'll head for the beach and swim seaward. Finally, if there are any friendly casualties," referring to himself, "well, Dick will just have to patch me up." Llina smiled and nodded. "If it's severe, Trinidad and Tobago has the closest medical facilities. Regardless, we won't return to Caracas and risk arrest. Any questions?"

Boucher knew the risk he was about to undertake was more about his personal revenge than it was about Cummings' sanction against Rajakovics.

"Sam, how much longer?" he asked leaning around her side towards the navigation display.

Sam checked her GPS navigation display and radar plot, "Forty-one miles - about another hour and a half, Jake."

Boucher began to turn away but she touched his hand stopping him.

"Why, Jake?" she asked softly.

Boucher stopped and stared into her eyes.

"We face a radical Islamist enemy who intends to dictate what we can believe, what we can think and tell us how we will live our lives. As long as I have a breath left in me I'm going to fight them."

"But, Jake, you must realize they'll never give up and you can't kill them all."

"Yeah, maybe, but I reckon we have more bullets than they do Islamists and at some point, with a little luck, we'll beat them back and contain them."

Sam saw the commitment in his steel-eyed gaze. She also saw a man who was capable of violent action.

"What are you going to do when there's no one left to fight?" she asked in a whisper.

"I suppose I'll go fly fishing with Mojo on Baker's Run in Renovo, Pennsylvania."

"I always wanted to try fly fishing," Sam said.

"Yeah, me too," Boucher replied turning away.

She squeezed his arm.

"Jake, you be careful. Promise?"

"Yeah," he smiled. "I need to catch a quick power nap. I want to be on Margarita before midnight. Please wake me up a half hour before it's time to launch."

Margarita Island, 2230 hours, Wednesday night

Mojo slowly motored the small inflatable boat toward shore, landing it on the narrow beach in the boulder-strewn area just north of the boathouse jetty as planned. Boucher was dressed in jungle camouflage and had his face painted in black and green. He stepped from the boat and gave the small inflatable a shove back out into deeper water. Mojo backed quietly seaward before turning and slowly motoring back out to rendezvous with Sam.

Scanning the back beach area and cliff side for movement, Boucher crouched behind a large boulder and waited until Mojo was completely out of sight before moving.

He cautiously made his way closer to the jetty and the boat ramp that led up to the boathouse. Using his night vision goggles, he carefully scanned the area around and above the boathouse. He could see the villa on the cliff above. It had a single mercury vapor streetlight which was mounted on a metal pole next to its seaward-facing patio. There was no sign of movement anywhere.

Boucher crept next to the boat ramp. The rails that the boat trolley rode on were rusted and appeared not to be in use. Remaining in the low vegetation,

Boucher slowly made his way next to the steep boat ramp incline to the boathouse. No guards were present. As far as he could tell he was alone.

Switching his night vision goggles to active infrared, he carefully examined the boathouse doors for signs of alarm systems. He found nothing. Surprisingly, the doors were only being held closed by an open padlock. He removed the padlock and opened the hasp. He carefully opened the door just wide enough to squeeze through, then pulled it closed behind him.

The active infrared feature on his night vision goggles provided ample illumination inside and what he saw astounded him. It was a low silhouette boat about sixty feet long with a small window-sided cockpit sticking up a few feet above its deck. The boat's deck was otherwise flat and had what looked like black foam neoprene rubber glued to its top surface all the way down the side to the water line mark. *Radar absorbent material, a RAM covered hull?* He rubbed his hand over the spongy material, *Ingenious.* He walked around it to its stern. It had a conventional propeller and rudder protruding from its hull.

There was a ladder leaning up against the boat's side. Boucher climbed it and peered down inside the small cockpit. *Basic navigation compass and a dash-mounted portable GPS.* Looking aft he could see it was powered by a small diesel engine. Two large fuel tanks fabricated from sheet metal were mounted low on each side of the inside hull frames. The tanks' seams were skillfully welded and perfectly formed. *At least one hundred and fifty gallons each. This damn boat probably has a thousand mile range between fill-ups.* The engine exhaust was piped outside, exiting below the waterline. *Exhaust muffling? No, heat signature and sound reduction, humm. This thing is a damn semi-submersible submarine with stealth.*

He studied the boat's interior, noting it had a heavy-looking container about the size of a thirty gallon trash can fixed against a keel-mounted rack located approximately amidships almost directly beneath the cockpit where the coxswain stood. The rack had reinforced rails on the bottom capable of supporting considerable weight. Cargo straps with tightening ratchets on the ends ran from one side of the rack to the other obviously used to secure the strange cargo in the rack.

He glanced up at the boathouse ceiling and noted it had a heavy lift chain hoist hanging from a steel I-beam. The hoist had the number 12 placarded on its side meaning it had a 12 ton lift capability. He climbed back down the ladder and crouched down to look beneath the strange craft. Its cradle was riding on a rail trolley. The back end of the trolley was attached to a winch cable running from the back of the boathouse. *Gravity launched and retrieved using the winch cable to pull it back up into the boat house. Ingenious, but what's this boat's purpose, drug smuggling?*

Boucher left the boathouse and propped the door closed using a metal bar he found lying on the ground outside next to the wall. From there he crept up the overgrown access road running diagonally up the side of the cliff to the villa above.

At the top he carefully reconnoitered the villa area for signs of life. There was one snoring guard sitting at the edge of the patio in a lawn chair. Boucher melted into the dense foliage northeast of the villa without anyone's notice.

The USS Independence, 0100 hours, Thursday morning

Two Dogs and his men launched from the Independence in two rigid-hull, semi-inflatable boats or RSIs as they were called. It was a perfect night for SEAL operations. The seas had a low, windblown surface chop which served to help hide their boat wake and the sky was filled with low clouds completely obscuring the moon. There was a line of rain squalls headed their way from the southeast.

Two Dogs and his men knew it would be a very dark night as they motored toward Margarita Island. They also knew the forty minute ride would be the easy part. Once ashore they would head for the villa and take up offensive positions from which they could neutralize the villa's defenses if or when it became necessary. There they would wait for Perez to arrive and then call in the Black Hawk helicopters that would deliver the DEA assault team.

Two Dogs actually enjoyed working with the DEA supporting their counter-drug operations. From a SEAL's perspective, South America was actually a better operating area than Iraq or Afghanistan, and he had operated in all three locations. Supporting the DEA always seemed to be black or white. It was either sheer boredom or adrenalin rushing terror – there was no middle ground. He also liked the DEA agents he worked with. They were top notch professionals. Many were ex-military and even those who weren't seemed to have a warrior's mentality. Like the SEALs, they would bend the rules and even occasionally break them if that's what it took for mission success.

He stared into the darkness knowing that somewhere ahead there was an island veiled by a passing rain squall. His mind drifted back to their encounter with the Virgo a couple of weeks earlier and his chance meeting with his old boss, Commander Boucher. He silently vowed to rekindle that relationship following his current deployment. Two Dogs pressed himself back into his foam-padded bolster seat and smiled as the RSI sped toward Margarita Island.

Margarita Island, 0330 hours, Thursday morning

Boucher had positioned himself in a hide that gave him clear visual access of the entire front, west side and rear patio area of the villa. To his right, he had an open view of the driveway leading to the villa along most of the airstrip. To his left, he could see the rear patio on the villa's seaward side.

He had concealed himself by digging a shallow pit just big enough for him to fit into while lying on his back. It was a very effective hide technique no longer taught to today's SEALs. Using a sharp-edged entrenching tool, he first cut the sod from the pit top and placed it on a poncho, carefully piecing it back together in the order he cut it from the pit. He then dug a shallow trench-like pit just large enough for his body to fit in and put all the fresh dirt he scooped out of it on a second poncho which he carried a short distance from the hide. He disposed of the fresh dirt beneath some dense foliage and pulled some grass and dead leaves on top of it to make the area look undisturbed.

Returning to the shallow pit, he lay down on his back inside of it and drug the sod covered poncho back across like a blanket, completely covering himself. He adjusted the sod and folded the poncho beneath so the surface looked undisturbed and normal from above. Using his fingers he carefully pulled the foliage up around the pit and the top of the surrounding sod back into an upright natural posture. He positioned his P-90 so it was at the ready resting on his lower abdomen and had a flexible straw-like tube by his mouth that led to a water-filled bladder which he used as a pillow.

He was now peering through a small raised slit beneath a large piece of sod that covered his head. All that could be seen of him at this point were his eyes and that would require that you knew exactly where to look. At ground surface everything looked normal. The only way his hide could be compromised was if someone stepped directly on top of him.

He noted a lone guard slowly headed his way around the villa's jungle perimeter. As he lay there watching, his mind drifted off to an operation that he ran many years earlier where he and his SEALs had effectively employed this hide technique to avoid detection. Under the cover of darkness they dug hides in the rough area next to a golf course putting green and waited to snatch a VIP who would be playing there the next morning. As the VIP arrived by the green to play his ball, Boucher and two of his SEALs exploded from the ground only feet away from his golf cart and grabbed him. The man was so surprised, he wet his pants. His two golfing companions never saw what hit them.

The SEALs drug the man's two companions off into the rough where they duct taped their hands, feet and mouths, then administered a syringe of strong sedative to each and put them into the same hides the SEALs had just used. The total action at the green took them less than a minute. Boucher and his men had dressed like golfers so they simply carted the VIP off to a rendezvous point using his golf cart, stuffed him into a waiting van and no one was the wiser. But this night's operation was not a body snatch and he had no intention of taking Rajakovics prisoner. He refocused as the roving guard passed about three yards to his front, stopping dangerously close to the right of the hide.

There he stepped into the tree line, slung his AK-47 assault rifle over his shoulder, unzipped his pants and urinated. Upon finishing, he lit a cigarette and stepped back almost directly in front of the hide. He was now standing just inches from Boucher's feet. The man leisurely puffed away totally unaware of his precarious location.

Except for the sleeping guard on the patio, Boucher had detected no other signs of life anywhere around the rear of the compound. As far as he could determine, all the manned guard positions were located in the front of the villa along the access road and the airstrip. Even so, he couldn't risk compromise. It was now or never. Boucher reckoned he was close enough to make it over to the villa without detection but he needed to eliminate the guard standing in front of him.

He slowly pushed himself upward exposing his silenced P-90. Aiming at the back of the guard's neck, he squeezed off a single shot severing the man's brain stem. The man crumpled forward sprawling face down. Boucher emerged from his hide and pulled the guard's body backward into the shallow pit he had just occupied. He quickly covered the body, mussing up the grassy sod on top of the hide and nearby foliage to make it match the surroundings. Taking one more look around to ensure he was alone, he stalked like a cat to the side wall of the villa disappearing beneath a hibiscus hedge.

From there he crawled around to the rear of the villa. There was a large patio overlooking the sea surrounded by a low stone wall. The mercury vapor light was mounted high on a pole on the opposite side of the patio. Numerous moths and other bugs orbited the light, casting small moving shadows onto the area beneath the light. The guard he had seen earlier was still asleep in the same chair facing the sea with his back to the villa. Boucher scanned the area for other guards. There were none. He cautiously made his way to the rear patio screen door. No lights were on inside. He switched his night vision goggles to the active infrared mode and entered the villa.

The room inside was large and beautifully decorated. Ceiling fans revolved slowly above. A well-stocked mahogany bar protruded from the right side wall. A heavy marble-topped table with ten wicker chairs graced the area between the bar and the back door. The other side of the room had leather sofas and arm chairs facing toward a huge wall mounted flat screen TV. The whole room reeked from the pungent scent of cigar smoke. It was a party room, plain and simple.

Boucher proceeded down a wide hallway toward the front of the villa. Other rooms opened off the hall to the left and right. Arriving at the foyer behind the front door, he cautiously peered up spiral stairs that led to the second floor bedrooms. He quietly made his way up the stairs pausing at the top to assess the doors that lined the second floor hallway. He knew Rajakovics had to be inside one of them.

With his P-90 at the ready, he began his search at the far end of the hall. Slowly turning the doorknob, he pushed it open and peered inside. A man and a woman were asleep in the bed. The man was not Rajakovics. He quietly pulled the door closed and moved to the room across the hall.

He pushed that door open. The bed in that room was unoccupied. He returned to the hall and worked his way down to the next room. When he peered inside this room he immediately recognized the man in bed. Gen. Perez was sound asleep beside a beautiful young girl. His uniform was hanging on a valet next to the bed. Boucher knew Perez desperately needed to be killed but he would not do it now. Rajakovics was the primary target and he couldn't risk mission compromise until Rajakovics was dead. He pulled the door closed and quietly latched it.

There were two more rooms opening from the hall. One of them, he reasoned, had to contain Rajakovics. He opened the next door ready to shoot. Again, the room was empty. Finally, the last room and he would get what he came for. Boucher approached the door. As he turned the knob and cracked the door open he heard a groan from inside. He stopped short of opening the door and instead listened again. He heard the sound again. It wasn't a groan; it was a growl – *a dog?*

Then a dim light inside flickered on and he heard movement. Boucher flipped up his night vision goggles and pushed inside. A woman lay sleeping in the bed. A man was standing in the bathroom over the toilet with his back to Boucher unaware of Boucher's presence, but the Pit Bull beside the bed was. The dog angrily sprang at Boucher who was able to successfully fire a short burst into him from his silenced P-90 killing him before he hit the floor at Boucher's feet. Hearing the ruckus, the man in the bathroom partially turned, slamming the bathroom door behind. *Rajakovics!*

The woman awoke and began to scream. Things immediately became chaotic.

Boucher raced to the bathroom door and tried to force it open with his shoulder. Five shots from inside splintered through the door barely missing Boucher. Unfortunately, three of the rounds hit the woman in the bed - one in her right temple, one in her neck and one in her right chest beneath her armpit. She died instantly in a geyser of blood.

Boucher shot back through the door emptying the remainder of his fifty round magazine into the bathroom. He snapped a fresh fifty round magazine into the top of his P-90 and kicked the door open expecting to find Rajakovics lying on the floor but it wasn't meant to be. *Son-of-a-bitch!*

There was an adjoining door that led into the vacant bedroom next door. Rajakovics had again escaped certain death. Boucher ran back out into the hall in time to catch a glimpse of a man jumping down to the ground floor from the bottom of the stairway. Boucher pursued.

As he reached the bottom of the stairs, lights were being switched on in the above hallway. He could hear voices shouting excited warnings in Spanish. He disregarded it all and continued down the first floor hall toward the rear patio from where he had entered earlier. One of the previously open doors to a room slammed shut ahead of him. Boucher shot into the latch and kicked it several times before it finally yielded. He pushed his way inside.

He quickly scanned the dark room with his night vision goggles using the active infrared mode. *No Rajakovics.* The room looked like an office. There was a desk with a computer on it. Pictures adorned the walls along with a collection of antique swords. The windows were closed and latched from the inside. There was no way Rajakovics could have escaped. *Unless...unless there is another way out of the villa?*

Boucher began a detailed search of the walls, pushing and pulling in an attempt to uncover a concealed door. *Nothing!* He checked his watch, it would be first light in another thirty minutes and daylight was not a friend on missions like this. He had to get out of the villa and soon. He then heard people stomping toward the room in the hallway. *Damn!*

He ran back to the door and wedged a chair under the knob. He turned and looked for cover. He needed a place that would provide protection; a place he could fight from. The furniture was wicker, hardly a material that would provide substantial enough cover for a fighting position.

He overturned the heavy mahogany desk. It would provide a bullet-stopping barricade from anyone shooting through the door with anything but an AK-47. Then the voices were in the hallway outside the door. Boucher knew he had to seize the offensive in the coming fight.

He shouldered his P-90 and stitched the length of the office wall bordering the hallway at waist level with automatic bursts of deadly 5.7 rounds. The voices outside immediately stopped and he heard a thud by the door. He quickly reloaded his P-90 with a fresh fifty round magazine pressing it into the top receiver with a snap. He realized if he didn't escape from the room quickly he would surely die there.

He peered outside through the window. He knew the guards would soon converge around the villa, if they hadn't already begun to do so. He glanced down at the floor where the desk had been. He noted a square cut seam in the carpet area that would have been centered under the middle foot section of the desk. He pushed at it with his foot peeling the carpet back exposing a trapdoor. He crawled over to it and lifted the trapdoor upward. Looking in, he saw a ladder leading down a vertical shaft some twenty feet beneath the office.

So that's how he got out. Boucher jumped up and unlatched the window pushing it open. He moved one of the wicker chairs beneath the window. He wiped some of the blood he had on his hand and sleeve from the guard he killed outside onto the chair and the side of the open window frame. It would serve as a decoy long enough to make his pursuers doubt he had discovered the trapdoor.

The sky was just beginning to brighten. He could have sworn he heard the distant sound of approaching helicopters. He quickly returned the desk to its former upright position above the trapdoor, and then climbed down the ladder, making sure the carpet was again in place over the trapdoor as he eased it closed.

Chapter 36

Margarita Island, minutes later

Two Black Hawk helicopters suddenly appeared above the villa. One hovered above the front of the building and the other hovered almost directly above the back patio. Both of them threw out fast ropes and like firemen sliding down a pole, a number of heavily armed men streamed down the sixty foot-long ropes to the ground.

They immediately formed an assault stack at the front door and rear patio door. They forced open the doors and threw flash-bang stun grenades inside. A second later both flash-bang grenades detonated and the men stormed inside. They returned outside the front door moments later with one prisoner.

The lead Black Hawk briefly touched down on the villa's front driveway, its rotor wash whipping up swirling clouds of brown dust, while the second chopper circled above with its door gunner suppressing sporadic fire from the guards. The entire assault team piled onboard the helicopter with their prisoner in hand. The Black Hawk's jet engines spooled up to full power and it lifted off barely clearing the villa's rooftop as it turned toward the ocean and disappeared over the seaward cliff. The second chopper followed close behind. It was all over in a couple of minutes and, except for the shouts from some excited guards in the distance, all was quiet once again.

Surprisingly, the guards were not converging on the villa. In fact, most all of them were still strangely hunkered down in their sandbagged bunkers in apparent fear of the helicopters' return.

Beneath the Villa

Boucher arrived at a closet-size room at the bottom of the ladder and closed the steel blast door, effectively sealing the small room off to the secret access shaft leading down from the villa above. Using his night vision goggles on the active infrared mode, he studied the strange room he was now standing in. He estimated its size to be about twenty by thirty feet with a ceiling around fifteen feet high. Its walls and ceiling were concrete. It was a purposely designed reinforced bunker. It was also a well-equipped workshop with heavily constructed work benches and a heavy lift chain hoist that ran along a centrally located ceiling rail high above the benches.

The benches appeared to have various functions and were all equipped differently. Some had electronic test and circuit assembly equipment on them while another had precision cutting and welding equipment. Another had tools for micro repair and assembly.

Larger machine shop equipment, like a metal lathe and milling machine, were mounted on sturdy raised floor foundations. A trolley-like rail system ran down the middle of the floor with its rails disappearing beneath a large steel door on the opposing wall. A flatbed trolley car, which had been removed from the rails, sat empty to the side of the door. The trolley had an odd wooden semi-curved cradle-like rack bolted to its bed. Boucher judged that whatever it carried was about the size of a fifty-five gallon barrel.

He switched on additional overhead lights brightly illuminating the laboratory and pulled off his night vision goggles. He stopped by a centrally located bench crowded with electronic equipment. He lifted a wiring harness from the bench and slid it into his backpack. *I can't wait to find out what this is for.*

He noticed two doors on the far side of the room that he had missed in his haste. He approached at the ready and cautiously opened the door on his right, switching on the lights inside. It contained living rooms with a full bath and two small adjoining rooms with beds. It even had a small kitchenette with a refrigerator, a small stove, and a microwave oven. He opened the refrigerator. It was stocked with beer and assorted soda. The freezer section had several frozen dinners stacked inside and the ice maker had a full bin. The trash can beside the counter contained some empty beer bottles and some cardboard and foil wrappers. The place was being used.

"I don't believe this shit!" he whispered to himself. *They sure as hell aren't making crystal meth down here. Incredible.*

Boucher cautiously exited the living room door and opened the other door on the left. The room was a clean room, the type used for handling and working with contaminated objects. There were two glove boxes located against the opposite side wall and more test equipment. It even had a decontamination area with a shower and an isolated changing room. Then Boucher saw something familiar - radiation detection equipment. *This is laboratory bench equipment and here is a portable gamma-neutron detector. They're installing nuke weapon fire sets in this lab.*

Then it dawned on Boucher. He suddenly understood what the mini-sub was intended for. *That sub out there in the boathouse is a delivery vehicle.* The strange cargo rack inside the sub was similar to the one on the cargo dolly by the door. It was a bomb cradle.

He returned to the main room and approached the large steel door. He studied the trolley rails running beneath it. The rail tops were worn shiny and used. He cautiously cracked the steel door open and peered down a winding tunnel. He couldn't see the other end. The concrete-lined tunnel snaked downward in a gentle five degree slope. There were shafts of natural light coming from small ceiling vent holes that had been cut vertically up to the surface. He thought he detected a shadow - a flash of movement - ahead along the side of the tunnel wall. Then he heard a door creaking open and close in the distance. It echoed when it latched shut.

He proceeded cautiously down the tunnel towards the sound. He arrived at another large metal door about the same size as the one behind him. Like the door he passed through at the other end of the tunnel, the trolley rails disappeared beneath it. He slowly opened it being careful to remain next to the bullet stopping concrete wall. To his surprise he was back inside the boathouse. The semi-submersible submarine he had investigated earlier was directly to his front.

He worked his way around the side of the strange craft toward the outside boathouse doors, pausing at the ladder leaning against its side. He noted that one of the outside doors was partially open. He hurried toward it exiting in time to see a man running into the cliff-side foliage about one hundred and fifty feet off to his left. It had to be Rajakovics.

Boucher crossed the narrow scrub area from the boathouse into the jungle as fast as he could. A short distance into the jungle he stopped and listened being careful to maintain concealment. He estimated he was about two hundred feet behind Rajakovics, assuming Rajakovics continued into the jungle and didn't stop short to listen like he did.

After hearing nothing abnormal, Boucher angled his direction toward where he anticipated he would intersect Rajakovics' path. His senses were at their keenest as he guardedly moved through the dense foliage. He estimated that he had only gone about one hundred and fifty feet when, from the foliage to his right side, he heard the unmistakable sound of a gun safety clicking to the off position.

"Hands up and don't move," a voice gruffly commanded in perfect English.

Boucher complied with the order slowly releasing his grip on his P-90 sub-machinegun allowing it to hang freely next to his side by its sling as he slowly raised his open hands above his shoulders.

An ominous-looking camouflaged figure slowly emerged from the foliage on his right. A second man emerged from his front. Both were holding assault rifles with large scopes mounted on the top Picatinny rails. He recognized the guns to be Mk-17 SCARs – Special Operations Combat Assault Rifles, and they were both configured with sniper barrels. Boucher knew only U.S. Special Operations Forces carried SCARs. Without showing it, he breathed a sigh of relief.

The man approaching Boucher from the side put his gun muzzle in Boucher's back as he removed Boucher's sub-machine gun and his pistol. The other man remained in front of Boucher holding a covering gun on him throughout the disarming process. The man finally spoke.

"Who are you and what are you doing here?"

"My name is Boucher, Jake Boucher. I'm an American."

The man in front lowered his gun slightly.

"Commander Jake Boucher? You're the guy who slid down the highline and rescued the flight surgeon a couple of weeks ago?"

"Yeah, that's me."

"Fuck'n-A, sir. I was on the Indy pulling hard from the other end of that highline. I saw the whole thing."

The man pressed his squad radio throat mic against the side of his larynx.

"Two Dogs, I got a man here who says he's Commander Boucher." The man listened pressing on his earpiece and nodded, "Roger that, be there in a sec. Follow me," he said to Boucher, "and keep your hands where we can see'm."

Minutes later they arrived at a shallow indentation in the hillside where the foliage naturally thinned. There were four other camouflaged men laying around a makeshift security perimeter with their guns at the ready. Boucher was brought into the center and told to sit down. He glanced around first looking to see what weapons the men were carrying. He saw two were carrying Mark 46 machineguns; the others carried MK-17 SCARs with under-barrel 40mm advanced grenade launcher modules. Their guns were all modified differently and none of the men were dressed or equipped exactly alike. Boucher smiled because he knew exactly what he was looking at - Navy SEALs.

"Commander?" a voice questioned from behind. Boucher turned to see the camouflaged face of his old friend, Two Dogs. "What the fuck are you doing here?"

Two Dogs bent down to Boucher and offered him a hand pulling him up to a standing position.

"Oh," Boucher sighed, trying to act as nonchalantly as he could, "I was in the area and thought I'd check up on you."

Two Dogs laughed, his white teeth gleaming through the black and green camouflage paint on his face.

"Seriously, Jake, my guys almost shot your dumb ass back there."

"But they didn't," Boucher countered, "which is a credit to their fire discipline." Boucher paused, "Doing drug ops?" he asked as he glanced around the shallow perimeter at Two Dogs' men.

"Yeah, just a temporary assignment. We'll be going home in a week. They stuck me and my guys with a lieutenant who just returned from Afghanistan to give him some detox time. Seems like he's a pretty sharp officer."

What's his name?"

"Morgan."

"Lt. Morgan?"

"Yeah, I never worked with him before. Do you know him?"

"Yeah, I've run across him several times over the past couple of years. He's a damn fine officer."

"Well," Two Dogs smiled, "your endorsement is good enough for me. Hey, Jake, are you here doing drug ops too?"

"Nope, never touch the stuff. I'm here to kill a terrorist by the name of Rajakovics. He's the guy who orchestrated the LNG tanker attack on New York City a couple of weeks ago. I was in the villa just before your guys did the snatch and somehow he got away. "

"The DEA did the snatch. We just acted as the security and blocking force for them in case things turned to shit. I was monitoring their squad communications and they reported a dead woman and dog on the second floor."

"Yeah, I shot the dog but Rajakovics shot the girl."

"They said they also found a dead guy in the hall on the first floor and that the place had been pretty well shot up."

"Yeah, I guess that was me too. Look, Glenn, Rajakovics ran into the jungle from the boathouse and headed this way."

"We saw a guy run out of the boathouse ahead of you. He looked like he was unarmed and we figured he was just one of the villa servants so we let him run."

"Son-of-a-bit... why didn't you shoot the bastard?"

"Sorry, Jake, but how were we supposed to know? Besides, you gotta be afraid to shoot the bad guys anymore because some fucking lawyer is always looking over your shoulder. Hell, my guys only stopped you because you were armed and coming up our ass."

"Can you help me nab him?"

"Sorry Jake, no can do. I'm hooking up with Lt. Morgan and his sniper element a click to the east and then we're on to our beach extraction point."

Sniper elements? So that's why the guards were all hunkered down. Morgan had his sniper teams plinking anyone who stood up to take a shot at the helicopters. Outstanding! He forcefully redirected his thoughts back to Rajakovics.

"Did you see which way he went?"

"The guy was headed west, following the coast," Two Dogs said pointing in a westerly direction. "He's probably a quarter of a mile ahead of you by now. Bet he's heading for the populated area on the southwest end. By the way, we saw two other guys head the same way. They were already a good distance from us when we saw them. They were both cammie'd up and packing heat. They must have been outside somewhere observing the DEA do the take down at the villa. Since neither of them was our target and they posed no threat to us, we didn't engage them."

Boucher shook his head in frustration and cussed under his breath.

"Sorry, Jake, we can't help you go after your guy. We got to make our extraction rendezvous in forty mikes. By the way, what's up with the boathouse?"

"I don't know but I got a look inside it last night and it's not what it appears to be from outside. You and your boys might ought'a check it out."

"We can't, it's not in our mission profile. We're not authorized to take any action outside that explicit profile or we risk punitive action. It's the fucking lawyers, Jake."

Boucher grabbed Two Dogs' shoulder and squeezed it, "Good see'n you, Glenn."

"Yeah, you too, Jake. Be safe, Brother."

Boucher turned away.

"Hey, Jake," Two Dogs grinned, "I'll buy the first five rounds the next time I see you back home."

Boucher momentarily turned back, "Sounds like a plan, Two Dogs. I'll buy the second five and bring Morgan with you. I'd like to see him again."

Chapter 37

U.S. Department of State, Washington, DC

"Boss," an excited Jimmy Bruce exclaimed as he burst into Blackburn's office, "I got two hot items!"

"Shoot."

We just received a flash cable from Embassy Caracas. Joel Lopez, the Deputy Chief of Mission there was assassinated."

"Assassinated? How? Who did it?"

"Apparently a high tech shaped charge, like a Claymore, was hidden in a bag on a bicycle that was strategically parked along his route home. Dip Security says it was fired remotely as his armored car passed by. The thing was aimed so the slug would pass through the back door into the passenger compartment at seat level. The DS driver and his shotgun caught frag but their injuries are not life threatening. No one is claiming responsibility. Our guys don't know who did it but they do know the FARC has never used anything that sophisticated."

"Holy shit, Jimmy. I know Joel Lopez. He's a straight shooter."

"Yeah, and it apparently cost him his life."

"What else do you have?"

"I got a call from Sam just before I came in here."

"And?" Blackburn impatiently beckoned.

" She said the DEA, supported by Army Black Hawks, ran an air assault a short while ago at the same villa where Commander Boucher was trying to get Rajakovics. She said Commander Boucher reported that Rajakovics somehow escaped from the villa. The Commander reported that he ran into some SEALs who were in the process of exfiling from the villa's perimeter during his pursuit of Rajakovics. They were apparently the same guys from the USS Independence who helped out with the Virgo a couple weeks ago. This was a major operation that obviously wasn't properly deconflicted."

"You're shit'n me, right?"

"No Sir, it's almost as if Boucher was set up."

"Damn it, Jimmy, we run an operation to whack Rajakovics and some other agency runs a simultaneous operation to snatch some druggies at the same time and the same place. Go figure what the odds of that are. Where is Jake now?"

"He told Sam that he's headed west in pursuit of Rajakovics. That's all I know for now, Sir."

Blackburn sat back in his chair and sighed.

"Is Sam doing okay?"

"Yes, Sir. Yellowhorse, Llina and Mojo are with her. She's holding the boat on station a few miles seaward of the villa where Boucher wanted her."

"How about Moss and Doyle?"

"They're standing by with the helicopter at the Caracas airport. Reilly is with them. They have their helo ready to go if Boucher calls."

"So right now Boucher is on foot chasing Rajakovics somewhere along the coast of Margarita Island?"

"Yes, Sir, apparently so."

"I don't like it, Jimmy. Something doesn't sit right with all this but I can't put my finger on it."

"One more thing, Sir, and I'm not sure if it means anything or not."

"Shoot."

"I did a cursory search of all shipping currently reported in the general area and there is a container ship by the name of Kingston loitering just west of Margarita Island. It's been there for about twelve hours."

"Damn it, Jimmy, what's that supposed to mean?"

"Sir, remember the Russian ship that disappeared off France?"

"Yeah, the Artic Mist."

"Well, Sir, the Kingston is one of the Israeli Corporation-owned Ofer ships like the one that was loitering in the area of the Artic Mist just before she disappeared."

Margarita Island, the same time

Boucher slowed his pace. He had been following freshly broken branches, bent-over foliage and boot prints in the dirt. He knew he was definitely tracking an active trail and judged he was getting close but unlike the desperate pursuits Hollywood heroes always portray, the heat was taking its toll. He was sweating profusely. Boucher realized he needed to rest a few minutes.

He knelt down on one knee, listening for movement in the surrounding jungle. A nearby bird chirped and flew to another tree. All seemed normal. He drew in a mouthful of water through the plastic tube leading from the water bladder in his day pack. It was warm, tasteless and far from refreshing but it served to keep him hydrated.

The sun had disappeared behind black moisture-laden cumulous clouds. *A rain squall*, he judged, would arrive soon and cool things off. There was a lightning flash close by and the near instantaneous crack of thunder. He could hear the roar of approaching rain on the jungle leaves. It sounded like a fast-approaching train coming down the tracks. A cool breeze swept by and turned into windy gusts, followed intermittently by large drops of rain, then an all out downpour. The jungle foliage was dancing as the windblown rain pelted down upon it. For Boucher, it was reminiscent of the jungles of Southeast Asia and the many years of his life he spent there. It was just another day at the office.

Refreshed and at home in his element, Boucher resumed his pursuit. The trail he was following had disappeared, but the rain also gave him an advantage. Its pelting noise covered his movement and allowed him to pick up his pace. He assumed Rajakovics would do the same, especially if he didn't know he was being followed. *How could he know?*

Boucher spied fresh shoe prints in the soft jungle floor filling with rainwater. He was close. He slowed his pace and tried to focus his senses on differentiating human form, standing or moving, from the storm-driven movement of the surrounding jungle foliage. All he needed was a glimpse. He moved methodically, taking four or five steps, then standing perfectly still while scanning the surrounding jungle, then repeating the process. Like a jungle cat, he was stalking his prey.

The tropical rain squall had intensified. Thunder cracks were so near it sounded like an artillery barrage bracketing his position. The leaves of the jungle foliage twisted in the wind and rain creating a kaleidoscope of flashing colors ranging from various shades of green, gray, yellow and purple. Boucher was no stranger to hunting his prey under these conditions. In fact, he was very much at home. He concentrated on form – human form, not colors. Then off to his right he got a glimpse of what looked like the back of a man's shoulder and head. *Rajakovics?* The man was cautiously easing his way through the jungle about thirty feet in front of him.

Boucher fell in directly behind the man, being careful to remain just far enough behind him so the man would not see he was being followed. Boucher needed a positive ID before engaging the man, but if it was indeed Rajakovics, there would be no warning and Boucher would not hesitate. He felt the feeling of revenge warm over his body. It would feel good to kill him and end another evil that infects the planet.

The man stopped short of a small clearing and carefully surveyed the surrounding area before crossing it. Boucher crouched down. The man quickly crossed the area and momentarily turned back toward Boucher before disappearing into the foliage. His positive ID impossible. *Rajakovics?*

Boucher's radio ear piece cracked with Sam's excited voice.

"Jake," her voice blared, "someone at the villa is shelling me with artillery. I think it's coming from the cliff area above the boathouse."

"Head seaward and zigzag. I'll get the helicopter and we'll be there in minutes."

Boucher checked his map and his compass heading.

Mossman, Jackie, you guys hear Sam?"

"Roger all, Jake. We're already on the way. There's a suitable LZ a few hundred yards due south of your position. Be there in five mikes. Mark with smoke."

It couldn't have been five minutes from the time Boucher ended his call before he heard the distant sound of an approaching helicopter. The familiar shape of the twin rotor Boeing 246 briefly came into view. He ran to a clearing next to the road and popped an orange smoke flare. The helicopter gradually descended, passing directly above Boucher at about seventy-five feet. Moss banked steeply, decelerating by spinning the mammoth helicopter around and landed it in the clearing in one fluid motion.

Moss kept the helicopter's powerful jet engines turned up at full power so he could conduct a maximum performance takeoff without delay. Boucher was no stranger to this tactic and jumped onto the helicopter's open tail ramp. Reilly pulled him forward and held on to him. Moss commanded the chopper back into the air accomplishing both a heart stopping vertical climb to one hundred feet and accelerating to a forward air speed of one hundred knots in under three seconds. Boucher made his way forward to the cockpit clawing his way around the auxiliary fuel tank in the cargo area. He grabbed a spare headset and put it on.

"Head back to the villa."

Chapter 38

On the Boeing 246 helicopter

Mossman flew just above the wave tops speeding the massive helicopter parallel to the shoreline toward the villa. The sky was clouding as another string of rain squalls fast approached from the east. Visibility was quickly diminishing and Moss knew it would be severely limited once the storms arrived in full force.

Boucher was crouched behind the radio console between Moss' and Doyle's seats holding on to their seat backs as a means to steady himself. Reilly was still standing behind Boucher like an umpire at a ball game. Yellowhorse was opposite of Reilly holding on to the back of Doyle's seat. All five men strained through the windshield and the mist beyond, trying to catch a glimpse of Sam's boat offshore.

Off to the west, a boat came into view. Using binoculars, Boucher recognized it as the fishing yacht Sam was driving. She was on a heading seaward.

They all saw a flash and a puff of smoke on the water's surface in front of Sam's fishing yacht. The water's surface rose upward forming a waterspout a hundred yards to the front of the yacht.

Boucher saw the boat's wake snake away from the settling waterspout. Then a second much closer explosion erupted off her forward port quarter flinging hot shrapnel into the boat's fiberglass hull.

"Jake," Sam's frantic voice blared through his headphones, "they have my number. You better do something real quick."

Boucher strained through his binoculars at the distant villa. He focused on the old Russian T-34 tank sitting on the cliff top. Its barrel was now elevated and its turret had pivoted toward Sam's boat several miles seaward. He saw a puff of smoke leave its gun barrel. He swung his focus toward Sam's boat in time to see a waterspout erupt just behind her boat. It was a near miss.

He clicked open his mic, "Sam, steer a radical zigzag course. You got to get out'a range of that tank."

"No shit - Yah think, Jake?" Sam sarcastically replied. "That S-O-B almost hit us with that last shot. Now would be a good time for you to do something really clever like putting that gun OOC."

Boucher thought for a second, *OOC? Out of commission. Exactly.* He clicked his intercom mic open. "Mossman, you feel'n lucky today?"

Moss repositioned his black ball cap with the letters DILLIGAFF embroidered in dirty white thread above the brim. "I'm always feel'n lucky. Why do you ask?" he replied with a crooked grin.

Boucher saw his men glance over at him like whatever he was about to say was going to be luminary. He glanced seaward at Sam's yacht then over to the tank on the cliff. The rain squall was now upon them.

"Okay boys, let's go get that tank."

Moss banked hard to the right and headed toward the villa at full speed. Boucher saw the tank fire again at Sam's boat raising a geyser directly in front of it. He knew that a shot that close had to fling its deadly shrapnel into the boat.

"Sam, you okay?" he shouted into his mic.

There was nothing but static.

'Sam, are you okay?" he asked again.

Still nothing but static. *Sam?*

"Jake, we just took a bunch of frag through our bow. Mojo caught a piece in his forearm. He says it's just a scratch but he's bleeding. Llina is patching him up. We're taking on water but I think the bilge pumps can keep up with the flooding but I might need to slow down so I'm not scooping water into the holes."

"No, don't slow down! You hear me, Sam? If you slow down they'll drop a round into your boat for sure. I'm gonna take out that tank. Keep your speed up and head seaward. Keep zigzagging."

Reilly looked over at Boucher, "I know this is probably a dumb question, Jake, but how are we going take out that tank? All we have onboard are pistols and sub-machine guns."

Boucher thought for a moment again. "We're gonna bomb the son-of-a-bitch," he confidently replied.

"Okay, Boss, bomb him with what?" Doyle questioned.

"Mossman, can you fly this thing by yourself?"

"Does a bear shit in the woods...I only bring Jackie along for comic relief. He doesn't help me fly these things; he keeps me from falling asleep at the controls."

Boucher nodded and put his hand on Doyle's shoulder, "Jackie, come with me. Billy, Johnny and I need some help unhooking the auxiliary fuel tank on the cargo deck."

The men knew what Boucher was going to attempt without further explanation.

"Mossman, give it a wide circle around behind the villa. Then come in over the villa from the landing strip side. When you're on top of the T-34, flare hard, and we'll shove the aux fuel tank off the tail ramp and drop it right on top of him."

"How you gonna ignite it?" Doyle asked.

"You got any flares?"

"Yeah, should have some in the emergency survival kit."

"Okay, that's the plan. Let's get the aux tank un-gripped, the fuel lines unhooked and rolled back onto the tail ramp."

Moss came across the beach at treetop level about a half mile northeast of the villa.

"Feet dry," he reported over the intercom.

Staying at treetop level he turned, making a wide circle, back toward the villa's landing strip.

"Twenty seconds," he reported setting his course so he would pass directly over the villa's rooftop.

"Ten seconds, standby" he calmly reported.

All of a sudden the fabric insulation bordering the helicopter's rear cargo area shredded, throwing pieces of insulation and metal fragments to the opposite side. They had been hit by machinegun fire from the ground. Like Boucher, neither Moss, Doyle, Yellowhorse, or Reilly were strangers to the experience.

Unfettered, Moss flared the helicopter bringing the nose up into a twenty degree angle. This maneuver bled off his air speed effectively stopping the helicopter directly above the T-34. Boucher could see the Russian-built T-34 directly beneath the open tail ramp.

"Now!" he shouted as they pushed the partially full auxiliary fuel tank off the helicopter's open tail ramp.

The fuel tank plummeted down onto the T-34's turret landing directly on its open top hatch. Several hundred gallons of jet fuel splashed over, in, and around the tank as the fuel tank ruptured.

"Mossman, go, go, go!" Boucher shouted into his intercom mic.

Boucher and Yellowhorse ignited and dropped flares onto the now ruptured tank just as Moss dropped the nose of the helicopter and headed over the cliff in an attempt to escape the explosion that was certain to follow.

Moss swooped down almost hitting the water and banked east following the coast beneath the cliff elevation. Behind, an instantaneous explosion erupted upward in a ball of red flames. A billowing plume of black smoke rose upward. The tank's turret was blown skyward coming back down behind the tank on the villa's patio.

The dull thud of a distant explosion reached the helicopter at the same time Moss realized the helicopter had a problem.

"Jake, we got a minor problem," Moss advised over the intercom. "Jackie, I need you here in the cockpit, quick."

Boucher didn't like the sound of Moss's voice and knew it meant trouble. Both he and Doyle raced back to the cockpit. Doyle crawled back into the co-pilot's seat.

"What's going on?" Boucher asked.

"We're going down. The ground fire must have damaged our hydraulic lines and also perforated our main fuel tanks. I'm getting hydraulic pressure fluctuations."

"Not good," Doyle added.

"So, you want me to put this crate down on Margarita or drop her in the water?" Moss asked.

"How long can you keep us flying?"

"Oh, I don't know, maybe a few more minutes or so."

Doyle carefully checked the fuel gauge levels and hydraulic pressures, "Mossman, we're losing hydraulic pressure. Our hydraulic fluid reservoir is bleeding out. We got to set down now!"

Boucher clicked his mic open, "Sam, head our way. We're going to set this thing on the beach east of the villa."

Moss gave Boucher a thumbs-up.

"Sam, we're landing now."

"Roger, I hold you visual, I'm on the way."

"Roger, keep your eye on us."

Moss landed with a hard jolt on a broad strip of beach just east of the villa where the cliff tapered down into a close by mangrove swamp. He immediately shut down the engines and turned off all the auxiliary electrical systems to reduce the threat of fire.

Looking seaward, Boucher saw Sam's boat headed their way. Mojo was motoring his way toward the helicopter in the inflatable dinghy. Boucher strode back into the helicopter's cargo bay.

"Let's get all our stuff off this thing and get it to water's edge for recovery."

Boucher led Moss, Doyle, Yellowhorse and Reilly to the beach. Ten minutes later Mojo beached the small boat in front of them.

"Come on boys, I'll take you out to the yacht."

"No thanks, Mojo. I still have unfinished business here. There's a bad guy who still needs killing."

"Okay, Jake, where to?"

"I need to take another look inside the boathouse beneath the villa. Something isn't right there but I don't know what."

"Okay, I'll put you ashore by the jetty. You mind if I tag along?"

"Glad to have another shooter."

"Wait a minute, Jake, Mojo isn't going to go without the rest of us," Reilly bellowed.

"Good, you're all welcome."

Boucher's radio crackled. It was Sam. He put it on speaker so all could hear the conversation.

"Jake, I just found a boat adrift out here."

"What about it?"

"I found Perez in it. He's dead."

"Great, who shot'm?"

"He was already dead."

"Already dead?" Boucher replied in surprise. "How?"

"I don't know but Llina says he was shot by something big like a fifty cal or a Lupua, probably sniped from shore. I saw his body. There was a hole blown through his chest the size of two fists. We left his boat adrift with him in it."

"Good call, Sam. Me and the guys are going back inside the boathouse. We'll catch up with you when we can. Hang tight off shore."

"Be careful, Jake."

Boucher gave his men a bewildered look. "We must have company?"

"Well, there's definitely somebody else on this island who didn't like Perez," Reilly replied.

"That's for sure," Mojo offered. "The good news is they're not shooting at us."

Boucher nodded, "Put us ashore by the boat ramp, Mojo."

U.S. Department of State, Washington, DC , the same time

Bruce burst into Blackburn's office, notepad in hand. "Boss, Sam just reported they ditched their helicopter on the beach a mile west of the villa.

Her description was sketchy but they were apparently shot down after they bombed that Russian T-34 tank we saw in the overhead imagery. She said it was shooting at her yacht. She also said Perez was killed by someone from shore. Jake is with four of his guys and they're going back to the villa to find Rajakovics."

Blackburn held up two open palms, "Whoa-wo-wo, slow down, Jimmy. Let's take this a piece at a time. How did they bomb a Russian T-34 from an unarmed helicopter?"

"They dropped their auxiliary fuel tank on top of it and ignited the fuel. Boom! She says it's still burning."

"And they got shot down in the process?"

"Hit by ground fire."

"Then they crash landed on the beach?"

"No, Moss landed it just before they crashed."

"How did they get from the beach back to the villa?"

"Mojo picked them up with the yacht's dinghy. Jake thinks something bigger than drug smuggling is going on there."

Blackburn calmly sat back in his chair contemplating the information.

"What's Jake going to do now?"

"He's going back to the villa's boathouse. Sam said he's intent on finding Rajakovics. He's determined to finish the job he went there to do."

Blackburn took a sip of cold coffee and swallowed hard, curling his upper lip from its foul acid taste.

"I don't like it, Jimmy. This mission has been compromised in multiple ways. The Independence has to be watching what's going on. We have a shot up helicopter sitting on the beach not far from the villa. There's a burning Russian tank on the cliff above and probably a bunch of crispy critter Venezuelan nationals lying all around it. Now we have an assault team going ashore composed of a bunch of retired SEALs, to do a search of the villa's boathouse while the rest of Boucher's crew are offshore standing by in a fishing yacht they leased using false identities. There are just too many people watching. Get a hold of Sam and Boucher and tell them to abort. Their cover has been blown and there's no way for us to backstop them. Cummings is going to shit herself when she hears this."

"Yes, Sir."

"When you're done, let's walk down to Washington Harbor. I'll buy you lunch at Tony and Joe's. I need a friggin beer.

"One more thing, Jimmy. When we update the Secretary, I'll do all the talking."

"Aye, Sir."

A half hour later Blackburn and Bruce left the Department of State and walked toward Washington Harbor. The infamous Watergate loomed off to their left. As they stepped into the street to cross, a panel truck ran the red light. Bruce was slightly ahead of Blackburn and didn't see it coming. Blackburn yanked Bruce from the path of the accelerating truck. The truck only missed them by inches.

"Son of a bit...!" Blackburn yelled as the truck sped down the street towards the Kennedy Center. "You okay, Jimmy?"

"Yes, Sir. That's the second time today."

"What do you mean?"

"Driving in to work this morning I was almost run off the road along the Route 28 stretch close to Poolesville. It was like the guy was trying to run me off the bridge into the Monocracy River."

Chapter 39

The boathouse, Margarita Island, the same time

The sky had quickly darkened and another rainsquall was bearing down. The wind had picked up again and was hurling large, gust-driven rain drops into the sea with enough force to erupt into thousands of tiny geysers. The rain torrent had reduced visibility to half the length of a football field. Lightning angrily flashed instantaneously followed by claps of ear-splitting thunder.

Mojo beached the dinghy and they took defensive positions behind the rock jetty. Boucher and his men could hear screeching metal coming from the boathouse above. It sounded like fingernails on a chalkboard, only a thousand times louder. Suddenly the mini-sub appeared outside and began sliding down the trolley rails gathering momentum as it rode toward the water. At the bottom it plowed into the sea like a ship launching immediately following the christening. Boucher could make out a man's silhouette moving inside the small sub's pilot house as the boat floated free of its trolley.

"We gotta stop that boat!" Boucher yelled.

Boucher squinted through the rain using his hand to protect his eyes from the windblown drops. The semi-submersible boat bobbed on the surface, slowly taking on ballast, as part of a controlled process to partially sink itself and reduce its detectability. Its small diesel engine was now revving. It was closely paralleling the rock jetty and slowly heading to sea. Boucher knew it would only be a few more minutes before the boat would be impossible to see in the rain and if it dove underwater it would become undetectable. Sam would never be able to intercept it.

There was a horrendous explosion from above. The entire boathouse erupted upward, taking a portion of the cliff with it. As the ground collapsed, the still smoldering tank tumbled down onto the boat ramp below and skidded into the water with a splash. Rock and rubble arched high into the sky above the villa and began raining back to earth. The explosion was so massive and the destruction of the boathouse so complete, it looked surreal. Boucher and his men hunkered down trying to protect themselves from falling debris. Several large pieces of rock landed squarely on their inflatable dinghy, puncturing the main sidewall inflation tube. Their boat was now inoperable. Boucher peeked up to see the semi-submersible heading seaward while taking on ballast so it could submerge. The rain squall was subsiding and visibility was steadily improving.

"I need a diversion!" he yelled pointing at the submersible.

"A diversion after that explosion is like hearing a fart in a diarrhea ward," Mojo yelled.

"Keep him hunkered down," Boucher yelled pointing at the small submarine.

His men weren't sure what Boucher was about to do, but they knew what to do. They all began taking aimed shots into the water close to the boat – close enough to look threatening but not close enough to hit it.

Boucher ran along the rock jetty to the left of the boat and reached its seaward end a good fifty yards ahead of the boat. He dove into the water and swam out into the path of the approaching craft.

Nearly fully ballasted, the semi-submersible's deck was awash, with only its small window-sided pilothouse protruding above the surface of the water. Boucher could see that the man driving was looking back in the direction of the boathouse launch ramp. Boucher positioned himself directly in front of the approaching craft.

It was now or never. As the boat's bow reached Boucher, he pushed himself up and over it, sliding like a circus seal along the forward deck back to the pilot house. He hit the small windshield with the full weight of his body, barely able to wrap one arm around it in time to stop his momentum. He swung to its side, aiming his feet toward the partially open rear access hatch. Using his other arm he reached inside for the man at the controls. The moment he grabbed the man, the struggle began.

Boucher was frantically trying to pull him outside through the small access hatch while the man was bracing himself inside using his legs and holding onto the boat's steering wheel. If it had not been a life and death struggle it would have otherwise been comical.

The man finally twisted sideways and Boucher identified him without question - *Rajakovics*. Boucher was able to get one of his hands around Rajakovics' throat and shifted his body position enough so he could reach for his pistol, but Rajakovics parried. Boucher lost his grip and nearly slid off the boat.

Boucher pulled himself back up and grabbed inside again. This time he snagged Rajakovics by the back of his shirt collar and yanked him backward from the controls. In a single motion, Boucher pulled his upper body inside the cramped cockpit overtop of Rajakovics. Elbowing Rajakovics down against the boat's instrument cluster, he was able to reach the throttle lever and yank it backward. The engine instantly slowed to an idle and the boat stopped its forward progress.

Sliding backwards, Boucher grabbed Rajakovics with both hands and pulled him backward through the hatch onto the boat's partially awash deck. Rajakovics countered by pushing himself sideways, knocking Boucher off balance. They both regained their balance and the two men came at one another punching, kicking and gouging. They were formidable fighters.

After struggling to the point where both men were nearly spent, Boucher landed a few lucky blows and wearily drew his pistol. It was a moment of sweet bliss; he finally had the drop on Rajakovics.

He watched Rajakovics slowly pull himself up into a kneeling, almost devout position. Oblivious to everything else around him, Boucher painfully pushed himself against the small pilot house holding his pistol down by his side. He sat there cocking his head from side to side watching Rajakovics. Rajakovics stared at his opponent.

"So, once again we meet, Commander," he slurred, wiping the blood from his frayed lip.

Boucher steadily raised his pistol toward Rajakovics until he was pointing it squarely at his face. "Pizdets tebe otmorozok obosraniy," he said in near perfect Russian.

Rajakovics began to laugh. "I did not know you speak Russian, Commander."

Boucher lowered his pistol slightly, leveling it at Rajakovics' midsection, "I don't."

Rajakovics laughed again, "So, are you going to shoot me?"

Boucher locked eyes with him, "No, I'm going to kill you."

"No, you won't. You will not murder me. Besides," he said glancing up at the two Black Hawk helicopters circling above, "there are too many people watching. You will take me prisoner. Maybe then you will learn what your enemies have in store for you in this submarine and the others just like it that already delivered their cargo to your shores."

"Others?"

Rajakovics laughed recklessly, "Yes, they're all carrying special surprises for your cities and this time it is too late to stop them. You have no idea who you work for."

Boucher snapped the pistol's thumb safety down to the off position. "Maybe not, but I can stop you from killing more good people."

"Why do you risk so much for them? I told you before, for me it is nothing personal. I am only a soldier."

"No you're not. You're a murdering piece of shit."

Rajakovics smiled, "And so you will become if you pull the trigger."

Boucher was so focused on Rajakovics he still didn't hear the Black Hawk helicopters circling above. Rajakovics knelt down on his knees in front of Boucher in full surrender and kept his hands over his head. The helicopters circled several hundred feet above. Sam was now only a few hundred yards away and closing fast.

Suddenly, Rajakovics wrenched violently backwards as if a sledge hammer had hit him. His body hit the boat's slick deck and he splashed overboard. For a moment Boucher wasn't sure if he had pulled the trigger or not. *Rajakovics has been shot, no, sniped by someone from shore and they used a big bore rifle.* None of his men had one of those guns on this operation. *The shooter was a third party.*

Without the least fear of also being shot by the sniper ashore, Boucher stood over Rajakovics' partially floating, face up body. A gaping hole had been blown completely through him and his lungs were slowly filling with water. Boucher kept pointing his pistol at the lifeless body below him like it was going to resurrect any second. He could see his own reflection on the blood stained surface of the water as he watched Rajakovics' body slowly sink into the shadowy depths.

Still staring, Boucher spoke aloud. "Here's the English translation for the only Russian I know, 'Now...die in the shithouse you miserable bastard.'"

Chapter 40

Dirksen Senate Office Building, Washington, DC, two days later

Classified hearings held behind closed doors always seemed to provide opportunity for its members to grandstand and Senator Kelly, the co-chair of the Senate Select Committee on Intelligence took full advantage of her position as she continued her assault on Boucher.

"Mr. Boucher, based upon the imagery taken from a National Guard helicopter and on-scene eye witness testimony, all of which we have reviewed, it appears to this committee that you committed a heinous act of murder by executing a prisoner in your custody during your Venezuelan escapade."

"No Ma'am, that's not true. At that point the terrorist you're referring to was not my prisoner and I didn't shoot the SOB."

"Well, all our video and eye witness accounts reflect a different picture. How did you know he was a terrorist?" Kelly leaned forward. "Let me answer that for you – you didn't." She now pointed her finger at Boucher. "You executed an unarmed man. And one more thing, Mr. Boucher, don't refer to me as Ma'am. It's Senator. I've worked very hard to become a senator and achieve the position I hold."

Boucher tightened his jaw but kept his cool. He sucked in a long cleansing breath and exhaled it slowly.

"Let me address your statements in the order you made them. First, I knew he was a terrorist about a year ago when he supervised the al Qaeda operation in the Canary Islands. I'm sure even you remember that. It was the al Qaeda attack where they intended to explode several nukes along the Cumbre Vieja Volcano's caldron fault line on the Island of La Palma. That blast was intended to break loose and drive a huge chunk of the mountain into the sea to create a manmade tsunami that would have devastated the entire

U.S. Eastern Seaboard. He was also the terrorist who I personally witnessed murder a CIA operative. Her name was Sandra Morrison. Then the son-of-a-bitch tried to kill me. He's also the mastermind of the LNG tanker attack on New York City a couple weeks ago. Surely you can remember that. So I caught up to him on Margarita Island a few days ago and he almost killed me there." Boucher pointed to the fresh stitches in his forehead. "So don't trifle with me about how I knew he was a terrorist unless you're prepared to argue that al Qaeda is not a terrorist organization."

Kelly interrupted, "Mr. Boucher, your attitude and unwillingness to cooperate with this committee…"

Boucher raised his voice and continued, cutting her off in the middle of her sentence. "Secondly, if I could have killed this guy I would have. You're correct about one thing; I've been trying to kill him ever since he killed Sandra Morrison. I freely admit whoever sniped him on that boat did me a favor and made me feel real good because my intention was to kill him."

"Seeing an unarmed human executed made you feel good?" Kelly fussed.

"Yeah, it sure did because I knew this particular human would never again kill Americans. As I told you, someone sniped him from shore. I didn't execute an unarmed man and neither did any of my people. I really don't care what the video or eyewitness accounts from a helicopter that was circling five hundred feet above indicate." Boucher thought for a second. "Now, if you're asking me if I would have shot him anyway, I'm unsure. The guy definitely needed to be killed. So maybe I would have shot him. Regardless, you can't accuse me of murder for thinking about killing him."

"Mr. Boucher, I…" Kelly again tried to interrupt but Boucher continued on.

"Last, I am here before this Select Committee on Intelligence voluntarily and, as you all know, it is not the first time." Boucher focused on Kelly, "You wanna be called senator because for some reason you think 'ma'am' isn't respectful enough for a person of your elitist office. Well, that isn't going to happen because I've given you about all the respect I can during this lifetime. So, if you want me to testify on the terrorist attack we foiled against New York City or about the potential nuke rework lab we found beneath the villa on Margarita, I'm willing to continue. If you expect me to sit here and accept your politically motivated attacks against me and the other good guys involved – well, I guess all the talking I'm gonna do is done. So make the call, ma'am."

Senator Rowland, Kelly's co-chair, opened his microphone and locked his gaze on her. A Vietnam veteran himself and former presidential candidate, he was especially attuned to the politics involved in hearings like this.

"Perhaps, Mr. Boucher should provide his evaluation of our counterterrorism and intelligence shortfalls involving operations such as these."

Kelly grudgingly waved her hand, gesturing her approval.

"Mr. Boucher," Rowland continued, "we asked you to testify here today because you have come from the front line, or, maybe I should say, the last line. You have again succeeded in stopping a catastrophic attack on our country when our intelligence community appears to have failed. You have proven yourself to be our last line of defense time and time again. This committee would be grateful for your unabridged evaluation."

Boucher sat forward glancing individually across each of the eight member panel.

"Senators, our intelligence community hasn't failed. I think it's important that we begin by understanding the purpose of terrorism. Terrorism succeeds when public fear drives its government to the point where it can no longer function. Its basic goal is to create public insecurity. Terrorist attacks are planned to cause circumstances that the public will interpret as failure of their government system."

"But Mr. Boucher, why are terrorists like Rajakovics so difficult to locate?" one of the other senators asked. "You said you've encountered him before and each time he showed up you had no warning that he was even involved. Wouldn't you agree that our intelligence community failed to detect his presence?"

"Well, Senator, you have to remember that those who head terrorist networks intentionally keep the numbers of their senior people who know what's going on to a bare minimum. They're masters at compartmentalization so the extent of their terror network along with their specific intentions is largely unknown by their membership. This usually makes finding a key terrorist more like finding a needle in a haystack than it is tracking down a murderer like Rajakovics."

Rowland interrupted again, "Do you actually believe Rajakovics was a member of al Qaeda?"

Boucher smiled, "Well here's the bottom line as I see it, Senator. While all Muslims are not members of al Qaeda, all members of al Qaeda are Muslims. Rajakovics was a Kazakh-born, Russian-trained, soldier of fortune, not a radical Islamist. He told me himself, he was just a contract employee and had no personal attachment to al Qaeda or their radical Islamist cause."

"So," Kelly loudly insisted in an attempt to make a political point, "President Banner rightfully reasoned United States forces should focus its efforts in Afghanistan and neighboring Pakistan, since that is the last remaining al Qaeda stronghold. Isn't that right, Mr. Boucher?"

Boucher slowly shook his head disapprovingly. "There are several issues you're overlooking. The first is the fact that the vast majority of all the recent al Qaeda attacks against U.S. interests have been relatively low level, requiring limited planning, human resources and minimal cost."

"Wait a minute, Mr. Boucher," Kelly cautioned. "You can't expect this committee to sit here and accept that last year's nuclear bomb attack in the Canary Islands or that tanker ship attack against New York City a couple of weeks ago was low level. If either of those attacks had succeeded I am certain we would not be sitting here right now - now would we, Mr. Boucher?"

Rowland answered the question. "Perhaps not, Senator Kelly, but Mr. Boucher and his team successfully stopped both attacks. Please continue, Mr. Boucher."

"Secondly," Boucher explained, "these attacks have not come from Afghanistan or Pakistan-based al Qaeda.They have originated from places like Yemen, Algeria and Somalia. I'll bet all the indicators and warnings were there well in advance of these attacks. The biggest problem our intelligence analysts face is that you guys have handcuffed them in their ability to ferret out the reliable intelligence from the erroneous noise they must assess. It is from the analysis of that noise that they target the bad actors or their associates for the purpose of collecting more substantially valid information from which a mosaic can be pieced together. You simply can't put our CIA operatives and military interrogators in jail because they may have violated some dirtbag non-U.S. citizen's civil rights. Hanging that sort of threat over our most trusted people doesn't motivate aggressive collection."

"So you think Congress has inadvertently taken the CIA's authority and motivation away?" Rowland asked.

"It's not inadvertent, Senator. Congress has succeeded in screwing up the entire intelligence community by forcing reliance on a technological process for data analysis and product distribution. Today, our analysts just operate the system and are restricted to do anything outside it. If they take any initiative to work outside the system they get screwed because you guys have created a system that disallows risk and prosecutes initiative. So, where's the motivation to do anything else but stay within the system?"

"So today, if I understand you correctly," Rowland slyly urged, "following the process is more important than success."

"I think most everyone wants success and sees it as important," Boucher responded. "The reality is that any poor bastard who steps outside the process gets skewered by the media, the Justice Department and you guys."

Kelly interrupted, "Like you murdering your prisoner as he begged for his life – right, Mr. Boucher?"

"Wrong!" Boucher seethed, visibly repulsed by her indictment. "You don't get it, Senator. Our Islamist enemies are a bunch of badass, very mean, sons-of-bitches who are willing to die for their cause. And they're as imaginative in their targeting and mission planning as they are mean. We continually underestimate them and generally hold the view that they are a bunch of cave-dwelling rag-tag rag-heads when the contrary is true. They're ruthless fanatics who don't have to deal with bureaucracy to come up with a good plan and run with it. And one more thing – a third party killed Rajakovics."

"And of course you know who that third party is," Kelly sneered, "don't you, Mr. Boucher?"

"As a matter of fact, I might."

A man in a dark suit who Boucher didn't recognize approached the head of the table and bent down between Kelly and Rowland whispering to them. They both seemed to agree.

Kelly picked up her gavel. "This committee hearing will recess until further notice." She rapped once on the table with a loud knock. Two Capitol Policemen escorted Boucher into an adjoining room. Shortly afterward, the man in the dark suit entered.

"Commander Boucher, my name is Christopher Malone. I am on the National Security Council staff and work for General Gregory Cline, the president's National Security Advisor. General Cline would like to meet with you. Would you please come with me to the OEOB?"

Old Executive Office Building, Washington, DC

Malone and Boucher were driven to the "OEOB," as it was known in Washington downtown circles. Their black Towne Car entered the White House grounds through the 17th Street gate and parked in a narrow access alley located between the OEOB and the White House.

Flashing his ID, Malone led Boucher past the uniformed Secret Service guards to Cline's office and ushered him inside.

"Mary, General Cline's guest is here," Malone informed the lady sitting at a desk outside Cline's inner office.

Cline's secretary picked up the phone and dialed.

"General Cline, your guest is here," she informed her boss. "Shall I send him in?" She hesitated before responding. "Yes sir. Right away." She stood and smiled at Boucher and Malone. "Please go in, gentlemen."

Boucher followed Malone inside.

Cline stood and approached Boucher with his hand extended for a handshake.

"Jake Boucher, Greg Cline, I'm pleased to finally make your acquaintance. May I call you, Jake?"

"Of course, General." Boucher wasted no time. "Why am I here?"

Cline smiled. Please sit down, he invited, motioning Boucher toward a brown leather couch located across from a small oblong table that was situated in front of his desk. Cline rolled his desk chair over to the table and sat down.

"Jake, I asked you here at the direction of the president."

"President Banner?" Boucher asked in surprise.

"Yes, last time I checked he's still the president."

Boucher slowly nodded. "Guess you're right about that one."

Cline smiled. "Look, Jake, the president is concerned that there may be certain elements of information that you have been exposed to over the past few days that should not be revealed. He's hoping you will protect that information and if need be, sacrifice as necessary to prevent its disclosure."

Boucher shifted uncomfortably. "General, are you asking me to take a fall for the president?"

"No. I'm asking you to consider the damage that could be done to the Office of the President and our national security by the information you possess should you reveal it."

"General, you're going to have to excuse me, but I'm not sure what specific information you think I possess that is so sensitive."

Cline glanced at Malone, "Please leave us and close the door."

"Yes, sir," he replied and departed the office.

Cline returned his focus on Boucher. "The Israelis are in the final planning stages to conduct an attack against Iran's nuclear weapon development facilities."

Boucher let out a grunt. "Okay, that's not something that's much of a secret. Everyone knows it's just a matter of time."

"No, Jake. It's far more serious than that."

"How so?" Boucher soberly asked. "I'm sorry, General, but I guess I'm not following you."

Cline leaned back in his chair and drew in a long breath. "It goes something like this. When Secretary Cummings asked you to go to Venezuela she did so, on behalf of President Banner. She was unaware of all the players involved."

"Players? What do you mean by players; the Israeli Mossad?"

"Partially," Cline flatly stated. "We know that Mossad has been tracking your activities for a number of years."

"What?"

"We also knew they were tracking Rajakovics'."

"They were?"

"Yes. We only recently discovered that Rajakovics was a double agent working for the Israelis."

Boucher sat straight up. "A double agent?" he repeated in surprise.

"Yes. We have been feeding him information that we wanted him to reveal to the Israelis."

Boucher was clearly astonished. "Are you saying Rajakovics worked for you too?"

Cline sat quietly staring at Boucher without answering.

Boucher's mind coursed the events of the last couple of years that involved Rajakovics.

Two years ago Rajakovics was a main player in a CIA-backed operation that I led in the Caspian Sea. We boarded a Russian ship that was smuggling a rogue nuke to Iran that had been purchased on the Russian black market. The Kazakhs blew up the ship and sank it. Then I was introduced to Sandra, a CIA operative, who I later learned had links to the bad guys. And she was murdered by Rajakovics. Rajakovics was a key player again only a few weeks ago in the LNG tanker attack against New York City. If it hadn't been for Sam he would have succeeded. Then Secretary of State Cummings asked me to go to Margarita Island and kill Rajakovics. When I finally caught up to Rajakovics someone sniped him from shore rather than risk having him talk.

Boucher sat up straight as if he'd been given an electric shock. His eyes narrowed, as he repeated his question, "General Cline, are you suggesting that I was sent down there to kill Rajakovics to prevent him from potentially compromising his relationship with the U.S. to the Israelis?"

Cline stood and walked over to the window. "Jake, the president asked me to make you an offer. I hope it's an offer you can't refuse."

"An offer?"

"We would like to bring you into the administration – you know, join us. The president would like to appoint you as an Under Secretary in the Department of Homeland Security. Or, if you like, you can work here with me as a member of the National Security Council. I'll make you the Counterterrorism Czar. If that isn't appealing enough to you, then you tell us what position you want and we'll make it happen."

Boucher's head began to ache. *The Luminous? Not again...God help us.*

Boucher had crossed paths with the Luminous before, shortly after he recovered the gold from the crash site in Cambodia a couple of years ago. The Luminous, or The Committee, as they were sometimes referred to by Washington insiders, were only ever whispered about. In fact, their existence had never been investigated much less admitted. The Luminous was a powerful shadow organization that operated outside the bounds of Constitutional and legal authority. They consisted of a little known group of powerbroker elitists who manipulated politics, high finance and government on an international scale. Since World War II no president had ever been elected without their sanction. And Boucher knew it went much deeper than that. Key administration officials throughout the Executive Branch, Congressional Chairs, even Supreme Court justices were sanctioned by the Luminous and complicit to assuring its direction.

Boucher thought he had exposed their network to the light of day almost two years ago. He now realized his assumption was wrong. They had merely stepped back into the shadows while they regrouped and replaced key positions. The man standing before him was undoubtedly one of them and that meant President Banner was either wittingly compliant or being unwittingly manipulated.

"And if I don't join you?" Boucher asked. "What then?"

Cline smiled. "Oh, but you will, Jake. This is your opportunity to do really good things. It's an opportunity for you to steer instead of ride in the back seat. Doesn't that appeal to a man like you?"

"Frankly, General Cline, I don't think you know anything about men like me. I have been watching our country slowly decline for a number of years. It sickens me at the direction you and this administration have been moving our country. You are systematically disassembling our Constitution and our national values. You are bankrupting us and stifling business growth. You are grabbing more power while at the same time you make the rest of us more dependent upon the government. And you guys do this with a smile and without guilt."

Cline sat listening unemotionally. "So you have decided to work against us?"

"General, everything I've seen over the last several weeks leads me to believe there's another major attack on the way here. I believe they may already have several nukes hidden within some of our major cities and I think they're going to use them against us. Surely you and the president must realize that."

"Of course we do. We've done the analysis and it comes down to this. This country can absorb the loss of a few cities and still survive as a nation. The president has determined that the only thing that will galvanize this nation again is a major attack. If that attack is clearly linked to Iran there will be no stopping our retaliation. The American people will want revenge and they will unequivocally support our efforts to eliminate the Islamo-fascists from the face of the earth. All we need is a catalyst; a wake-up call and a cause everyone can rally to."

Boucher shook his head. "What you need is a psychologist."

Cline frowned. "I truly expected more from you, Commander. You are free to go but let me give you some friendly advice, if you so much as reveal one syllable of any of this conversation to anyone, ever, things will not go well for you or those close to you. I believe your friend Patterson has a family and you friend; what's her name, Samantha could have issues"

Boucher stood up and locked his steel-eyed squint on Cline. "If I ever feel threatened by you or your people, or if you fuck with any of my friends, I'm coming after you. If you get me first, a SEAL buddy of mine will catch up to you and I promise you General, you will hate the very day you were born. So let me give you some friendly advice, General, don't threaten me!"

Boucher turned away and left Cline's office.

Fells Point, Baltimore, Maryland, later the same day

Boucher returned to the Fells Point Marina where he kept his yacht and walked up the pier. Because of its size, his yacht was moored outboard of the last slip. As he climbed aboard he noted that a large yacht, about sixty-foot, was now occupying the slip opposite to his. The boat was moored with its bow facing towards Boucher's yacht. The boat's white fiberglass hull was sleek and new. Its windows were all tinted black. It had two radars and a score of other antennas protruding upward from its pilot house. It looked fast and badass, as yachts go. What he didn't see was the yacht's name boldly painted across its stern in eight inch high gold trimmed black letters, "Sasbatzar."

Nice boat, he thought as he opened the mahogany door to enter the after cabin on his all mahogany 1962-vintage Chris-Craft Constellation. Boucher was pleasantly surprised to find Sam, Moss, Doyle and Reilly sitting in the air conditioned enclosed lounge area in the main cabin sipping beer.

"What are you anal savants doing here? Sam, you weren't included in that question," he light-heartedly joked.

"I invited them to join us for dinner, Jake," Mojo announced. "We're celebrating Sam's new appointment."

"Appointment?" Boucher asked. "What appointment?"

"She's going to be the new Deputy Administrator of the U.S. Maritime Administration."

"MARAD?"

"Yupper, Jake. The president announced her appointment himself about ten minutes ago during a press conference on maritime security. He made a big deal of crediting Sam with saving New York City."

The look on Boucher's face was telling.

"Did you know it was coming, Sam? I mean, did they check with you first?"

"Not exactly. My employer, EISC, contacted me this morning and told me they wanted me to take an extended leave of absence to kind of let the dust settle before reporting for duty aboard my next tanker. I didn't figure that was anything abnormal. Then, on the way back here I got a call from the MARAD Administrator himself. He asked me if I would come to work for him. MARAD is apparently reorganizing the U.S. merchant fleet to better meet the evolving maritime terrorist threat. I know that's a worthy initiative so I told him I'd do it, but only for a year or so. The next thing I know President Banner announces my appointment."

"Great, Sam, you're a perfect fit for the job." Boucher turned his attention back to Mojo. "So what am I cooking us for dinner?"

"We're having sushi delivered. Should be here any minute."

Boucher forced a weak smile. He seemed troubled and they all noticed.

"How did the hearing go today, Jake?" Sam asked.

"It was like getting my ass wire-brushed. Then I was taken over to the White House for a private meeting with General Cline, President Banner's National Security Advisor."

"And how did that work out?" Moss asked.

Boucher uncapped a beer bottle and took a long swallow. "He threatened me. It's the Luminous again. I'm sure of it."

"I thought we put them out of business." Reilly commented.

"Me too but it seems they're back and they control the White House."

Sam scratched her head. "The Luminous? What's the Luminous?"

Just then the dinner delivery arrived. Over dinner, Boucher methodically explained every last detail of the meeting he had with Cline and all about his past dealings with the Luminous.

"Geez, Jake," Doyle commented, "These guys are some serious players. They just don't stop, do they? You really think they'd try to whack you?"

Boucher drained his beer in one long swallow. "I'm not too sure what they might try but my insurance plan is you guys."

Sam handed Boucher a fresh beer. "What's next?"

"All we can do is hold our cards close to the vest and wait and see how they play their hand."

"Going back to Bakers Run camp is looking better to me every day,"

Mojo grumbled. "Sons of bitches try to mess with me there and they'll end up worm food."

Boucher's cell phone rang. Pressing it to his ear, his face suddenly went ashen. Then he grimaced in obvious grief. He slowly closed the phone and put it back in his shirt pocket. He stared at the ceiling for a few moments. Everyone suddenly became quiet as they observed his emotional behavior. They knew it was bad news. He drew in a deep breath.

"That was Dean Blackburn. He called with some bad news. Jimmy Bruce is dead." His voice broke. "He was crossing 23rd Street on his way to the Foggy Bottom METRO station. A van ran a red light. He was killed instantly. The van was stolen and the driver left the scene." Boucher hesitated. "Dean doesn't think it was an accident." He paused again. "Jimmy was a good man."

The men nodded. "A good man," echoed from various mumbled voices.

Moments later, Boucher's cell phone rang a second time. This time it was Deb, Patterson's ex.

"Hey Deb, what's up?" He listened. "Wait a second, Deb. Let me put my phone on speaker so the guys can hear this." Boucher put the phone on speaker.

"Jake, when the kids came home from school today they handed me a note they said was given to them by a man in the school parking lot. The note says I'm supposed to read this to you."

"Okay, Deb, go ahead."

"It says, 'Anytime, anywhere.' What the hell is that supposed to mean, Jake?"

"Deb, don't let your kids out of your sight. I'll call you later."

Boucher returned the phone to his shirt pocket.

"It has started," he cringed. "Mossman and Jackie, make sure our Gulfstream and the helicopter are fueled and ready. We might need to move in a hurry. Billy, get a hold of Dick Llina. Tell him we need'm here ASAP." Boucher stiffened up and narrowed his eyes. He cleared his throat and swallowed hard. "We continue to face a cowardly enemy who hides in the darkness of big government and who wants to change life as we know it." Boucher paused and stared into his men's eyes. "Well, I don't want my way of life to change and I don't want my government or anyone else telling me how to live it."

On the yacht opposite Boucher's, the same time

Two men sat at a desk-like control console wearing head sets. A third man entered the small cabin area and stood behind the other two men observing over their shoulders.

"What are you learning?" the man asked.

"He was just told about the kids. He understands the message." The man chuckled. "He thinks it's his own government."

"But it is – with a little help," the man replied in a sinister voice. "How much have they figured out?"

"Not enough to compromise our operation."

"And Boucher?"

"He is manageable. Besides, everything is in place and there is nothing he can do about it."

"Then we will keep watching him. And - for now, we'll leave him alone."

"So we will proceed as planned?"

"Exactly. Let's get this boat out of here. We have an outbound ship to catch."

Epilogue

Jimmy Bruce's funeral service was attended by his family and friends. Boucher, Sam and all the men attended. Dean Blackburn gave a moving eulogy. Sam took Boucher's hand and gave it a soft squeeze. He responded by putting his arm around her. Both feel a special fondness for one another but their relationship is progressing slowly. Neither knows if it is love or just a deep affection and respect based upon what they have shared. Regardless, neither of them is ready to make a commitment. The timing just isn't right.

Sam was sworn in as the Deputy Administrator of the U.S. Maritime Administration. She moved into a small apartment in Rockville, Maryland located close to the White Flint METRO station so she can take the subway to her downtown Washington, DC office. While she feels she's contributing, she spends many days mindlessly staring out of her office window at the Potomac River longing to be back at sea.

Boucher has kept his marine repair company working out of his Baltimore Fells Point warehouse. He occasionally helps out on a local contract if the water is warm and the job is easy. Otherwise, he spends the preponderance of his time fly fishing for native brook trout with Mojo on Baker's Run in Renovo, Pennsylvania.

Patterson is steadily recovering from his brain injury and is helping Boucher with bookkeeping and the underwater repair business. He now manages the entire operation for Boucher and hired several commercial divers to do the preponderance of the work. He met a nurse during a routine neurology checkup and they are now dating. His children approve. He claims he's not getting serious with her but Boucher says he hears wedding bells every time he sees the two of them together.

Secretary of State Cummings has recently become more vocal in her negative comments about the Administration's policies. Some believe it is a sign that she is distancing herself from President Banner because she realizes the administration is heading down the wrong road. Others believe she is posturing for a potential presidential run the next election. The truth perhaps lies somewhere in the middle. Boucher suspects she could be affiliated with the Luminous. He keeps his distance from her and General Cline.

President Banner and his merry men continue to largely disregard the grassroots concerns of the American majority. No one is sure if his aloofness and elitism is a result of his socialist entitlement culture or if he is being manipulated and/or ill-advised. As political parties seem to be less different in their message and share corrupt motivations, citizens' skepticism and unrest grows exponentially. President Banner exacerbates this distrust in government by abusing the fundamental Constitutional tenants of his office with increasing arrogance and disrespect, mostly aimed at the middle class. As the national debt soars and Banner's radical appointments to the Executive and Judicial branches of government go unchallenged, there are some who feel so disenfranchised that they believe a government-wide cleansing is in order. As the next presidential election nears, the form in which that cleansing will manifest remains unclear.

Iran revealed that it has procured four ground-based, Russian built, ultra-sophisticated S-300 air defense systems. Two systems were reportedly purchased from Belarus while two others were acquired from an undisclosed source. The missile systems are not believed to be operationally ready. Should there be indications these systems are being readied for operational deployment, Israel will undoubtedly launch a devastating attack against Iran aimed to both destroy Iran's S-300s and its nuclear weapon development facilities. The Israelis are watching closely and realize they have little to lose, as far as their U.S. relationship goes, if they attack. And to be sure - attack they will.

The End.

Fact

Fuel-Air Explosives (FAE) is reality and in the military's inventory. FAE operates by explosively atomizing a volatile liquid fuel (liquid benzene and propane work great) that forms a "cloud." The cloud mixes with the air and becomes oxygen-enriched in the process. At precisely the right time of maximum enrichment and at precise location within the cloud, charges are detonated causing the cloud to subsequently detonate. Depending upon the size of the FAE, the blast over pressure can easily equal that of a small nuclear weapon. Under ideal conditions a LNG tanker could be made to detonate as a FAE.

As it stands today, Germany is the key to the European Union's survival, but Germany has more in common with Russia than it has with the EU. Russia continues to reassert its influence over the former Soviet satellite nations in an effort to reestablish its security buffer zone aka, the Soviet Union. Per the scenario revealed in this book, Russia may well emerge as the last remaining superpower without having ever fired a shot. Stay alert.

As farfetched as it may seem, Israel has reportedly established a secret intermediate operating base located in an obscure area five miles outside the city of Tabuk in Saudi Arabia where it has forward deployed assault helicopters and fighter-bomber aircraft. Its naval forces are forward deployed to locations close to Iran in the Indian Ocean. Israel is poised to attack Iran in a three pronged operation that will employ the Israeli Air Force launching strikes from both Israel and from Saudi Arabia. Israeli naval forces, that include several submarines capable of firing cruise missiles, will attack shore and near shore targets from both the Indian Ocean and Persian Gulf. Commandoes will surgically strike point targets acting as a diversion and force multiplier. The goal will be to destroy Iran's missile batteries and annihilate their nuclear weapon program. The U.S. will inevitably be drawn into the conflict and it will get ugly.

There is growing evidence that Venezuela is facilitating drugs for arms trade between al Qaeda and communist-backed forces friendly to Venezuela. Margarita Island, located just off the east coast of Venezuela, is an al Qaeda hotbed and hosts the single largest Islamic population in South America. Venezuela's communist dictator, Hugo Chavez, is sympathetic to both the FARC and to al Qaeda, allowing both to use Venezuela as a strategic sanctuary to further their anti-American and his pro-socialist agenda.

Existence of the Luminous has been rhetorically argued throughout the media and university classrooms since the assassination of John F. Kennedy. Whether acknowledged or not, there is a highly exclusive group of likeminded international powerbrokers who operate without allegiance to a single country or government. They are known as the "Committee," by some and the "Luminous" by others. They are the same organization. They exist in the shadows, throughout high finance and government. While they, themselves, are largely transparent, their influence is not. One only need recognize that political parties have little influence on the politics forced upon us, or the direction that government imposes both domestically and outside the U.S. The Luminous issues and dissolves power to achieve its goals and maintain its influence over government, finance and you. You may not believe the Luminous exists but, at some level, you must feel its presence.

Glossary of Terms

ARIP – Air Refueling Initial Point, agreed upon location where the tanker aircraft arrives, at 110 knots, configured with flaps seventy percent down and the refueling hose extended, pressurized and ready to transfer fuel to the receiving aircraft.

BDU – Battle Dress Uniform. Camouflage uniform worn by the troops operating in the field.

Big Apple – nickname for New York City originating from jazz bands that played in NYC's numerous night clubs. Playing the "Big Apple" was a big deal.

Boat School – Navy slang for the Naval Academy. Sometimes also called "Canoe U."

Boeing 234 – Civilian variant of the military's CH-47 twin-rotor, heavy-lift helicopter.

BOHICA – Bend over, here it comes again.

BUD/S – Basic Underwater Demolition / SEAL Team training.

Bulkhead – Nautical name for a wall, both interior or exterior, and most other flat vertical surfaces on a ship

CBRNE – Chemical, Biological, Radiological, Nuclear, Explosives.

CH-47 Chinook – Military version of the civilian Boeing 234 twin rotor heavy lift helicopter.

Claymore mine – Directional explosive charge that can easily penetrate armor with a range of 100 yards.

Corvettes – Term given to small, fast, heavily armed, guided missile surface ships.

Color Revolution - Protesters used the Iranian national colors as their symbol for revolution. Hence, the media branded it a "color revolution."

DILLIGAFF – Does it look like I give a flying fuck.

Dogs on the watertight door – Term given to the steel locking levers that surround a watertight door that are manually tightened once the door is closed. Most watertight doors have four dogs equally spaced along each side from top to bottom.

Drogue – A receptacle trailing on a long hose behind the transferring tanker aircraft.

EMP – Electro-magnetic Pulse. EMP is created by a nuclear detonation. Its effects literally destroy unshielded electronic equipment.

ETA – Expected time of arrival

EU – European Union

Euro – European Union currency

Exfil – Short for Exfiltration.

FAE – Fuel Air Explosive

FARC - acronym for the Revolutionary Armed Forces of Colombia – People's Army. In Spanish it's Fuerzas Armadas Revolucionarias de Colombia – Ejército del Pueblo, or FARC-EP. FARC is a Marxist-Leninist revolutionary guerrilla organization with somewhere between fourteen and eighteen thousand well trained, well equipped troops. They're basically the military wing of the Colombian Communist Party and they've been fighting the Colombian government in an attempt to overthrow it for over sixty years. They're considered a terrorist group by the Colombian government, the U.S., Canada and the European Union.

Flaps – located on the trailing edge of an airplane wing, can be extended to increase the wing's surface to achieve greater lift at slower speeds.

FRAG - Short for fragmentary order, or a specific mission part of a complete order. To FRAG an aircraft is to commit it to complete a specific mission as part of a larger operations order directing Fighter Groups or Squadrons to perform general missions.

Gitmo – U.S. military base Guantanamo, Cuba.

ICE – Immigration and Customs Enforcement, subordinate agency of the Department of Homeland Security.

IR – Infrared

Jacobs ladder – A rope ladder that has wooden rungs, used primarily onboard ships because of its storability and portability to ascend/descend a ship's side. It can simply be secured to the deck and unrolled down the hull to the water.

LANDSAT – Satellite imagery commercially available over the internet.

LAW Rocket - Light Anti-armor Weapon. Small man-carried short-range rocket made popular during the Vietnam War and still in use today.

LCD – Liquid Crystal Diode

LDO – Limited Duty Officer. The Navy promotes deserving enlisted men and warrant officers to regular officer ranks as LDOs. LDO commissions are granted by the Secretary of the Navy, not by Congress. Thus, they are not considered Line Officers and are not permitted command.

Littoral – Any land area bordered by the sea.

Lizard Line – Nautical term meaning a rope with knots tied in it to make it easier to hang onto.

LNG – Liquefied Natural Gas

LZ – Landing Zone

MARAD - Maritime Administration, headquartered in Washington, DC.

MLAT - Mutual Legal Assistance Treaty

M.S. – Motor Ship. Unlike ships driven by boiler-fired steam turbines, motor ships typically have large diesel engines turning electrical generators which, in turn, power large electric motors that power the propeller shafts.

NSA – National Security Agency. A super secret spy agency of the US government.

Novak .45 – Wayne Novak is a premier custom pistol builder specializing in the 1911 model .45 pistol and the Browning Hi-Power pistol. www.novaksights.com

OEOB – Old Executive Office Building, located beside the White House on the corner of 16th Street and Pennsylvania Ave. in Washington, DC. Serves as office space for the president's and vice president's staff and the National Security Council.

Old Man – Navy nickname for the Commanding Officer of an afloat command.

ONI – Office of Naval Intelligence

OOC – Out of Commission.

Pad Eye – A reinforced steel, D-shaped, hook up point welded to the hull or bulkhead of a ship. Used to secure shackles, block and tackle, lines, etc. to the ship at specific commonly used locations.

Pave Hawk – U.S. Air Force special operations variant of the Black Hawk helicopter.

Picatinny rail – a common geometry, grooved and slotted accessory attachment rail used on most modern military firearms. Given the name Picatinny from its origin, Picatinny Arsenal.

PJ – U.S. Air Force Parachute Jumpers, highly trained rescue medic and commando.

POTUS – President of the United States

RAM – Radar Absorbent Material, significantly reduces radar detection by absorbing the Radar signal. It comes in the form of special paint, coatings and more obvious rubber foam-like material glued onto a surface.

RPM – Revolutions per minute. Also can mean rounds per minute when addressing automatic weapons cyclic rate of fire.

RSI - Rigid-hull Semi-Inflatable boat. Uses a rigid fiberglass lower hull with inflatable upper tubes attached to the gunwales. RSI's are widely used by the U.S. military and police because they are relatively fast and extremely seaworthy.

Sasbatzar - Means, 'keeper of the fire.' The term dates back to the biblical days of King Solomon.

S/CT – U.S. State Department's Office of the Coordinator for Counterterrorism headed by an ambassador at large.

Shaped charge – Directional explosive charge designed to penetrate armor and/or for precision cutting of all materials, e.g., concrete, steel, wood, earth, etc.

SOB – Son-of-a-bitch

SOS – Special Operations Squadron (U.S. Air Force)

SPECAT – Special Category, designation given for special handling requirements for extremely sensitive need-to-know classified programs.

Spooky – Nickname for the Air Force's Special Operations Squadron AC-130 gunships.

T-34 – Main Russian battle tank used against Hitler during WW-II.

VFW – Veterans of Foreign Wars

WTF – What the fuck

About the Author

Paul Evancoe is a retired, career Navy SEAL with significant combat experience and numerous military service awards, including the Purple Heart. Following his military career, he continued government service at the U.S. Department of State, the National Nuclear Security Administration, and the Department of Homeland Security. He is the author of *Own the Night* and *Violent Peace*. *Poison Promise* is his 3rd novel in a planned series of five.

www.ingramcontent.com/pod-product-compliance
Lightning Source LLC
Chambersburg PA
CBHW030243030726
47493CB00023B/570